# Brian McNeill



# The H[illegible] That Swoops

# Copyright

This novel is entirely a work of fiction. The names, characters and incidents portrayed in it are the work of the author's imagination. Any resemblance to actual persons, living or dead, events or localities is entirely coincidental.

Published by High Hold Books
www.brianmcneill.co.uk



Paperback Edition © 23.10.2020 ISBN : 978-1-913957-02-5

Robin Blecher, in memoriam

For ideas, conversation, guidance and the very best of company, my warmest thanks go to:

Mike Brooks, Herschel Freeman, Margaret Gravitt, Ros and Paul Shepherd, Jiggernaut, Clandestine, Jim and Jinty MacLachlan, Amy Brady, Craig VanWinkle and Jacqueline France.

As a musician, I have toured the USA with pleasure and fascination for the best part of four decades now, revelling in the wild complexity of its different musics and the boundless beauty and grandeur of its landscapes—and wondering at the endless variety of paradoxes its people have to face.

Nowhere is the cult of celebrity stronger—and the possibility of living there and evading its reach, in these computerised times, becomes daily more remote. When I wanted my busker to confront the way that celebrity status—positive or negative—affects complicated lives, it was the obvious setting.

This story began in a decrepit Dodge van back in the early eighties, after the steering column had decided, without warning, to part company with the rest of it near Norfolk, Virginia. The three hour wait for the tow truck left me with a fine view of an old red barn bearing the legend *Chew Mail Pouch Tobacco.* Somehow, it made the right backdrop for musings on plot and character.

The winding back roads of Appalachia, the abandoned industrial behemoths of the rust belt and many, many miles of freeway gave me the rest.

# 1

# FREE

THE VIEW FROM the Ambassador Hotel's window could have been a recruiting poster; the huge stars and stripes flag, rippling slowly in just the right amount of breeze, the vapour trails emerging from behind it at exactly the right angle, the distant dome, brooding, portentous with power, its whiteness intensifying as the surrounding sky's blue hardened into darkness.

"Yessir, sure can't complain about the view. Land of the free. I expect you'll be glad to leave it, though, Mister Fraser, get back to Scotland."

I said nothing. The voice's determined optimism ploughed on.

"I'm of Scottish descent myself. They tell me it's beautiful this time of year. Not like here—can't believe it's only April, doesn't usually get this muggy till the end of summer."

"I don't live in Scotland."

I regretted the bluntness as soon as it came out, but the only reaction was a leisurely consultation of the Rolex. The movement segued smoothly into the attaché case's arc up on to the cheap bedspread. The double click of the catch sounded oiled, expensive.

"Let's see... Itinerary, return ticket, Homeland Security departure clearance, transcript of your evidence. That's about it, I guess."

The four brown envelopes went down on the table in a precise line, as though symmetry could compensate for the chipped surface. I sat down beside the open case, pulled off the tie they'd so pointedly given me to wear and tossed it away. It landed on the air conditioner. The vent's draught lifted the fat end into a futile tweed wave.

"And then there's this, of course."

I turned, catalogued him—razor-parted short blond hair, dark blue suit, immaculate white shirt with a button-down collar, striped tie with a gold pin. Twenty-four? Twenty-five? In jeans and t-shirt I'd have said younger, just a boy, really... Did it matter? I watched the signet-ringed hand make a fan of three crisp new twenty dollar bills beside the line of envelopes. The smile became even more self-satisfied; a novice, pulling off the winning flush in a poker game...

"Cab fare. And a little extra, in case you want a beer or something, a sandwich. Before the plane."

Yes, it did matter. *Tipped. By a child…*

"Rank's outside, I suggest you leave no later than seven-thirty," he went on, "they like you there early for transatlantic, security's no cakewalk at Dulles. Oh, and in case you run into any difficulties..."

The cream-coloured card went down beside the envelopes and the cash. It bore a stern government eagle perched on a Stars and Stripes shield, circled by the words Department Of Justice and a Latin motto. His name, F. Carlton MacDonald, was embossed along the bottom beside a phone number. I watched the sight of it sober him; the proof of his power, the icon of his authority. Its appearance signalled the end of informality.

"Mister Fraser, on behalf of the DOJ, I'd like to express our thanks for your help in this matter. When we couldn't trace you in Europe, we found ourselves in serious difficulties—after Mr. Eve's unfortunate demise last month, we were even considering dropping the whole case. If you hadn't co-operated when the Italian police located you..."

I looked away. I knew how rude I was being, but it didn't stop me. Behind me I heard his voice ignore the snub and cling stubbornly to its gravitas.

"The testimony you gave today could be decisive. Add that to the evidence you've agreed to give the German authorities and the prosecution looks unassailable. My superiors want you to know we're grateful."

I turned back to face him. "Grateful enough to help with my other request?"

He averted his eyes, closed the attaché case as camouflage. The recital came out rehearsed; polished, buffed smooth with polite regret.

"I wish we could help, but I'm afraid that would be handled by—"

"—a different department," I cut in. "Frankly, Mister MacDonald, I would have thought you might show a little more initiative, especially in the light of what I'm doing for you at the moment. Make your gratitude practical, then I might believe in it."

Finally, a dent in the bulletproof smile. A flush of embarrassment captured him. Suddenly he really was just a boy, suddenly the briefcase and the clothes looked awkward, wrong. The trappings of the up-and-coming had been devalued, and he didn't like it. He spun round, ready to retreat—and then, hand on the door handle, he stopped. I watched training reassert itself.

"OK, Mister Fraser, have it your own way. You might be on the right side of the dock this once, but let me remind you of one fact—one *legal* fact. Your temporary visa runs out at midnight tonight, April 22nd. If you're not on that plane to Glasgow at 9pm, inside three hours you will be in breach of its terms." Defiance stripped away the manicured voice and gave him boldness. "And therefore subject to arrest—though I expect you're used to that, given your record. You better realise that in this country we don't hand immigration waivers around like candy, especially to convicted murderers." He nodded at the flag outside the window. "Land of the free, like I said. Don't confuse it with a free lunch."

The door gave the punchline as much of a slam as the thin plywood could muster. I listened to the receding footsteps, then let myself fall backwards on the sagging bed. I stared up at the ceiling. *Wonderful,* I thought, a *boy made into an enemy. Exactly where does that get you?*

I lay there, sweating, letting my annoyance simmer. Most of it was directed at myself—my behaviour had been pointless as well as rude. *Tipped, by a child…* Yes, but if I'd been on the street, busking, I'd have been happy enough to take his money... What was wrong with me? My life was getting angrier, I knew. Why? Was it age? I thrust away the questions, pulled myself up on to my elbows and looked at my fiddle case.

Unopened. Since I got here, three days ago...

Should I take her out, at least try to play a tune? Had I brought her all the way to Washington DC just to ignore her? What would my friend Luther Eve have said about that?

No, it was wrong, I decided—and Luther would have agreed. Maybe later, maybe somewhere in the open, once I had these pitiless people and this hellish room behind me. Now, I just didn't have the heart. I forced myself up, wiped the sweat from the back of my neck and turned to the window.

It was almost dark. The vapour trails were gone, the flag hung limp, showing a forest of aerials behind. Their grimy geometry was thrown into sudden relief as Capitol Hill's battery of floodlights came on. The white dome seemed to expand in their glare. As I stared, I gradually became aware of sounds—engines, sirens, the squeal of brakes... Voices, running feet, honking horns, the distant rumble of aircraft...

A city. A real place with real life, not just a symbol—the conjunction of a million stories, messy, intertwined, complicated...

Human.

As though in response, canned laughter came from a TV set through the wall.

As the unintended irony died away, it was replaced by a harder sound, the arthritic roar of the air conditioner, cranking itself up a protesting gear.

I watched the blast of refrigerated air reanimate the awful tie. It kept trying to reach my leg, flickering like a tartan serpent's tongue.

*

The beer didn't taste much like beer, but it was fine and cold, just like the two before it. I drank off half of it in a silent toast. Absent friends. Had Luther's passing been painless? I could only hope so—a coronary, they'd said, sudden. The world would be a poorer place without him. A fine man and a wonderful musician. An example.

A friend.

I could have used a friend's voice, now. In the mirrored wall behind the bar, I watched the occupants of the hotel lobby. At the counter there was one other drinker, a distinguished-looking white man, older, bearded, with slicked-back reddish-grey hair and thick spectacles, sipping his drink in silence and scratching at his beard. He gave my fiddle case a doubtful look, then buried his face in his *Wall Street Journal.* Apart from him, there was only me and the barman.

And my half-empty glass... I ran a speculative finger down its frosted side, then downed the rest of it in one and eyed the gantry along the back wall.

Whisky...

The bottles glinted invitingly, old friends ready to renew acquaintance. They were arranged around a framed poster.

A triptych, all but religious. The object of worship was a girl—a temptress, full-breasted and plump-lipped, perfect. She had flawless skin, a Rapunzel mane of blonde hair and a smile that said a hint would always be sexier than a promise. In each of the three panels she was decked out in a different style of stars and stripes dress—but the glass of liquid in her hand was always the same, tricked by the photographer into a luminous smokiness which somehow stayed brighter than the patriotism she was wearing. The legend below the pictures was even less subtle than the images.

*DRINK LIKE AMERICA'S SWEETEST SWEETHEART!*
*TASTE SCOTLAND'S SCINTILLATING SOUL!*

Scintillating... I heard laughter and realised it was my own. Land of the Free, Home of the Brave...

Territory of the Trite.

Whisky wasn't Scotland's soul. Whisky was what Scotland's soul used for camouflage. It was what that ever-elusive entity hid behind whenever its realities got too raw. It was the consolation prize—easy excuses by the bottle, amber absolution by the glass, the pub philosopher's maudlin manna.

It was single malt self-pity.

And it was what I wanted.

I sat back on the bar stool, avoiding my own reflection, eying the triple image. The effect was seductive. It was meant to say *sophisticated, urbane.* It was meant to say *sensuous,* it was meant to say *success.* My eyes went back to the bottles grouped around it. All I wanted them to say was *oblivion.* The question simmering in my subconscious finally boiled to the surface. If I got drunk, really drunk, right now, right here in this soulless hotel bar, who would care? The barman appeared in front of me.

"Another?"

"How did you guess?"

His face stayed professionally expressionless. "You want to last in this job, bud, you learn to recognise a man on a mission." He jerked a thumb at the wall behind him. "Nobody here to see it but her and me. You want I should run a tab?"

I almost succumbed, but then my left foot touched the fiddle case. It was enough to sober me. I shook my head.

"My opinion, good call," he said, drily.

As he left with my empty glass, I took the envelope from my jacket pocket and spread its contents on the bar. The single sheet of paper was what I reached for first. It was creased, worn from constant re-reading.

*Alex,*

*I hope this gets to you, I've sent it to the last address I had.*

*There's no good way to say this. Your mother's in trouble. Bad trouble. She's been diagnosed with cancer, lymph glands, aggressive, and it's spreading. I have to take her away for treatment. Soon. It's a long shot, but it's the only one we have left.*

*She won't see you. I've tried everything, reasoned, pleaded, shouted, but as usual, her useless bloody god's in the way. Ironic, isn't it? First you won't see her, now this. The waste of it all, I'll never understand.*

*But there is one thing you can do for her. You're either actually in the States now or you're on your way, you told me the last time we talked. You've an uncle there, her brother George. You've never heard of him. The reason for that's a long story and a hard one, but you'll know about it soon enough.*

*He's a strange man, Alex, always was, even more religious than her when he was young. He lives near a town called Fayetteville, in Arkansas. He won't answer the phone, and every single letter she sent came back unopened, which is why what I'm about to ask has to be done exactly the way I'm asking. The photo's the last one she has of him, by the way. It's older than you are, but it might help. He looks like you did at the same age, a lot.*

*What it comes down to is this. They haven't spoken since he left Scotland, sixty years ago, and all that seems to matter to her now is making her peace with him. The letter that's contained in this one is what she was going to send. I think if it was returned like the others, it would be the end of her, so this is what you have to do. Go to the man, open her letter in his presence. I know what's in it. Read it to him. That way, you'll know the truth as well.*

*I know this is a hard thing to ask, given how she is about you, but it's the only thing I have left to give her. I'm hoping that if you can do this for her, before it's too late, it might unlock something. Something that might let some mercy out of her heart for you.*

*For both of us, in fact. Because I'm not sure how much more I can take on my own.*

*Your father.*

The letter within the letter stared up at me. For the hundredth time, I looked at the severe copperplate I knew so well, addressed to a person I'd never heard of until a week ago.

*George MacBeth, 430 Demon's Lair, Fayetteville, 72764 Arkansas, USA.*

Should I open it now? Now that I was sure I had no chance of fulfilling my father's wish? I lifted the next part of the puzzle. Though I'd examined it dozens of times, the creased photograph still made me uneasy.

It wasn't entirely in focus. It showed a shy young man in all the nonsense of full Victorian highland regalia—kilt, Glengarry hat, tweed jacket, *sgian-dhu* and brogues. In one hand he gripped a bible, its page edges gilded, the shimmer of light told me. The other hand was holding out a presentation watch in an ornate cardboard box. In the background, fuzzy but unmistakable, a pit wheel loomed over a row of roofs.

The resemblance in the sepia portrait was obvious. It was me, or at least a version of me. Was this what I might have become? The idea was disturbing. Once again, I turned over the picture to find her elegant writing.

*To George MacBeth*
*For Good Works In The Name Of The Lord*
*SPCK*
*Fallin Parish Church 18.12.1956*

SPCK. The Society For Christian Propagation… The organisation in large measure responsible for the joyless Scottish sabbath—the Sunday Killers, my father called them, with his vengeful atheist bitterness. Sadly, I put all the component parts of the mystery back in their envelope—and as I put it away in my pocket I found myself thinking, as I had done so often in the last few months, about my parents.

My mother. Mary the upright, staunch servant of the Kirk, untiring handmaid to her Protestant God...

For ten years, I hadn't seen her. I had banished her through fear, that much I could admit. Fear of forever—fear of being cast out for all time as Cain. Then, by the time I'd admitted how cowardly that was, it was too late, for the tables had turned—and with a vengeance. Her Calvinist judgement of me had become flint, impenetrable, something which couldn't even begin to be challenged. Could we start again with each other, now? Or ever? However long *ever* might last...? I just didn't know.

And then there was my father. Andrew the angry, incessant learner of the world's lore, tireless disciple of the mechanics of its turning... The fighter whose sense of injustice kept banking the fires of his fury, the striver after understanding who had never understood his own son.

I hadn't helped. I'd been a withdrawn child, wary, perpetually unsure of why the quick-tempered man across the kitchen table always seemed such a stranger. For most of my early life we'd stared at each other through a fog of doubt and disappointment, pierced only by awkward moments of wild companionship when love, like clumsy lightning, had managed to strike both of us at the same time. It had taken the pain of a death and a prison sentence for us to acknowledge the bond between us. We were still trying, each in our own stumbling way, to comprehend it.

And now, when all he wanted in the world was a crumb of comfort to give her, I had to deny him it.

*Arkansas.*

I'd found it on the map, I knew roughly where it was. I even knew a tune with the name in it, *Arkansas Traveller,* one of Scotland's perennial country dance favourites. But how far away was it? I looked round, ready to ask, but the barman was busy wiping tables. I caught a glimpse of the grey-haired man in the mirror, polishing his spectacles. As he donned them he gave me a bleak frown, as though I'd caught him doing something disgraceful. He put money down on the bar, then slid off the stool and walked out.

My eyes found my own reflection in the mirrored wall. What did any of it matter, anyway? Given my current status in this country, Arkansas might as well be on the moon. For the twentieth time I wondered why my parents' phone went unanswered—I must have tried three times every day since getting here. Had he taken her for treatment? And if so, where...? He'd had no way of contacting me since I'd left Italy, I realised. At least, I thought bitterly, they were sending me back to Glasgow, from there I could—

"Hey!"

The flash was an explosion beside me. As the barman yelled, I spun round on the stool. The blitz of light came again, twice. Dazed, I threw up a defensive hand—and then I saw the face behind the mobile phone.

Acne-scarred cheeks, a thin mouth, blue eyes, a tousled shock of fair hair...

A teenager. Girl? Boy? The skinny body wheeled round, began skipping away between the tables. I shouted, launched myself, caught a fistful of collar.

"Lemme go! I didn't do nothin'! Lemme *go!*"

The squirming bundle had surprising strength. I yanked backwards. As the jacket's denim ripped, my quarry turned. The phone swung round, caught me hard on the temple. As my vision jarred, a kick took the legs from under me. I went down in a clatter of chairs. Everything swam—and then the barman was pulling me to my feet. I stood, breathing hard, looking at the baseball bat in his other hand.

"What the hell was that, buddy?" he said, softly. "You bring trouble into my bar?"

I felt a trickle of blood run down my brow. I was just sober enough to check my temper. He glared, then pushed me away.

The kid's phone was at my feet. I picked it up, surveyed the cracked screen. Where to begin? I knew next to nothing about these things... I went along the top row of buttons, pressing one at a time.

Three bad pictures of me, blurred with movement...

An icon for email.

A calculator.

A music selector.

Games.

What did I have to do to find the owner's name? I came to the last button, pressed it.

And then just stared.

This picture of me was in perfect focus. I recognised it—a mugshot, a police photograph taken many years ago.

On the night I'd been arrested.

Without warning the phone's speaker gave a tinny cartoon clang. Jail bars were superimposed on the image of me—followed by text in bright red lettering. A website...

*THEY GOT AWAY WITH IT!*
*WHERE ARE THEY NOW?*

*Yup, you got it, guys! If justice really meant justice, these bozos would have been roadkill long ago! Take the specimen above, a stone killer from Bonnie Scotland who offed his wife, got a sentence that was a slap on the wrist, then...*

I was aware of footsteps from the bar's doorway, a hurried tattoo of heels. Only when the sound reached me did I look up from the ruthless screen; a blonde, her face concealed behind huge sunglasses.

"Excuse me," she said. "I think you have my niece's phone."

I said nothing. She waited a moment, then took off the glasses, rubbed at her eyes and looked at me.

I stared. The hair was up in a careless topknot, and a creased raincoat had replaced the bright dresses. There was no come-hither smile.

But there was no doubt, either.

It was the woman from the triptych poster. I was looking at America's Sweetest Sweetheart.

*

The table was in an alcove, as far from the bar as possible. When we reached it, she gave the fiddle case a puzzled look before taking a chair. I sat. She leaned forward, let her eyes search my face. The proximity of her gaze was uncomfortable. What did she want? When her voice came, it tried to be combative, but the brittleness beneath undercut it.

"Are you really who my niece says you are?"

My anger spilled over. "Nice to meet you, I didn't catch your name," I said. "Mine's Alex Fraser. I made a bad mistake once. I killed my wife. In a fit of rage. I went to jail, served my time. In Scotland, more than twenty years ago. Since then I've been a street musician, trying to get by any way I can. If that's who your niece thinks I am, fine, bring her back in here, I'll be glad to accept her apology." I slid the phone across, stabbed a finger down on the cracked screen. "On the other hand, if *that's* who she thinks I am, tell her to get herself some new adults in her life. Ones who can teach her about judgement. And decency. And privacy."

She flushed bright red. "She's not here, I—I sent her home. In a cab," she stammered. Her eyes dropped. "You're right, I apologise. I was just so shocked, when she told me..."

I watched her try to pull herself together. "I'm Rose Vannier," she said, finally. "You might have heard of me."

"I haven't." I stood up. "I have to go, now."

She grabbed my wrist. "Wait! Listen, I really am sorry. It's just that you being who—what—you are... I mean, it didn't look like a coincidence! I'm sorry, obviously I got it wrong..."

I looked down at the hand that gripped me so tightly. It was dominated by a large red-stoned ring on the middle finger. She let go of me and sat back, defeated.

"It's complicated, you couldn't be expected to know." Her eyes fastened on the cut above my eye. "You're hurt," she said, as though the fact offered some kind of solution. She reached down, hurriedly, brought up a handbag. "Look, let me give you some money at least. Just to—I don't know, compensate you or something."

I was so angry I didn't trust myself to speak. It made her even more desperate.

"I mean, she's just a kid! Who can understand kids, now? They're like a different species! They're out of control, they're..."

The words were a mantra, a lament. As her despair petered out, she held up a fistful of crumpled money.

"Will this cover it?"

The contempt in my face turned hers away. The other voice came just in time.

"Ms. Vannier, perhaps you'd be kind enough..."

I turned. The barman scowled at me in passing—and then his expression became sickly, something between deference and worship. He was holding the framed poster of her in one hand, a felt-tipped pen in the other.

Anger claimed me completely, hot and raw. Before it could explode, I lifted the fiddle case and strode out of the bar.

*

By the time I was due to leave, I was calmer. Holdall in one hand, fiddle in the other, I came out of the hotel. The air was warm, humid and oppressive. I heard distant thunder, saw the flat flash of sheet lightning off to the south. How soon before it rained? Would a storm delay the flight? I turned left for the taxi rank.

And saw her.

There was no avoiding it. The *Wall Street Journal* reader I'd seen earlier was the only other customer, waiting patiently beside the yellow diamond sign that told people where to queue. I walked along and took my place beside the girl. Neither of us spoke. A cab arrived. The man got in, the door slammed, the cab drove off. The two of us were left in silence, determined to ignore each other. She brushed an errant lock of hair from the edge of the sunglasses, turned up her collar as though it could ward me off and tightened the strap of her handbag. Her hands were shaking, I saw. Clumsily, she adjusted the handle of her plastic suitcase and rolled it closer to the taxi sign, as far away from me as she could get. I stared down at the pavement, my head throbbing, desperately tired, desperately trying not to think.

The engine noise which rounded the corner was odd, but only for a split second. *A scooter? Here?* Scooters were Europe, scooters were France, Italy—and what was a scooter doing in a taxi rank, anyway? Its silver body wobbled slightly as it came toward us, and its exhaust rattled. The black-helmeted rider and passenger looked awkward, less than steady. As they came closer, the one on the pillion reached into his leather jacket.

I caught the glint of steel as his hand reappeared. I spun round, grabbed the girl's sleeve and pulled as hard as I could.

"What—"

I heard curse turn to yelp as she fell. The two shots were thunderous.

The scooter skidded to a halt beside me. I dived. My shoulder caught the passenger square in the chest, hard enough to dislodge him. We went down in a tangle of limbs that ended in a loud grunt as his helmet smashed against the kerb. The gun clattered across the pavement. As I scrambled up I caught a lungful of fumes and heard the tinny rattle of the scooter's exhaust as it sped away. Coughing, I turned.

She was half-sitting, half-lying, propped against her case, her left hand bleeding, her handbag and her smashed sunglasses a few feet away. She was shivering, her mouth working in panic.

Time slowed. All I could hear was my own heartbeat. I stared at the charred hole in my holdall, then turned back to the assailant. He hadn't moved. I got down beside him. No blood... A knife fell out of his jacket, an evil little switchblade. Behind me, I heard the girl whimper. I lifted the limp white hand, saw the red freckles on its back, tattooed with a crude green letter M in a circle. I placed finger and thumb round his wrist.

Nothing. No pulse.

*No pulse... Christ!*

I scrambled to my feet. The helmeted head's odd angle was plain to see. His neck was broken. My heart raced.

*I had killed.*

I turned to her.

*Again.*

She sat there, fists tight on her knees, head bowed.

*By accident. Who would believe me?*

Tears were coursing down her cheeks. I tried to speak. Finally, I managed to get words out.

"The police..."

Slowly, jerkily, she got up, blinking, rubbing at her eyes with her bleeding hand. I watched the blood smear itself across her cheek—and then she got herself under control. She breathed deeply, then looked both ways along the dingy hotel's facade. We were alone, separated from the passing traffic by a withered hedge. When her voice came it was a whisper.

"No cops. Please."

She looked at the gun, then the knife, as though she was committing the shape of them to memory. Then she shouldered her handbag and gripped the handle of her case. As though it was a skill that was hard to remember, she began to walk, fast. The thought rushed in on me.

*They'd lock me up. For Life.*

Overhead, the lightning flashed.

*Or they'd execute me.*

My mind tried to run from the words, but it couldn't. The thunderclap came. I stared up at the dark sky. Had my panic triggered it? As the fat, greasy drops of rain began to fall I took a last, terrified look.

The body, the weapons....

I grabbed the fiddle case and my holdall and stumbled after her.

# 2

# DUST

*THE HAWK THAT Swoops On High...*

Above me, the buzzard wheeled, catching the thermal and riding it effortlessly, turning the old bagpipe tune's title into poetry. I stopped and leaned against the wooden rail fence that lined one side of the dirt road, feeling the sun on my neck. A chilly dawn had quickly become a warm spring day, with none of the muggy humidity of—

*The foul air...*

*The clammy feel of the dead boy's hand...*

My eyes fled back to the big bird. It was turning, patiently, waiting for the scared dash, the giveaway scurry that meant prey, food. Briefly, I let fantasy rule.

*I was being guarded, watched over—at the first sign of danger the talons would descend, grasp, I'd be lifted...*

The noise of a vehicle killed it—something big, coming round the bend behind me. I began walking again, my pulse quickening. Cops? Had someone become suspicious? At the store? I stuffed the newspapers I'd bought into my jacket's inside pocket and pulled up my collar. It was still damp from the previous night's downpour. The engine noise grew.

A black van. A few yards past me, it stopped. Willing my face to some kind of normality, I kept walking until I was level with the driver. The window wound down to reveal a handsome man with a shaved head, perhaps in his fifties. A pale puckered scar ran the length of his jawline. What had made it? A knife? Impassively, he shifted the wad of tobacco he was chewing to his cheek. Finally he produced a solemn smile.

"Dusty day for walking, sir. Could a working man and his lady wife interest you in a lift?"

A slow delivery, made less intelligible by the chewing tobacco...

"Thanks, no," I said. "I'm fine. Enjoying the sunshine."

A head of chestnut curls leaned forward in the passenger seat. A woman with an attractively lined face gave me a wide smile.

"Sir, I have to tell you—" Her mellifluous voice, more cultured than her husband's, paused. "—I just *love* your accent! Where do you hail from?"

*Accent…*

I stood, numb with shock, staring at her. *No easier way to identify a stranger…* She smiled on, undaunted—and then a big green and yellow tractor rumbled round the bend behind us. The impatient blast of its horn saved me. The driver and his wife exchanged a quick glance of annoyance.

"I guess some folks just never learned manners," the man said, gravely. "Whoever that gentleman is, sir, we apologise for him. Good day to you."

As soon as the van began to move, the tractor roared into the open gate of the field opposite and stopped. As if in response, the van drew to a halt as well. I watched the window come down again. Anxiety gripped me. Were they going to rebuke the tractor driver...? The fiddle case handle was slick with sweat in my grip; *no incidents, please God, nothing anyone might remember…* But it wasn't what the van driver had in mind. A brown stream of tobacco juice hit the road's dirt. I had a brief view of the scarred face in the wing mirror, unsmiling now—and then my would-be benefactors revved away in a cloud of red dust. As they ascended the hill, I read the legend above the number plate.

*WENGER'S SEED & SUPPLY*
*YOU HOE 'EM 'N' GROW 'EM, WE WEED 'EM 'N' FEED 'EM!*
*CALL 1—800 WENGER*

The big tractor started up again. Without so much as a glance at me, its driver rumbled off across the field—and as the sound of both vehicles faded, the sweat broke on my brow. Was I still safe...?

*Accent…*

I'd have to be more careful. Dizzy, I forced myself forward. At the brown line of tobacco juice I stopped, my eyes drawn to the buzzing life, the frantic convergence of insects.

*Food…*

*Prey…*

I looked up and let my eyes find the bird. It was still etching its perfect circle, tethered to some invisible stake in the sky's blue heart.

*The Hawk That Swoops On High.*

I would have given anything for him to descend and lift me.

*

I walked on, taking refuge in movement. As I reached the top of the next ridge, a lone cloud blocked out the sun and made a cave of shadow that darkened the red earth. It triggered thought.

*The rain. The two of us, half-walking, half-running in grim silence…*

*Her, soaked, sitting on a bench in tears, hair plastered to her head, waving her hands, shouting desperate orders at her mobile phone…*

*The long black limousine, its driver in a separate compartment…*

And then my waking at first light, alone on the car's back seat, outside a white wooden house, far from city or town.

Where was I? Somewhere in the state of Virginia, somewhere deeply rural, that much I knew from the masthead of one of the papers. But it was all I knew. Why had she brought me here? And, more importantly, why had she *left* me here? I sat down on a fallen tree trunk and tried to take stock.

When I'd woken alone in the big car, my intention had been simple—to run, to get as far away as possible. That had lasted as far as the country store, as far as the chink of the till and the change from the twenty-dollar bill. After buying the papers I had exactly fifty-six dollars and twenty-five cents to my name, the remains of the crisp bills the cocky young lawyer had given me the day before. I fished his card out of my pocket. *F. Carlton MacDonald…* My contempt for him seemed an unimaginable luxury now.

No, as things stood, running was out of the question. To

vanish and remain free, in a land where I knew no one and had no money, was impossible. I pulled out the sheaf of newsprint.

*USA Today, The Washington Post, The Winchester Star.* For the third time, I started to go through them, page by page, story by story, line by line.

Presidential pronouncements, a chemical plant fire, the middle east, high school pageants, congressional committees, elections for sheriff, polls, storm warnings...

Used car sales, supermarket discount coupons, roofers for hire, best deals on central heating, personal ads...

Scandal, gossip, opinion, outrage, full page endorsements, tiny sentences of condolence...

But no dead bodies outside cheap Washington hotels.

I looked up at the sun and calculated. Nearly overhead... Midday? Maybe sixteen hours since it had happened—more than long enough for something like this to make the papers. A broken-necked body in the street, surely that was news... Or was America so jaded, so inured to the violence of its cities, that it meant nothing? It was beginning to dawn on me just how little I knew of this country's workings. Again I looked up. The bird was still circling in the sky, not much more than a speck above me. The logic was obvious; the more height, the further the view, the bigger the picture.

But who needed a bigger picture when one fact blocked out everything else? One brutal, inescapable fact.

Once again, Alex Fraser had taken a life.

That meant being on the run. That meant danger, and doubt, the always-watch-your-back uncertainty of the fugitive. It would be unleashed by every unexplained silence, every quizzical look, every suspicious noise.

By every lift offered by a stranger...

But it meant more as well, much more.

I knew myself. The mire where conscience met reality had been a questionable place often enough in my life—and, like every other time violence had occupied it, the canker of it would grow and work its way through me. What could I call the boy's death? An accident? Self-defence? It didn't matter, because I knew the law would never see it that way.

So where did that leave me?

The patch of shade disappeared. The dirt road gave me no answers. I got to my feet and lifted the fiddle. There was nowhere to go but forward.

*

My destination was marked by a hanging sign at the roadside. I hadn't noticed it earlier.

*GALLANT FOX FARM*

The wrought iron name presided over a metalled driveway, guarded by two ancient oaks. It led me down to a perfect acre of manicured lawn, bordered on two sides by thick walls of pine. The house was three storeys of white wood clinging to a rough trapezoid of stone chimney and surrounded by a covered porch. The scene's only movement was the gentle undulation of the two-seater swing seat which hung from the porch roof beside the front door.

Just the breeze, or had someone been sitting there…?

My eyes searched the slope that fell away behind the house, and I now saw what the dawn's mist had hidden, a line of outbuildings. Through the open door of the first, a black horse's tail swished away flies, and from further along I heard a cackle of hens. At the hill's bottom stood more buildings, in various states of repair. Finally, my eyes went to the car which had brought me here.

The long Cadillac limousine hadn't moved. It sat in front of the house like an emissary from a different planet, its sleek blackness totally at odds with the rustic setting. But now there were two other cars drawn up beside it.

Just as big, just as shiny, just as forbidding.

The authorities? Had she thought better of our flight? Was that why she had abandoned me? The porch door opened. Three women came out.

The first was tiny, elderly and thin. She wore a faded pink apron over a drab brown dress. A blue baseball cap, incongruously new, sat on her unkempt white curls.

The second was young, perhaps in her early thirties. She was athletic-looking, shapely in jeans and tight green t-shirt. Her face was pale and strong-featured, her black hair pulled into a heavy knot behind her head.

The third strode out past the other two. She was middle-aged, formally dressed in business two-piece and low heels, the grey of her crisp clothes exactly matching the shade of her short, sculpted hair. She took hold of the porch rail with both hands, as though it fenced off a courtroom she intended to address.

None of them spoke.

*I was the enemy,* I realised. *Why?*

They watched me. They were waiting for something, I knew. When the door opened again, I almost didn't recognise the figure that joined them.

The woman I'd saved was no longer the whisky siren of the hotel bar. She'd become rural, a farm girl in cutoff jeans and denim shirt. The only evidence of the madness we'd shared was a sticking plaster on her left wrist. When she saw my eyes find it, she hid her hand in her pocket. I watched the other three close ranks round her. What was going on here?

I didn't get time to ponder the question. Without looking at each other, they all turned and filed back inside. I was left alone in the spring sunshine.

Until the door opened again.

A man came out, a fat wreck of a man in a wrinkled, sweat-stained white suit, wearing a straw hat which had seen better days. He supported his bulk on a shiny black cane until he subsided on to the porch seat. The chains creaked as they took his weight. He took off his hat and began to fan himself. The pink baldness of his head glistened with perspiration as he finally acknowledged my presence with a wintry smile. As if in reflex, I looked up at the sky to escape his gaze.

The circling buzzard was still there.

*Tomorrow, hawk,* I thought, *if I'm still free, I'll play you the tune.*

*

I had been interrogated often enough, but never quite so ineptly.

Power... People who were sure they had it could never understand when it didn't work, could never conceive of opposition as anything other than a negotiating tactic. I watched the well-dressed woman's cool smile compress itself into a thin line as she wound herself up for another try.

"I don't think you understand. I am Ann Savoy of Atlantic Style." When I didn't respond to the title, she suppressed a frown. "We're the biggest modelling agency on the east coast. I am Rose

Vannier's manager—the heart of her team, she's like a daughter to me. We have no secrets from each other. At *all."*

The strained emphasis on the last word gave the lie—she obviously knew nothing of the night before's brutality. She leaned forward to give me the full bore of her brown eyes.

"All we want is to *understand,* so we can help Rose—protect her, if need be, whatever it takes. We simply *have* to know, and we have to know *fast*. Many things—important things—depend on it."

*Important things*... It didn't take a genius to work out that the phrase was shorthand for *money*. I repeated what I'd been saying for the last hour.

"I've already told you. Get Miss Vannier. I have no intention of talking to anyone else before I talk to her. Alone."

The grey-haired woman tried for a poker face and failed. What next, I wondered. Promises? Appeals to reason? She shot a despairing glance at the girl in the green t-shirt; *help me*. The blank look she got in return irritated her. Brows creased, she turned back to me, more determined than ever. As the uncomfortable silence stretched, I looked at the black-haired girl and wondered; what were the politics here...?

A side door opened. The smell of coffee filled the room as the tiny woman came in. She marched up to the table and set her tray down beside the cracked phone which had started the whole thing. As she began placing cups on the pine top, I heard my interrogator's voice change.

"Let me put this another way, Mister Fraser. You're obviously in some kind of trouble. I'm sure the authorities would be interested in talking to you."

So, threats, not even veiled. If I couldn't be cajoled or tempted into the fold...

Whatever the fold was. Why hadn't Rose Vannier told them about last night? I stared at the steam from the coffee pot, then looked up—to find the eyes beneath the blue baseball cap searching my face. Shrewdly. Calmly.

"...if you help us, we'll help you. As I said, Rose is like a daughter to me. So—"

The metal pot went down on the wood with a thump. A black gout of liquid jumped from the spout. It killed the sentence. The tiny woman's gaze left my face for the middle distance and went from stare to outright scowl. When the clipped drawl came again, it was glacial.

"Thanks, Mattie, we'll take it from here."

*An underling, admonished…* The old woman retreated to the open doorway without a word, then lingered, tray in hand, making it obvious she intended to take her time leaving. Again, politics... When the door finally closed, the black-haired girl took up the slack.

"My name's Sandy, Mister Fraser—Sandy Hunter. I'm Rose's personal assistant."

The voice was a surprise—English, home counties, educated. Moneyed?

"She's having some down time at the moment," she said. "We don't disturb her during that. But meanwhile," she went on, "why don't you tell us about yourself? What we do know, after all..." She gestured at the phone. "...hardly seems biased in your favour."

When I stayed silent she accepted defeat with an indecipherable smile.

The new awkwardness didn't last. The door flew open. The white-suited man came in, moving nimbly despite his girth, a tall glass in one hand, his cane in the other. He put the drink down with slow precision, plucked a red spotted handkerchief from his jacket's breast pocket, wiped his brow, then replaced it with exaggerated care, patting its folds straight. Then he placed the black cane on the table top, carefully. The action invested it with significance; a marshal's baton, a vizier's rod of office... I watched him peruse it, then shift it minutely on the polished wood, as though its comfort was important. Only once all the theatre was over did he smile at me. When the voice came it managed to sound lazy and animated at the same time.

"How nice it is to see us all here on the farm, enjoyin' the simple life. Wouldn't you agree, Mister Fraser?"

So they had my name… I didn't reply. The smile widened.

"I have to say, sir," he went on, "that it's a genuine pleasure to make your acquaintance. In all my years at the bar, I don't believe I've ever had the thrill of meetin' such a one-off individual, a man with such a truly determined talent for self-destruction. I had always thought the type genetically restricted to my home state of Alabama, but I have to confess—" The smile stretched even further, without touching the porcine eyes. "—the utter error of my ways. It's obvious to me now that the mother lode lives high in the mountains of Scotland, listenin' to the bagpipes, waitin' for the bygone howl of the wolf to energise its wild and troubled soul." He raised his glass. "I salute you, Mister Alexander Fraser, so help me God, I do." He swivelled round in his chair to address the room. "Save your breath, ladies, this gentleman's not the talkin' type. He's a jailbird, all right—" He gestured at the phone. "—but forget all such sensationalist trivia. What we have here is a good ol' moral murderer. The fact that he's a musician's just a bonus, because to date, this highly interestin' individual's existence has been one long, sad song."

He drew out the last three syllables as the rubbery mass of his torso wobbled back into the chair, then took a sheaf of papers from the copious folds of his jacket and put them down on the table.

"Here's the story. Pretty much right after they're married, Mister Fraser's lovely wife does a Your Cheatin' Heart number on him. With his best friend, no less. He kills her. Maybe an accident, maybe not—either way it's Jailhouse Rock. When he gets out, he's a one-man justice department, corrupt cops killed our speciality." He shook his head in mock amusement. "I Shot The Sheriff, all round Europe. Now he's here in the good ol' US of A. He's just taken part in the trial of a USAF officer, in the name of helpin' Uncle Sam put the guy away for life. For bein'—" He grinned. "—a thoroughly *bad* man."

He finished the drink in one swallow and slapped his left hand down on the papers. His right hand came up in parody of a legal oath.

"Sworn testimony, right here in Our Great Nation's Capital. Prosecution witness in the case of—" He consulted the sheets in front of him. "—Pentagon v. Lieutenant Wesley Willis, accused of the distribution of counterfeit pharmaceuticals while on service in Germany. And a witness, I might add, on a damn short leash. You see, ladies, Alexander here should have been on a plane home to Scotland last night, but he skipped, so now—and this is official—the Feds are after him. No joke, nothin' counterfeit on this one. There is definitely a Hellhound..." He paused. "...on Alexander's Trail."

No one in the room moved. I felt his gaze settle on me.

"Care to comment, sir? My people get anythin' wrong? Somethin' I need to go back to our private investigators and complain about, spend another eleven thousand of Ms. Vannier's hard-earned dollars checkin'? Anythin' I missed out?"

Still, I said nothing. It was too much for the iron-haired woman.

"For Christ's sake, Saul, of course there is. You can let him know you'll initiate legal proceedings against him if he keeps interfering with the rights of my client to continue doing her job! My client, who, I might remind you, is one of the world's top models. All—"

The snort of laughter from the doorway stopped everything. All of us turned.

Her.

They all waited for her to pronounce.

"He has no idea who I am."

They all swivelled round to stare at me—and then the fat man let out a whoop of genuine mirth. "My stars, that's priceless! An honest-to-god caveman! A primitive vigilante! A proper—"

Rose Vannier's fist smacked hard against the wall beside her. "Enough! Out! Now! All of you, except him."

The English girl was the first to go, carefully not meeting her employer's eyes as she brushed past her. The fat man's merriment went on, but eventually, he got to his feet like the others. Only the grey-haired woman had the courage to confront her.

"Rose, for God's sake," she said. "Why?"

Rose Vannier's reply was menace, pure and simple. "Maybe I just want someone to talk to, Ann. Someone whose eyes don't turn to dollar signs every time they look at me."

The Savoy woman regrouped fast. She put her fists on the table and leaned forward.

"I know we disagree about a lot of things Rose, but I've never been less than honest with you. When you're right, I tell you so—like the sweatshops thing. I admit I got it wrong and I apologise for my opposition. But candid cuts both ways. I've got to tell you that with this guy, I think you're shooting yourself in the foot. Everything about him screams *liability,* and having him around could damage us—you know what the *Opulence* people are like, image is everything to them, the slightest whiff of anything less than squeaky clean could jeopardise the whole deal." She stabbed a finger in my direction. "Talk to him all you want, do whatever else you have to with him, but whatever has to happen, it happens *now.* By the time we're round the table with them, he has to be *gone."*

The silence simmered. This time it was the fat man who filled it. Beneath the deed-to-my-plantation playacting, the voice was hard as nails.

"Well, Annie, I reckon I've got a solution for you. To the problem of our friend here, at least." A malevolent chuckle found his voice. "Bring him along to the big meetin', somethin' exotic, make these French bastards sweat, let 'em speculate which one of us—" He lifted the stick from the table, then paused for effect. "—is fuckin' him."

The word was a lightning rod. Rose Vannier turned away. Ann Savoy stood like stone.

And then the tight set of her mouth began to quiver. She lifted her briefcase and marched out of the room. The man called Saul shrugged, shouted after her.

"He passed the first test, didn't he? He didn't steal the damn Caddy." He turned back to me, reprised the glacial smile he'd given me outside. "Maybe if we're nice to him he won't piss in the soup, either."

*

The last of the outbuildings opened out on to an enclosure for the hens, a big sloping coop that went halfway down the hill. There were hundreds of birds. They rushed up to the wire fence in a red and brown boiling of wings and combs, frantic for the food pellets, clucking, scratching, pecking at each other. Plastic bucket in hand, face once more hidden by a new pair of sunglasses, Rose Vannier threw, watched them scramble, then run back to the wire for more. *Like her employees?* I thrust the thought away—not my business. I watched her complete the cycle three times. I hadn't the slightest idea whether the the activity was affording her fun, or satisfaction, or solace. Was she still as angry?

But how to proceed? Half an hour ago she'd demanded privacy for us, but she hadn't said a word to me since. I put down my fiddle case and raised my voice over the din.

"Why did you abandon me after we got here?"

The hand hesitated in mid-throw. "You get to where I am," she said, flatly, "your life isn't always your own."

She went back to feeding the hens.

"Someone tried to murder you last night. Why?"

She dropped the bucket and whirled round. The glasses

came off. One finger of the hand holding them came up against her jaw in mock speculation.

"Gee, I don't know. Maybe the last *Elle* cover sucked. You think that could be it, mister wife killer?"

The bravado struck a note as false as a cracked bell. How close to the edge was this woman? I picked up the dropped bucket, walked over to the nearest of the feed sacks and scooped half a dozen handfuls of pellets into it. Her voice, high with tension, came from behind me.

"All the stuff Saul came out with. Is it true?"

"Every word."

"That's really why you're here, in America? For this trial? That's why you were at the hotel in DC?"

I carried my load of pellets to the fence and flung it into the coop. The birds raced. I dropped the bucket and turned. As I crossed the barn I took out the lawyer's card and thrust it at her. Without letting her eyes meet mine, she took it.

"If you still can't believe me after last night," I said, "that man will identify me. Asking him to do it might put me in jail for the rest of my days." I heard bitterness claim my voice. "It might even get me killed. But I can't see that mattering to anyone here."

I closed my eyes, desperate to check my temper. When I opened them again she was staring out at the hens, trembling. Shame filled me, but she was so deep in her own misery she didn't even notice. When her voice came it was battened down, fierce with the suppression of tears. The words tumbled out.

"The trouble you're in is my fault, all of it."

She faltered. A single tear ran down her cheek.

"In the circumstances, *thank you* is pretty lame..." She let out a deep, shuddering breath. "...but if you can use it, it's there."

"Miss Vannier—"

Still shaking, held up a hand to silence me. Then she unclenched the fist which held the crumpled card. She wiped her face, smoothed it out and brought it up close to her eyes. I watched her brows furrow as she read.

"This visa thing..." she said, finally. "What will happen?"

The tension between us had died. I walked deeper into the barn's shadow.

"I don't know," I said. "But I know it's nothing compared to a dead body."

The words hung in the dusty silence—and then a soft knocking sound came from behind us. We both turned. The fat man was leaning against the door frame, cane in one hand, his pink face neutral beneath the brim of his hat.

The pact was instant. The girl didn't look at me, I didn't look at her. How long had he been there? Had he heard the words *dead body?* He came into the barn, paused, then walked right up to me. He planted the cane down between us like a territorial marker, then examined my face. For a long time. When he finally spoke, it was her he addressed, but his eyes never left mine.

"Rose, my apologies for intrudin'," he said, softly. "Ann wants to check with you, for Missouri. Ritz-Carlton, St. Louis, less 'n' forty-five minutes to the St. Charles show, we have it three days, take your meetin's right there in the suite. That OK?"

Rose Vannier said nothing.

"Cars'll be leavin' shortly for the Foundation conference in Richmond," he went on. "Fifteen minutes?"

Eyes on the ground, she gave a curt nod. None of the three of us spoke or moved. And then, after a last look of thoughtful scrutiny, the man called Saul turned and went slowly back towards the daylight.

When he reached the fence, the hens rushed up in a squall of sound.

The cane moved fast, lashing at them, slapping them away from the wire, once, twice—and then it came down firmly before him, as though it was vindicated, sated. Without a word, he resumed his progress. His ascent of the stone staircase seemed to take an age. We listened to the ferrule's careful punctuation of each step. When all that was left was the noise of the birds, Rose Vannier's voice, barely more than a whisper, came from my side.

"I'm sorry."

Before I could reply, she hurried after him.

# 3

# ENCOUNTERS

TWENTY MINUTES LATER, I was alone.

No explanations had been given, no expectations expressed. The whole menagerie had decamped minutes after she'd left me—her, hidden behind the inevitable sunglasses, the entourage swathed in self-important silence. Watching them leave was yet another unreality.

I was numb, I had no idea what to do. I was dog-tired, but I dreaded sleep and its inevitable haunting. The image of the boy I'd killed would come, I was sure of it. Fiddle case in hand, I wandered along the row of outbuildings.

The organisation of it all was meticulous. Next to the chicken barn was a lean-to full of firewood, the logs regimented into tall pyramids. It led into a vast storage shed. What did the piled sacks contain? Feed? Fertiliser? Had this been where 1—800 WENGER was heading? I kept moving.

Nothing was locked. I found a workshop filled with the smell of freshly-sawn pine. Fencing? The measured lengths were stacked high, the big power saw was surrounded by neat mounds of sawdust. After that came a tool store with brushes and paint sprayers, compressors, hedge trimmers, long shelves piled with masks and overalls. The main barn followed; racks of drills, rakes, shovels, nail guns, ten different varieties of axe. Half the floor was neatly partitioned into bays for generators, arc welding sets and motor mowers, the other half was given over to bigger items, a digger and its attachments, a brace of mini-tractors, a detachable trailer. I was intrigued. Was it normal for fashion models to be farmers? Or was a working farm merely the current accessory of choice? Money had been spent here, a great deal. The room which led off it was a surprise.

A couch, filing cabinets, a folding screen on wheels, scales… A surgery? *This place even had its own doctor…?* The stethoscope lying on the corner desk confirmed it. What next, I wondered—its own vet? The walls were bare except for one huge framed photograph, placed to catch the window's best light. It took me a second to recognise it as her, Rose Vannier.

Artifice free, fresh-faced, a laughing teenager...

I turned away from it, went back out into the sunshine. Another few yards brought me to the stables.

I didn't know much about horses, but the animals I found in the stalls looked expensive. The black stallion whose tail I'd seen earlier stood next to a clutch of hunters, and a gentle Appaloosa was nuzzling the ear of a soulful-looking bay mare. There was even a pair of working horses, huge, a head higher than the others. Clydesdales? If not, they were certainly first cousins to the beasts I'd watched as a boy on the farms around Stirling. I stood with them a long time, drinking in their size, their patience—until the nearest one gave an impatient snort and a stamp of hoof to remind me of my side of the bargain. I found the the row of feed bags by the far wall and let each of them steal a handful of oats from my palm. The rasp of their tongues was home, childhood.

*My parents…*

Roughly, I thrust the thought from me; *not now.* I patted the two big horses one last time, then went back out, skirted a stone mounting block and continued on the path. It narrowed, then wound me down round a series of tight bends to the hill's bottom.

To what had once been the settlement's heart, I was sure, the gallant fox's original domain—a small hidden valley, sheltered, the lush green of its banks watered by a placid stream. Half a mile away, a waterfall trickled down from a high limestone ridge which curved away into the distance.

The old stone house at the valley's centre must have been grand enough, once, but now it was a building site, hemmed in by a tight skeleton of scaffolding. I rounded its corner to find a large tent. Inside were plastic-covered palettes of brick and dressed stone, rows of copper piping and stacks of slates. I pulled up one side of a tarpaulin to find oak beams, massive, each one nearly twenty feet long. How old were they? Beside them lay piles of broad hardwood planks. Flooring? Reclaimed from some other house? I let my fingers run along the fine grain, then turned and surveyed it all. This wasn't just construction, it was renovation—and period renovation at that. Again, money... On a workbench my eye found a splash of colour.

A workman's tool belt. I went across and lifted it. It was heavy, its leather loops hung with hammers and pliers, files, spanners. I looked at it and felt a small tug of satisfaction; a working thing, with all the inherent beauty of good, functional design. But this had been made even more beautiful. The colour came from rows of turquoise stones, worked into the leather above the tools.

*Work....*

As I replaced the belt on the bench the thought came.

*She could give me a job...*

As soon as the idea surfaced, I swatted it away as ridiculous. Back outside, I walked along a row of wooden garages. Inside the third one I found a van.

An ugly van, an old Ford, big and battered. Once it had been blue, now it was more rust than paintwork. I opened the back doors and drank in the cocktail of smells; diesel, exhaust, stale heat. One cardboard carton, surrounded by jerry cans and coils of hose, took up most of the space. It was the kind big electric appliances came in—refrigerators, washing machines. When I pushed open one end, my brows rose in surprise; a sleeping bag, pillows, a torch, packets of biscuits and soft drink cans...

It looked snug enough, I'd slept in worse. Someone's bolt hole? Thoughtfully, I got out, closed everything up, then went round to the driver's door. It was open. The key was in the ignition. I pulled myself up on to the seat and turned it. The instrument panel came to life. The gauge told me the tank was three quarters full. I looked back at the cardboard box. Whose vehicle was this? Someone who worked on the site? The owner of the tool belt?

And then I felt my heart, beating faster, thrusting blood painfully at the scab on my temple. The maelstrom of thought I'd kept at bay for the last hour burst through the dam my brain had built against it.

*Take it. Run. You're not safe, the man Saul knows... By the time they're here again you're a hundred miles away on the back roads...*

It was almost irresistible. And then the flip side surfaced. If Saul did bring the authorities, there could be no more obvious admission of guilt than flight...

The decision was balanced on a knife edge.

I waited until my pulse slowed, then got out and slammed the door.

Mouth dry, fiddle case in hand, I began the climb back up the hill.

*

Dusk was strange, a state of grace in which the colours intensified as the light failed, a serenity that refused to be buried in fear or worry. Calm came in its wake, along with a heightened sense of perception. The sounds around me became clearer, more resonant; wind, the rustle of leaves, the crickets, the hens, the whinnying of the horses.

Had I made the right choice?

If I hadn't, then I was at least getting a fine equivalent of the condemned man's final meal. I sat on the porch steps and watched the last of the sunset, trying to hope.

And then, through the dying light's garland of birdsong, one sound began to dominate.

A broom. It was at work somewhere at the other end of the house. The old woman? Why hadn't she gone with the others? The long sweeps were comforting, regular.

Rural...

And right. The rhythm was subtle, but it was compelling. I opened the fiddle case.

*The Hawk That Swoops On High.*

I looked up at the darkening sky. Was the bird there? Perhaps... It didn't matter, though, the vision of the broad wings hadn't left me. I lifted my fiddle out and tuned her.

It was a slow beginning, tentative, a reaching—for some kind of rightness, for something that mattered. An antidote. I closed my eyes as muscle and shoulder tensed, letting my fingers search out the notes, letting the bow carve out its cadences and tie them to the rasp of the broom—and then, as always, inside a few phrases I was in the music, lost in it. Nothing else mattered. Before I knew it I was at the end of the second part, pushing back into the beginning, eager to let the instrument speak, to get to the raw modal jump that stamped it as a pipe tune and defined the whole melody. When I had gone round it for the third time, I just sat, eyes closed, satisfied that what I'd played had earned me, at the very least, a place in my surroundings.

And when I opened my eyes, the old woman was standing at the other end of the porch, about thirty feet away. She was gripping the broom handle with both hands, holding it before her, leaning on it like a pilgrim's staff—and the dusk's light let me recognise what age had tried to conceal.

She had been beautiful, once...

As beautiful as her daughter.

Before I could digest the revelation, more steps came.

The man who appeared at her side was big, at least six and a half feet tall. He stood erect, naked from the waist up, calmly watching me. His upper body was massively muscled. The blue-flecked tool belt I'd seen earlier hung from his waist. Above it I saw skin of a dull red, a dark ochre that seemed to hold a layer of luminosity below its surface. His hair, long and lustrous, was the blackest I'd ever seen.

An American indian. A god of a man...

How old was he? I couldn't tell, but somehow, being seated in his presence seemed wrong. I laid the fiddle in its case and got to my feet. The solidity of him was mesmerising. I watched him put a huge arm round the woman's bony shoulder—and then a voice cut in.

"Well, now, what we got goin' on here?"

The voice was rich, its southern tones playful and amused. I turned. A thin man in spotless white jeans was standing at the top of the steps which led down to the outbuildings, holding a black cowboy hat which looked newer than the rest of him. A smaller figure arrived behind him. I took in the clothes; scruffy denims, trainers, a red hoodie. Only when the hood was pushed back did I recognise the face.

Pale, unsmiling, the rash of spots and scars like a brand on her cheeks...

The kid.

The tomboy from the night before, from the hotel bar, the one responsible for the whole mess I was in now. She avoided my eyes, thrusting her fists into the hoodie's pockets and scowling down at her feet.

The thin man paid her no attention. He came towards me, limping slightly, one hand dusting at a white leg with the hat's broad brim, the other scratching at his mop of blond curls. When he reached the corner, he saw the woman and her companion. The friendly grin turned itself down a notch, but the change didn't stop me recognising his features. Again, revelation—the third side of the triangle. This was another version of Rose Vannier's beauty, but male, and withered rather than weathered. I watched the confrontation between mother and son. The red man's face stayed unreadable.

The newcomer turned and stepped up on to the porch, the easy grin back to full wattage. I watched it wait for reaction as he faced me. When none came he turned, quickly.

"Howdy, momma. Still keepin' fine comp'ny? Just like the old days, I guess, first come... What's next? Our dark brethren? Me-hi-canos?"

The venom was a mismatch with the smooth smile. Neither the old woman nor her companion reacted. The newcomer turned back to me. The movement brought me a whiff of his body. Beneath the heavy aftershave was the hint of something bad, something stale and decaying. The smile widened.

"And I guess you gotta be the man, the guy ripped the jacket—" He jerked a thumb at the slight figure behind him. "—offa my Mary Lou last night. Where'd you get off layin' hands on my kid, fella?" He paused, gave a laugh that was meant to menace. "I oughta beat the shit outta you for that."

The casual contempt was all the excuse my anger needed. I took a step forward. It killed his poise. He shied back, stumbled against the porch step and dropped his hat.

Somehow, through my rage, I found my eyes locked on the red man's. The calm I found there was a rebuke. It checked me. Slowly, I bent down, picked up the hat and held it out. After a second's hesitation, the thin man's hand reached for it.

It was a bony hand, a poor hand... It was the truth of him, raw and mean, the nails bitten, the thin fingers misshapen and ugly. It snatched the hat from me. He put it on, carefully. By the time our eyes met again, the smile was nearly back in place. He put his hands in his pockets with studied casualness and turned again to his mother.

"End o' the month, momma. You tell Rose I'll need a little extra, kid needs stuff. Clothes. Gotta get her new shoes." His mouth twisted into a sarcastic grin. "An' a new jacket."

Without looking at me he strolled away, back towards the steps. The girl was gone.

"Mary Louise Vannier! Where 'n' hell are you? Get your ass in the car! I'm outta here in five minutes, you ain't there you can walk, you little shit!"

I didn't move until the petulant shouting had stopped—and when I turned, the old woman and her companion were no longer there. In the silence, I looked up at the darkening sky.

But then I closed my eyes. The hawk had left me, somehow I knew it.

*

"Where did you learn your music?"

The red man's voice was a bass rumble. The urbane formality of it was a surprise, its impact doubled by the clothes. In the hour since I'd first seen him, he had changed. Now he wore a three-piece charcoal grey suit, a white shirt with its collar pinched in by a gold pin, and an immaculate tie. Had its deep red been chosen to match his skin? I found myself remembering the young government *apparatchik* of the day before. This was a version of the same uniform, undoubtedly—but the man before me projected a different rank entirely. The Washington boy lawyer would have given anything to look like this, to radiate, so effortlessly, such authority. We were in the room where they'd tried to question me. I leaned across the table for the whisky bottle; amber absolution, finally...

"I was taught," I said. "Well taught by a thorough old lady. Who are you?"

"I'm the handyman."

A handyman dressed like a banker... We sat in silence, letting that paradox settle. I watched him drink, his massive hand all but obscuring his glass.

"The one with the hat, he's Rose's brother?"

He nodded. "Mr. Lee Vannier, ladies' man, drug dealer and general failure of this parish. Fading movie star looks, five-star gee-shucks smile and—" He paused. "—sad little felony record. Three years for possession with intent to supply—remarkable, really, that they couldn't hang more on him." He took a sip from his glass. "An entirely unreconstructed redneck, tolerated due to the happy accident of his birth. Tolerated on this farm, and in the apartment his sister bought for him in DC, but pretty much nowhere else. Here for his monthly handout."

"And the old lady? Their mother?"

"A complicated story. But yes, Mattie is their mother."

"And you? What's your story?"

He smiled, said nothing. I took a mouthful of whisky before trying again.

"At the moment, my life could do with a little less mystery. Could we start with your name?"

He considered it, then nodded. He reached into his waistcoat pocket, brought out a business card and put it down on the table between us. I picked the card up.

*John Walks-Over-Ice MD.*

The occupant of the surgery…? The name held me, an atavistic mismatch to the letters which followed it and the twenty-first century row of phone numbers and email addresses beneath. I put it in the back pocket of my jeans.

"Are all indian names so poetic?"

The face didn't change. "Full marks," he said. "First reaction's usually polite surprise that one of us Native American noble savages could aspire to anything as sophisticated as medicine."

I smiled. "So what do I call you? Doctor Walks-Over-Ice?"

The massive head shook. "Nobody else round here does."

"What do they call you?"

"To Rose and Mattie and Saul I'm John, to the rest...." The shoulders gave a massive shrug "Johnnie Walker. Or Big Chief. Sometimes even Tonto or Hiawatha, if they think I'm not listening." He nodded at his glass. "Depends how bold the other Johnnie makes them."

The irony in the voice never showed on the stone face.

"You prefer being a handyman to a doctor, John Walks-Over-Ice?"

"You prefer being a fugitive to a fiddler, Alexander Fraser?"

I felt my anger flare, then dissolve. Other than letting me know I should mind my own business, he had done nothing to deserve it. The standoff lasted until he lifted the bottle again and poured a generous measure into both our glasses.

"A job is a job," he said, finally. "Not much call for a doctor here at Gallant Fox. I give some medical advice now and then." Without warning the voice became a deep parody of officialese. "But surprising though it may seem, and despite a sincere commitment to the facilitation of non-racial stereotyping and equality of opportunity from everyone involved in Ms. Vannier's entourage..." He swirled his drink around. "...not a single person round here, not even the stable boy or the old guy who does the hens and the horses, wants their vitamin shots from a three hundred pound Cherokee injun."

I didn't reply. He sat back, his eyes examining me, calmly.

"You planning on staying long, Mister Fraser?"

"I'm not sure."

Outside, I heard cars draw up, doors slam. The man Saul's high tones drifted in, hectoring and mocking at the same time. When the red man spoke again, the deep voice was carefully neutral.

"If I was you, I'd make that the subject of some serious thought."

A warning? A threat? Before I could probe, he put down his glass and rose.

"Circus is back in town," he said. "Better get to it, top-of-the-line vehicles to polish."

I stared at him. Calmly, he looked back at me, the same steady assessment he'd given me when his arm was round the old woman's shoulder.

"Yes. I'm also the chauffeur. It was me who collected you and Rose from Washington last night."

*

One day, no matter how strange, at a time.

Since my conversation with John Walks-Over-Ice, no one had said a word to me, but for the moment it seemed I was safe. The room the old woman had shown me to was under the house's eaves. It was spartan, comforting in its simplicity—a polished pine floor, a single window, a bed with a patchwork quilt, a table with a chair. I lay, smelling the wood, listening to the outside sounds, exhausted with the effort of trying to work out what had happened to me.

Mothers, daughters, brothers, managers, lawyers, assistants, chauffeurs...

And then there was Rose Vannier, the strange creature at the middle of it all. She seemed almost simple by comparison. I knew why—hurt people, damaged people, those were people I could understand.

But then I checked myself—damaged people who were some kind of huge success, that was new to me...

I finally acknowledged that sleep was impossible, got up and went to the open window. The night air was cool, pleasant. I put on jeans, shirt and shoes and took the fiddle from its case, along with the cloth I used for cleaning her.

When I reached the porch, the moonlight showed me a single sheet of paper lying on the swing seat. I picked it up and sat down, holding the fiddle as I read.

*Isn't it just the best kind of American story?*

*Adopted from a Mississippi orphanage, Rose Vannier was brought up in Lexington, Massachusetts. The girl who was to become one of the world's best-known models grew up surrounded by love and comfort, but her new parents were determined that, just like every other kid, America's Sweetest Sweetheart...*

The words *not again, too damn much! Get to the point!* were scrawled in the margin in a different hand.

*...worked all the way through High School. She bagged groceries at her local supermarket, she worked the carwash at weekends, she was the neighbourhood's star babysitter. All with the fantastic smile the world now knows so well! If...*

A yellow stick-on note that said *Friday lunchtime absolute deadline!!!* obscured the next line.

And as I bent the paper back to read on, I felt it.

*It.* The knowledge, from my jail days...

*...a stable home. Add to that the fact that she learned the value of a dollar while she was growing up, and you'll understand why she founded the Rose Vannier Foundation For Family Life, the charity which has been so successful in giving financial help to struggling parents, help-*

*ing them give their kids a better start in today's tough...*

It was the sixth sense, the one I'd grown in self-defence, in Glasgow's Barlinnie prison...

*...to date, this ambitious organisation has supported hard-pressed families across America to the tune of seventeen million dollars, and is endorsed by no less a person than...*

I was being watched.

No sooner had I realised it than the patrician English voice came from the porch's far corner.

"What do you think?"

I turned. Sandy Hunter, the personal assistant. She was sitting on the decking with a glass of red wine in her hand, ten feet away from me, knees pulled up in front of her face. Her grey eyes looked huge against her pale skin. She got to her feet effortlessly, still holding the glass. It was like watching a serpent uncoil—or rather, a nest of them, for the thick tendrils of black hair seemed to possess separate lives, each one taking an extra millisecond to settle on her shoulders. She slid a shapely denim hip up on to the wooden rail.

"Sixth form English prize and I end up writing one of these a week. Or rather, rewriting the same one. Depressing, really."

I found my voice. "So why do it?"

"Money." Her expression was serious. "The almighty dollar." She swirled the wine round. "The stuff that rains down from a benevolent sky."

She drank, then threw back the black mane and looked out at the dark. When her eyes finally came back to me, they seemed even bigger. She unleashed an ironic smile.

"And of course, there's always the matter of a career in—" She let the red nails of her free hand make parentheses in the air. "—*fashion.* The Holy Grail for a nice girl from Surrey. It was either that or the bimbo route."

"Which was?"

"Secretarial school," she said. "That was my mother's advice. Remember it's your backside that matters, Alexandra, not your brains. Keep your nails nice, your skirts short and your heels high. Wax your legs, swing your hips, bag yourself a banker." The plummy vowels became prosaic. "Or a doctor or a lawyer, shit, even a bloody dentist, if they can pay the Harrods' bill." She turned away, gazed out at the darkness. "So I chose modelling rather than mediocrity. The trouble was, I was crap at it. A genuine catwalk catastrophe, about as much poise as a sheep waiting to be shorn." She turned back to me. "Luckily I had other assets—they do love an accent, the Yanks, don't they? So thank you, Cheltenham Ladies' College." She took the barest sip from her glass. "Your turn…" Again, the hard smile came. "…Alexander."

I said nothing. Her voice became a purr, completely unabashed in its efforts to coax.

"Your moment in the lights. What exactly happened in the big bad city? I'm curious." When I said nothing, she pressed on. "Some great epiphany, was it? Some divine transformation which told you fashion was your life?"

When I still didn't answer, she laughed. It wasn't a sound which had much to do with humour.

"You think fashion's nothing to do with you, don't you? Well, as of whatever went on last night in the fleshpots, you're wrong. You're part of the entourage now, Rose wants you, that's obvious, and what Rose wants... Shouldn't be too difficult to make you fit, as long as you keep your mouth shut. You're a good enough looking bit of rough. Eye candy, up to a point."

The Americanism seemed out of place in the home counties drawl. Was I being flirted with? Still I didn't speak. It didn't daunt her.

"I'm thinking, Armani suits, darkish, a couple, lightweight. No tie, of course. Half a dozen shirts, collarless, muted colours." She smiled lazily as she assessed me. "Not silk, no, not really you. Cotton, high thread count, J. Crew do some great ones, a bit downmarket, but that doesn't matter. Gucci loafers, shades. And some decent aftershave. Splash a bit on some of that lovely macho designer stubble."

She undulated herself off the rail, glided across the space between us and let her perfume envelope me. It was heavy, sultry. The voice matched it exactly.

"Like a bit of a scent, do you, Alexander? This one's expensive, very. Maybe you could buy a poor girl who shares a name with you a bottle. Out of your first paycheck, perhaps?"

No doubt about what was being offered, none at all. As she reached across me, the hem of her t-shirt rose. The smooth flesh of her midriff brushed against me. A puckered scar made a long white seam across its left side. Finally she plucked the paper from me with one hand and handed me her wine glass with the other. It was still nearly full.

"Let me know when you're ready to hit the mall," she whispered. She gave the swing a shove that was a shade too strong to be playful. "Love to help you choose."

I let the seat rock, watching the red liquid in my hand undulate with the movement. As her footsteps disappeared into the house, I stopped the motion with my foot and raised the glass to my lips.

The wine tasted bitter.

*

It was another hour before I made it back to the room. Exhaustion had finally claimed me. I was ready to swap the fiddle for sleep—until I saw the bag on the seat by the window. A leather bag, big, a larger version of a Victorian doctor's bag. An envelope and a mobile phone lay on the seat beside it. I lifted the bulky envelope with my free hand. It wasn't sealed. Inside I found a sheaf of notes, tens and twenties. Two thousand? Three? There was a credit card as well, in the name of A. Salinger, and a scribbled note.

*Go. Quickly. It's not safe to stay, I'm not sure how much Saul knows. There's an old van in the last garage, the keys are in it, nobody'll miss it for a couple of days. Use the cash first. When it runs out, use the card. Name's Salinger, the pin's 9843, it's got plenty of credit and I can cover the withdrawals with farm stuff. My cell's 0202 435622, Hole up somewhere out in the sticks, call me in a week or so.*

*The bag, After last night I thought you could use a new one. I took the liberty of adding some clothes, in case there's any kind of description out.*

*I'm sorry for all this, so sorry. I'll get you out of it, I swear.*

*R.*

Frowning, I sat, trying to work it out. Who had brought this? The bag, the money...? Rose Vannier herself? The girl, Sandy, after she'd left me? I hadn't heard anyone on the stairs.

But if Rose Vannier was right about Saul...

I decided. I tucked the envelope away in my jacket's pocket, then stood and looked at the bag, smelling the expensive leather. With my free hand I took the handle and lifted. It was heavy—heavier than I thought it would be. As I held it, it seemed to shift in my hand. The catch fell open.

I heard the rattle too late.

Fiddle and bag were wrenched away as the snake launched itself. I staggered backwards, fell, felt the floor slam the breath from me. The room swam. I scrambled away in a frenzy of shins and elbows. Again I heard the rattle.

*Was it coming?* I made myself look. It was on the bench, a sinuous cartwheel of brown and black. The head rose, then crooked downwards. Mesmerised, I watched it slither down towards the fiddle. The instrument was lying face down, rocking to and fro at a precarious angle, its peg box caught on the bag's handle. The sinuous body's passing dislodged it. The neck fell on to the diamond-patterned back. The strings sounded, the trapezoid head snapped round. Again, it struck—this time so fast I never saw it happen. As the instrument clattered away, there was a loud bang. The rattle was everywhere, surrounding me.

And then the snake seemed to hesitate. It reared up from its coils, swaying, then pushed itself back up on to the seat. The forked tongue flickered out as though it was testing the air—and then, with infinite slowness, the head zig-zagged up to the window sill. I watched it cantilever itself obscenely out into the night.

I didn't dare move. All I could hear was the rasp of my breath. Finally, I made it to my feet. Still shivering, I checked my right arm.

*Nothing*. It hadn't got me.

Relief brought dizziness. Despite it, I reached down. The fiddle was still in one piece, the bang had been the bridge collapsing. I angled the wooden body round in the moonlight. Some of the purfling was gone. I laid her on the bed, then got down and searched. When I found the bridge, my gorge rose.

Two puncture holes, an indentation in the shape of a reptilian jaw... Still dizzy, I slumped down on the bed.

My fiddle had saved my life.

It took a shaking age to pack the instrument away. Once it was done, I lifted the case. My other hand reached out for my old canvas holdall.

I stood in the middle of the room and closed my eyes, then let out a long breath. I was alive.

Everything I owned in the world was now in my two hands. I made for the stairs, wondering how long it would take me to stop shivering.

# 4

# BOND

A MAP. I'D NEED a map.

The back road out of the farm was narrow and potholed, and the darkness robbed me of any sense of direction. The old van rattled and groaned, her suspension bouncing wildly on the deep ruts, but despite my clumsiness, she never stalled. I'd only driven an automatic vehicle once before.

But the strength she demanded of me was good. To have something to struggle against was a relief—something to smother thought while I got as far from Gallant Fox Farm as possible. For once in my life, logic and instinct were in exact agreement—I had to put as many miles as possible between me and my assailant. And then? Somewhere sheltered, somewhere I could claim a breathing space and camouflage my presence long enough to sleep. If sleep was possible.

I drowned big thoughts in small practicalities. Food. It was a long time since I'd eaten. How long could I go without a meal? One more day? The biscuits and cans in the back might stretch it to two... The more serious problem was going to be fuel. Inside half an hour's driving, the gauge had already plummeted. Where would I find petrol? On the back roads, in the middle of the night...? Petrol and a *map*. Did rural America have filling stations out in the wild? Any knowledge I had of this country came from the sugar-coated television of my childhood, but it seemed logical to expect a town or a village at some point. And—

Without warning the dirt road became a ramshackle bridge. Beneath me, traffic roared, loud with horns and bright with light. Even though it was the middle of the night, the huge road was busy in both directions, with cars and vans, massive trucks. I slowed. Should I take the chance? Service stations would have what I needed... Would they be better camouflage or worse? And then my headlamps found the rural darkness again. I accelerated.

*Away from all that...*

I couldn't trust the modern world, not yet—and then the memory of the snake slithered through my defences; the obscene rattle, ancient and evil. I shuddered.

There were worse things than the modern world.

*

I needn't have worried about sleep. After another hour of pitting myself against vehicle and road, it became an imperative. I was beyond fatigue, past rational thought. I found a clearing, took off my jacket and just sat in the driving seat, watching the rain spotting the windshield as I listened to the engine clicking itself cool. The sound reminded me of something else.

A cane on stone steps...

Had that been just half a day ago? Was Saul Morgan the one who'd planted the snake? It had been an act of cold cunning, one that required planning... Slowly, I felt my body begin to surrender itself.

The images which claimed my unconscious were a jumble of inchoate fears and inarticulate desires. I was on my knees in a darkness far deeper than I'd ever known, aching with longing for something I couldn't name, something beautiful which was waiting just out of reach. But even as the longing filled me, I knew a monster was watching. Its reek was sulphurous, its breath a long, rattling hiss. No matter how I turned it was always behind me, patiently measuring me for revenge. How had I wronged it? Above me the buzzard circled. Its call was the creak of the van door, the chill air I felt, the fanning of its wings. I knew I was weeping, but the tears were Rose Vannier's.

*Could it have been her?*

The touch of the dead boy's hand killed it, brought me back to consciousness. Wet with sweat, terrified, I saw with relief that it was still dark outside. I slumped forward, exhausted by the dream.

I reached for the keys. If I couldn't sleep, then I had better keep moving.

*

By three am, the van was running on empty. I came to a junction with a metalled road. The toss of a mental coin took me left. After a few miles I came to a round shield.

City of Brunswick, MD, population 6171.

MD, was that Maryland? Didn't that mean I was going north? Did I want to go north? Rows of houses began to appear. I scanned them. No sign of life. Slowly, I drove on. A bridge rose out of the darkness. Another sign told me I'd reached the Potomac River. I drove across it, the tyres singing on the metal mesh surface. On the far bank I saw lights and movement and heard sound; a railway marshalling yard. In the distance I saw a stubby diesel locomotive shunting a line of wagons along a tracery of tracks, silvered by the moonlight. The first thing I saw on the other side was a flickering gasoline sign. I pulled in. It was deserted, but there was an automatic pump.

Credit cards only, a torn-off sheet of paper taped to the kiosk told me. I stood, shivering. Risky or not, I had no choice. I reached into my pocket, then took off the filler cap and pushed the Salinger card into the slot. The pump handle's metal felt cold as I stuck the nozzle into the tank's neck. I pulled the trigger. Nothing. I frowned. Broken? Had I done something wrong? I took it out and repeated the process in a different order. Still nothing.

"That ain't the way you do it."

I whirled round. The kid, the tomboy. She was standing just behind the van. From the depths of the red hood, the blue eyes surveyed me, warily.

"You gotta lift the lever." Eyes still on me, expression unreadable, she came forward, then reached out to the pump. "Like this."

She pulled up a steel flange, took the hose from my hand, inserted it and pulled the trigger. As the fuel began to flow, she looked up at the scar on my forehead.

"I do that?" she said.

Slowly, I nodded.

"Hot damn," she muttered. A brief smile flickered. "Musta

got you pretty good."

*

The ancient waitress brought ham and eggs and coffee for me, and set a stack of pancakes down in front of my companion. As she waddled away, the girl lifted her fork and examined my face. It was an adult's look, not a child's. Appraisal was the aim, not approval.

"It's where I go, on the farm, when my old man gets rough," she said, matter-of-factly. "The van, I mean. If he can't find me he just leaves, comes back the next day. When I was little, it'd buy me a lickin', 'cept if Aunt Rose was around. Or John." She paused. "When you stopped, I had to get out to piss. I got back in, you were cryin'. In your sleep."

Observation, not accusation... I watched her search my face for reaction, file away the fact that none came.

"Nobody knows about the van 'cept me and John. And now you, I guess."

This time it was a probe. I watched the intelligent eyes wondering if they'd made an accomplice of me. Finally, she reached across for the plastic bottle at the table's end. She upended it and squeezed syrup on to her pancakes.

"Guess we're tight, now," she said, "buddies."

I didn't contradict her. She bent her head and attacked the food. After a few forkfuls she spoke again.

"Where we goin', anyway?"

I looked round. There was a blue-suited businessman with a choleric face, frowning at a laptop, and two elderly farmers in overalls. None of them was paying us any attention. I hesitated. What was the best way to do this...? I heard the awkwardness in my voice as I spoke.

"Where I'm going doesn't matter. You're going home. It's an accident you're here, but it's still my fault. I have to get you back to your parents."

She snorted. "Parents? There's just my old man, momma's gone. Long gone." The two final words elongated themselves into an exaggerated southern drawl. "I never even knew her. The old man says she was just a hooker anyway." The look she gave me was a challenge. "Says he's been surrounded by chippies spreadin' 'em all his days. Says it's an even bet I'll go the same way, make my livin' on my back."

Her face retreated to its default blankness as she waited for my response. I kept my voice neutral.

"Then I'll get you back to your aunt."

A lank lock of hair fell over her brow, hiding her eyes as she bent again to her food. Like the blank face it was deliberate, camouflage... I let the silence stand and lifted my fork. Only after the first mouthful did I realise how hungry I was. After she'd eaten half her food, she swept back her hair. Her eyes stayed on the table as she fingered the angry line of spots on her left cheek.

"I don't wanna go home," she said, quietly.

*Careful, now...* "Mary Louise, that's your name, right? Can I call you that?"

Her mouth hardened into contempt. "Mary Louise sucks," she said, succinctly. "Sentimental southern cornpone shit. I hate it."

The vehemence was a surprise. "So what do I call you?"

"My friends call me Lou."

"Lou, I know your aunt cares about you. She'll be worried."

The only answer I got was the lowering of her head. I watched her, scowling at the remains of her meal. It was the first time her face had shown her as less than adult. She pushed her plate away, still not looking at me.

"I have no choice," I said.

Her head jerked up as she fastened on the words. "That's because you're in trouble, right? On the lam. That's why you stole John's van."

I said nothing. She leaned across.

"I can help you. I'm smart, I know the street and you don't. Shit, Alex, you can't even pump gas. Make it to Fayetteville on your own? Yeah, right—you wouldn't last a day."

The shock of it was like a physical blow. "How do you know about Fayetteville?"

She brazened it out. "Whaddya think I am, some kinda retard? I went through your jacket. When you were asleep."

The envelope... Automatically, my hand went to my inside pocket. The letter was there. Her lip curled as she misread my response.

"I didn't touch your money."

Her bitterness killed my anger. I sat back, looking at her sad defiance. How old was she? Thirteen? Fourteen? None of the hardness was facade, somehow I knew it. She looked away.

"What'd he do, anyway? Your uncle?"

Something in the girl's voice made it important to reply.

"I don't know," I said, quietly.

As soon as the words were out, I wished them unsaid—it was a revelation too far. I finished my coffee and angled myself out of the booth. Warily, she watched me put down too much money for the food.

"Ten minutes," I said.

Outside, the sun had killed the mist. The van was parked a few yards away. At the diner's corner, I saw the dilapidated phone booth I'd missed in the darkness. I took out Rose Vannier's note as I went toward it. I had to trust the woman, I had no choice. But how to do this? Leave the girl somewhere to be picked up? No, she could run... Put her on a bus or a train? What guarantee would I have that she'd go where I sent her? No, I thought, it had to be personal. America's Sweetest Sweetheart would have to come to me—I had to physically give her niece back into her care, nothing less would do. I tried to do a mental computation. It was morning, now. How long would it take Rose Vannier to get here? Four hours, five? I stared at the chipped black plastic of the handset. *If I got this wrong...* I reached for the receiver. Perhaps I could—

"I'm not goin' back."

I turned. The kid was standing behind me, fists bunched in the hoodie's pockets.

"You try to make me, I'll run. Before you're a mile down the road, I'll tell everyone you kidnapped me. They'll get you in an hour."

It was all said calmly. Her face was unreadable. The moment stretched between us, confrontation on her part, confusion on mine. Slowly, I hung the phone up. Again, she misread me. She turned to run—and collided with the blue-suited businessman, briefcase in hand, coming out of the diner. Tie flapping, he leaned down and caught her with his free hand. Gently, he turned her round.

"Whoa there, little lady, what's your hurry?"

She scanned his kindly face, then looked at me. As she turned back to him again, I watched her expression change.

"Can I get a ride with you, mister?" she pleaded. Before he could reply, she shot out an accusatory finger at me. "That man there says he's gonna rape me!"

He let go of her as though she was made of brimstone. Consternation and distaste came to his florid features. As he turned to me she stepped back, out of his sight, the smile on her face a mixture of calculation and pure mischief. Then she ran past him, grabbed my hand and grinned back at him.

"Just kiddin', mister. He's my dad."

He looked at both our faces, amazement turning to outrage. Finally, he scowled at me.

"Mighty strange sense of humour your kin has, sir," he said, stiffly. "Goes with a dirty mouth, I guess. Was my daughter, a stunt like that, I'd whale the ass off her. Good day to you."

Without looking back at us, he got into an old brown sedan. As he drove away, carefully not looking at us, she gripped my hand even tighter. She looked up at me.

"See how easy it would be? See—"

The anger in my face stopped her. I pushed her back against the van's side, too hard.

"You think this is a game? That man won't forget us, now, *ever.*"

I felt her trembling before I saw it. Shocked at myself, I let my hand drop. She scrambled into the van. The door slammed.

No other sound came. I closed my eyes tightly, trying not to think about the fear in her eyes.

*

"Alex, we need a motel."

"Isn't that risky?"

"Safest way to get internet."

"And we need that?"

"We need that." She paused. "And you need a bath."

I felt myself smile as I slowed for the traffic lights. I watched her register it, then add it to her store of victories. Then I went back to perusing the street.

*We...*

It was a strange idea, but it had become real—neither of us was quite so solitary any more. Here, in the drab suburbs of Wheeling, West Virginia, I finally admitted it to myself.

And she was right about one other thing, at least—she was, by a long chalk, smarter than me about American street life. Fugitive life. Maybe even criminal life...

A map.

*Don't just buy a map, dummy—people remember folks who buy just one thing. Get a bagful of stuff…*

Food.

*Don't go for the hot dogs, let me. Nobody remembers a kid buyin' dogs at a stand…*

Fuel.

*No freeway truckstops, ever, they got security. Busy urban gas station, evenin' rush hour. Tired people don't notice, lots of 'em fillin' up on the way home. Park a ways away, send me in first to buy candy, scope out the cameras…*

The lore of the hunted... As we quartered the matrix of streets at Wheeling's deserted centre, I stole a surreptitious glance at her. She was intent on the street, carefully scanning the shop fronts from the passenger seat. For what? I had to force myself to concentrate on what she was saying.

"...don't ask for ID. We want a shitty one, a mom & pop place where they don't care 'bout nothin' 'cept the money. The strip won't be good, all big chain jobs where you got to register. We need one of the old main roads out of town, from the time before the freeways. You—"

She stopped, suddenly aware of my scrutiny.

"What?" she said.

The default blank face... I heard the wariness in her voice.

"Where did you learn all this?" I asked. "All this stuff about how to live on the road, how to survive?"

She looked away. "Pull over," she said.

We drew up in front of a grimy shop window, crammed with plastic dolls, camouflage jackets, fishing rods, rifles, hunting knives, every conceivable variety of battered consumer electronics. A somnolent grey cat cast one eye over us from a precarious pile of old LPs, then went back to sleep. The flaking lettering above the dirty glass told me we'd stopped at the *Jesus Is Lord Gun & Pawn*. Lou examined the window in thoughtful silence, then turned to me.

"I need two hundred bucks," she said.

"Why?"

Her face still expressionless, she held out her hand. I didn't argue. I reached into my jacket pocket, opened Rose Vannier's envelope and gave her a handful of bills. She stuffed them into her pocket and got out. As she pushed open the shop door, her eyes found mine. I caught a millisecond of a new look, a lost look, before she turned away.

*Worry...*

I understood it. She was waiting for the axe to fall. She had to go home, that fact hadn't changed. All day long, since the diner, the question had been avoided—by both of us. I'd caught occasional glances from her, furtive ones, as I drove. In the morning, they'd been anxious, as the day wore on, less so.

Why hadn't I done it? Sent her back? I'd told myself it was a breathing space after the morning's events, but it wasn't the truth and I knew it. At bottom, the truth was fear.

A new fear, to add to all the others... I was afraid of being alone here, in this strange place, this incomprehensible country. I looked out over the choppy waters of the Ohio river, its waves flecked by the rising wind. Practicality overran my thoughts; a storm? We'd need to be off the road, and soon...

*We...*

As I backed away from the thought, the passenger door opened. Grinning now, Lou put a brown paper bag down on the seat between us. I looked inside, then drew out two rusting red rectangles. Number plates, old ones.

"Ohio plates. You're still usin' John's. We need to change 'em, first thing they'll circulate. See what else I got."

I put my hand back in the bag, felt a sleek piece of black plastic, cold and heavy. I lifted it out.

"What is it?"

She shook her head in amazement. "You never seen an iPad? What planet you from, Alex?"

She reached into her pocket. Her hand came out with a paper clip.

"You're on the lam, in a stolen van. You—"

She straightened the clip, then inserted it into a hole in the device's side. A tray slid out.

"—gotta check the news to see what's out on you. On us. This way—"

This time her pocket yielded a tiny card. I watched her fit it into the tray and push it back in.

"—you can do it any time, anywhere there's wi-fi, without anyone lookin' over your shoulder. Gets us email as well, stuff we might need." She saw the doubt in my eyes. "Relax, Alex, it's untraceable. I got a dozen different accounts, I'm an ace, ain't a better hacker in DC."

The bravado died as quickly as it had come. She slumped back, deflated. Then she reached over and handed me a crumpled fistful of notes.

"Beat him down to a hundred 'n' sixty," she said, quietly. "We got to save our money, right?"

*We…*

For the very first time, I heard the child in her voice, the longing, the fear of rejection. And then I watched her find courage. Honesty came in its wake. She stared out at the darkening street.

"The thing you asked..."

She shrugged. Once more, the fists bunched in the hoodie's pockets.

"When your daddy's a dealer, you learn stuff." She hesitated. "You learn it *fast,*" she said. She turned away. "You gotta."

*

The erratic flashing of the hotel's neon sign, just outside our door, meant there was no real darkness. There was no real silence, either. The storm's strength had grown, hurling the wind up the steep hill from the river to skirt nature's barriers with ease and humanity's with contempt. The force of it rattled the cheap windows and underpinned the noises which surrounded us; from the room on our left, a steady snoring, from the one on our right, the clink of glasses and giggling voices, male and female, playing out the age-old rituals of seduction. From the railway line down at the water's edge, a deep train whistle blew its mournful comment. I watched the plastic digits of the bedside clock's calendar slowly begin to change.

Midnight on April the 24th… Just over two days now, since I'd become a fugitive… How much had my life changed in these two days?

I looked across to the other bed. Lou was asleep on it, still in her clothes, a skewed tangle of limbs that looked as though she had burst through the ceiling at a wild run and collided with the mattress. Beside her, the iPad's screen played and replayed an endless series of cartoon characters; friendly giants, wild-eyed villains, spiky-haired girls.

Tomboys, like her...

But once again, she'd been right. After she had given me my

first ever computer lesson, we'd monitored the news channels. There was nothing about us. It was a relief.

And it was a puzzle, for it was a strange echo of the scooter boy's death in Washington. Once again, no reaction... Nothing. There was no search out for us, or at least, none that had been made public. Had my panicked exit from Gallant Fox Farm been enough? To satisfy whoever had planted the snake? Had death been the objective, or had disappearance done the job well enough?

Whatever the job was...

But through all the other confusions, one conviction was growing in me.

Everything which had happened to me was linked to that first encounter, to my initial confrontation with Rose Vannier.

I had no way—yet—of understanding why, but my endless mental replay of it had made me sure. My temper had stopped me seeing it at the time, but one thing about that first meeting had been wrong. Very wrong. The Ambassador Hotel was not the natural habitat of the Rose Vanniers of this world.

She been there to meet someone. Someone she hadn't met before.

Someone violent.

*...you being who—what—you are... I mean, it didn't look like a coincidence...*

After the episode with Lou, she had assumed that someone was me, because of my record. Sooner or later I'd have to know the reason behind that. But exactly how late could sooner or later afford to be...?

I reached across to my jacket, took the envelope of money from the inside pocket and counted. Sixteen hundred dollars and change. How long could it be made to last?

As if in malevolent answer, the wind gusted, rattling the windows even more, threatening every frame in the building. On the other bed, Lou turned. In the half dark, with the notes in my hands, I saw the forelock fall, the anguished expression on the pale, blotched face.

Sixteen hundred dollars. Food, fuel, lodging... Maybe ten days, I thought, if we're lucky, two weeks. And then what...?

There was no choice, I knew, I had to do it. I got up, put on jeans, shirt and boots, then looked down at the sleeping child. If I got her away now, there was still a chance of doing it cleanly.

Outside, the wind's howl was ferocious, catching at my shirt, billowing it out like a sail. As I walked, dust and litter blew across the wooden walkway, sticking to my legs and clanging against the vehicles. I passed the van and went along to the block's end where I'd seen the pay phone. Before me, the dirt road which had brought us here curved down under the railway through a concrete tunnel. I rounded the corner, lifted the receiver and began dialling—but before I could complete the number, another sound came.

A tapping, slow, measured... Just loud enough to be heard over the gale. As I replaced the receiver, a familiar figure rounded the next corner.

White suit, cane, a pink dome of head...

"Good evenin', Mister Fraser. We decided to let you take some rest before comin' to find you."

He raised a hand in signal. Somewhere behind him, the light changed.

"I bring a flag of truce, sir, I do not think either of us would suffer from sittin' beneath it, sheltered from nature's displeasure. If you'll trust me, I can offer you a small libation in a warmer place." He saw my hesitation and smiled. "Take it from me," he said, gently. "You don't have any choice."

He turned, began to walk away. The resentment rose in me—*all the running, and for what?* Slowly, the wind whipping at my shirt, I followed the sound of the cane.

Because I knew he was right.

I rounded the corner and walked behind Saul Morgan towards the blaze of light that was illuminating the hotel's shabby rear.

Towards the luxury limousine which had brought myself and Rose Vannier out of Washington DC, two nights before.

# 5

# EXTREMES

THE WIND ROCKED THE BIG CAR on its springs, but the insulated pod of its passenger compartment translated the movement into something more languorous, more expensive. The American whisky tasted like sweet chemical fire. As the cold seeped from me, I watched Saul Morgan savour it.

"Bathtub bourbon, Mister Fraser. Workin' man's poison, blue collar balm. Drink it long enough, it'll eat your innards. I can afford better, but once in a while—"

The red spotted handkerchief appeared from the breast pocket. Carefully, he dabbed at an imaginary spot on his lapel, then smiled at me as he replaced it.

"—one does like to be reminded of how far one could fall."

"How did you find me?"

He examined the contents of his glass, as though it was the liquor's right to answer. When the southern voice came, it was dry.

"Your atavistic soul seems to have acquired a degree of boldness since our last meetin'. I applaud that." He kept his eyes on me as he took another sip. "Especially as it seems to have kept its love of romance in the process." He brought the glass up in ironic toast. "Even in your hour of extremis, you let it take you on one of the last real journeys on this sadly homogenised continent of ours. It has given me great satisfaction, sir—" He drained the liquor in one. "—to watch your flight follow the line of the great

Baltimore and Ohio railroad."

The glass went carefully down on the tray table that separated us. The voice relinquished showmanship.

"The plastic. For gas, last night. Rose, sweet child that she is, imagines her own people don't monitor her." He shook his head, fondly. "Not that it matters, under the circumstances, but still... And then, a few hours ago, a sim card known to us logged on from this palatial establishment." He read my frown and smiled again. "The arrogance of youth, Mister Fraser. I'm sure your teenage protégé imagines her online privacy inviolable. It's not. We know every internet address, every alias she uses." Still smiling, he opened the briefcase on the seat beside him and took out a sheet of paper. "And that's not all we know. You might want to cast an eye over young Mary Louise's cv, get an idea of just how serious your position is."

I read. Absconded four times, marijuana possession, attempted computer fraud, breaking and entering, assault with a deadly weapon... I looked up, let the fat man's eyes meet mine.

"Interestin' readin', is it not? A disturbed young woman."

I said nothing. He leaned towards me.

"Such arcana is my job, Fraser. Anyone even remotely connected with Ms. Vannier, my brief is to know about them."

I put down my glass. "I thought you were her lawyer."

"Alas," he said, "in this modern age, the definition of that proud callin' has become severely debased." He motioned at my empty glass. "Another?"

Behind the smoked glass partition at my back, someone moved. I willed my head not to turn. Who was there? John Walks-Over-Ice? He was the chauffeur, he'd been at pains to tell me... And they must have had someone watching our room door, I reasoned. Had it been him? My eyes went back to the fat hand's painstaking pouring. Both glasses filled, Saul Morgan sat back. As the leather creaked to accommodate his body, I watched the theatrical mask slip effortlessly back into place.

"Morgan," he said. "Used to be Morgenthal. Granddaddy was a merchant. Lithuanian, thought of himself as Kraut. Natural-born dollar turner, got out of Kaunas just before the first war, half a ringlet ahead of the next pogrom." His eyes stayed on me as he talked. "Reached Alabama, found it less objectionable than anywhere else he'd been, started making his pile in Birmingham as a cotton broker—till the Klan objected. These particular gentlemen didn't like clever jewboys any more'n' they liked coloured folks, so he bought himself a wife. Local. Irish, transplanted landed gentry. Not a red cent to her family's name but red hair down to her aristocratic and alcoholic ass." He shook his head. "Jewish money machine marries crazy Mick lush. A piquant mix, people tell me. Add the fact that they both screwed the help, then stood back and let their kids, including the feckless failure I had the misfortune to call father, do the same, and you have—" A fat finger pointed in accusation at his own chest. "*—moi.* Lyman Ward Military Academy, then Tulane, resultin' in a highly average degree in law. After that, forty years of bendin' that remarkably pliable entity to keep it from applyin' to rich assholes. Married twice—hell, I tried. Talented as the Torah, slippery as sin and—" He gave a lecherous grin. "—gay as Gomorrah." When I didn't respond, he looked at me levelly. "Don't worry, you're not my type—I like 'em young, sweet an' docile. You fail on all three counts."

"Why are you telling me this?"

Again, he drained his glass and settled back. "Because I know all about you, Fraser, which makes it only fair you should know all about me. It's my firm belief that partners in negotiation start out better if they start out even. I have an offer for you."

He opened the briefcase again, pulled out another sheet of paper and handed it to me.

"We don't know why you decided to run. Or what in hell's name possessed you to take the kid. Perhaps in time, you'll tell us. But for the moment, sign that and your legal troubles are over."

As the implications sank in, I had to force my face to stay expressionless. Could I believe him? Fighting the unreality, I read through the document.

*... of the state of Virginia... ...special circumstances... ...to be reviewed at three-yearly intervals...*

An indefinite extension of my visa. How? I came to the signature at the bottom.

*F. Carlton MacDonald.*

My eyes found Morgan's.

He answered the unspoken question. "Rose insisted it be signed by that particular official. Exactly why, I don't know, but I gather it might be a source of some personal satisfaction to you. Once the shock's worn off, of course." he finished, drily.

"How—"

He held up a hand to stop me. "Rose Vannier is about to announce her support for the Virginia State Attorney General's upcomin' Senate campaign. On all social media outlets, any day now," he said, evenly. "Makes you just die of excitement, don't it?" His face became serious as he shook his head. "Don't know what it is you've got, Fraser. You steal a van, you do a midnight run. You even kidnap her niece. But still she goes out to bat for you, big time. Made me call in a huge one." He took a pen from the briefcase and put it down on the paper. "You seem, my obstinate Scotch friend, by some roll of the divine dice, to have landed with your ass in the gravy."

I stared at the pen. When I didn't pick it up, Saul Morgan's face creased in annoyance. He shook his head.

"Grand theft auto, abducting a minor... It would not seem to me," he said, with quiet irony, "that you have too many other options—but if that won't convince you, maybe this will."

A third sheet of paper came from the briefcase. He laid it on top of the others.

"What's this?"

"A contract."

I stared at him. The grin returned.

"Your new job. Freelance consultant to Ms. Rose Vannier. Eighty thousand a year, full benefits, health insurance, the whole dee-luxe-all-singin'-all-dancin' package. Only condition is, you bring back the kid under your own steam, just in case anybody picks up on it. The episode will never be mentioned again."

Still I didn't speak. At the end of a long, wind-filled minute, the gentle laugh came again, a mixture of admiration and menace.

"Well, you're a stubborn one and no mistake. How close to your pecker does the hatchet have to fall?" He leaned across to me. "Don't you get it? She's decided she wants you. I tried to talk her out of it. Till I was blue in the face—the others did too, but there's no shiftin' her. Despite..." He hesitated. "...the events of several nights ago in Washington, DC."

It was like a punch in the gut. Before I could react, he held up a hand.

"Before we get to the minutiae, let me explain the facts of life to you. Right now, Rose Vannier is, as her niece would no doubt say, *hot*—one of the most sought after women in the world, goddess to millions. As *Vanity Fair* magazine so aptly put it last month, she has become an icon of desire. She's also one of the biggest cash cows on the planet. Not that it's always been that way, mind—her social conscience gets her into scrapes. Takin' on the sweatshop owners in Asia, callin' out the big cartels on workin' conditions, that crusade damn near finished her—but she never once thought of backin' down. Same with blood diamonds, animal testin' of cosmetics, a dozen others. But despite all that..." He swirled the liquor round in his glass. "...she has managed to remain one of the top five models in the world. Social media, over sixty million followers. Public adores her, no matter what crap her family—" He gestured at the printout about the girl. "—pulls. Ninety per cent of her earnin's go into charitable trusts—kids, animals, environment, whatever. She puts somethin' on two days in a row, half the teenage girls in the world're wearin' it the next mornin'. Three days, new factories open in China. Endorses a perfume, the whole damn country stinks of it till she changes. She farts, they're talkin' about it on chat shows. She's not just a name any more, she's not even just a brand—" He leaned across towards me. "she's an *industry.*"

He paused on the word, then reached for the bottle once more. As he poured, he eyed me.

"She's also a strange mixture. Never met a savvier woman in my life about money, but there's times when she simply does not comprehend what it takes to keep the lid on stuff around her. Which brings us—" His voice took on a serious edge. "—to the Ambassador Hotel."

The silence between us seemed to press in on me, solidify. He sighed.

"Sometimes my damn job is a nightmare, Fraser. What the hell did she *expect,* pullin' a stunt like that? America's Sweetest Sweetheart goes into a bar after her idiot niece starts a fight, beggin' your pardon, with some Scotch lowlife! Then she autographs a poster! That asshole barman had it on eBay half an hour later! Cocksucker got nearly six thousand for it, we've had to pull in dozens of favours to keep the story off the wires." He looked across at me, grimly. "I knew about her bein' there inside twenty minutes of the first bid. Like I said, it's my job." He stopped. "So now I expect," he said, in a measured voice, "you're wonderin' exactly what else I might know. About the events of that fateful evenin'."

Still, I didn't speak.

"The answer, my friend, is..." He sat back. "...nothin'. Beyond a series of minor occurrences. Things of no account, events outside the aforementioned establishment. A pair of designer sunglasses with a smashed lens, found by the cab rank sign. A damaged corner of the brickwork, splinters lyin' around. What caused these phenomena is not exactly clear, but I understand the management is pursuin' no further enquiries." Once again, he held up a hand. "And just in case you should be wonderin', Alexander..." The voice became even smoother. "...no body was found that night, anywhere within a long country mile of the Ambassador Hotel."

*

As soon as I got out of the limousine I saw the big Cherokee. He was dressed in jeans and t-shirt. I watched the cloth in his hand, polishing the car's wing in careful circles. In the mirror I could see the shirt's front—a picture of Geronimo holding a rifle, above the words *sure you can trust the government, just ask an indian.* Suddenly it came to me that I'd stolen his van. I stood, awkward, trying to think of the right words of apology. He didn't look at me as he spoke.

"She's as heavy on oil as she is on gas. A quart every couple of hundred miles should do it." He had to walk round me to get to the limousine's rear. "Wouldn't rely too much on the spare, either. Pretty old."

He stowed away the cleaning utensils, let the trunk lid fall, then walked back round to the driver's door, got in and closed it. The engine's start was almost inaudible. The big car circled me, slowly, before gliding out on to the main road.

As the wind tried to tear Saul Morgan's papers from my hand, I watched the tail lights disappear.

*

The gale's force was reality. Shivering, hunched forward, I began retracing my steps through it. I had to shake off the effects of the alcohol—if ever I needed a clear head, it was now.

Stick and carrot…

Could I trust this offer? I rounded the building again. The carrot was huge—a clean legal slate, money...

Safety.

Was that really possible? I stopped. Down on the railroad tracks, a big diesel locomotive's triangle of lights probed the darkness as it slowed for a signal. The line of flat wagons it pulled seemed endless, stretching back out of sight. The metallic ring of the buffers threw a long line of echoes up the valley behind it. Saul Morgan's voice filled my head; *one of the last real journeys...*

But what about the journey being offered to me now? If it sounded too good to be true, then it usually was, wasn't that the rule? I walked on, round the last corner, into the full force of the wind.

The row of vehicles was the same. Above them, the neon sign swayed alarmingly, illuminating crazy corners of ground and sky at random. I scanned the darkness outside its reach as I walked—and then, halfway to the room, a huge gust almost knocked me over. Only the van's rusty blue side kept me upright. On the ground beside the driver's door a sudden flash of illumination showed me a long smear, brown and wet. It seemed familiar. Why? As the crazy light stole it away again, other thoughts crowded in.

The stick… How much choice did I really have? If I refused, would I be thrown to the wolves? *He knew about the body.* Who had told him? Rose Vannier? I levered myself off the van's side. When I got to the room I reached for the door handle.

But I needn't have bothered. It was open. I pushed it.

Lou was gone.

The papers fell from my hand. I stood in the doorway, staring at the fractured vision of the interior thrown up by the stuttering sign outside. It took me an age to reach for the light switch.

*My fiddle.*

She was nowhere to be seen. I forced back panic. My bag was gone too—and my jacket.

With the money.

Lou...? No, surely, she couldn't have—she *wouldn't* have...

I took a step forward. The only thing left was the iPad. Propped against her bed's pillows, it was still emitting the same endless round of cartoon happiness which had guarded her fitful sleep. I lifted it and touched the screen as I'd seen her do.

The anodyne pastel figures vanished. The image that replaced them was brutal.

It was Lou's face beneath the tousled hair, but the thick strips of silver tape across eyes and mouth made her look more like a mummy than a human being. The blood trickling from her nose was the only thing that told me I wasn't looking at a still photograph.

The sign hung round her neck was a torn piece of cardboard, the writing, a thick scrawl of marker pen.

*SHE'S ALIVE*
*FOR NOW*

A hard slap knocked the girl's head out of vision. The screen blurred. Then a hand yanked her back into sight by her hair. The sign had changed.

*THE DOOR*
*OPEN IT*

I did it. A red dot appeared on the jamb to my right—then vanished. It reappeared in the middle of my chest. Paralysed, I waited for the shot. Instead, the picture in my hands changed again. Now the girl's head was being forced sideways by a blued steel gun barrel. The knuckle holding the trigger was white with tension. I watched a red weal spread itself across her face between the strips of tape. This time the message was longer.

*YOU DISAPPEAR, SHE LIVES*
*GET IN THE VAN*

The screen went black. I stood, the pulse throbbing at my temple, the manic darkness roaring round me. Slowly, still holding the iPad, I started taking measured paces forward. With every step, the red spot stayed on my chest. I reached the van door. Again, I found myself staring at the long brown smear on the ground. The red dot disappeared. For a split second I couldn't see it—and then logic came.

Terrifying logic. The laser beam was on my forehead.

Very slowly, I put the iPad in my jacket pocket, opened the door and hoisted myself on to the driving seat. The key was in the ignition. My right foot touched something hard—the fiddle case. My bag was beside it. When I looked up again, I saw the spot directly before me, refracted through the windscreen. Heart hammering, I reached for the key.

The van started. I put her in drive, inched forward, then swung her round. The dot appeared in the side window, then vanished. I revved for the dirt road—and then, on the downward slope, she stalled.

But she didn't stop. I stamped on the brake. Nothing. *Why?* She rolled on, picking up speed. *Christ, the brakes!* Suddenly the steering was leaden in my grip. *They'd cut—*

I heaved round to the left, only just keeping her on the road. She careered into the tunnel below the tracks, smashed into one side, then the other. *No!* Jarred from the driving seat, I lost my grip. The back doors burst open. A tyre exploded, gunshot loud. The train whistle echoed above me. We skidded out of the tunnel in a long, banshee wail of tortured metal.

A telegraph pole loomed out of the darkness.

*

I came to.

Blood... *Why could I taste blood?* A sudden smell brought me out of it—a sharp smell.

Petrol.

The van was canted over at a crazy angle, almost on its side. My fiddle was on top of me. My blood-covered hands took hold of it. As I heaved myself up, ragged ends of cable sparked down by my left leg.

The driver's door had been torn off. I tumbled out on to wet tarmac and lay, gripping the fiddle, gulping air.

A new smell came—burning. I rolled, made it somehow to my feet and tried to run. *My leg... What was wrong—* A loud *crump* came from behind me. The explosion bowled me over—and then the world was smoke, oily, black, thick and bitter. Coughing, retching, I made it to my hands and knees. *The fiddle, where—*

And then, somewhere above me, the deep whistle came. *The train!* The acrid black clouds cleared. I was at the foot of the embankment, the case at my feet. I grabbed it and began a limping run up towards the line of moving wheels.

The train was beginning to pick up speed. Sobbing with effort, I forced myself to go faster. *Now!* I flung the case up on to the nearest wagon, saw it bounce, then grabbed a stanchion and heaved myself up—and felt my knee crash into a wheel. Pain shot down the length of my leg. *Keep hold!* I let myself be dragged along, half skipping, half staggering, until I had enough purchase to try again.

I made it. Just in time to dive across the greasy surface and grab my fiddle before it slid off the other side.

And then, with no warning, I was in the storm. I lay there, pummelled by the force of it, fighting for breath, watching the wind-whipped pillars of flame and smoke disappear round the bend behind me.

# 6

# SUCCOUR

THE CLANKING woke me, as it had done a dozen times through the night. I knew what it meant. The locomotive had changed speed, its load was transmitting the shock along its spine, jarring the long line of wagons together like vertebrae after a fall. I braced myself, one hand grabbing the iron bar behind me, the other anchoring the case to my chest. Twice, I'd nearly been thrown from the train, but this time, when the shock came, it was gentler. We were slowing down.

It was nearly light. We were in a cutting, at the top of a winding valley. To either side I could see the drab backs of old wooden buildings. I pulled myself round, my lacerated hands painful on splintered wood and flaking rust, my body stiff. The rain had stuck my clothes to me, and I ached from the effort of keeping myself and the fiddle on the slippery wood. Every joint in my body throbbed, but the wound on my right thigh was the worst. It was bloody, swollen enough to chafe painfully against the ripped cloth of my jeans. A hundred yards further down the track I could see coal hoppers and sidings and platforms.

A station.

Before I could even begin to think, two faces appeared at the wagon's edge.

Kids.

The train's pace had slowed to less than theirs. They walked alongside, their eyes huge. Watching them watching me, the memory of Lou wrenched itself loose.

*Her face, terrified…*

These two were younger, freckle-faced siblings with snub noses and red hair, wearing identical striped sports uniforms, laundered and pressed. The logo on their caps said *Evergreen School Little League.* The boy was holding a baseball, the girl, an oversized leather glove. They were both frowning. It was the girl who finally shouted up to me.

"Bulls'll be comin', mister. You better get off 'fore they find you."

"'Sright," the boy chimed in. "Mean motherfuckers, throw your ass in jail sooner 'n' shit."

She rounded on him. "Quit cussin', Tom Shelton! You'll go to hell!"

He didn't even look at her. "Cuss if I want to, hell don't bother me none. That a fiddle?"

I managed to nod.

"Grannie McClintock plays real good."

I made it to my knees and pulled myself towards them, dragging the case. When I got it to the edge, the boy read my intentions and reached up. He wasn't tall enough. I pushed it over the wagon's side. He caught it. I got down on my stomach, turned, and began levering myself off, trying to keep my dangling legs from the huge moving wheel. Then a last clank lurched the whole train a final foot forward and dislodged me. I fell heavily, felt myself land on gravel, then roll, tumbling downwards. The bottom of the ditch was wet. My head plunged into brackish water. Raising it again took the last of my strength. Without warning the smells assailed me—burned clothes, vegetation, rank water. I retched. When I opened my eyes, I saw both children, still frowning at me.

I heard the words *take care of my fiddle.* I had no idea who said them. Everything swam.

*

Darkness. Hunger. Pain. How could my head be so hot when my body was so cold? I felt hands gripping me, big hands. I was aware of being lifted, but I could see only a faceless face, eyes and mouth hidden by strips of silver tape. As someone carried me, I heard voices. Water was forced between my lips. I coughed, nearly choked.

"Easy, now, feller," said a deep mutter by my ear.

But the sound wasn't as real as her face.

*Lou…*

My mind tried to reach past her name—for logic, for comprehension.

For rage.

I didn't have the strength. My head lolled back against a strong arm.

*

It was music which finally brought me to. I knew the melody and I didn't—but I knew it was my fiddle that was playing it, somewhere near. I lay, bathed in sweat, struggling for the tune's name. Finally, it almost came.

*Campbell's? Cameron's?*

It was a tune I'd played often enough... Except it wasn't, quite. The music stopped. I forced open my eyes. My hands hurt. I brought them up. My fingers and knuckles were bruised and swollen. Despite the pain, I made them search the space around me. They found cold metal, then rough cloth; a bed... I was lying on an old-fashioned iron bedstead, beneath a blanket. I pulled myself up to a sitting position. I was naked—but at least, except for my throbbing thigh, I no longer ached. I looked down at my leg, saw the fresh bandage. Who had done that? My eyes found my jacket and jeans, hanging on the unpainted frame. Who had undressed me?

The tune came again. Why was it so different? The tone was thicker, I realised—every note was double-stopped, two strings playing at once. I'd never heard my fiddle sing like that before. It was strong, rough and beautiful at the same time. Again, it stopped. A bizarre notion came; *were my thoughts controlling it?*

The sound was coming at me through an open door that didn't fit its frame. In the dim light I saw a room with yellow-brown walls and an uneven floor of wooden boards. Apart from the bed, a three-legged stool and a pot stove in an alcove, there was no other furniture. I reached for my jeans. Someone had washed them and sewed up the long rip in the right leg. I struggled into them and tried a tentative step forward. Movement was painful, but it was possible. I saw my boots, neatly paired, at the bed's end. They were clean, shining. *Who...?* Carefully, despite the difficulty of bending, I managed to put them on.

The yellow walls were newsprint, old, tinted almost to illegibility by a patina of smoke. I ran my fingers across it, then stopped at a fragment of headline.

*...INCHEON SEPTEMBER 12TH, 1950*

I frowned. *Incheon...?* What was Incheon? Or where, or who? I entered the next room. It was just as bare, except for a cellophane-encased suit of clothes hanging on a wire hanger from a nail on the wall.

A uniform. A U.S. Army uniform.

A U.S. Army *dress* uniform, a sergeant's, the chevrons on the olive sleeve told me. It looked as though it had never been worn, its buttons gleaming, its creases razor-sharp beneath the clear plastic. The name tag above the row of medal ribbons was *McClintock.* I'd heard that name, not long ago... Thoughtfully, I turned back to my explorations. As I progressed through the next two misshapen rooms, the tune began again.

When I finally made it to the light, it was strong enough to make me shade my eyes. As they adjusted, I saw I was standing on the whitewashed stone step of a cabin, beneath an overhanging roof of wooden shingles. To my left was a clutch of sheds, to my right, a tree stump levelled off as a chopping block for wood, and a pen for pigs. A trio of chickens was pecking round its fence, and a rutted dirt track wound away past it, descending out of sight. On the other side of the track, a fast-flowing stream was making a fine job of polishing a line of flat boulders. It was bridged at its most placid point by a lashed-together pair of pine planks. On the water's far side, a tethered mule grazed in a small half moon of pasture, walled off by a curved curtain of grey rock. A narrow path led up to its tallest point, then disappeared through what looked like a man-made fissure. On the steep slopes above, the pines loomed. Once again, I heard the music, somewhere to the left of me. Stiffly, I followed the sound round the cabin's corner.

A flat outcrop of rock hung over the stream. On it, a woman with long silver hair was sitting on a kitchen chair, playing my fiddle. My case, smoke-blackened, lay beside another, battered and fastened with string. Both were nearly hidden by the grey hem of her skirt. I watched her boot tap along with the tune. Her playing was effortless, elegant and strong.

She heard my approach. She stopped, placed instrument and bow carefully in her lap. When she turned and faced me, I saw the white stare of her eyes.

She was blind.

Her voice was nervous. "Mighty fine fiddle, sir. I sure hope you don't mind. She needed testin' after I set her up, bridge was down. Didn't reckon the old un'd hold no more, so I used my spare—ten year old, but she's well made, hand cut by a young feller over to Elkins. Hope it don't inconvenience you none." She let her right hand stroke the wood. "But Lord, I ain't played on a fiddle this good since my husband come back from Ko-rea on his first furlough. She sure likes to sing out, don't she just! *Campbell's Farewell To Red Gap,* that's a tune suits her right well." Her hand patted the instrument's shoulder. "Learned it from Mister Franklin George, one night in Charleston, forty year back. Never did get it quite right, but I keep on tryin'. You feelin' better now, sir?" She didn't let the question pause her. "Reckon you should be, now your fever's broke. I poulticed up some mustard an' give you some meadowsweet 'gainst the pain an' the swellin', 'cause you sure was mighty poorly when my boy Seth hauled you in yesterday mornin'. Betsy Shelton oughta be right proud o' them two young 'uns o' hers, Lord knows they done right by you, runnin' up here to git Seth come git you, bring you on up to ol' Grannie McClintock. Hope you'll 'scuse me for washin' your clothes, by the way, but there was a powerful reek o' smoke on 'em. You a hobo?"

The question startled me—until it struck me how well the title fitted.

No money, no direction, no luck...

No future.

Finding my voice was an effort.

"Yes."

Her fine features creased into a sudden frown. Her voice sharpened.

"What's a hobo doin' with a fiddle this good? You a thief? You a bad man?"

I looked into the sightless eyes. Nothing but the truth would do, somehow I knew it.

"I've done bad things in my time, but I'd like to think I'm a good man, now," I said. "I try to be."

I watched the foreignness of my voice register. *Accent...* Slowly, she nodded.

"I'd call that an honest answer. All a person can do is try. You outta money, sir?"

"Yes."

"Ain't nothin' to be 'shamed of, happens to folks. This land of ours sure ain't drippin' with milk 'n' honey's far as I can see—less'n' you're a politician, or leadin' young folks into trouble with drugs, like them bastards makin' that crystal meth up the next holler. You just plain outta luck, then?"

"Yes."

Again, her voice took on its suspicious edge. "You runnin' from somethin?"

"Yes."

"Somethin' bad?"

I closed my eyes. "I tried to do something good. Something right. It turned bad."

After a long moment, she nodded a couple of times more. From somewhere near I heard the sound of an engine. She heard it too.

"No call to worry," she said. "My boy Seth."

The chickens scattered as a gleaming red pickup nosed into the space between the pig pen and the shack. The man who got out was wearing a faded version of the khaki military jacket I'd seen hanging on the wall. Despite the grey of his cropped hair, he was strong and muscular.

And he was black.

As the truck door closed, the woman pulled herself erect on the chair. "I tried to do right, once," she said. "Married Seth's daddy. Problem was, Booker McClintock wasn't the right colour for some folks. Right colour to go fight for his country in Ko-rea, but the wrong colour to get tret like a regular person here'bouts, no matter how fine a man he was." She shook her head. "Boy marryin' a girl he'd give a misfortune to, that was no problem. A *black* boy marryin' a *white* girl he'd give a misfortune to, that was sump'n' else..." Again the silver locks shook, slower this time. "Folks took offence—'n' more'n' offence, if you git me."

She paused. I watched her gather resolve.

"We went down to the dance. Once, only tried the once. We was wed by then, but it didn't signify. Minute Booker come in the door, it went quiet, then a banjo started playin'. *Run, Nigger, Run.* Ol' Uncle Dave Macon tune, hateful thing." She frowned at the memory. "Near shamed the music outta me, didn't lift the fiddle for a year." The sightless eyes turned to me. "That's why we lived out here. In my daddy's ol' cabin. I'd had my druthers, would've been a white house with a picket fence, down by the church..."

Her voice tailed off, then found its courage again. Her pointed chin jutted out defiantly.

"Seth says folks've changed now, but I reckon me an' ol' Steady—" She nodded across at the grazing mule. "—better just stay put right here in Chimney Holler with the hogs an' the hens. Don't reckon stupidity's gone from these mountains yet, ain't no tellin' when it's gonna come a-knockin' again."

I watched her staring into the past. Finally, she lifted the bow. But then, before it reached the strings, she stopped herself. She turned back to me.

"You're from the old country, ain't you?"

I watched the unasked question grow, then turn itself into an unexpected smile, tinged with a girl's shyness. She held out fiddle and bow. Hesitantly, I took both. Despite my ravaged hands, the fiddle felt right. I put her under my chin. Again, I had to fight to get out the words.

"We call it *Campbell's Farewell To Redcastle.*"

The girlish smile widened, casting off the years and restoring beauty to her. Her son sat down on the flat rock beside her.

As my skinned and battered fingers fought through the pain for the notes, he gave me a solemn nod and took her hand.

# 7

# HOLLER

FOR THREE DAYS, they fed me, changed my bandages, let me rest—and asked no questions beyond a name to call me by. They gave me theirs in return, formally; Jane Gillespie McClintock and Seth Booker Gillespie McClintock. It was the simple courtesy of simple people, hospitality given without stint—and no matter what they thought I might be, without the least intention to pry. A decision had been made to take in a stranger. The acceptance which followed was without quarter or qualification. After the chaos and violence of the preceding days, it touched me deeply.

A lifeline.

Without it, I'd have been lost, for the things which stalked me were close, now—and getting closer.

I knew I had to keep them at bay; my parents, the dead boy in Washington, the two attempts to kill me—the questions were all there, waiting, sharp and savage, at the edge of my consciousness. Each time they loomed, I took cover, each time they became too insistent, I shied away. When I managed to sleep, it was restless, plagued by versions of the same dream which had haunted me the night I'd fled Gallant Fox Farm. The monster was still there, still hovering, feral and anarchic, at the borders of my darkness.

*Lou...*

The memory of her obscenely taped face was the worst of it. What could I do? I couldn't abandon the girl, she had become my responsibility. But what could I *do?* Every time the question came, it haunted me, unanswerable.

In the end, it was the music which saved me.

Jane McClintock was its advocate, as gentle as she was persistent. After hearing me play that one simple Scottish march, she seemed to know instinctively that my fiddle was what would heal me. She shepherded me back towards it with tact and patience, using her own playing to lay out a row of Appalachian tunes as bait. Despite my damaged hands, by the third day I had grasped the lure and had my fiddle in my hands once more. The decision wasn't a conscious one. It came from somewhere deep inside me, somewhere deeper than anything rational, a whisper which told me my music was the only part of me which no fears could touch.

And so it began, master and apprentice...

It was so long since I had been either.

*Push on up that E string run, Alex—she wants to sing out on the top A, you got to set it up for her...*

It was the old way, and it was the right way. Jane McClintock would play, I would listen, then I would try.

*More bow on the bottom double stop—that phrase's near 'nuff the start of a shuffle beat, gotta come out loud for folks t'get the rhythm...*

She would correct, gently, I would try again, over and over—and when I finally got it right, she was unstinting in her praise.

*That's it, Alex! That's exactly it! Sounds like you was born 'n' bred right here in Upshur County...*

By the morning of my fourth day with her, I had learned two tunes, to her satisfaction and my own, *Lost Indian* and *Billy In The Low Ground.*

And then, as I was flexing my left hand, her voice came, even gentler than usual. "Why'n't you play me some o' them Scottish tunes, Alex? Maybe even teach me one."

It was a moment which could have gone either way—and then the victory I'd won tipped the balance and brought me down on the right side.

Apprentice and master...

I spent much of that day, between the household tasks she now let me share, playing the sparser Scottish cousins of her own tunes back to her. She took great delight in the differences, in the arcana of the different Scottish regional styles, in the pulling around of rhythm in the airs, in the subtle differences of structure between melodies which had begun their lives on harp or pipes.

And above all, in the mystifying snap of the strathspey's driven bow.

*That's a hoss gone lame, Alex, I swear! You tellin' me folks can dance to that?*

I assured her she would get the stroke, it would just take time.

*Got enough o' that partic'lar commodity, I reckon—no place like the mountains for time. You reckon you could draw some water from the stream for me?*

And that was the way we learned, stopping to collect eggs from the hens, pausing in mid-tune to tell the stories of the players who'd played it, or how or why either of us had learned it. Sometimes it was her music, given to me, sometimes it was mine offered to her.

Master.

Apprentice.

Somewhere between these two shifting roles, a calm grew between us—until, that evening, shyly on both sides, Jane upon her rocking chair and me upon the three-legged stool from my room, we came together and played with each other.

The tune was that staple of the mountains on both sides of the Atlantic, *Soldiers' Joy*. I watched her smile, uninhibited and passionate, as we let our two versions mingle into wildness—and then I caught my reflection in the cabin's only shard of mirror. The sight of my face in the oil lamp's light was a shock. I watched it change as the guilt rushed in.

*Lou…*

*Joy…*

What right did I have to joy? Or even contentment…?

"What's wrong, Alex?" Jane asked, gently.

"I can't tell you."

Silence descended. When she broke it, I could hear how carefully her words were being chosen.

"Hidin' from trouble only works awhile. Sharin' can help. Anythin' you want to let out, it'd go to my grave with me."

I was ashamed to look at her. I was desperate to confide, to confess—but somehow I couldn't. Something inside me forbade it. Finally, I managed to find my voice.

"This tune, it's part of it."

Her brows creased briefly, then she sat back, accepting the

offering. I began.

*The Hawk That Swoops On High.*

*

It seemed to take an age to play.

I wasn't conscious of exactly when she joined in. All I knew was that the two instruments in harmony were somehow lonelier than the single fiddle could ever have been. I shut my eyes tightly against it. When we came to the end, all I could hear was the creak of the cabin's timbers in the wind, and all I could feel was the slow tracking of the tears down my cheeks. We both sat, totally still, for a long time.

A familiar sound from the rocking chair ended it. I opened my eyes to find Jane's left hand holding a white object, its ceramic surface spidered with age.

A rosin holder, Edwardian. As she passed the length of the bow briskly along it, I read the legend.

*Excelsior, for superior tone and control.*

I caught my breath.

In Scotland, as a child, I had owned its twin.

Jane put down the bow, then rose and stood in front of the cracked triangle of mirror. Her free hand reached out to the glass.

"Only thing my daddy ever gave me," she said, gently. "Day I started on momma's fiddle, eight years old. I was standin' right here, in front of this ol' mirror, brushin' my hair—wouldn't think it to look at me now, Alex, but I had fine blonde hair when I was a girl. He come up behind me, made me close my eyes, then put it in my hand."

She held up the rosin holder. I saw it catch the light, watched her fingers fondle it.

"Come from his daddy afore him, he said, won it in a card game up in Vicksburg, eighteen eighty-five. Leastways that was the story, don't know's I rightly believe it."

She turned, sat again, rearranged her skirts. I saw the faint blush on her cheek as she smiled.

"Only bow my daddy ever drew strong was the long 'un."

The smile died at the edges as it turned away to a private place. I saw her grip tighten on the holder.

"Only thing he ever gave me," she repeated.

*The only thing I have left to give her…*

My own father's phrase, from the letter...

I grasped the courage the memory offered me. The words rushed out in an awkward jumble.

"There's a girl, a teenager—she's in trouble. Because of me. I have to find her."

*

The next morning, before Seth arrived, Jane asked my permission to tell him my story. As soon as I'd given it, she made me go through it all again, this time in forensic detail. In the face of my doubts about telling him, she was adamant—he could help.

But how? The idea seemed impossible—but her certainty was unshakable, and when he arrived, I put doubt to one side. As I told the tale again, Jane sat, shelling peas into a bowl. Her body stayed still as I talked, but her face was another matter. I watched her frowning at the occasional episode, nodding gently from time to time in understanding. My voice sounded strange to me as I recounted it all; events, emotions, suspicions. It was as though I was some kind of disembodied narrator, as though the facts I was relating belonged to another man's story, a man granted, somehow, a lesser version of life.

"...and I've no way of proving any of what I think."

As my words petered out, I searched both their faces—for disbelief, for distaste or condemnation. There was none. Jane McClintock had already decided I was a good man. That endorsement was enough for her son, I knew—but as I looked at his handsome black face, I saw that his eyes held something more. She broke the silence, turned to him.

"Well, Seth?"

He addressed himself to me. The voice was the same deep solace I remembered from my near-comatose journey up from the railway line.

"Let me see what I can find. If there's information out there about any of what you've told us, I can get it for you."

There was a long pause. I watched him register my disbelief.

"I'm a programmer, Alex. I know computers, I design 'em and build 'em," he said, matter-of-factly. "I know how to access pretty much any kind of file without leavin' a marker."

*Relax, Alex, it's untraceable...*

Lou's carefree bravado, Saul Morgan's casual contempt for her naiveté...

Instinctively, Jane knew what was wrong. Her hands came to rest above the bowl of peas.

"Gotta start trustin' some time, Alex." she said. "Seth says he can do it, means he can. I ain't never known him break his word."

It was the gentlest of rebukes. Again, the deep voice beside her spoke.

"I guarantee it, Alex. What's the girl called?"

I looked at Jane's sightless eyes and knew she was right. I turned to her son.

"Vannier. Mary Louise Vannier. She calls herself Lou. She's about thirteen, short blonde hair, blue eyes. Bad skin."

Seth nodded, then rose. "OK, till tonight. Sooner, I get anything quickly. Bye momma."

He leaned down and kissed his mother. Her smile widened. By the time he'd reached the door, she was working again. I watched her, cracking the pod, squeezing out the peas, discarding the debris... And then I looked up from the certainty of the fine hands to the utter serenity of the fine face—and wondered if either she or her son realised the legacy of the days I had just passed with them, here in their crevice of mountain and stream.

But how could they? How could they know that this was the first time I'd freely trusted anyone since I'd set foot in America?

*

It was late when Seth returned, carrying a bundle of newsprint. He read the anxiety in my face.

"Relax, more good than bad. Strange, though."

He crossed to the kitchen table, then spread out the top newspaper, the *Record Delta.* It was dated Friday, April 26th.

*VAN CRASH IN WHEELING.*
*CREWS FROM TWO STATES ATTEND FIRE.*
*DRIVER MISSING.*

"You're still safe enough," he said. "No follow ups for the next two editions, means the sheriff's decided to file and forget."

"How do you know?"

He looked at me, levelly. "I didn't tell you this earlier, didn't want to spook you. You know what a snowdrop is, Alex?" He didn't bother waiting for an answer. "Snowdrop's slang for a military policeman, 'cause o' the white helmets. I was one, when I was a marine, a long time ago, over in 'Nam. Means I know cops, the procedures—an' the mentality, how their minds work." He stabbed a finger down on the headline. "This guy's department hasn't even bothered identifyin' the cause, just wrote the whole thing off as mechanical failure. Which means that, unless the Feds take this over, all they want it to do is go away. Only one thing'll change that. New information."

"And the girl? Lou?"

He pulled out a sheaf of computer printouts from inside the newspaper and handed them to me. "No connection made with the crash, but a kid called Mary Lou Salinger was arrested the day after..."

*Salinger…*

"...doped up to the eyeballs on tranquillisers, caught tryin' to steal a sandwich from a supermarket in Steubenville. That's in Ohio, not far over the river from Wheeling. Sheet as long as your arm, fits the description you gave me."

"Is she still there?"

He shook his head. "No. She was charged immediately, hearin' date set for three days later. Two hours after she got her statutory phone call, a limousine appeared, high powered mouthpiece. Sprung inside of ten minutes. I got a friend at the courthouse over there, Sheronda. She says money changed hands, enough for the supermarket not to press charges."

The calm, intelligent face watched me take it in. *What did it mean?*

"If you need more, we can keep diggin'. We got other resources, too." His voice became slightly more guarded. "I got buddies, more'n' a few, guys I was in the service with. Kind of a network. We keep in touch, anyone gets in trouble."

He straightened up, folded away the newspaper, then carefully didn't let his eyes meet mine.

"Extends to friends 'n' kin, one of us vouches for them. You know what I'm sayin'?"

I heard the kindness in his voice.

"Seth…"

He held up a hand to forestall my thanks. "Main thing is, you know the girl is safe," he said, finally. "Other stuff, we can make a start on takin' care of."

*

The next morning my leg seemed better, and as the day went on I felt well enough to help with the heavier tasks. By late afternoon I was chopping wood, stacking it at the cabin's gable end, then chopping again, getting into a rhythm of work as I listened to Jane playing *Grey Squirrel Eatin' Up The New Ground Corn.* It was a Kentucky tune, she'd told me, she'd give me it later, once the pigs and chickens were fed. What would I give her in return? *The Jig Of Slurs? South Of The Grampians?* Or a reel...? *Mickie Ainsworth,* perhaps? As well as *The Hawk That Swoops On High,* I'd already taught her *Dunkeld Steeple* and *Center's Bonnet* and *Villafjord.* If she—

Suddenly the axe in my hands felt strong and good, right.

*Lou.*

Had she escaped, or had her kidnappers let her go? Had keeping her somehow become dangerous for them? Had they acted before the news got out that I'd survived the crash? The information Seth had brought meant I could face the questions, now. The girl was alive. That one fact let light in on everything else.

I dug the axe into the block and stood, letting the breeze dry my sweat, feeling resolve grow. There was one thing left to do. I went back to my room and took the little computer from my jacket pocket. The girl's words came back to me.

*You never seen an iPad? What planet you from...*

I felt the hatred grow in me as I stared at it, and then I forced it away. It was just a box, a slim packet of wires and circuits. A device, maybe even a useful device...

But I didn't care. All I knew was what the thing meant to me. I walked back out and slammed it down on the oak block.

The impact switched it on. The last image of the girl's kidnapping was somehow still there. Rage rushed in, so strong I could taste it. Lifting the axe was elation. I brought it down with every ounce of force I could muster. The sound of the plastic sundering was totally different from the sound of logs being split. It stopped Jane's fiddle. She looked across at me, first in alarm, then in puzzlement, her brow creased. Should I explain? At least try...?

I didn't know how... I bent down and picked up the remains of the thing. It was neatly sheared in two. As the silence gathered, I finally looked again at Jane McClintock, but hers was not the face I was seeing.

*The silenced mouth.*

*The blue gun barrel.*

Revulsion robbed me of my new-found strength. Breathless, dizzy, I sank down on the white step. Where was Lou now? Back with her wastrel father? What kind of future would that mean for her? Was—

And then, through the chaos, I heard the sound, distant, but growing—a vehicle. Jane's hand touched my shoulder.

"I don't know what your sorrow is, Alex, but troubles don't come single. That ain't Seth's engine."

*

The rock above the mule's pasture was the only place, its top a natural hollow deep enough to keep me hidden and near enough to let me monitor events. I lay, cradling the fiddle in its case.

I'd only just made it. The car appeared a bare second after I'd reached the top, its arrival punctuated by the unnatural stopping of Jane's playing halfway through a reel. I risked a cautious look.

A white man in a tan uniform, pink-faced, wearing sunglasses and a stetson. He was short, bow-legged and grossly overweight, his stomach hanging so far over his waist that his belt buckle was invisible. Jane let him reach her chair. He tipped his hat in greeting, then stood, one foot up on the flat rock, one hand on the gun handle protruding from his right hip.

The law.

I watched the dumb show of their conversation, then hid myself again. Head flat against the stone's cool smoothness, I listened to the wind and the stream, trying to catalogue what I'd left in or near the cabin. Had I cleared all the remains of the iPad...? Would this man be suspicious if he noticed them? Would he search? After what seemed an age, I heard an ignition key turn. I wanted to look, but I forced myself not to. The sound was followed by a sentimental strain of country music from the vehicle's radio. Jane's fiddle answered, a rebuke of authenticity. Still, I waited. The engine took a long time to recede—and then, after another few minutes, the melody she was playing changed.

*Camp Chase.*

It was one of the tunes she'd promised to teach me—and it was our agreed signal that it was safe to come down. Slowly, I got to my feet.

*

A few minutes later, I crossed the plank bridge. When she heard my step on the wood, Jane stopped playing, then got to her feet, holding her fiddle tightly to her. Her smile was elfin, mischievous.

"Sheriff Roly Barger, my, my."

She shook her head and gestured at the white step. An empty plate lay on it. It held a fork and a few crumbs. She chuckled.

"Like father, like son. Same dumb cracker manners, same greed." She turned to me. "His daddy, Big John Barger, owned the store in town. Used to come a-courtin'. Like I said, dumb—never did work out that a bouquet o' magnolias in his hand didn't signify 'gainst the bourbon on his breath." The laughter left her face. "Couldn't stand the man, couldn't get rid of him neither—till I got together with Booker, a-course. Then John Barger, Mister High 'n' Mighty with his big money five an' dime, wouldn't give me the time o' day, no matter how much o' my pie he'd et, the summer o' forty-six."

She reached down for the case at her feet, lifted it on to the chair and let her anger take refuge in packing the instrument away, the bony hands working with their usual spare efficiency. Abruptly she turned back to me.

"Word's out on you. The Shelton boy told his buddies, one of 'em told a teacher. All round town, now. Sheriff Barger knows you was brung here."

She read my silence. Her voice came again, stubborn.

"We done made our bargain, me 'n' Roly Barger. I told him we give you some food and you left on foot the same night, he wrote down what I said in his book, or leastways he says he did. Don't know if he believed me or not, but it don't matter. All one to him if you're here or halfway to Hawaii, he just wants to get to tickin' that box, says he checked us out. Fine example of our tax dollars at work, Sheriff Barger, 'specially with the 'lection comin' up. Says he'll be back Thursday to make sure I'm all right, 'case you're still hangin' round somewheres." The humour returned to her as she gestured at the empty plate. "Means he wants another couple slices. Just like his daddy."

Witout warning her right hand reached out and grabbed my arm. I felt her grip tighten, as though she could transmit strength to me. When she spoke again, it was a pronouncement.

"I feel it, Alex. You do too, I know you do. Bargain's bought us time, ain't no knowin' how much." She let go of me and turned away. "Hope it's enough to git you gone."

*

The leavetaking was awkward. Jane and Seth both took refuge in practicalities. She decreed the main road too risky, even at night, then busied herself finding supplies. He saddled the mule and packed its load with obsessive care—and then the three of us hammered out a plan. When there was no more to be said or done, we broke bread together, and then, when it couldn't be put it off any longer, I went round the table and kissed Jane's brow. She took my hand.

"Good luck, Alex."

"Jane—"

"Moon'll be up. Hope that bridge o' mine don't buckle." She turned away to hide the tears. "The Lord go with you."

*

Seth walked the mule and me up past the chimney rock, then helped me mount. He held the reins while I settled in the unfamiliar saddle, going over it all again.

"Don't hurry ol' Steady. Once he's on that trail over the tops, ain't nothin' gonna stop him, he's a workin' mule, likes havin' a job to do, knows the way better'n' I ever did. He'll git you there by mornin', maybe sooner. He wants to stop 'n' graze, you let him, just as long's he needs."

His hand found the animal's velvety right ear, fondled it. He looked at me earnestly.

"Remember what I told you. Cabin's a bare mile south o' Weston, couple hundred yards from the highway. You'll make it by first light. Ain't no door. Use the torch, check for critters, copperheads in the corners, up on the crossbeams too. Rest up there if the leg's givin' you trouble, long's you like, nobody's gonna bother you, folks reckon it's haunted." He smiled, patted the pannier. "Momma give you 'nough to keep you a good three days, I reckon. Once you're at the cabin, all you got to do is give ol' Steady a slap, he'll make it home on his own."

I watched his fine features settle into resolve. A muscled black arm held a leather pouch up at me. I took it, opened it. It was full of twenty dollar bills. I thrust them back at him.

"We already had this conversation."

"Momma says you don't leave without it."

"I have food. I have my fiddle. I'll get by."

I didn't move my hand. He laughed, then, shaking his head, he took the money. Before I could stop him, he'd rammed it down behind the bag of food in the pannier. The mule snorted at the disturbance.

"You tryin' to git me a whippin'? Ain't nobody argues with Grannie McClintock, she's set on somethin'. She says she won't sleep easy, you don't take it, so you call it a gift or a loan or whatever the hell you want, but them bills's goin' with you." He held up a huge hand against further protest. "I make good money, you ain't leavin' nobody destitute here." He took a step back, out of my reach. "You still remember the drill?" I nodded. "When you get to Terre Haute, follow it. Exactly." His handsome face became serious. "Good operations fail when orders ain't followed."

Again, I nodded. When he spoke again, his voice was softer.

"I'm grateful, Alex. Ain't nobody 'cept me touched my momma like that, not in a long time." Once more he paused. "You still minded to follow the plan?"

"Yes," I lied.

"Remember, mornin' bus goes straight into Charleston, then you gotta wait three or four hours for the long distance. Be cops around, so be careful, could be descriptions out on you. You need to hide awhile, get off the street, a church'd be good, nobody gonna bother you there. Indiana to the Canadian border's about four hundred miles, maybe a couple hundred more if you want to avoid the big crossin's. Even on the back roads, you should do it in two days, easy."

His voice tailed off. Again, he fondled the mule's ear.

"Chimney Holler gonna see you again?"

This time it was the truth. "I hope so."

He reached up and offered me his hand. His grip was fierce.

"Be safe. You got friends here, remember. Look in the bottom of the bag, you get a minute." Before I could say anything, he hit the mule on the rump. "Git, now."

I swivelled round and watched him, standing erect on the rock like a hidden monument, black on black. And then he was gone. The animal seemed to sense it. As it took its first sure steps, I turned again and faced the pines.

Endless, immense, forbidding...

My resolution faltered. Loneliness descended on me. What had I told Seth? That I had fiddle and food...

I'd left out fear. I'd thrown off its grip on my memories, but that didn't mean it had left me. What did I have to fight it, here in this dark glen on the wrong continent? The answer came when the wind took a brief respite from its relentless prowling through the pines.

A thin strand of melody, already changed from what I'd taught.

*The Hawk That Swoops On High…*

Eerie in the cold night, the raw Appalachian strains cloaked the tune in beauty until the rustle of the trees ruled once more—and then a sliver of moon pushed away the clouds. Its light illuminated the images that seemed to swim around me.

A silver head of hair above the shoulder of my fiddle.

A teenage girl's face, blinded and gagged.

And a long stream of brown tobacco juice beside the rusty side of an old van…

Just like its twin, a week ago, on a dusty Virginia back road.

I grabbed the reins tighter and let Steady carry me forward through the darkness.

# 8

# GREYHOUND

"LEAVIN' PROMPT, FOLKS. You ridin' the St. Louis dawg, be on board in five."

*Ridin' the dawg...*

A fine piece of slang, the poetry of the impoverished; the Greyhound bus, the dog… It was proof that language would always have life, that it was virile, unquenchable...

And irrelevant. I put down my paper water cup, forced my mind back from fatigue and prised myself off the counter stool. Before the tannoy's echo had died, I was heading out through the truck stop's swing doors. It was important to be the first back on, over the last two stops I'd worked that out. I reached the bus and waited, glad of Seth's jacket as I watched the wind rearrange the discarded fast food containers around the huge front tyres. The black driver gave me a sullen look through the glass, then loosed the blast of compressed air. The door opened in a smooth, pneumatic movement. I climbed the steps and nodded my thanks. She didn't acknowledge me, staring morosely ahead through the windscreen. Quickly, I moved up the aisle and swung myself into the back seat.

My fiefdom, my citadel...

My vantage point. From here I could scan new passengers, or perceive any changes to the behaviour of the old ones. I was incredibly tired.

My stomach rumbled. Jane's food had lasted a day so far, but

I had no idea how long I might need to make the rest of it stretch. After the second bus ticket, I had exactly four hundred and twenty-three dollars and forty cents to my name. I reached into the canvas bag and unwrapped a corn biscuit from its foil wrapper. Delicious. Her voice came to me. *Meat won't last more 'n' a day, Alex, corn'll keep a good long time…* As I wiped my lips, the memory of her seemed more real than anything surrounding me now. Would she forgive me if she knew what I was planning? Would Seth? As the rest of the bus's human cargo began to board, I examined them.

The ageless black man in dungarees, careful to let his eyes meet no one else's.

The teenage Hispanic mother with her tightly swaddled infant and her huge straw bag of baby paraphernalia.

The two middle-aged gay men in matching bright sweaters, snuggling up to each other as they sat down.

The no-longer young redhead with the brittle face and the short skirt, reaching for her compact the minute she was seated, crossing her legs conspicuously as the three uniformed army cadets passed her. They all looked.

The solemn quartet of Asian girl students, the white-suited man with his arm in a sling, the sleek black youth in his jogging suit…

And then the pace of it all slowed, as though the boarding process had somehow been elevated to a different plane.

The elderly couple's progress up the aisle was ceremony. I watched; the manners of millionaires, the punctiliousness of potentates... She held his arm, he leaned on his stick. Clad in their threadbare nineteen-fifties pastel finery, they inched their way forward between the seats, greeting to right and left as they passed, deferring to each other with elaborate courtesy. As always, tiredness spread its net of fantasy for me.

*The passing of discarded gods…*

*The last salutation of deposed royalty…*

And then, abruptly, fantasy vanished. The final passenger was all too real, a pale boy, barely in his teens, crackling with tension. He sidled sinuously up the bus as though contact with either side might contaminate, scowling at anyone who looked at him, just as he'd done all the way from Charleston. I felt the impact as he flung himself down into the seat in front of mine, then saw him don the headphones which kept the world at bay.

I put on my own pair—instant public privacy, the best *Do Not Disturb* sign I'd ever discovered. Once again, I mentally thanked the boy for the idea. It had been five dollars well spent at the journey's first halt.

I finished the biscuit and settled back into my seat. The hiss of the doors came, the air of expectation descended, the susurrus of conversation petered out. The big motor coughed into life, the driver's unhappy voice came over the speaker.

"Next stop, six am. Columbus, Ohio."

As we began to move, I felt myself begin to relax. I was safe... Once again, being cocooned in this travelling silver pod had brought its strange bonus.

Camouflage.

The only way to stand out on a Greyhound bus was to look prosperous. If you were weird or poor or alternative in any way, this was your natural habitat.

*Ridin' the dawg...*

I felt body and mind disconnect. I touched my shirt pocket once, to make sure the treasure was still there, then closed my eyes.

*

I woke to panic—where was I? And the sounds? What—

Automatically, my hand reached for the fiddle. Touching the case's cracked leather unlocked logic—the vibration was the bus, the faint heavy rock was spill from the seat in front of me, from the kid's headphones. Slowly, piecemeal, memory kicked in; *the dead boy, the snake, Lou, the crash, Jane, Seth...* I willed it away, all of it—the present was where I needed to be. I had gone to sleep an hour ago, on a bus heading west through America... That was enough.

Warily, I scanned the heads in front of me. Most were lolling sideways in sleep. The baby's gentle wail and her mother's soothing lilt were the only audible signs of life, I was alone as I could be. I unbuttoned the pocket of my shirt and brought it out, the fine thing I'd found at the bottom of the saddlebag as I'd waited in the abandoned slave hut.

*Excelsior, for superior tone and control...*

The ceramic holder's rosin still held the marks of her bow. Again, her voice claimed me.

*Only thing my daddy ever gave me…*

For it to be in my hands now was evidence of a bond which went a long way past friendship. Would Jane McClintock and I meet again? I grasped the rosin holder tightly, felt her courage flow from it—and swore to myself that we would. Some day I'd return to Chimney Holler. I put the treasure away and reached into the bag for the second of the secret gifts I'd been given.

A plastic oblong. It was foreign, an intrusion into my life, just as the last one had been, the only difference being that this one was khaki, not black. The note was still taped to the screen.

*I found the shards by the block, so I reckoned you could use a new one of these. Military issue. Fully charged, ready to go, all service paid for a full year, internet, everything. Email, you're steady@gmail.com. Don't use it to contact me, we stay separate, too easy to trace. Other than that, if privacy's an issue, don't worry, the account's in the name of a friend of mine overseas.*

*Follow the instructions on the first screen. Some of the buses have wi-fi.*

With a mixture of curiosity and trepidation, I fingered the screen of my new iPad.

And then I realised I was smiling. Email wasn't something I'd ever wanted, but if I had to have it, I liked sharing an address with a mule…

*

Seth's instructions were precise. Added to the rudiments Lou had shown me, I found I could cope, however mystifying it all felt. It took me an hour to achieve kindergarten level.

Hesitantly, the headphones shielding me, I typed the name I wanted into the search engine. I chose one from the list of results—to be swamped, instantly, with sound and image. Over the roar of the engine, as the bus pierced the darkness, I tried to take it all in.

*"…and the new shades in Lauren's collection are simply fabulous! The surprise is that the silhouette is so fifties, but it's no surprise it's so beautifully tailored—that's why all of us ladies love you, Ralph! But the question is, will the other designers follow suit? Add that to the speculation that America's Sweetest Sweetheart really is set to become the new*

*face of Opulence and we have a couple of humdinger stories for you here on Fashion Update tonight! Later, we'll get the real skinny from our correspondent Kay Elliott—but in the meantime, here's our girl Rose at the Milan show six weeks ago, looking drop dead gorgeous as always. Awesome isn't the word..."*

Unable to bear it, I turned off the sound. The pictures were enough, a collage of shots that zoomed, twirled, split and dissolved into each other at frenetic speed. I saw Rose Vannier pout, preen and pose. I watched the luxury being poured on, relentless—every shot a different mood, every mood a different outfit. From all sides, hands claimed her, deferring, brandishing, pampering. They wielded brushes against her cheeks, they hung jewels round her neck, they painted gloss on her lips and lacquer on her nails. Combs and dryers swept her blonde hair down into hanging waves and up into artful towers. Mirrors caressed her in close-up as she beckoned and strutted, captured by brilliant flurries of flash. Strangest of all, in an almost subliminal burst of shots, I saw her mouth widen, fracture by fracture, in the millisecond it took to change from pursed sulk to widescreen smile.

It was fascinating.

It was frightening.

And above all, it was repellent. It was as though I was being offered the chance to buy the woman rather than watch her.

But if it bothered her, she didn't let it show. In the midst of all the commotion, she looked confident and poised. In charge. I watched the fabled smile, turning on and off like a capricious tap, feeding on the ecstasies of applause as she loped along the catwalk. Was it genuine, her smile? It certainly seemed to inspire. I caught a fleeting glimpse of familiar faces, upturned and rapt, as she passed; Ann Savoy and Sandy Hunter. Even with no sound, I could see that the show was reaching its climax. As I watched her lead a phalanx of other models along the runway, half-walking, half-dancing, the eager forward surge of the faces and bodies to either side triggered a memory.

It took a second to solidify, but then I had it. I smiled; the chickens in her barn, rushing up to the wire fence...

But then my smile died.

Confident, outgoing, poised.

This was a different being from the distraught woman whose life I'd saved on a Washington pavement.

A very different woman.

*...At the Milan show six weeks ago...*

Six weeks... What had happened to Rose Vannier in those six weeks?

*

Again I slept. The release was bliss, the duration, brutally short.

The pattern of it hadn't varied since I got on the bus. I was never allowed respite for longer than an hour—it was as though my unconscious had made a bargain with my body. If I reached for wakefulness at regular intervals, the nightmares would be kept at bay. All I could do was accept that I had no control. When would the cycle end? How long could my brain refuse me rest? By the time of my third waking, my mind was fit to do little more than wander.

The day's light was beginning its grey rise. Landscape came with it. As we wound down from the mountains, I tried to take it all in—tumbling rivers and vast acres of forest which looked virgin, untameable. The black ribbon of highway we were thundering down seemed puny by comparison, a grudging concession made by the wild, something nature could wipe away with one disdainful flick. Rain came on the thought, heavy, insistent. As I stared through the bus's wipers, the only things which seemed alive were the huge billboards looming out of the half-darkness, beacon-like on their towering stalks.

*MCDONALD'S, FAMILY DOLLAR, TASTEE CHIKIN*

They gathered before each settlement like sentinels who'd been warned of our approach, guarding neat towns with strange War Of The Worlds water towers, or mile-long agglomerations of oil tanks, or grey depots housing endless lines of huge trucks. Once the sun was fully up I saw that the concentration of them was increasing.

*ARBY'S ROAST BEEF, THE WORLD'S BIGGEST GUN SHOW,*
*WBNS SPORTS RADIO, JIFFY LUBE, WOK 'N' GO,*
*APPLEBEE'S*

What would come next? In answer the downpour stopped and showed me my first American shopping mall, huge, sprawling across both sides of the road, neon-lit despite the daylight.

*FRY'S APPLIANCES, LOWE'S, BARNES & NOBLE,
TACO BELL, BURGER KING, PIZZA HUT*

I couldn't see a human being, only cars, cruising like a new species on patrol—and then we were back to wilderness. The bus changed gear and began to climb a steep hill. At the top came a different vista. Below and before us was a vast patchwork of geometric squares of farmland, stretching as far as the eye could see. It came to me that I was looking at the midwest.

The heartland...

The first of the billboards on the downward slope was the biggest so far, its floodlit lettering dominating the glowering sky.

*FEEL HIS GRACE BAPTIST CHURCH.
ALL WELCOME!*

The image entwined in the lettering was of an overweight man, arms extended to the sky, smiling in ecstasy. What ecstasy would there be for me, I wondered. A man who had killed…? An outcast who had let a child in his care be kidnapped...? The second board was even bigger, the man's expression even more delirious.

*COME FEEL THE POWER!
COME FEEL THE GRACE OF GOD!*

I felt my anger stir. God... Where did God fit into what had happened to me? If there really was—

*REPENT!
REJOICE!*

The third board was the biggest of all, the human figure surrounded by celestial sunlight. As I closed my eyes to blot it out, the driver's voice, neither repentant nor rejoicing, came over the tannoy.

"Terre Haute. Twenty minute stop."

*

*Left out of the bus station, N. 8th Street, past the Eugene Debs museum, right on Spruce Street…*

Canvas bag over my left shoulder, fiddle case gripped tight in my right hand, I walked. By the time I reached the turning, I'd convinced myself I'd find nothing. If there was no vehicle, what would I do? The rain had begun again. It fell like doubt, incessant, unavoidable. After two hundred yards I turned, trying to look casual as I scanned for prying eyes, checking off the cars along the road, four of them, a hatchback and two sedans to my left, a minivan to my right. It was what I'd been told to expect. At the bottom of N. 9th Street, a lone vehicle stood beside a row of trees.

*Chevy pickup, ex-army, brown camouflage, tarpaulin over the back, Michigan plates. No other vehicle near. Anything else on the street, do not approach.*

Square and squat, it was the right shape and in the right place. I crossed. I was alone on the wet pavement. As instructed, I willed myself to stay unhurried.

*Good operations fail…*

As I reached the vehicle the rain became heavier.

*Keys on the kerbside rear wheel…*

After a glance to each side, I leaned down, reached into the wheel well and ran my fingers along the rubber.

Yes! Triumphantly, I grasped the metal bundle. I straightened up, then took a last look along the damp street. Nothing. I opened the driver's door, got in with my twin burdens, wiped the rain from my face and smelled the stale tobacco fug of someone else's life. A page of cheap paper was folded over the steering wheel.

*Long box in the back, everything you need—fatigues, binoculars, trench tool, k-rations, bug spray, duct tape, sleeping bag, blankets. Pup tent will do, but check for tears in the groundsheet if it's wet. Stove is good, enough spirit for a couple of weeks. Keep the jerrycans tied down. When it's time to lose her, how is not important, she can't be traced back to me, or to any mutual friends we might both have.*

*Burn this—prints.*

*Semper Fi.*

I folded away the note, then put the key in the ignition. She started on the first turn. I adjusted the mirrors, then sat back, exhilarated.

*Semper Fi…*

The famous Marine motto. Seth had been as good as his word. His network of buddies had saved me.

*

The phone booth behind the supermarket was third in a row of four, the only one unvandalised. It smelled of too many bodies, of cheap perfume and old sweat. I read the graffiti.

*Suck My Dick, Asshole!.*
*Fuck all State Troopers!*
*Leanne, you a slut, but I still love you.*

I looked right and left, but in the bright morning light which had come after the rain, no one was paying me the slightest attention. I watched the supermarket's customers shuffling their trolleys through the doorway and tried to sort out my thoughts.

I'd made my choice, I had to do this. Before my courage could fail me, I dialled. An automated message filled with fake politeness told me how many quarters to use. I fed the money into the slot. Finally, a deep voice answered.

"John Walks-Over-Ice."

"You know who this is?"

There was a pause. "Sure. Where are you?"

"Never mind, listen. The kid, Lou. I think I know who abducted her in Wheeling."

The silence seemed to go on forever. He broke it.

"Things have moved on, Fraser," he began, slowly. "If you want to meet, I'll explain—"

I slammed the receiver down and forced my way out into the sunshine. As I walked towards the pickup, a fierce joy rose in me—if they knew more than I did, that was fine, I'd done my duty. I stood in the middle of the car park, giddy, stupid with relief—now I could go my own way with a clear conscience.

And then the elation drained away.

*No, I couldn't go yet…*

I still owed one person an explanation. I turned, went back to the booth. This time, after all the rigmarole, it was a tinny version of Rose Vannier's voice that I reached. It spoke to me in a breezy sing-song.

"Hi, you've reached Annie Salinger's machine! I'm not here, so after the beep, you're it!"

I waited. Finally, the electronic noise came. My voice sounded strange to me.

"I know Lou's safe. I just want to apologise to her. I'd never have left her alone if I'd thought she was in any danger. Will you tell her that for me?"

I heard the clatter of the phone being lifted at the other end.

"Fraser? Where—"

Once again I slammed the receiver down and pushed myself out through the folding doors. This time I ran towards the vehicle.

Not Rose Vannier's voice…

*Saul Morgan's voice.*

# 9

# DEBONNAIRE

AS SOON AS I saw the narrow cobbled road's dead end, I pulled over and switched off. Frustration filled the sudden silence. A wrong turn? The map, misread? If I went back to the main highway…

And then, slowly, it came to me that I had come to the end of endurance. My limbs were like lead. I sat, dully, letting the tendrils of tiredness strangle purpose—and then, head swimming, I simply let go; sleep, no matter how short, no matter how troubled. All I was conscious of was the absence of the engine's noise. The fifteen hours of back roads I'd just driven replayed themselves as a jerky series of stills somewhere behind my eyelids; rusting county line signs, small towns full of suspicious stares, red barns daubed with faded exhortation.

*Chew Mail Pouch Tobacco.*

Was that what he chewed? Wenger's Seed and Supply? *Why had he let Lou go…?*

I woke in cramped discomfort behind the wheel, the newness of the military fatigues chafing. A few miles away, I saw a line of moving headlights. The main road I'd avoided? Behind it, the dawn's first light was cutting an angry red line between the peaks of the Ozark mountains and the dark sky. Across everything I could make out a fine layer of mist, hanging just above head height like a thrown grey shroud.

I got out of the pickup, stretched, took the torch from the

glove compartment and walked slowly towards the gothic silhouette which loomed over the cobblestones.

A gateway.

Or rather, the remains of one. Built to impose, it was still impressive, even as debris—huge rectangular blocks of dressed stone, lying where they had fallen, impervious to the vegetation's guerrilla creep. One pillar was still standing, a massive tower, pitted and flaking, stretching up into the half light at a crazy angle, as though the only things stopping its fall were the thick hawsers of ivy anchoring it to the undergrowth. I let my torch beam scale the thing, following the path of an intricately carved serpent as it threaded its way up through patterns of vine leaves, past eroded coats of arms, beneath the bellies of snarling animals, limbless and unrecognisable. What was this place? An estate? There was something unsettling about these ruins... But what?

And then I had it—they didn't fit. They didn't fit America—or at least the America I'd been driving through for the last fifteen hours. This gateway was aristocracy, privilege, it was older than democracy. Had my father simply given me a wrong address? The strange, long-faced beast at the column's top scowled down at me, offering no answers, expecting no pity for its crumbled wings.

I let the beam search further. The one remaining iron gate was only just still attached, its huge weight anchored to the column by a single twisted and tenacious hinge. Above a massive lock, I saw half of an oval plate. Between the bullet holes of someone's target practice I could make out letters, wrought in serifed capitals against the rust's flat surface.

*DEBON*

A name? Half a name?

I wandered between the fallen blocks until I found what was left of the other gate, hidden behind the second pillar's stump. It had been reduced to a neat stack of iron bars, ready for the scrapyard. Again the question found me. What *was* this place? I fingered the newness of the saw cuts, then turned back for the pickup—and stumbled over a single stone, smaller than the others, hidden in the grass. I reached down and pushed away the vegetation.

It was the second column's top—a carved animal, sinuous and sleek, perfectly preserved despite its fall. I didn't recognise the beast, but it looked lifelike enough to speed away from me at any minute. Beside it I found the second half of the oval name plate. It took all my strength to prise it off the ground.

*NAIRE*

The letter E crumbled in my hand. In the rising light, I stared, first at what I held, then back up at the other half.

*NAIRE...*
*DEBON...*

*DEBONNAIRE*

My mother's voice jumped five decades to find me.

*You are of fine blood, Alexander, on both sides of your family. On your father's side you are a Fraser. A Fraser of Lovat, never forget that. You are the descendant of a great clan. My own family is even more noble. I am a MacBeth, descended from Kings of Scotland. You know our motto? Debonnaire, Alexander. It means gracious, which is what a young man like you must always strive to be, no matter how low circumstance has brought us...*

I stood in the mist, lost in remembrance; *her voice, her perfume, the strokes of the brush, quick and harsh, as she readied my unruly hair for church...* I shone the torch back down on the stone beast at my feet, recognising it now. Again her voice came.

*...the otter. That was the animal which graced our coat of arms, along with the serpent...*

My beam followed the snake up the column to the wingless beast at the top. A thread of mist hung from its snarling stone face.

*...and the dragon.*

Again, memories; *her hands, spinning me round to the mirror, the sliver of happiness which for once pierced the grave melody of her voice as we examined ourselves.* Before I could stop it, the thought came, unguarded.

*Was she still alive?*

And then, before the question could possess me entirely, a shaft of light broke free from the silhouette of the jagged peaks and showed me what filled the valley before me.

It was vast, a sea of identical white boxes, stretching as far as the freeway. As I took the sight in, a garish artificial light suddenly illuminated its far edge. It came from a high-stalked sign, like the ones which had loomed over the Greyhound bus.

Two devils, bright red, horned, tailed and grinning. One held a frying pan, the other a fishing rod. The words they were dancing upon began to flash on and off.

*DEMON'S LAIR TRAILER PARK*

*Demon's Lair...*

*Debonnaire...*

The motto of George MacBeth's clan. My thoughts flew back two nights, to the tired insight of an Appalachian truck stop; *language, virile, unquenchable…* One name, twisted by the usage of common people into another...

*Debonnaire...*

*Demon's Lair...*

The conviction grew in me. I hadn't come to the wrong place after all…

I turned my back on the view and forced my weary limbs back towards the pickup. I was sure, now.

Somewhere down there, among the regimented ranks of caravans between me and the dancing devils, was the next step towards the uncle I'd been sent to find.

*

"How long you fixin' to rent for, sir?"

Beneath the manager's jovial tones, I heard the calculation. I tried to make my voice as neutral as possible.

"I'm not sure. How much for a week?"

The glint of greed in his eyes became more open. Good, it would trump questions about my accent. I watched him mask the look quickly.

"Normally, that'd be 'bout a hunnerd 'n' sixty. Course—" The swivel chair creaked as he shifted. "—if you'd don't need any paperwork, we could, ah, *adjust* that a little.." He searched my face for the right guess. "Hunnerd 'n' ten sound 'bout right?"

I nodded and reached into my jacket pocket. As I counted out five twenties and a ten, he registered the notes one by one and eyed the thickness of the roll they'd come from. When the money was safely in his hands, he looked across at me.

"You a fisherman, sir? Bass're jumpin' pretty good. You want, we can rent you a real fine rod. Be up there on the lake right now m'self, wasn't for the 'mount of shoutin' I gotta do to get stuff done round here, lazy bl—"

I watched the word being swallowed and gave him what I hoped was a smile of complicity. If I was to get the information I wanted, I had to be an actor, now. I needed this man at his ease.

"Nothing wrong with the word *black,*" I said.

He shifted his frame in his chair and gave me a sideways look. He seemed to approve of what his eyes found. He nodded.

"Damn right, friend" he said, solemnly. "Amen to that. Political correctness, ain't that what they call it? Be the death of free speech in this country, we let it."

I nodded in my turn. "What was this place originally?" I asked.

It was the cue he'd been waiting for. "History, sir, that's what it was and is—pure history. I gotta tell you you've landed in one o' the most fascinatin' outposts of our nation's heritage." He sat back in the creaking chair. "Demon's Lair was the ol' MacBeth plantation. Kinda colourful, every sense o' the word—" He gave me a sly grin. "—if you get my meanin'. Ol' Man Macbeth, the first one, way back, the seventeen hunnerds, he came to raise cotton, went bust, hocked the place to the hilt, drank 'most every cent he raised on it, then spent whatever was left raisin' any other kinda hell he could find. Guess that wasn't so hard." The grin widened into a gap-toothed leer. "Fields full o' black-assed temptation, my friend, every curve of it bought 'n' paid for."

He leaned forward, put his hands squarely on the desk. The voice became conspiratorial.

"But there was other stuff, too. Devil worship 'n' such. Folks even called his wife a witch, jus' like in the ol' play. They say that's how the name got changed, how the demons got in. Fact is, till recently, we still had MacBeths here at Demon's Lair." Again the grin came, but this time it turned into a chuckle. "Never saw none o' that ol' voodoo hoodoo from 'em personally, mind."

I bit back the question. He turned the chair, kept talking as he busied himself counting the bills away into the safe behind him.

"Yessir, used to live right here in this park, number 430, fanciest double wide on the lot. Reverend George MacBeth, was the preacher at Promised Land Baptist, right here in downtown Fayetteville. Got married there, second time I b'lieve. Moved on out to better things a while back. Him 'n' Lady Mac—"

Once again he caught himself, but this time it was an indiscretion too far. By the time he'd turned back to me, the lecherous grin was gone. He slid a key across to me.

"Two-twenny-three, far north corner," he said, abruptly. "Gas cylinders at the store, ten bucks deposit, 'lectric'll be turned on by the time you get up there."

*

*Married...*

And twice... Did my parents know? There was no hint of it in my father's letter. I stood, staring at the huge metal box which had once housed my uncle and his second bride. It was double the size of the one I'd just rented—bigger, in fact, than the house in which I'd grown up.

A static caravan, a travelling home unable to travel... Had this one ever been mobile? It looked as though it had long since shed its wheels and settled, let itself be seduced into permanence by its stone surround, by its neat tomato frames and its garlands of shrubs and flowers. I fought disappointment. How was I to proceed from here?

"You lookin' for the Kramers?"

I turned to find a small woman on the other side of the road, surrounded by an untidy vegetable patch. She had a squat, muscled body, a red kerchief knotted across her brown hair, and horn-rimmed glasses which turned up at the ends to make a permanent question of her eyebrows. She dug her pitchfork into the earth, then waddled across to me and wiped the sweat from her brow with a gloved hand.

"Be a while yet, Saturday mornin's, them two're flat-out, busier 'n' a lizard drinkin'. Ruby's doin' the football run for the boys, Ed's gettin' the groceries."

"Actually, it wasn't the Kramers I was trying to find."

She giggled. "You talk funny, hon. Who you lookin' for?"

"Mister—sorry, *Reverend* George MacBeth."

A huge smile lit up her face. "The Reverend! Ain't heard o' him in a long while—a damn long while, come to think on it.

Moved outta here, oh, maybe, eleven, twelve years ago. Must be a fair age now. Still see his good lady wife, though, just about every damn where—big deal in the Rotary, Daughters of the American Revolution, all that. Cut the ribbon on the State Fair last October. Big boss lady, finger 'n' every pie. Runs the radio station, KZTX, outta Zion Junction, 'bout forty miles upstate. Reverend George used to preach on it every Saturday night, even when he was at First Baptist. Kep' it up for more 'n' thirty years. The gospel hour." Her smile changed, became tinged with fondness. "Used to listen to him when I was a young 'un. With my kid brother, under the covers. Scared us both shitless. Never knew a man could talk up hell so many different ways. Yessir, wasn't many round here didn't listen."

*

*"...And the Lord said, all of you who are afflicted, come unto Me! That's right, that's what He said, folks!"* There was a murmur of approbation. *"Wasn't, Come unto Me, you got the time 'fore your favourite TV show!"* This time the congregation was louder. *"Wasn't Come unto Me, you don't win the lottery!"* Again the response grew, with cries of *That's Right!* and *Praise Him! "Wasn't Come unto Me you couldn't get tickets for the ball game, no sir! It was COME!"* The thump of a fist punctuated the word. *"UNTO!"* Again, the fist. *"ME!"* The congregation went wild. A blissful female voice sang out over the uproar. *HE IS THE LORD!* The preacher chuckled. *"Amen, sister, you sure got that right! And because He is the Lord, folks, He—"*

As I negotiated the downward slope's last hairpin, the radio's reception died. I listened gratefully to the static. Sanity, relief... After all the hectoring, the no-right-thinking-person-could-believe-any-different... Was this what had happened to my Uncle George? Had he been seduced by this fervour, this rabid witch-doctor's call-and-response? *And if that was the case, did I want to meet him...?*

I pondered it as I drove slowly along the valley bottom's crumbling road, beside a rushing river in full spate—and then a shaft of sunlight pierced the overcast sky and reminded me of the beauty around me. A leaping deer bounded out from the tangle of flowers which bordered the pines and raced me along the road's edge before disappearing again. It was one of the most graceful things I'd ever seen.

*Grace...*

Was that what I was on my way to find? A man in a state of grace? If that was the case, I could respect it, even if I couldn't believe in it. But why had he sent back every letter? Was there something about his new life which had made him reject the old one?

I came to a covered wooden bridge, stately in its stubby functionality. As I drove slowly through its artificial cave, listening to my tyres negotiate the rough wooden boards and the echoing river beneath, I let myself dream. Maybe, in a few hours, this strange mission of mine might come to some kind of fruition. If it did, perhaps I could come back here. I had a tent, I had a stove and a sleeping bag. I could buy food and make a fire, sit with my fiddle and remind myself of the tunes Jane had taught me.

I could claim a little peace.

I could claim solitude.

I could claim the right to take something good from this country before I had to work out how to flee it...

But none of that was possible yet. Once I reached the sunlight, the road's inexorable rise up the valley's other side began, and the radio filled the pickup's cab again.

*"...because today we have with us an old friend, Pastor Elmore Cairney, from North Fork Baptist in Waxahachie, Texas, one of our sister congregations in Christ. Let me bid you a warm welcome to KZTX, Pastor Cairney, broadcasting the beautiful length and breadth of Arkansas, right here out of downtown Zion Junction."*

*"Mighty pleased to be here, Reverend Seiler, always a pleasure to help you folks up here in the Ozarks fight the good fight. Praise The Lord!"*

*"Praise Him indeed! Now, Pastor, in your capacity as one of our most respected Christian political commentators, I'm sure you would agree that this wonderful land of ours has never been in greater moral peril. When we look, for instance, at the godless legalisation of abortion and marijuana cultivation in so many states, not to mention the current attitudes to homosexual so-called marriage..."*

Again, the reception died—and this time, my composure died with it. It was all too weird, too much to process—I couldn't just keep driving, I had to stop, to *think*. There was a layby on the next bend. I pulled into it, switched off, and closed my eyes. For the first time since I'd reached Arkansas, my fears surfaced in full.

What was I going to find in Zion Junction? Welcome? Rejection? What if my uncle wouldn't see me? Or refused to believe who I was? Or refused to let me read him my mother's letter?

The sound of another engine, straining up the steep hill behind me, broke the train of thought. I'd hardly seen another vehicle since I'd left the trailer park. I'd no reason to think anyone was following me, but...

A small yellow hatchback pulled up alongside me. Its driver was a young woman, attractive, her chestnut hair pinned up behind her head in a careless bun that held a pencil. She smiled at me as she got out, then went round and lifted the rear hatch. I watched her rummage through a mountain of luggage, unearth a plastic box, place it on the car's bonnet and take off the lid.

"OK, you guys, food!"

Three small girls, in identical pink-and-white checked gingham dresses, emerged slowly from the back seat and stood, regarding me doubtfully as they waited for their lunch. As I watched each of them being given a sandwich and a carton of juice, I realised that their car's radio was tuned to the same station as mine.

*"...in Washington DC itself. And now, for the first time here on KZTX, brought to you courtesy of Golden Harvest Produce in Fayetteville, the best fresh produce this side of the Mississippi, please welcome, live and raised in praise, straight from Nashville, Tennessee, the beautiful voice of Megan Mallinson!"*

The applause quickly gave way to a country rock beat; guitars, drums, bass and dobro. A sentimental fiddle line wove itself into it. Instinctively, my hand found the morocco case by my leg. As I watched the young mother brush crumbs away from her jeans, a female voice floated effortlessly from the car's speakers.

*"Praise Him, for He is the glory!*
*Don't waste what you got, 'cause He knows the story!*
*You got to do what's right and Praise the Lord today!*
*Yes, Praise Him!*
*Lord, Lord, gotta Praise Him!*
*Lord, Lord— "*

Anger gripped me—so lush, so professional, so slick. Every emotion cued to the last second, every endorsement seamlessly positioned, every opinion expertly manipulated...

I got out, desperate to get away from both the sound and my own anger. I ignored the little family and walked across to the road's edge. The view had become more than beauty now. It was spectacular, steep slopes of pine, endless, soaring up before me, pointing ramrod-straight at the sky like some ultimate magnification of Scotland. As I stared at it, an earnest voice came from behind me.

"Sir, excuse me, but could I interest you in a tuna sandwich?"

I turned. The plastic box was being held out to me. The woman shrugged.

"The kids've all had theirs, an' heaven knows, I've been snackin' on Cheerios an' chocolate since we got in the car at seven o'clock this mornin'."

Her face was open and kind, guileless. The smell made me remember how hungry I was. I hesitated, but only for a moment. I reached out and took the sandwich.

"Thank you. You're very kind."

She grinned, then jerked a thumb backwards at the car. "Like the Good Lord says, ain't no point in wastin' what we got! You have yourself a fine day, sir." She turned and yelled. "OK, kids, back in the car! Let's move it, now! Gotta git to grandma's 'fore suppertime."

She waved to me as they left. With shy smiles, her daughters followed suit. I returned the wave, then stood and watched them disappear round the bend.

Kind, thoughtful, friendly... And obviously, believers.

*But in what, exactly…?*

Sandwich in hand, I turned back to the pines. My opinions, I realised, were perhaps a little less certain than they'd been half an hour before.

# 10

# ZION

THERE WAS NO DOUBT that I had arrived in a place which did not believe in equivocation. I surveyed the sign.

*ZION JUNCTION*
*POPULATION 2714*
*THE LORD LIVES HERE!*

Which of the 2714 was responsible for the upkeep of the rusty lettering, I wondered—and given the state of it, would there be retribution…?

The place was a grid of six streets by seven, spread out neatly on either side of a much-mended road. There was a Family Dollar supermarket, a post office, a cafe called Mona's, a bar called The Shack and four gleaming white churches. I found the radio station easily.

The building was large and flat, a single storey concrete box untainted by any concession to architectural style. It was topped by an aerial dish of science fiction proportions and flanked by an extensive car park on one side and a lush carpet of lawn, mowed to perfection, on the other. As I walked up the path, I counted—over thirty cars, not a negligible operation, God was obviously a serious employer... One vehicle towered over all the others, a massive black four-wheel drive with gleaming alloy wheels. As I passed it, a noise from behind made me turn.

A big lawn mower rounded the corner and chugged across the grass. It was being driven by an old man with abundant white hair and a thick walrus moustache. At the sight of me he stopped and switched off the engine. His puzzled frown lasted a few seconds, then morphed into an unsmiling nod. It was slow and dignified, as though he'd decided, after decent deliberation, that I was a fit person to gain entry. I nodded to him and walked on—and then, as I neared the building, the huge aerial seemed to contradict him. Its tortured grind stopped me. I watched it turn, with threatening slowness, until its thick central stalk was pointing up into the sky directly over my head.

The thought was instant. *Was God's opinion of me being sought?*

I almost smiled, but the fantasy stopped just short of being comic. I pulled my eyes away and pushed open a glass door emblazoned with the station's logo, a silver cross with an old-fashioned fifties microphone at its centre. The words *KZTX – Where The Lord's Voice Shall Never Be Silenced!* ran diagonally across it in red cursive script. Nothing remotely rusty about the lettering here...

The receptionist was a twenty-something blonde in a virginal white blouse, coiffed and made up to doll-like perfection. She looked my fatigues up and down, unimpressed, gave my fiddle case a puzzled glance, then remembered her job description. Her right hand came up to her jaw to show me her perfect nails. The smile showed a lot of teeth.

"If y'all're looking for work, the stations's music comes direct from Nashville, we don't do any actual hirin' here."

"I was hoping to speak to Mrs. MacBeth," I said.

The smile turned itself down a notch. "Oh..." She decided to take refuge in formality. "And what is the nature of your business?"

"It's private."

*Private* seemed to be a problem. The smile retreated even further as she wondered what to do with me.

"If you'll just take a seat."

I perched on an uncomfortable chair, put the fiddle case on its twin beside me and waited. The station's current broadcast was leaking softly from speakers built into the ceiling. As the woman dialled, I listened.

*"...and a transcript of today's broadcast, along with many others, is available from Christian Family Radio of..."*

"...says he wants to speak to Miz Lillian."

*"...at a cost of only seven dollars fifty. Simply attach a stamped addressed..."*

"Well, gee, Josh, I don't know, he won't say!" The call ended. "Be someone here in a minute," she sang out.

*"...and Pastor Cairney's latest book, Jesus—How To Bring Him Back To His Rightful Place In Government—one of the most significant political works of recent times, can be yours for a donation of just fifteen..."*

A door slammed down the corridor to her right. The sound galvanised her into action. A lipstick appeared between the red-nailed thumb and forefinger of her right hand. Using the back of her mobile phone as a mirror, she applied it quickly, then unleashed the smile's full dazzle in the direction of the approaching footsteps. A man's voice, warm and friendly, not young, reached her desk before the rest of him did.

"Well, the Good Lord has surely blessed you today, Millie. Lookin' fine, real fine."

"Why, thank you, Josh!" she said, coquettishly.

The smooth bulk of him arrived, silver haired, tanned and smiling. She basked briefly in the flirtation, then pointed at me.

"Gentleman over there."

He turned; white shirt, red-and-blue striped tie, immaculately polished shoes, grey flannels, blue blazer, cut to accommodate the outsize shoulders and biceps of a weightlifter. He was a handsome man in his forties, ageing well, and he knew it.

And then my mouth went dry—the clothes said *politician* or *businessman,* but the bulge under his left shoulder said something quite different.

*Security.*

And professional security at that. His scrutiny of me was brisk and methodical. I watched it travel over the fatigue jacket's blank name tag, then come to rest on the fiddle case.

"Miz MacBeth'll be available momentarily. Before we go see her, though, you mind if I take a look inside that case o' yours?"

I reached over, snapped the locks and lifted the lid in silence. He grunted at the contents, as though finding the instrument was the wrong surprise, then bent over. Without touching the fiddle, he poked a thick finger into each of the case's three inside compartments. Then he pulled himself up to his full height and gestured that it was all right to close it. As I did, I watched him decide to read the look on my face as disapproval.

"Necessary precaution, friend. We gotta be real careful here, lotta crazies around. Let's get you signed in."

I looked back at the desk. A plastic clipboard had appeared on it.

*A visitor's log.*

I felt my grip tighten on the case handle. It was something else I hadn't anticipated—but I couldn't afford to let confusion show. Pulse racing, I kept my face straight as I rose. Real name or false...? The choice had to be instant—the man's eyes were firmly on me. As the phone beside the red nails rang, I signed my own name, as illegibly as I could. The receptionist answered, then gave the big man a reprise of her arch smile.

"Miz Lillian'll see him now, Josh."

He nodded, then looked over my shoulder at the sheet. "This way, Mister Fraser."

Not illegibly enough, obviously... Case in hand, I followed the massive back down the corridor, and wondered. Ex-cop? Ex-military...? He stopped at the last door. The silver-lettered name plate was imposing.

*MRS LILLIAN MACBETH*
*STATION DIRECTOR*

Underneath, a smaller plastic sign, slightly askew, said

*Until The Almighty Decides Different!*

The big man knocked.

"Come right in."

He opened the door. Inside the spacious room, I saw a grey-haired woman standing with her back to me, bent over a desk littered with papers. She was smartly dressed in a two-piece bottle-green suit with matching low-heeled shoes. Her voice was both annoyed and amused.

"Josh, will you raise a prayer to the Good Lord for me, ask Him to do somethin' 'bout my memory!"

"Yes, ma'am, I surely will."

"An' if you put in a supplementary, maybe He can tell me, right now, right this minute, where in tarnation I put the recordin' of last night's second show."

As her hands went on sifting through the desk's confusion, the enormity of what was about to happen hit me. This woman, this total stranger, was part of my family. Part of my history, part of my *life...*

"There, that's where you went, you li'l devil, you!"

She unearthed a plastic box from the mess, then filed it away on a shelf behind her. Then she straightened up and began to turn.

"Now, Josh, where's this mysterious gentleman caller you've brought to see me?"

*Should I smile?*

*Should I offer my hand?*

Before I could do either, I saw her take in my features. Her mouth dropped open in shock. Her brown eyes filled with alarm. The colour drained from her face.

And then Mrs. Lillian MacBeth, station director of KZTX radio, swayed to one side, uttered a small cry, and collapsed.

*

The only decoration in the first aid room was a huge poster of Jesus, sad-eyed and haloed in ethereal light, head turned meekly to one side, with both arms outstretched. The words *Rest In Silence, I Will Heal You* were written in gold between the open-palmed hands.

At least one part of it had been achieved, I thought. The silence...

But it was a silence which differed on opposing sides of the table. For me it was a silence of regret. Unthinkingly, I had ripped open a wound. I had brought pain.

And for her?

If it hadn't been for her hands, I'd have called it a silence of catatonia. I watched them, emerald-ringed, lined with age, perpetually working, winding round each other as they shook in her lap.

Washing each other...

*Lady MacBeth.*

The trailer park manager's cruel nickname... Accurate by accident, I thought. I forced myself to speak.

"I'm sorry to have brought back your grief, Mrs. MacBeth. If I'd known..."

It drowned in awkwardness. I watched her attention fight to return from wherever it had fled, then struggle even harder to grasp my words. Finally, she managed to look—at me, for the first time, instead of past me. Then, slowly, the tendons of her neck taut with strain, she turned away again, as though she didn't understand what she had found. Her eyes returned to their secret place in the middle distance—until she found strength from somewhere. She delved into the voluminous handbag by her side. Her hand emerged with a small leather wallet. With great care, she took out a photograph and put it down on the plastic table top. Her forefinger pushed it across to me.

A black and white print, old, grubby from handling, torn at the top edge. I stared. The out-of-focus picture in my father's letter had shown the resemblance, but this...

It was of George MacBeth, taken many years ago. My uncle...

...was my double. My *exact* double. Over the upturned collar of a bulky leather flying jacket, my own face was looking up at me.

It was beyond uncanny.

His smile was mine. His hair, hanging in exactly the same way over his brow, parted in the same place, was mine. His eyes were exactly the same colour as mine, the brows above them arched in exactly the same way mine were.

For some endless unit of time, reality shifted.

I was looking at myself.

It took her voice to bring me out of shock. "You understand now?"

Eyes still fixed on the image, I nodded. She reached for her lighter, fumbled a slim cigarette from the packet on the table, lit up, threw her head back and took a long draw. I watched her exhale, slowly. She nodded down at the photograph, then started to speak in a flat voice.

"September third, nineteen seventy-one," she said. "My Kodak. Presbyterian Church picnic, up on Beaver Lake. Fell in love with him in less 'n' a heartbeat, handsomest man I'd ever seen in my stupid little life. Just swept me away. I was sixteen years old, thought I knew it all. Silly little dyed blonde in a miniskirt. I'd been fightin' my momma over the length of it for a month."

She ran out of words.

"How old was he in this picture?" I asked, to break the silence.

Once more I watched her struggle to thrust away remembrance. She gave the table a puzzled frown, as though the question had been put by some intruder she'd only just noticed. A knock saved her from answering. The door opened; Josh, the security man.

"You OK, Miz Lillian? Folks're worried."

I saw her make the effort to hide her feelings; *not in front of the troops…* "Thank you, Josh, please tell them I'm fine. Mister..."

"Fraser."

"...Mister Fraser and I just have some matters to discuss. Some *personal* matters."

The word was a dismissal. He didn't like it. He gave me a promissory scowl as he closed the door. I'd made an enemy, definitely... I looked back at Lillian MacBeth. Once more, she avoided my eyes. She got up, cigarette in hand. When she reached the window, the dead voice continued.

"'Course, no matter how much he set my heart a-flutter, he was off limits—even at sixteen, rebellious little hellion or not, I knew better 'n' to try. First thing my eyes found was the ring on his finger. It was her left him the money, his first wife, Louise—rich family, the Duggans, coal, owned half Sebastian County. But he'd noticed me, all right, I'd made sure of that."

The edge of triumph gave the voice life. She turned, gave Jesus a stare of defiance, then let herself fall back against the window ledge, left arm supporting the right elbow in the classic female smoker's pose. She took another quick draw of the cigarette. The smoke somersaulted up in a question mark which curled into the hanging grey wave of her hair.

"It didn't happen till six months after she died. He was ordained by then, had his pulpit at First Baptist. I'd joined his congregation, couldn't keep away, waylaid him every chance I got—all proper, mind you, I knew I'd have no chance if it wasn't. Finally he told me he wanted to use Louise's inheritance to do the Lord's work, said he had a vine to plant, told me about his plans—Christian radio, reach thousands every day, not just a few hundred every Sunday. I just took my heart in my hands and told him I knew I could help him make it bear fruit." She paused, let her eyes find the spiral of smoke. "We were at the altar inside the month. Day after the weddin' we were workin'." Her head shook fondly. "No honeymoon, not even a night in a hotel room. I didn't care. Every cent we had went on gettin' the station up an' runnin'." Now the voice began to slip back into the vernacular. "First buildin' was a raggedy-ass ol' barn down in Fayetteville. George, me an' Reuben, bugs near et us alive. I did the admin, took care of the licence, sold the air time, wrote the scripts, sweet-talked the sponsors. George did the broadcasts 'n' found the other preachers. Reuben ran the transmitter, kept us on the air." She nodded at the window as the mower passed. "Still here, Reuben, cuts the grass now, brings the sandwiches, doesn't understand all the new tech stuff. Drinks."

She let an indulgent smile find her face. It disappeared when she went back to her story.

"Sixteen hours a day, that was normal. We did everything ourselves, even the grunt stuff—cable trenches, drywall, restrooms, we couldn't afford to hire. Lived in a trailer park on the ol' MacBeth place, that's what'd drawn George down here in the first place. Told ourselves it'd be jus' for a while, till we got established. Thirty years later we were still there." She paused, lost again. "Best years of our lives," she finished. "Praise the Lord."

The three word coda wasn't much more than a whisper. She went back to staring out of the window.

"What did he die of?" I asked.

I watched her back tense, her head bow. "We never really found out. He was out walkin' in the woods, he did that sometimes, when he needed inspiration. There'd been storms, flash floods, we think he might have got caught in one, been incapacitated somehow. Then a mountain lion, or maybe coyotes, there were marks. Four years ago next October. Took us the best part of a year to find the remains, never got 'em all. We identified him from this."

From the wallet, she produced a battered square wristwatch. My mouth went dry as I turned it over. The inscription matched the one on the back of my father's photograph.

*To George MacBeth*
*For Good Works In The Name Of The Lord*
*SPCK*
*Fallin Parish Church 18.12.1956*

"Never took it off, 'cept to sleep. We buried what was left of him right here in Zion Junction. Near on a thousand at the funeral."

The hand holding the cigarette had begun to shake again. Was she going to break? I watched her shoulders rise as she took a deep breath—and then I felt the determination radiating from her. She had tapped, once again, into some deep well of resource. Only after she had taken her fill of it did she turn and finally face me.

"Forgive me, Mister Fraser," she said, her voice resolutely even. "Forgive me first of all, for faintin' on you like some young girl at the Saturday dance. And then forgive me, in the name of the Good Lord, for givin' you the news of George's death so bluntly after you've come all this way to find him. You've had just as much of a shock as I have." She walked back across to the table. "Now, if you'll excuse me, I must look a sight."

Before I'd managed to stand, she was gone. I slumped back down on the seat, my thoughts in turmoil. Finally, my eyes came back to the black and white photograph beside the smoking cigarette in the scallop shell ashtray. I turned it round.

The man my father had sent me to find, the brother who meant so much to my mother, the man who looked so much like me...

The man who was dead.

Why had the possibility never even occurred to me? Was it just the force of my father's command?

*Go to the man...*

The iron certainty of his will?

*Read it to him...*

I sat, holding the picture. My mission was over. I thrust away my own feelings—to be faced later. My hand went to the pocket of my jacket. The letter, my father's letter, it was still there. Should I show Lillian MacBeth the other photograph, the one of the young George? Should I read the letter, now? Should I read it to *her,* let this woman know what the sister-in-law she'd never known had been so desperate to tell her husband?

Would it be a kindness to do these things, or just another burden, more hurt?

And then Lillian MacBeth was there again. As she slid into the seat across from me, I sat back.

The shock was palpable. It was like meeting a different woman. I was no longer looking at the grieving widow, I was facing the director of the Christian Radio Station, the poised executive, in complete control, cool and scented, elegant, make-up perfect, not a grey curl out of place. She looked so much younger—and attractive with it. She reached across and took my hand in both of hers. Her smile was solicitous.

"What in the Lord's name must you think of me, Mister Fraser? Where are my manners? Here we are, two complete strangers joined together in tragedy, not exactly kin, but the next best thing to it. We need to get properly acquainted, don't you think?" Her voice became resolute. "I want you to know, my house is your house, for as long as you want to stay. I just telephoned my maid, told her to get the spare room ready—"

*No!* The panic was sudden, imperative—it was all I could do to keep it from my voice.

"Thank you, I have a place to stay. My luggage is there already."

She let go of my hand. I tried to keep my face immobile as I cursed myself; *always the same, always—why did my words never come out right?* I reached for an olive branch.

"But if the offer could be postponed by a day..."

It went against the grain, against every solitary bone of my loner's body, but I had to do it, I knew. She rose.

"Of course it can," she said, briefly, her face unreadable. "I'll look forward to that."

And then she was all bustle. The solicitous smile reappeared.

"I'm going back to work, now, Mister Fraser—if for no other reason than my own sanity. And then I'm going to Zion Baptist. To pray." She nodded up at the poster on the wall. "He and I have some talkin' to do."

Awkwardly, I got to my feet.

"Come tomorrow, I would welcome that."

She reached into her handbag, brought out a card and put it down on the table. Then she offered me her hand. Its grip was firm, not old at all.

"Come in the early evening, when the light's good. I'll take you..."

She faltered briefly, then recovered her poise.

"I'll take you to see George's grave."

*

I took the first road I could find out of Zion Junction, heedless of where it might lead. It wasn't a decision. It was an action with no rhyme or reason other than the need, overwhelming and insistent, to escape. To be free of all of it—my doomed quest, the people, the worries. I followed the tortuous Ozark back roads in a trance, fighting the pain of failure. I was all too aware of the bleak paradox waiting beyond.

I had never been more afraid of being alone—and yet alone was the only place I could bear to be. I was close—and I knew it—to breaking.

How long it lasted, how long I drove or how far, I had no idea. It took a rusting green sign to end it.

I stopped. It mocked me in the fading light.

*ZION JUNCTION*
*POPULATION 2714*
*THE LORD LIVES HERE!*

My confusion had let the mountain roads trick me into a circle.

I didn't even have the strength for frustration. I gave in, pulled over and switched off the engine. I wasn't even conscious of closing my eyes.

*

It was the chill which woke me, clawing at my limbs through the rough clothes. Shivering, I started the engine, turned up the heater and wiped the condensation from the windscreen. The sign was barely visible against the night sky. I looked at the dashboard clock.

I had slept for five hours. My body had allowed it.

The realisation brought me close to tears. It was a break in my darkness, a tiny crack of light—a small enough thing in the scheme of it all, but something to cling to. As the warmth began to flow, I summoned every last ounce of mental strength left to me.

Back to the trailer park, get one night on my own, begin again tomorrow, prepared, fresh...

I pulled out on to the road and drove slowly along the deserted main street, the lightless buildings ghostly to either side except for the occasional blue flicker of a television. At the other end of the town I came to a fork in the road. A sign showed me the entrance to the freeway which would take me straight back to Demon's Lair. As the headlights flashed past, I fought to organise my thoughts.

Zion Junction and Lady MacBeth, my uncle's suddenly glamorous widow...

To probe someone else's life—it was anathema to me. But could there be a plus side? Surely, the more information I could take home, the better—and then there were the unanswered questions. Did the woman know anything at all of her husband's Scottish family? Did she know about the letters? About them being returned?

How long would it all take, I wondered. A day? Two, for decency? I reached into my jacket and brought out the card she'd given me.

*Mrs. Lillian MacBeth*
*Station Director, KZTX Christian Radio*
*42 Gethsemane Trail*
*Zion Junction*
*72712 AR*

Gethsemane... Reality dawned as I faced the size of the stone that would need to be rolled away.

*Tell me about yourself, Mister Fraser...*

*Twelve years ago I killed my wife for sleeping with my best friend. Currently, I'm wanted by several police forces across your country...*

My bubble of optimism vanished. I let the card fall. How naïve could I be? It was, of course, impossible. In fact, given the parting scowl of Josh the security man, it was even money that, by now, the station's computers would already have traced everything there was to know about me.

My time in Barlinnie, everything that had happened to me since—and above all, my current fugitive status.

Two complete strangers joined in tragedy or not, I couldn't see any of it sitting well with the ethics of a religious radio station. In fact, returning to Zion Junction might just put my head in the noose I'd been running from since I landed in America.

Finally, thankfully, the dancing red devils beckoned. I'd never thought I'd be glad to see them, but now they were a refuge, a hiding place. I took the exit and followed the bumpy road, past the racist manager's office, up the curving fork that would bring me to my rented caravan. What was the number? I reached across, took the keys from the glove compartment. 223... It was the last in its row, the trees a waving black wall behind it. I pulled up on the driveway and switched off.

And as I wound down the window, it all rushed in on me; the scent of roses from one of the nearby garden plots, the remote hum of traffic, a distant radio from one of the other caravans. One by one, the smells and noises laid their small, searing, imprints on me—the faint traces of other peoples' lives, the mundane borders of a world I never seemed able to be part of.

*Alone, the only place I could bear to be...*

I closed my eyes tightly and reached for the radio's knob.

*"...and we beseech Thee, O Lord, give us a sign! Let us know that Your divine purpose has not excluded us! Show us, miserable sinners that we are, that we have not been been cast out from Your kingdom! A sign, Lord! That's all we're askin', just a sign!"*

I punched at the radio with my fist, killing the voice. And then I heard a metallic creak. I opened my eyes.

From the caravan's open door, Rose Vannier was staring down at me. As I stared back at her, Sandy Hunter appeared at her side.

# 11

# SAND

"HOW DID YOU find me?"

I heard the anger in my question. So did she.

"It wasn't difficult." Her voice was ghostly in the gloom of the unlit cab. "It was Lou who told me. She knew you'd make it here eventually, she'd read the letter you carry, the one from your father. Once we knew that, it was simple—research, detectives, money, then just stake the place out and wait. Saul organised it."

"Where is she?"

"Lou? She's safe, hidden. She wanted to come, but I wouldn't let her. She's had a rough time, she needs rest. Care, too—we're still not sure what she was given when she was being held."

"Why are you here?"

She ignored the question. "You're under no obligation," she said. "Not even to hear me out. You have a life, you deserve to live it on your own terms. You can walk away right now." I saw the silhouette of her mouth try for a smile. "Me, I've got a twenty-four hour pass." She nodded up at the caravan. "Sandy's riding shotgun," she said. "In about two hours, she'll remind me it's time to saddle up and head back." She shrugged. "Till then…"

"So why waste your freedom on me? I'll ask you again. *Why did you come?"*

This time, my aggression triggered hers.

"Because I owe you! Because you're in danger, worse than

before! I wasn't the only one Lou told about Demon's Lair. The man who took her from you—under the drugs she told him everything. His name is Jack O'Malley. He's coming after you."

"How do you know that? If—"

*"Listen!"*

She spun round. Her face came up close to mine. Her brows furrowed.

"I don't how much time we've got, he could be watching us right now! My brother Lee's body was found yesterday morning. In the ocean, just off Virginia Beach. It could only have been him. O'Malley."

She read the shock in my face. When she spoke again, I could hear the emotion being kept at bay.

"Don't waste your regrets, Alex. He's had enough of mine. It wouldn't have happened if he hadn't employed O'Malley in the first place."

"Employed him to do what?"

She took a deep breath. Finally, she put on the sunglasses. To hide.

"To kill me," she said.

*

"Lee Vannier. I need to know."

Saul Morgan's eyes catalogued me from head to foot, slowly. Then, without speaking, he lifted the stubby handgun which lay on the ancient iron table before him. I watched him click open the chamber and empty it. With what looked like a pipe cleaner, he pushed an oiled cloth through each of the barrel's chambers.

"Sand. I hate the damn stuff—gets everywhere. If the entirely illogical entity who created this misbegotten planet ever decides on a makeover, then I sincerely hope She will decide—" He inserted the bullets one by one, then clicked the barrel shut. "—to dispense with it."

He clipped the gun into the holster at his waist, then lifted his cane. Shaking his head, he began unscrewing the metal tip. When the ferrule came away he upended it and tapped it once, hard, on the table's iron rim.

"I need to know *now.*"

He gave the little pile of sand a baleful look, then swept it away with an impatient hand. "Ease off, Fraser," he said. "You're runnin' too rich, take your foot off the gas."

As I sat, he poured for us both from his bottle of bathtub bourbon, then began fanning himself with his hat. My eyes went to the ramshackle wooden edifice behind him. The sign over the door said *Cormorant Cove Cottage* in roughly carved letters. Did she own it? Was this another hideaway, the North Carolina equivalent of the Virginia farm? Did she have one in every state? I examined the building's salt-seared wood. It had been white once. Now, its corners rubbed to roundness by the elements, the colour was only visible in random patches. A stack of paint tins waited by the door to repair the winter's ravages, their bright primary colours incongruous, a misdirected threat of modernity. My eyes went to the beach beyond, stretching for a perfect curved mile in the shelter of a blunt headland. Its smooth surface was like molten gold, its tide lit by a blood red orb of sun which was slowly admitting defeat behind the horizon.

*A far foreign shore...*

Wasn't that what the old songs called it? As I sat watching it beside Saul Morgan, the two adjectives had never seemed more apt. The crickets, shrill and insistent, were its chorus. Listening to them, it was hard to believe that these waves had any connection with the relentless breakers which slapped so angrily at Scotland's west coast. Was my father gazing out over the Atlantic now? For solace, as I'd seen him do so often? Not for the first time, my mind went back to the painful revelations of two days ago. In the seemingly endless drive here from Arkansas I'd had time enough to brood over them, but I was no nearer any kind of decision. What was I meant to do now? How was I meant to convey what I had learned of my uncle's life and death to the other side of this ocean?

My uncle...

*His widow...*

Had I ever really meant to go back to Lady MacBeth and Zion Junction? Before I could examine the question, Morgan began to speak.

"Yes indeed, Mister Lee Vannier. Pillar of every community he was ever thrown out of, curse on the lips of every woman he ever ran out on. Proof providence does not ignore the shallow end of the gene pool. Finally, R.I. —" He paused, then shook his head firmly. "No. If there's any justice, there'll be no damn P. No peace for the son of a bitch. He might have gone to meet his maker, but knowin' Lee, he'll probably try to hustle him when he gets there, deal him some meth or a few lines of coke. I hope his gravestone tells it like it is, Fraser. I hope it says *Here lies a connivin' bastard who never told the truth once in his whole goddam life."*

The vitriol's intensity surprised me. "There's no doubt about his death?" I asked. "Or that this man O'Malley is responsible?"

"None on either count. We have Lee's computer, it documents the whole sorry mess between them—an' then there's the small matter of two bullets, one to the head, one to the genitals. Body was ripped up pretty good by the sharks, that's the only leeway—pardon the term, no comedy intended—we have. An' sickenin' though that fact may be, it has allowed me," he continued, drily, "to persuade the relevant authorities in Virginia Beach that a verdict of accidental death might just be possible. Or rather, a large donation to their benevolent fund has allowed me to persuade them."

I looked away. Was there anything in this country these people could not buy? The cynicism of it all was breathtaking. I saw my companion's brow crease and knew my thoughts had been read, but I didn't care. He went back to gazing at the whisky glass. Slowly, his fingers began turning it, as though each side could offer him a different revelation.

"What you're about to hear," he said, "is not an edifyin' tale. Easiest way to understand it is to strip it back to the root." He put the glass down, then reached for his cane and planted it solidly between his legs. "Under Rose's will, Mary Louise inherits the bulk of her estate—that's no secret. Like the rest of us, Lee knew it—and he knew, also, that in the event of his sister's death, as the girl's guardian he would have control of her money until she came of age. He had a wildly inflated idea of how much the estate was worth, by the way, given the extent of Rose's outlay on her various causes, but that's another story. As you've been told, he decided..." He paused, fondled the cane's silver top. "...to have his sister killed."

Again I let my eyes find the horizon. The sun had sunk further, the crickets were louder. Those were facts. The bald statement of inhumanity I'd just heard seemed too fantastic to be part of the same language. Morgan's eyes met mine over the table.

"Insane? Sure—but don't forget, Fraser, you're a new recruit to this particular family circus. Lee's resentment'd been simmerin' for years, everyone round Rose could see it. He hated her—

hated her for bein' everythin' he wasn't; rich, successful, loved, envied, idolised, perm any six from two dozen different coon-ass grudges. But once you accept that a crime like this was perfectly acceptable to a moral retard like Lee Vannier, a kind of twisted logic does come into play." His eye went back to the liquor glass. "A couple of months ago," he said, "through contacts in the criminal fraternity, he made his approach."

From the pocket of his jacket, he produced an untidy sheaf of computer paper. *Déjà vu,* I thought; *our first meeting, Gallant Fox Farm, my interrogation...*

"Professor John Milton O'Malley, to give him his full honorific, Chair of Celtic History And Culture, Symington College Of Fine Arts. Up in Illinois." He put the bundle down and smoothed it out. "Quite the intellectual, much respected—until he was let go, or whatever name a sackin' goes by in the groves of academe. Happened about a decade ago. His employers, it seems, took exception to him fakin' exam results for Asian students at sixty grand a pop." He pushed the papers across the table. "It was quite a fall. Inside a year, the good professor was doin' time in Joliet for bad cheques, but his ineptitude didn't last long. Once he learned the ropes, his rise was fast—fraud, blackmail, drugs. There were only a few hiccups, mostly caused by the voraciousness of his physical appetites—a need for sex to feed his ego. But that aside, once he'd worked out that the organisational skills behind his scam artist's career could leverage him into an altogether more lucrative field, he was unstoppable." He shook his head. "He has made money, a great deal of it, by offerin' a unique service. He's an agency."

He caught the puzzled look on my face. His expression became grave.

"A murder agency, but not just the usual hits for hire deal. The jobs are usually carried out by other people, although he'll get his own hands dirty if he has to. His unique sellin' point, as the marketers call it, is a guarantee that his work is virtually untraceable, because he plans—meticulously—to make it look completely random. Word on the street is, he has a near hundred per cent success rate—almost nothin' he sets up ends up bein' identified as a professional hit. I might add that he is utterly ruthless, an' that he makes it a point of honour never to leave business unfinished."

"And this is why you're now armed." I said, slowly.

"You have a problem with that?"

Instead of answering, I picked up the top sheet. A series of mugshots, their left/straight ahead/right format chillingly familiar from my own past. The printout was grainy. I saw the slicked-back red-grey hair, the unsmiling mouth, the beard, the thick glasses...

It was the lone drinker from the Ambassador Hotel, the man who'd been in the taxi queue before Rose.

Morgan watched me digest the information. "The proposition was simple," he said. "A contract, with a few caveats. O'Malley was to organise Rose's murder an' disguise it as a drive-by. Once Mary Louise had inherited," he went on, "Lee, with legal access to his daughter's money, would pay him one million dollars. As we now know, O'Malley accepted, an' in due course, the attempt took place, the kids on the scooter outside the hotel in DC." He turned to me. "You with me so far?"

"How did he know Rose would be there, at the hotel?"

He nodded. "That's the jackpot question—an' frankly, Fraser, I have to tell you that the Ambassador Hotel is currently a bone of contention between me an' my employer. She says she was in DC with Mary Louise to buy the girl a new laptop, and that she simply decided to wait there for the limo. Frankly, I do not believe her. I have told her so, but she is adamant. Maybe you can get the truth out of her."

Morgan waited patiently for me to take the bait. When I didn't, he leaned across the table.

"Whatever the reason, the main thing is that the attempt did not succeed. With admirable courage an' a fine degree of recklessness, you thwarted it. An' that—" His hand's grip on the cane's head tightened. "—is the moment when Professor Jack's troubles began to multiply." He counted off on his stubby fingers. "One. Suddenly there are witnesses to his presence, close to the scene of an attempted murder—you, an' the intended victim. An' two. He's sure you got a good look at him."

*The bar's mirror...*

"But the Ambassador Hotel was only the beginnin'. What came next was worse."

He paused. I sat, watching his unease, until the sky behind the cottage changed. A pair of headlights crested the hill. Rose? John? I turned back to Morgan.

"What do you mean?"

He exhaled, slowly. I watched his face become bleak.

"Wheeling."

The single word brought it all back; the motel, the wind, the obscene images on the iPad, the red dot... Once again, Saul Morgan reached into his jacket pocket. The note which came out was typewritten, pinned to a picture of Lou's taped mouth.

*Five million. Cash. Details to follow. Tell no one. Cops, tricks, she dies.*

"Slipped under Rose's door at the farm. The reasonin' is simple. If Rose cared enough to make the child her heir..."

I finished it for him. "...then she cared enough to pay a fortune to get her back."

Morgan nodded.

"Lee's idea or O'Malley's?"

"The discovery of the body off Virginia Beach," Morgan said drily, "does not leave too much doubt on that score. I would suggest that Lee Vannier had simply outlived his usefulness—no sentimentality among thieves. The cold logic of the professional criminal is what has ruled here, Fraser. A bigger payday, much, two and two addin' up to five million instead of one. No wait for probate, no unreliable partners. No drive-by uncertainty."

Once more, I looked along the beach. The sun was almost gone.

*No drive-by uncertainty...*

The question I'd tried to avoid for so long finally surfaced. "The boy with the gun, on the scooter, the one whose body you got rid of. Who was he?"

When Morgan's voice came, it was deliberate in its emphasis. "Fraser," he said, "as someone who has revised his opinion of you entirely, I counsel you to abandon that particular line of enquiry."

"Tell me."

The stubbornness of the two words registered. When he spoke again, his voice was slow and patient. as though explaining something to a child.

"I repeat—do not go there. The boy was employed by O'Malley for the hit, that's all you need to know. There is nothin' to be gained from takin' it further."

"My decision," I said, softly. "Not yours."

Saul Morgan shook his head in exasperation. "Not just a boy scout," he said, finally, "a *predictable* boy scout. When they put you away, Fraser, your damn fool conscience is goin' to need a cell of its own—maybe even a whole damn cell *block* of its own." He poured from the bottle again. "I sincerely hoped it would not come to this," he said, "but I confess I expected it might."

He threw back the liquor in one. I watched him choose his words with care.

"There is a professional organisation which can be called upon," he said, "to erase the aftermath of a certain category of event. Once their involvement is over, they provide all relevant details to the person who retained them. In this case, as you have rightly guessed, that person is me. The information has been duly sent. At a time of my choosin', I will pass the details on to you—if you agree to two conditions. One, whatever complications of your own you add into the mix, nothing happens to hurt Rose further. Two, the law does not get knowledge of this. Ever."

His eyes remained steadily on mine. What was I getting into, here…?

"Well, sir?" he said.

My mind still racing, I nodded. "All this," I said, finally. "The contract, O'Malley, Lee's story—how do you know it all?"

"I told him."

I spun round at the new voice. Standing on the crumbling patio at the cottage's front door was a slight woman. Her left arm was in a sling and her face was a misshapen mass of bruises and sutures. Under my scrutiny, she looked away. Sandy Hunter came through the cottage door behind her. The position she took up made their roles plain; prisoner and guard. Morgan gave the English girl a curt nod, then turned to the injured woman.

"Fraser, this is Ms. Nancy Bell," he said. "I believe you've already met."

The auburn curls... I knew them. But where from…?

And then I had it. *A dusty day for walkin'...*

Wenger's Seed And Supply.

I looked again at the battered woman—and remembered the curls, tumbling forward. *I just love your accent…*

She had been the black van's passenger.

I looked down at the printout. My mind superimposed the memory of the driver's face on it.

Shorter hair, no beard…

There was no doubt. Professor John Milton O'Malley had been the driver.

*

Her mouth was so lacerated, she could only use the right side of it. It didn't stop her good hand reaching for the bourbon. After drinking deeply, she turned to me. It was obvious that the movement caused her pain—and it was equally obvious that she was already a long way past sober.

"I did not know. I swear it."

Despite the drink and the mouth's constriction, the voice's accent was as cultured as I remembered. Native or acquired? I had a fleeting impression of gentility, hard won.

"Don't get me wrong," she went on. "I'm not playing the innocent. I knew Jack was trouble—knew it the first day he walked into the office. Me, the lowly secretary, him, the new professor, Mister Campus Big Shot. Call me the biggest fool in the world, but inside a week I was his. I worshipped him, plain and simple, I'd have done anything to keep him. It lasted ten years. Ten years of *Make me feel good* all night and *Take a letter, Ms. Bell* all day. Even after he was sacked, I swallowed every lie, every single lie—especially the one about being Mrs. Jack O'Malley some day."

She tried to smile, but the stitches stopped it. She closed her puffy eyes.

"But I swear to God, when he came for me that night, I had no idea how far this would go."

She stopped, abruptly, lifted her glass and emptied it, then held it out to the English girl. As it filled, her eyes never left the liquor's rising level. When it was full she shared a bleak stare with each of us in turn.

"If he knew I was here, he'd find a way to finish me. You OK with that?"

No one answered. The fact angered her, jolted her out of politeness. A red flush suffused the bruised features.

"You people..." she began, softly, shaking her head.

She cradled the glass in both hands. I watched the liquid tremble.

"You people are *mean fuckers.*"

The educated voice made the words worse. She bowed her head—and then our continued silence robbed her of composure.

The glass dropped. She fell forward. As Sandy Hunter caught her, she winced. The sudden movement made the wound over her left eye leak blood. It trickled down round the socket. Before sympathy could catch me, Saul Morgan's voice came from across the table.

"You've stalled long enough, Ms. Bell. We need what you know. *Everythin'* you know. Dates, times, conversations. Absolute honesty is your only chance. Aidin' an' abettin' the abduction of a minor, that could send you away for a very long time."

Her stare turned to a sullen scowl, her eyes glassy above the tears of blood—and then she brought herself back from the brink. Brows knitted, she fought dully for focus. Her head lowered, like an animal ready for fight. I watched her eyes fix on the cane's silver top. Her mouth became a grim line. When the words came, they were slower, louder, even more proper.

"Fuck you," she said, succinctly, "you kike bastard."

Saul Morgan's only reaction was to place a small recorder on the table top. When he spoke again, his voice was pitiless.

"Every last detail. Right now."

*

"My condo in Germantown."

"When? Exactly."

She frowned. "Couple of weeks back. April twenty-second—no, twenty-third, it was way past midnight. When I answered the door he just barged in past me, like he'd only walked out the day before." She forced her mouth into as much of a smile as the stitches would allow. "Seven years since I'd seen him, but he took up right where he'd left off. Orders right and left—get this, do that. Mister Masterful." The smile tried to become fond. "Always turned me on, the way he could *control.* He needed my help, he said, needed to find someone, some fool with a fiddle who'd got in his way." She looked away from me. "His plans had been screwed up, big time, he said—but it was more than just business, I could tell. He was cold, ice cold when he talked about it. Too cold." She reached for her drink. "Meant it was personal." Half the glass went down in one. "But once this obstacle had been dealt with..." Again, she didn't look at me. "...it would be plain sailing. That was where I came in. He needed someone who could take care of a teenage girl for a while. There was five grand in it for me, once..."

Her voice faltered, then petered out. We waited, but she didn't continue.

"How did you track me down?" I asked, finally.

She closed her eyes. When Morgan's voice came again, it was an order.

"Answer him. Now."

She looked at the ground. "A phone call, early in the morning," she said—and then her head whipped up as she fought for bravado. "While we were *fucking!"*

Sandy Hunter turned away. Once more, Nancy Bell tried for a smile—and then her face changed again, became blank. She turned to Saul Morgan.

"There's a lot more I could tell you, a whole lot, but I'm not saying another word. Not till there's some kind of deal on the table."

Once again, no one spoke. She began to weep, the blood leaking again, mingling with the tears. Misery fought with anger in the battered face as the cultured accent finally died.

*"Jesus, I let the damn kid go! After he grabbed her from that fleapit motel!* He was set to kill her, he told me when he brought her to me, soon's he had the money! I'd never have done that, I couldn't! When he found out I'd let her go he went ballistic! Crazy, batshit crazy! With a fucking *tire iron!* I thought I was *dead!"* Her fists were clenched as she faced us. "Doesn't that buy me some credit, here? Doing the right thing? Soon's I could stand I started tracking you down!"

The drunken plaintiveness was obscene. Still, no one spoke. The sobs started to tear themselves out of her in earnest. She buried her face in her hands.

"I'd've done anything for him, anything in the whole damn world, anything else! *But no matter how much I love him, I couldn't let him kill a kid!"*

She collapsed against Sandy's shoulder. I looked away again, at the sea, trying to take it all in—until a noise turned me. Mattie was standing in the cottage doorway, her face unreadable. Suddenly the battered woman's whispered grief was all there was.

*"I couldn't have done it, God's my witness, not even for him, I couldn't do that. I couldn't let a kid die..."*

The rage began its inexorable rise in my chest.

*On the Virginia back road, that first morning, if the tractor hadn't arrived...*

I felt it roar through me. I got up and leaned across the table till my face was only inches from hers.

"But you wouldn't have had any problem watching him kill *me,* would you?"

Her grief became hysterical—and then, as abruptly as it had started, it died. Her face went slowly blank. Then it twisted into a sneer.

"I don't know what you did to him, mister drifter, but you are *fucked! So fucked!"* She started to laugh, not letting the stitches stop her any more. "Jack O'Malley won't give up. *Ever!"*

Blood ran down her cheek, dripped into her drink. For a split second she watched it, then she raised the glass to her lips. Once she had drunk, she breathed deeply, looked straight at me and pronounced, calmly.

"You're dead, you just don't know it yet."

The edges of my vision reddened. I felt my breath shorten as I fought for control. I grabbed the bourbon bottle, turned away from all of them and headed towards the almost vanished sun.

*

"We ain't never spoke."

I was in a sheltered dip on the headland, staring out at the dark sea. Mattie sat down beside me on the peeling bench. The baseball cap was the same one she'd worn at Gallant Fox Farm. Without speaking, she took the bottle from my hand, wiped the top and drank.

"Was my weakness, once, whisky. Ain't touched a drop, a long while now." She handed the bottle back to me. "Ain't perfect, neither. Sometimes it just won't do the job, sometimes you cain't get drunk, no matter how hard you try." She kicked at the blown sand surrounding the bench's foot. "First off," she said, "I want to thank you. For savin' my girl's life. Don't seem to me like none o' the rest of 'em's ever goin' to get round to sayin' it. I think you're maybe a little naive, Mister Fraser, but you're a good man." She paused, choosing her words carefully. "You did a brave thing for my Rose. You should be proud of it." Again she paused. "I ain't sure how much heart's left in me, but what there is..." She shrugged, then finally let herself look me in the face. "You'll always have a place in it."

I took in the wrinkles, the lined cheeks. It was a long time before she spoke again.

"I'm from Mississippi," she said. "The north, two-bit dog 'n' pony town called Toccopola. Seven sisters an' a brother, Daddy was a truck driver. I wanted to be somebody, went at the book learnin' real hard, won a scholarship to nursin' college up in Philly." She gave a faint smile. "Family was proud of me, real proud, only one ever made it through high school." The smile died. "I had it all—brains, looks, the whole package." She turned, faced me. "Inside a year I'd thrown it all away. Love. Same kinda trouble's that woman back there. That sad woman. Ain't sayin' *sad* excuses what she done, 'specially to my granddaughter, but it makes it..." She shrugged. "...I don't know, more understandable, I guess." She looked down at her feet. "When I couldn't get over my own man trouble, I hated myself. Guess that's how I started." She paused. "Turnin' tricks."

She waited for my reaction. I took the whisky bottle and drank. I'd never been more sober.

"At first it was OK. High on excitement, high on uppers, bein' the centre of attention, bein' an outlaw... Vanity, thinkin' you got it made, thinkin' you're really somebody. It can kill hurt, but only for a while. Then the truth sets in, reality—bars, truckstops, cheap motels, Florida to the Mason Dixon. Three tricks a night, maybe four, never sure exactly what's comin' through the door." She shook her head. "But its' a hard life to get out of, bein' a whore," she went on. "I tried, a couple o' times. My pimp was a Cajun. Lennie Dutroux, Big Lennie. One night I mouthed off too loud. Wasn't a tire iron came out, it was a baseball bat, Lennie's good ol' Louisville Slugger. Didn't stop swingin' till it'd smashed up the whole crib. I hadn't been such good business, I hadn't been too good-lookin' to hurt, he'd've smashed me up too."

Footsteps came. Rose Vannier, her face expressionless behind her glasses, appeared on the rocks above the dip's edge, her blonde hair windblown, her hands deep in the pockets of a bulky quilted jacket. Mattie glanced up at her. I read the love in the lined face, and the determination.

"I ain't never told you, Rose, but that's what you was born out of. Violence. It excited him, Mister Lennie Dutroux. Got him all hard an' riled up. After it, he took me all night long, rough as he could. No chance to take any kind o' precaution. A month later

I knew I'd fell pregnant. I got up the courage 'n' ran, but not fast enough or far enough. By the time he'd got on my tail, you an' your brother was already born—Charity Hospital, New Orleans. I named you—that much I give myself—and then I took you to the nuns." She paused, gathered her strength. "I was livin' in a hot pillow joint behind Bourbon Street, less 'n' twenty bucks in my purse, still bleedin' from the birth. He bust the door down, middle of the night. Bat was in his hand. My heart damn near stopped—I thought my time had come, thought he'd surely beat me to death. But he was smart. He saw the blood, there was no hidin' that, worked the rest of it out. I tried to lie—said I'd had a baby boy, stillborn, but one o' the other girls told him the truth. For money. He said if I didn't go back with him right then, he'd make it his business to find you both..." Her eyes fell. "...and kill you." After a brief silence, she turned back to her daughter. "In the end, he got Lee. Held that over me for years. But he didn't get you. When you come for me, I near didn't believe it. By then I guess I just didn't think there was goin' to be anythin' else. Not ever."

She got up and dusted the sand away from her spindly shins. When her voice came again, it was determined.

"You tell Mister Fraser the rest, Rose. Now. All of it. I know you meant well, hidin' it, but this is a good man. He's had my truth. He deserves yours."

# 12

# BLOOD

THE SUNGLASSES HAD BEEN discarded. The moonlight left her face a pale cutout against the darkness.

"You ever had money, Fraser?"

"Enough to get by."

"Ever want it, bad?"

*Not as much as peace… Not as much as my music…* I shook my head. She nodded in understanding.

"Paul and Mimi," she said. "They were my foster parents, but it was a long time before I knew that. To me they were just Mom and Pop, like Sarah next door's, or Maggie Farley's round the corner." She paused. "They were the first ones to give me money. Biggest fortune I ever had. A blue piggy bank with yellow flowers. Took quarters, nickels, dimes, pennies. I was three years old. When I went to bed at night I used to lift it and rattle the coins. Made me smile." She let the memory hold her. "I learned I was adopted when I was sixteen. Mimi said the day she told me, my face nearly broke her heart. John said he watched me cry on the back porch for four hours."

"John? John Walks-Over-Ice? He was their son?"

She shook her head. "No. Next best thing, though. Lucius, Paul's father, was in the Marines in the Pacific. John's dad Ira was his driver." A smile found her mouth. "Major Vannier and Sergeant Walker, Oakland to Okinawa—when they'd had a drink, the stories would start. But when peace came, Ira couldn't get work—nobody would give an indian the time of day, didn't matter a damn about his service or how good a mechanic he was. Lucius set him up in Lexington, a gas station with a repair shop. Left money in his will for John's education, too, enough to put him through med school. They had a frame house at the end of our garden, we were in and out of each other's kitchens all the time. Fed each others' pets. I had rabbits, he had a three-legged coyote, and snakes—rattlers, copperheads."

*Snakes…?*

I fought to keep the word's effect from my face, but I needn't have worried. She was too deep in her memories to notice.

"He was three years older than me, John. High school track star, quarterback, swim champ. Dial in exotic movie star good looks and noble savage, add a big pinch of forbidden fruit," she said, wryly, "and you'll understand why every one of my girlfriends had a massive crush on him. Moths to the flame. Not me, though. Might have been easier if I'd joined the club, but it never happened. We were just buddies, me and John. Best buddies. Still are. Always will be."

An edge of defiance had crept into the last few words, as though I'd challenged her in some way.

*Snakes…*

She held up her right hand. The ring's red stone caught the moonlight. I recognised it from the hotel in Washington.

"This was Mimi's. I put it on it when I want to be private. Ann hates me wearing it, says I'm missing a trick, says I should be drumming up trade, wearing something designer for the cameras."

Her eyes stayed on it for a long time. Then she kissed it quickly and let out a long sigh.

"Lexington, Massachusetts. Paradise. New England frame houses and Paul Revere's ride, Girl Scout cookies, Halloween pumpkins. Everything America was always supposed to be." I watched her smile flower, then fade. "I never suspected I didn't belong, not once. Nobody else in town did either—I even looked a bit like Paul, same kind of bones, pretty much the same hair. Coincidence. So up until I found out, my life'd been like any other teenage girl's, school grades, boys—nothing serious—pop posters on the wall, babysitting. I even did my first modelling job, a charity dress show for the church." She shrugged. "So the shock of being told, you can imagine—all the sixteen-year-old kid questions. How could my parents not want me? What had I done to deserve it? Could people tell, just by looking? All that. And I was mad—stupid mad, enough to start hanging with the wrong set. For about a week I was the local teen sensation—good kid goes bad, what's the world coming to? When the gossip reached John, he dropped out of college for a month, just to try and get me back on the straight and narrow. He did his best, but I wasn't ready—nowhere near ready. I was stubborn and I was hurt—my best friend ever, and all I could do was tell him to go to hell. Then..." She shrugged. "A summer Saturday night. The drive-in. A little booze, a little pot, the back seat of the wrong car." She faced me. "It was just the once," she said. "I never even knew the boy's name. I didn't even enjoy it, it just hurt."

She closed her eyes against the memory. I watched the effort it took her to continue.

"I didn't know my body. At all. I'd only just started having periods, so when they stopped, I wasn't worried. I didn't tell anyone. For the first three months, it barely showed—and when Mimi finally noticed, I was wheeled off to the doctor. He told us a termination was out of the question—too late, too dangerous, I was anaemic, other stuff as well. It was a bombshell, you can imagine—but once the shock had worn off, they just took care of it, Paul and Mimi. They were good people, the best, old-fashioned north east liberals, Harvard academics, absolutely devoted to each other. And to me. They sent me away to have her."

She stopped, abruptly. Suddenly the question of snakes didn't matter any more. The silence seemed to last forever.

"We're talking about Lou, aren't we?" I said, gently.

She nodded.

"Does she know?"

Rose Vannier got up, put on her camouflage sunglasses and began walking down towards the water.

It was all the answer I needed.

*

The surf foamed round our bare feet. She looked straight ahead. The shelter of the sunglasses made it easier for her to tell the rest.

"They had it all planned. When I came home, they'd be the parents, that would be the fiction. They'd tell everyone she was adopted, they'd decided they wanted another child. No one we knew batted an eyelid—ever since old Lucius and the Walkers, the family'd had a reputation for being impulsive. So it worked. Paul and Mimi gave me space, they gave me time, they let me love my daughter. No blame, no moralising, what was done was done. I was her mother in private, they were her parents in public. Sometimes, when friends came, it got awkward, but we dealt with it—and if anyone guessed, they kept quiet. The only one I know for sure worked it out was Betsy, John's mom, and she wasn't going to tell. And that's how it was, for a year. One wonderful year." She looked out at the ocean. "You understand, Fraser? It was the best time. People who loved me had made me a safety net. I had a child who meant everything to me, I had the best home, the best family. I had to do a lot of growing up, fast, but I managed it. I could start planning a future." She shrugged. "It's so weird to think of, now. I wanted college, career, the whole nine yards."

She fell silent. I understood; futures past… They were the hardest things of all to contemplate.

"There was one last thing I had to do," she said, finally. "It crept up on me, refused to go away. So after a lot of thinking I went to Paul and Mimi, told them I loved them and I always would, that I'd always be their daughter, Rose Vannier..." Again, she paused. "...but I needed to know who my real parents were." She smiled. "They got it, immediately," she said. "They set it up, drove me everywhere till I was old enough to get my licence, then bought me a car. They dealt with the official crap, the files at the kids' home, finding the staff from back then, getting statements, all that. The whole thing took eighteen months. I finally traced my mother to Mississippi, to a waterfront joint in Biloxi. Lennie's Free 'n' Easy. It was supposed to be a bar. It was a front for a whorehouse, even an innocent like me couldn't have missed it. I watched the place for two whole days before I got up the courage to go inside. John was with me, but I made him wait in the car. I had to do it on my own."

She stopped again. Who else had she told this to? Anyone? She continued, her voice precise now.

"She was tending bar, but her real job was keeping the girls in line and cleaning out the cribs. When I told her who I was, she went nuts. I never saw anyone so angry, before or since. She marched me into the kitchen, pinned me up against the wall and let loose. What the hell did I mean, turning up on her like this?

Out of the blue, no warning! If she'd wanted me she'd've kept me! I was to disappear, get the hell gone, the Free 'n' Easy was no place for some sentimental dumb-ass kid!"

A wave washed round her ankles. Her voice softened.

"She was just trying to protect me, I know that now. To scare me off, get me away from the mess of her life. Keep me clean."

"And did she?"

She let her gaze find the ocean again. "For a while," she whispered.

*

By the time I stirred, the blown sand had moulded itself into a protective wall against my back. I turned. My head was on something soft. I pulled myself up and looked; her jacket, her quilted jacket... Some time during the sliver of night we'd snatched for rest, she had placed it beneath my head. I was touched. I got to my feet, then scanned the beach.

The first thing I saw was her clothes, a neatly folded bundle, just above the tide line. Fright rose in me—*she wouldn't…* But the panic was brief. I saw her head, bobbing among the waves as she swam back towards the shore. The patient strength of her was hypnotic. I watched the strokes, powerful, unhurried, regular.

And wondered at the rest of the tale she'd told me.

Paul, her foster father, dead of a heart attack a month after she'd found Mattie, Mimi gone a few weeks later, a stroke. No will, so a distant cousin got the house and the money—which left her alone with a baby, no income and no way out but the lowest of low-end jobs; supermarket checkout girl, waitress, cleaner…

And then a miracle—a model agency scout who looked at a motel maid and saw something more…

She'd reached the shallows, now. She stood up, shaking the droplets from her hair. When she saw me, her pace changed, became more deliberate. She waded forward, the water clinging to her, eddying round her thighs.

Then she stopped. The incoming swell caught up with her. The spume lapped at the dark vee between her legs.

The surge of lust was immediate. It ruled my body, overpowering reason, hardening me, quickening my breathing. I walked towards her, stopped at the pile of clothes. She didn't move. The next wave crashed around her, then died at my feet.

She was only an arm's reach away. Saul Morgan's phrase came to me; *an icon of desire...*

And then the voice came, from the top of the dunes. Mattie's voice.

"Fraser! Rose! Come quick! Come *now!*"

*

For a breathless moment I thought it was paint, something to do with the pile of tins—and then I knew exactly what was seeping out beneath the cottage's front door. As I pushed it open, the sticky redness smeared an obscene crescent across the rug beneath. Without warning, the slaughterhouse reek claimed me. My mind reeled. *How could a smell be a colour...?* And then the metallic pungency of the cordite superimposed itself and made a taste of it as well. It was the only thing that could have made it worse.

*Blood, so much blood...*

I stood, dizzy with shifting realities, my eyes seeing a different red lake, one my memory could never relinquish.

*My wife...*

*My rage...*

*My blow, the sickening crack of bone on metal...*

"Fraser, in here!"

The urgency of John's shout killed it. I skirted the red mess through to a small kitchen. Two doors led off it. The left one's panels were splintered. A small automatic pistol lay on the floorboards, its handle smeared with blood. Beside it, the remains of a head and a single arm were visible. I had to fight for calm. The torso was curled foetally round the shattered door jamb. The stickiness was already darkening, congealing round the mass of auburn curls.

"The other room! Open it!"

John Walks-Over-Ice was his massive red self, naked from the waist up, just as I'd first seen him. He was tearing his shirt into strips. At his feet lay a crumpled bundle of hair and limbs. *Sandy?* Her right thigh was a quivering red mess, the blood from it mingling with the dead woman's. She was whimpering softly.

"Hurry!"

The locked door gave at the first charge of my shoulder. By the time I was back, John was kneeling at her side.

"Sandy, can you hear me?"

She managed to nod.

"Brace yourself, this is going to hurt a lot. Fraser, under her arms."

As I leaned down, the heavy perfume enveloped me; *expensive…* I felt my gorge rise as it draped itself over the other smells.

"On three."

As we did it, she screamed, then passed out, her head lolling backwards. I watched the tangles of black hair brush the blood on the floor into hieroglyphics. Once she was on the bed, John lifted the leg, carefully. She groaned as he turned her.

"Flesh wound," he said. "Straight through, probably looks worse than it is. No bone. Nerves, we'll have to see."

He began tying his improvised tourniquet. "She's lost too much blood. She needs a hospital, now."

*"Sandy!"*

Rose scrambled past me, tumbled down beside the blood-stained bed and clasped the unconscious girl's hand.

"I'll get Saul," I said, "he's—"

I stopped. We looked at each other.

"Saul," Rose said, the panic mounting in her voice. *"Where's Saul?"*

*

Mattie was already on her knees beside him. He was lying on the beach at the other side of the cottage, face down, the pooled blood on his back already rimed with blown sand. His right arm was outstretched, as though it was trying to reach his gun. The revolver lay, half-buried, about a foot away. His left hand was balled into a tight fist, the silver-topped cane dug hard into the sand beside it, like a mountaineer's marker. Only the bubbles, forming and bursting at the edge of his mouth, showed he was still alive. As John leaned down, Mattie thrust a mobile phone at him. He began dialling.

"A blanket. Quickly. And my bag, from the car—and a card from my wallet." As she stumbled away, he put the device to his ear. "Emergency, we need a helicopter ambulance, Cormorant Cove, the cottage..."

I found myself staring at the inert form, then at the cane, then the gun.

*Sand. I hate the damn stuff, gets everywhere...*

I sank down beside him, prised open his fist. More sand, compressed by the tightness of his grip.

"...John Walks-Over-Ice. *Doctor* John Walks-Over-Ice—okay, *Walker*, if that's too hard. Ma'am—you have to *hurry!* Three victims, one deceased, one stable, one critical. No, ma'am, please put it in train right now, this minute. My associate will give you details."

Mattie arrived with his bag. He thrust the phone at her. As she began reciting credit card numbers, he kneeled down, talking as he worked.

"No way I can avoid calling the cops, Fraser. Which means you need to be gone. Fast. Take this."

He pulled the bloody pistol from his trouser pocket, put it in my hand. It felt slick, sticky. *Repellent...*

"Lose it somewhere, a drainage ditch, maybe—just make sure it's a long way from here. Use my car, keys are in the ignition. Take Rose."

"Why? Why take her?"

He didn't answer. I stood, holding the awful little gun, dimly aware of Mattie's voice, patiently intoning into the phone, of the red hands busying themselves with ampoule and syringe. Once the injection had been given he got to his feet, a stethoscope dangling incongruously across his huge red chest.

"You know Rose's history, don't you?"

I nodded. He pointed down at Saul.

"For ten years this man has kept her from being harmed by it. Surrounded her with the right people and kept the wrong ones at bay. Found every rumour, every dumb tabloid story that could hurt her, and killed it." He stopped, waited for a response from me. "Well," he said, harshly, "isn't it obvious?" Again, he gestured down at the body. "Look at him! He can't do that any more. *He might never be able to do it again!* She needs to be gone from here, Fraser. Before the vultures gather."

In the stark silence which followed, we all became aware of a new figure.

America's Sweetest Sweetheart...

Rose Vannier was standing a few yards away. She was all but catatonic, shaking uncontrollably, her eyes fixed on Saul. Caked with blood and sand, she was a nightmare vision, aboriginal, a primitive puppet of death. The memory of her, proud, naked, the icon of beauty in the waves, flashed back at me.

In two steps John had placed himself between her and the body. Massive, his long hair whipping in the wind, he towered over her, more godlike than ever. He took hold of her arms and shook her, gently. It had no effect. He tried again, harder. Her head, rag doll loose, fell to one side. A whimper escaped her.

The slap was hard. Rose staggered back and fell to her knees. Soundlessly, she began to cry. John reached down. Slowly, carefully, he brought the girl to her feet and held her to him. As her arms came round him in a jerky embrace, I watched the two of them merge into a single entity.

And then, even more gently, the big Cherokee disengaged and shepherded Rose Vannier across to me.

"Out of here," he said. "Right now."

I took one last look along the pristine beach.

*A far foreign shore…*

# 13

# STAKES

"A *LADIES'* GUN? I don't care what kind of damn gun it was! How the hell did she get within a hundred yards of any of you *with any kind of gun at all?"*

The long mahogany table was littered with laptop computers and magazines and papers. I turned away. I felt light-headed, detached—at one remove from all of it, the questions, the frustration, the anger.

Especially my own anger. Since the sight of Rose Vannier looking so helplessly down at Saul Morgan's body, so close to the mental edge, I had somehow been purged of my rage. Had that only been twenty-four hours ago? Half a dozen steps took me to the angled observation window. It was like a battleship's bridge, looking down over the deck of the gaming room below.

The Cherokee Nation Casino.

A hundred yards long and fifty wide, a collage of green, red and black, opulent at every turn, gilded at edge and corner. From this angle, the flat planes of colour made it look childish—a pop-up instruction book for the under fives; *money and how to get it…* As the furious silence simmered behind me, I surveyed it.

Blackjack, roulette, poker...

The stylised chief's head on the wall was the centrepiece. His stern uplifted gaze ignored the industrial ranks of slot machines, as though the manic obsession which drove their operators was nothing to do with him, as though the stylish drape of his neon war bonnet's feathers over the casino's name was some regrettable accident. His descendants, bulky in sharply-creased black slacks and powder blue blazers, their massive red necks spilling over their perfect white collars, quartered the room in slow-moving pairs, professionals with calm, roving eyes, whispering into headset microphones as they walked. The lenses of the surveillance cameras, recessed into the ceiling, swivelled restlessly above them, seemingly at random. I was reminded of the satellite dish at Zion Junction; a contrast... Or was it a contest, God's bargain with the airwaves versus Manitou's deal with mammon? *And the winner is…*

The largest of the roulette tables was directly below me. The gamblers gathered round it with the shuffling gait of penitents, reluctantly reminded of their devotions. Only when the chips were placed and the bets confirmed did the tension descend, drawing them together, binding them into congregation. I watched a delicate female hand reach out, the wheel spin. The resulting cone of light was an altar, a spontaneous outburst of faith. The white ball rolled. I watched its bouncing progress suspend disbelief, saw the hunger of chance became the mutual prayer, written across every face. Only when the glittering motion stopped did the bond break. The ball settled on a number. Success cried out in ecstasy and failure turned away, back to the default boredom which masked disappointment. The croupier, tribal and exotic, her straight hair falling like a black waterfall down the back of her embroidered silk waistcoat, pushed the pile of chips towards the winner, then smiled her reflex smile of absolution at everyone else; *money and how to lose it…*

"A criminal! An alcoholic! A convicted felon who's been in and out of psych wards and rehab half her life! She shoots the English kid, then she shoots Saul, then she tops herself!" Ann Savoy's voice had risen to a near shout, now. "Can anyone at least tell me *why* she did it?"

The ensuing silence redoubled her vexation. Suddenly she was on her feet, fists on the table, looming over her client.

"Jesus, Rose, what if you'd been there? What if this crazy bitch had taken it into her head to shoot *you?* You have to come to your senses and listen—"

Rose Vannier's voice was like ice. "I'm aware of your views on security, Ann. Everyone here is, you've rammed them down our throats often enough. Let it go, now is *not* the time."

She was no longer helpless, that much was obvious. It was the first break I'd seen in the threatening calm which had ruled her since the shootings. I watched the cold menace silence her manager. There was another pause, long, adversarial, framed by the muted echoes of the slot machines. As the grey-haired woman slumped back into her chair, John Walks-Over-Ice's voice, inflectionless, tried to take up the slack.

"Sandy says Nancy Bell was thoroughly searched as soon as she was brought to the cottage. She has no idea how the gun got through."

His words revitalised managerial frustration. "It beggars belief," Ann Savoy said. "A nut. A drunken bimbo with a handgun. And not only did nobody try to sober her up, *you actually gave her more alcohol!*" She shook her head in exasperation. "You people are unbelievable." She turned to John. "Are we safe here?" She waved a dismissive hand at the window. "In the middle of this, this—*pow-wow?*"

John's voice kept its politeness. "You're a guest of the Eastern Band of the Cherokee Nation, Ms. Savoy, we all are. Their police department is on the case, O'Malley's description's been circulated, not just here, the length and breadth of Oklahoma. He won't get in."

She gave a derisive snort. "And that's supposed to make me feel safe? What're you going to do when the cavalry arrives, Chief? Sharpen the tomahawks? Break out the war paint?"

Silence. The stone face didn't change. When the riposte came, it was in a voice which had dropped half an octave. He raised a hand in mock indian salute and gave her an unblinking stare.

"Great Spirit, he say, in big tipi, much wampum spent on x-ray machines. Also on security cameras, you bet your bony pale-face ass."

Ann Savoy flushed bright red. The thump of Rose's fist on the table finished it.

"Enough!" She pulled off her sunglasses. "The way we confronted the woman was Saul's decision. We didn't know where O'Malley was, how close he'd got, how much time we had. We needed her information, fast. He thought she might let more slip if we let her keep drinking."

"Was the right call, no matter what happened after. Woulda took half a day to sober her up, state she was in."

Ann Savoy whirled round. Mattie was standing in the doorway. I watched the rebuke form on the manager's thin lips—and then she looked back at Rose and thought better of it. But her frustration was determined to fasten on someone. The scowl found me. The thought was plain*; all this began when you arrived…* Ostentatiously, she looked away, then jerked a contemptuous thumb back over her shoulder.

"And Braveheart here. Where was he when all this was going on?"

"Leave Alex out of this," Rose said, sharply.

A new silence. It was the first time she'd used my Christian name in front of her manager—in front of any of them, in fact. Despite the battering she was taking, it was Ann Savoy who recovered first. I watched her eyes go round the table, measuring, evaluating, filing away my change of status. And then retreating.

"How is Saul, anyway?" she asked, grudgingly, as though admitting affection was above her pay grade.

"Still in a coma," Rose said. "He took three bullets, he only just made it. If we'd found him ten minutes later, he wouldn't have. The doctors say it's still touch and go. We'll know inside the next forty-eight hours."

Ann Savoy gave a shrug which didn't have anything to do with sympathy. "He'll make it all right, he's a tough old bastard," she said. "We could do with him now, though, for the press, before the feeding frenzy gets out of hand. We might have to hire someone. We need a strategy."

"We don't need anyone, Ann. I've already told you my intentions."

The grey haired woman ignored her, trying to postpone the confrontation. "And the English girl?"

Rose pushed her chair back from the table, stood up and put both fists down on the table in a mirror image of the pose Ann Savoy had struck with her.

"For your information, she's very nearly ready to walk. On crutches. And she's not a girl or a kid, she's thirty-two years old. For nearly five of these years she's been a dedicated member of my staff. In San Francisco two years ago she even took a knife in the groin to stop a stalker reaching me. You think your professional security could do better than that?"

Once again, the older woman changed tack. She tried to make her voice placatory, but the edge of desperation was obvious.

"Forgive me, I'm just so worried." She leaned over towards her client, appealing. "Look, I know you hate hearing it, but you have to let us put people round you when you're private. If you don't, it's only a matter of time..."

She finally ran out of words. Rose turned away from her and walked across to my side. She kept her back to the table as she spoke.

"It doesn't matter, Ann. As I said, I've already decided. Don't worry, I'll fulfil my outstanding commitments."

"You don't mean this, Rose, you *can't*. Talk to me, please."

Reluctantly, Rose turned and went back to her chair. As she reached the table, her manager unearthed three magazines from the mess at its centre. She splayed them out in front of her client.

"*Vogue,* cover of the summer issue. Sales of the sundress you're wearing have gone through the roof, the Armani lawyers are taking legal action against at least three of the knockoff operations. *Harper's,* cover again, Moschino two-piece, Saks have had to reorder twice, probably going to happen again next week. *Redbook,* two articles on you, makeup and healthy living." She gestured at the rest of the pile. "And on and on and on. You're huge, you've never been hotter—and now you're on the verge of the biggest score in your whole career—*the biggest modelling deal this country has ever seen.* If you walk away from this, it's all been for nothing. Don't screw this up, I'm begging you." She paused. "This man O'Malley," she said, finally. "We can find him." She took a deep breath. "And if we can't stop him, then we can buy him off or something, find some way of stalling him till the deal's done. Negotiate with him."

For a terrible split second, I didn't believe what I'd just heard. Rose went white. With rage, I realised. Watching her face, I heard her words of the night before, delivered tonelessly in the cabin of the private jet.

*...fashion... All about manipulation. Models don't have whores for mothers, so Mattie has to be hidden. Models don't have illegitimate kids, so Lee has to be Lou's father...*

Finally, she broke the awful, simmering silence. "For years, Ann, I've bowed to your will. Everything you ever asked for. Every adjustment in the name of image. Every denial, every half-truth. Every deception for the chat shows, the tabloids. But *this?* Murder? Kidnap? Extortion? Two of my people in hospital, one of them fighting for his life!" Her voice came down to a glacial whisper. "And you want to *negotiate?*"

The tension was unbearable, a miasma of hatreds primed to explode. Only the prosaic knock saved the situation. John went out into the corridor. I heard him conferring. When he returned, he looked straight at me.

"Fraser, the security people have examined your violin, but they're not sure how to repack it."

I managed to keep my face straight as I walked towards him; a pretext, an obvious one—my fiddle case had been checked with everything else on arrival. He closed the door behind us, then held out a bulky envelope. My name was just recognisable on the crumpled surface.

"Saul's writing," he said, softly. "The guys found it inside one of the limo's headrests."

In the room behind us, I heard Ann Savoy's aggrieved voice begin again. I tore open the envelope and reached inside.

A single sheet of paper.

*As agreed.*

This could only be one thing. I felt back inside the envelope. A leather object, soft, about five inches square... I pulled it out.

A battered brown wallet. I unclipped it. The first thing I saw was a photograph, encased in a grubby plastic holder.

The exterior of a pub. It was called Pat Riordan's and it had been captured at twilight. In the distance behind it, a floodlit obelisk pointed skyward. I recognised it. My eyes went back to the pub's brightly lit facade. Beneath the Celtic knotwork lettering stood a red-haired young man, smiling, surrounded by girls, his freckled right arm around the most beautiful. All of them were teenagers, flushed with drink and excitement, their faces ecstatic with youth and health. I saw the tiny green dot on the hand that rested on the the girl's collarbone and felt my mouth go dry. It would be a circled letter M, I knew.

I was looking at the scooter's pillion passenger, the boy I had killed.

I eased the photograph out from its yellowed protective cover and saw what the boy's left hand, curved under a full breast, held.

A carved brown scroll...

Four black tuning pegs...

*He was a fiddler…*

I fought my confusion. Did that make it worse…? I unzipped the back compartment and found a plastic card. An official head and shoulders photograph. I read the print beneath, then just stared. John's voice brought me out of it.

"What is it?"

Before I could answer, the door burst open. If Ann Savoy saw either of us, she didn't care. I listened to the furious clack of her heels, disappearing towards the elevator, and then I returned the picture to the wallet and went back into the conference room. Rose was standing at the window, arms folded, her back to me, the camouflage sunglasses once more in place. She was trembling with rage. I sat down at the table and looked across at Mattie.

"Even if we were prepared to negotiate with Jack O'Malley," I said, "we couldn't. Nancy Bell was right. This man won't stop until he's killed me."

Everyone heard the pain in my voice. I put down the driving licence and stared, first at the red-haired boy, then at his name on the card.

*Michael O'Malley*
*Apt. 6b 7200 Taylor St.,*
*20710 Bladensburg MD*

As John entered the room, Mattie turned the square of plastic to read it. Rose's eyes fastened on mine. Slowly, like a sleepwalker, she crossed to her mother's side. I watched her read the card, saw the brutal truth claim first her, then Mattie. John's deep voice came.

"Why, Fraser? Why should this man be so determined to kill you?"

Weariness washed over me. It was Rose who spoke.

"Because Alex killed his son," she said.

# 14

# CAPITAL

THE TARMAC WAS on the point of melting, the haze above it a shifting shimmer which added a layer of unreality to the view. It gave the illusion of movement, of breath, it made the towering industrial ruins seem alive, merely dying rather than actually dead. Angular and gaunt, they loomed over the man-made canyon as far as the eye could see, their cast iron gantries rusted, their intricate Victorian frames windowless and abandoned to the weeds. Built for the roar of long-gone industry, they now exuded a puzzled stillness, beasts waiting patiently in harness for the return of work which had long since abandoned them.

And now, progress had added contempt to the mix. Whatever grandeur these structures might once have claimed, it was now being mocked. By modernity—a grubby modernity, mundane and depressing. The litter-covered wire mesh fence was sagging, already breached in several places. Whoever had built it had obviously grudged every penny, and I could understand why—it was an exercise in futility, a barrier able to do nothing but corral indignity. My eyes went back to the huge skeletons. What had they been, these giants? Oil? Steel? Chemicals? The sweat trickled down my neck as I watched a cloud's shadow deepen the brick's red and the rust's brown. And then my eyes went back to the sign we'd been monitoring for five hours.

Five long, sweltering, hours...

*WENGER'S SEED & SUPPLY*
*YOU HOE 'EM 'N' GROW 'EM, WE WEED—*

A white styrofoam carton was impaled on the broken wood's splintered edge. Behind the tatty mesh, the black van I'd last seen on a Virginia back road stood beside a squat lean-to. It had taken us two days to track it down; two days of abortive leads across three states, two days of incessant phoning, of high speed acceleration down miles of highway, of snatched sleep. Had it been worth it? No one had come near the vehicle... At what point would John move things on? Beside me, I was aware of Mattie's voice, trying to soothe, to massage away the obvious blackness which surrounded me.

"...Rose, she ain't like the rest of 'em. The other models, I mean. Sure, she does the same shimmy—the catwalk stuff, TV, interviews, spreads in the magazines, ads 'n' such—but that's the job, ain't it? The rest—hangin' with pop stars, fancy parties, gallery openin's, on the phone night 'n' day to girlfriends, kiss 'n' tell, that just ain't her. Makes her an outsider, I guess, but it don't seem to do her any harm, never has done. From day one, America just damn well upped an' fell in love with her. 'Specially the girls, the teenage kids. 'Cause she looks like she come out o' the same mould, I guess—an' that means they get to hope they can be like her—hope they can *be* her. That's the dream—if Ms Average from the burbs can make it, the girl next door, so can they. Parents, well..."

Her mouth twisted in irony. To disguise it, she looked away. The sunset over the begrimed New Jersey town of Sayresville was spectacular, but her gaze was far beyond it.

"Good, ain't it," she said, softly. "Mother a whore, father a pimp, brother a pusher." I heard her voice harden. "An' they love her 'cause she's so damn wholesome." She turned back to me, her face serious. "Used to eat Lee up, the way they all loved her. Eat him up real bad."

The pain of that five word requiem... What must it be like to lose a child, even one like Lee Vannier? Again I scanned the industrial wasteland. The rust had turned to a glowing bronze in the failing sun. It was a valedictory colour, a colour of memorial.

"Tell me about him," I said. "Tell me about Lee."

*

"Kid never stood a chance. Didn't land lucky, like Rose. Folks who got him from the orphanage were Baptists, hard shell, dirt poor, worked a spread up in northern Kentucky. Had two daughters, told the orphanage folks they wanted a boy. Way Lee told it, what they wanted wasn't a son, it was a slave. Got him when he was nine years old, goin' on ten. No schoolin', don't know how they got away with that, but they did. Up at daybreak, milkin', pullin' plough, shuckin' corn, balin' hay. Made him sleep in the barn, wasn't allowed to eat with the family, got whupped regular if he looked at any of 'em the wrong way, 'specially the girls. Night of his thirteenth birthday he'd had enough. Busted open the cash box an' lit out. Money was gone by the time he was over the Ohio line—Cincinnati, ghetto called Over The Rhine, bad place. Then it was the old story—good-lookin' kid, not a cent to his name, barely a teenager, on the run. Picked up off the street by a guy who slipped him a mickey..." She paused, looked down at her folded hands. "No great trick to guessin' the rest." I heard her voice armour itself in mundanity. "Pretty soon he was peddlin' his ass round the local chicken hawks. Then he started climbin' the food chain—richer johns, more'n' one at a time, kiddie porn, magazines, movies. Then it was drugs—had to come, sooner or later. When Lennie found him he was fourteen, just out of Juvie. Lennie told him he was his father, Lee thought he was just another old guy after his ass, let Lennie take him to a motel—then tried to roll him for his watch an' his wallet." This time, the smile was grimmer. "Not somethin' you did to Lennie Dutroux." She turned to me. "He beat Lee senseless, three ribs, right thigh bone, kid limped the rest of his days. Then he brought him on down to Biloxi."

"Lee knew by then that you were his mother?"

She shook her head. "For two years, I didn't know Lennie had found him—didn't even know he was lookin'. By then he'd turned the kid into a version of hisself—dealin', loan sharkin', girls." She shook her head. "A sixteen-year-old kid, watchin' his father run whores. An' all to pump the boy up, make him feel big. Lennie told him he was bein' trained, told him one day he'd take over the whole Dutroux operation. One night he brought him into the Free 'n' Easy. Came right up to me at the bar, clapped his hand on Lee's shoulder an' said, *"This is your momma, son, she gave you up 'cause she was way too busy turnin' tricks to raise you."* She stopped. "Lennie's revenge," she said, quietly, "Big Lennie Dutroux's revenge."

The silence in the vehicle was thicker than the heat. Eventually she went on.

"I'd spent years, wonderin'. 'Bout him an' Rose both. Fantasisin'. The day would come, the three of us would be a family, Lennie would give us a bunch o' money, ride off into the sunset an' leave us be in a house with a garden an' a white picket fence. With horses, an' dogs..." Again, she shook her head. "Reality never come close to matchin' up—truth be told, reality was a sick joke. The minute my boy was brung back to me, it was worse than the hell I already had." She turned to me. "I tried to get close, Lord knows I did, but from that very first day, my son mostly despised me. An' that's how it stayed, till Rose came."

She fell silent, but only for a moment. I saw her come to a decision.

"You're family, now, I suppose, I guess you might as well know." A change came over her, a leadenness. "She went to him. Lennie. She tried to buy me, offered him every cent she had. But in the end, she couldn't meet his price."

"What was it, his price?"

Even as I asked, I knew the answer. She stared down at her hands.

"Her. He told her she could have me if she went to work for him."

"What happened when she refused?"

"A miracle," Mattie said, quietly, her voice carefully inflectionless. "Couldn't call it nothin' else."

She reached down into her bag. The cutting which emerged was fragile, folded, yellow with age. She handed it to me with something like reverence. It was from a newspaper called the Biloxi Sun Herald.

*MYSTERIOUS DEATH OFF GULF COAST*

*At seven am today, Central Time, a Coast Guard launch was called to the Biloxi Boardwalk Marina, where a Tiara Coronet 3900 cabin cruiser had been reported drifting out to sea. Observers from the shore had seen a body draped over the rear gunwale. Once the craft had been brought in, the corpse was identified as the boat's owner, night club proprietor and local gangland kingpin Lennie Dutroux. At first, death was thought to be due to natural causes.*

*In a sensational development, however, the Biloxi P.D. has now confirmed that two marks were found on the victim's ankle during autopsy, and the cause of death is now believed to have been a snake bite. The boat was thoroughly searched, but no snake was found, and the exact species responsible will not be ascertained until toxicology tests have been carried out. A source from the Mississippi Department of Wildlife, however, has told this newspaper that instances of snakes, particularly copperheads and rattlesnakes, falling into leisure craft from overhanging trees at their moorings, are not unknown. No snake was found in the craft, or near its usual berth.*

*Speculation is now mounting as to the future of Dutroux's extensive gambling and prostitution empire. Will his successor be obvious, or must the city endure yet another criminal interregnum before a new czar emerges? The last gang war cost over twenty lives.*

*See leader article P2 BILOXI'S CRIMINAL UNDERBELLY.*

I watched Mattie fold away the cutting, then looked out again at the stifling heat's shimmer.

"A miracle," she said again.

A statement of belief? Or a question... Once more I looked out at the haze.

*Snakes....*

*

The lights of Capitol Hill were hazy. *Me? Or the whisky...?* I heard footsteps and turned.

The second bottle went down on the coffee table with a thump, beside the one I'd just emptied. The blunt noise echoed through the motel's deserted reception area. A water glass came down between the two bottles. John Walks-Over-Ice sat, then began cleaning it with a spotless white handkerchief. I sat down opposite him, watched him pour, drink, then put the glass carefully down. Only then did he speak.

"It's three am. What's so important it can't wait till morning?"

It took a conscious effort not to slur my words. "I had a long conversation with Mattie today. She told me a lot."

He sat back. "About me?"

"Only tangentially." I leaned across to him. "We were talking about the death of Lennie Dutroux."

His face gave nothing away. *"Tangentially,"* he said, imbuing the word with contempt. "I like that. An articulate drunk. What do you want, Fraser? An explanation? A fight?" He emptied his glass. "Or just the chance to wallow in self-righteousness?"

"Who made the decision to kill Dutroux, you or Rose?"

"She knew nothing about it."

*No denial...* We faced each other. The exchange of looks was a mutual admission that we had, on some level, colluded.

"Mattie guessed, didn't she," I said. "Did Rose? Given that she used to feed your snakes, back home in Lexington? In the good ol' days."

The sarcasm had no effect. "Would it matter if she did?" he said, evenly. "Look on it as waste removal, Fraser. It set a decent human being free, someone who'd been abused for decades. Dutroux treated Mattie like shit. He was an animal. He spent his entire life exploiting appetites and profiting from misery. The planet's a better place without him."

"And the law?"

He regarded me sourly across the top of his glass. "You're going to lecture me about the law? *You?* How often have you killed, Fraser? Or doesn't that matter as long as you wear the hair shirt? And which version of the law are we talking about, anyway? Yours? Mine? Dutroux's? O'Malley's? Even Saul's?"

I said nothing. He refilled the glasses. Again, he drank.

"In case you haven't worked it out," he said, "here's how it plays. Civics one-oh-one." He leaned across the table. "The law in this country—anyone's version of it—is a bigger whore than Mattie ever was. It belongs to the highest bidder or the fastest gun or the loudest lawyer. That's justice, here in the land of the free."

*Land of the free...*

The alcohol hit me in a hot wave, jerking my memory back to another hotel room, only a few miles away. *The young lawyer...* I could still see his aggrieved face. Before I knew it, the words had tumbled out.

"I was told once not to confuse it with the land of the free lunch."

The big Cherokee's laugh was bitter. "Wow, Fraser, that's deep, really profound. Our homeland in a nutshell, you nailed it, you just defined its whole philosophy. Why bother with analysis when you can have the folksy soundbite? Especially when it doesn't mean shit."

He slammed the empty glass down on the wood. Through my drunkenness it dawned on me that this man was trying, very hard, to keep himself under control.

"You take care of your own," he said, finally. "You surround yourself with good people, people who know right from wrong, people who aren't afraid to fight for something better. People who'd put their hand in the fire for you because they know you'd do the same for them."

A creed, almost a chant... Again, the alcohol rode over me, anger on its back.

"Yessir! Must be great being Big Chief Morality—great to have principles. Especially such elastic ones—the kind that let you kill anyone you don't like. The rattlesnake in the bag, back at the ranch. Why?"

Once more he sat back and surveyed me. "I didn't know what the hell was going on, but it struck me you might just be the good guy in all of it—or if not that, at least the innocent. I reckoned you were safer gone until I knew more. When we talked, I saw I'd never persuade you, so I decided to scare you off."

The words burned; *so cool, so smug...*

"You self-righteous prick," I said, softly.

"Takes one to know one."

My head exploded. I launched myself, punching, clawing, shouting. I landed hard against the solid mass of him, heard him grunt with the impact and smelled whisky. Wood splintered beneath me. When the blow came, it was like being hit by a tree trunk. I felt myself fly until my back slammed into a wall.

The universe turned. And kept on turning. His voice came from somewhere above me.

"That's the first really honest thing I've seen you do since you played the fiddle at the farm."

The voice came nearer. I heard its tone change.

"I would do anything for Rose Vannier. *Anything*, legal or not. That's all you need to know."

I managed to focus. On his face, his implacable stone face... But somehow I was looking beneath the surface, deep inside him.

*We were just buddies, me and John. Best buddies...*

She had never loved this man, she'd told me. I believed her—but the feeling wasn't mutual.

John Walks-Over-Ice was in love with Rose Vannier, as completely as one human being could be with another. Again, the deep voice came.

"You weren't in any danger. She was a rescue, from a rattlesnake rodeo in Texas, her venom glands had been taken out. Her bite would've hurt you, but it wouldn't have killed you."

His hand reached down, massive, redder than ever. I stared. It was hard to comprehend that it wasn't a threat. I reached out, took it. He pulled me up. As I stood, trying to anchor myself somewhere in the spinning world, I heard the sound of whisky pouring.

*

The Unitarian Church's advert was unmissable.

*IF THE WAGES OF SIN IS DEATH, SHOULDN'T YOU QUIT BEFORE IT'S TIME TO PICK UP YOUR PAYCHECK?*

Mattie stopped in front of it. It was a begrimed plastic light box on wheels, its brightness luminous in the dying daylight, a battered oblong with slot-in black letters, most of them cracked. It sat as close to the traffic as it dared, right at the edge of the potholed pavement. Someone had covered the corners with black duct tape to make an arrow of it, pointing at the door of the pub across the street. As the engine noise of the passing cars died away, the strains of whistle and tenor banjo and guitar reached us from the green doors, a reel, played too fast... An Ulster tune? Donegal? Finally, I recognised it; *The Boys Of Malin.*

"Is that Scottish music?" Mattie asked.

"Irish," I said, "different page, same book."

"Can you play it?"

"A little," I said, "not well."

She nodded, filing the information away. We stood, listening. The pulse of the music seemed to keep time with the throbbing pain in my head. Briefly, I wondered if John was hurting as much as I was. I doubted it, but even if he was, I thought, he'd never let his face show it...

An ancient red convertible cruised past, its black teenage occupants slapping the bodywork in time with the thunderous rap music coming from its radio. Beneath the brows of their woollen watch caps, they eyed us with a casual mixture of resentment and boredom, as though our presence was too insignificant to merit a scowl. As the car pulled away, I looked once more over the street, to the pub's car park. Was John in place? Had he found anything at the boy's address out in the suburb of Bladensburg…? No sooner had the questions surfaced than a pair of headlights flashed, once. Good. If we needed a fast getaway... The corollary to the thought came; *if we actually found Jack O'Malley…*

I forced speculation away, let my eyes find the building again. It was square, unlovely, a rebuke to the spotlit grace of the grandiose official buildings in the distance behind it. How had it survived? The view for a hundred yards to either side was bleak beyond words—every building either derelict or demolished. As we began to cross, I turned and looked back. A knot of people, mainly men, had gathered at the street's badly-lit corner. All of them were black. Once they had catalogued us and estimated the speed of our progress, they looked away. Mattie's voice, matter-of-fact, came from my side.

"War zone. Every city's got 'em, DC more 'n' most." She took my hand, firmly. "Don't stare."

*

The tune changed as I pushed open the door; Ireland's session favourite, *The Bucks Of Oranmore.* It was borne on a familiar odour, heady and strong.

Beer—good beer, stouts and porters and eighty-shilling ales... For a split second I wasn't in America, I was in the Scotia Bar in Glasgow, or O'Connell's in Dublin, or The Favourite in London's Camden Town. I stepped forward, half expecting my foot to come down on sawdust. The smell enveloped me, familiar and forbidding at once, a refuge I had too often mistaken for home. I watched Mattie's eyes take it all in.

We were at the mouth of a long wooden cave, dominated on one side by a polished mahogany bar and a row of peeling stools. The drinkers, perched on them like parrots, didn't look up as we came in, except for the occupant of the nearest one, an immensely fat woman in a green satin jacket embroidered with orange shamrocks. She was well in her cups. She spun round too fast at our entrance and nearly overbalanced. As a lock of greasy grey hair flopped over her face, her neighbour's hand caught her.

"Steady, now, Bess."

She turned and scowled at her saviour, a young man with a long sweep of jet black forelock and dark good looks. He pulled her back up on to her stool and didn't let go till he was sure she was secure. When he withdrew his hand, the woman pushed her hair back and scratched at the bulbous appendage that served her as a nose. Then she took a long pull of her beer, put down her glass and patted the boy's arm. Her speech was slurred.

"Boy, Andy, ain't you strong! For a spigger, any roads." She spun round to us. "'S what you get when a spic fucks a nigger." She lifted her beer again and laughed before she drank. "A spigger, jeez, runnin' Pat Riordan's. But he's a nice kid just the same."

Behind her, the boy smiled, grimly. "And he's immune to insult, Bessie. You're done for the night. Finish your beer. I'll call you a cab."

"Andy, you're like a son to me, I swear. Why'n't you just take me yourself? I've a bottle of Paddy, we can break into it 'fore bedtime, watch the Redskins game."

"Bessie, I'm your lodger, not your keeper, and I've a shift to finish. And what makes you think you could stay on, anyway? First curve, bang, you're gone—then what do I get? The God Squad on my ass, that's what. You think Father Butler's gonna miss the headline—Irish Grandmother Makes Crater On Dupont Circle? You know what queen size coffins cost these days?"

She shrugged, belched, then shook her head. "Bastard," she said, equably.

He ignored her, pushed himself off the stool and placed himself before us. Nineteen, I reckoned, twenty at the most... He was dressed in the old-fashioned publican's uniform, dark trousers fronted by a long white apron, with a crisp white shirt, sleeves rolled up to the elbows. The black lettering of his Washington Redskins t-shirt was visible through the white cotton, and a bar towel was tucked in at his waist. He cleaned his hands on it as he looked us over. Mattie didn't seem to trouble him, but when his eyes got to me, they rested first on my bruised cheek, then on the fiddle case. He tossed back the forelock. When his smile came it was open, generous.

"You want to sit in with the band? I can ask."

"Thanks, maybe some other time."

If the Scotland in my voice registered, he didn't let it show. He nodded.

"Welcome to Pat Riordan's anyway, folks, always nice to see new blood." He nodded at the fat woman. "Don't mind the local colour, Bessie's harmless." His manner became even brighter. "So what'll it be? We got Guinness, Murphy's, Belhaven, Belgian Blue Moon—"

"Jim Beam over ice, twice," Mattie said, before I could reply. She pointed at a booth in the corner. "We'll take 'em over there."

Her brusqueness knocked the edge off his smile. He turned away, shouted to the back room.

"Two Beams on the rocks, Con, corner booth."

We threaded our way through a no-man's-land of three-legged tables with grimy marble tops. The booth was worn and comfortable, the curved wood of its seats scuffed and well-used, intricately carved with graffiti. I watched Mattie's puzzled eyes as she tried to decipher *Up The 'RA!* —and then I turned to take stock.

Over one end of the bar's gantry was the inevitable green, white and gold flag, braced by a pair of Glasgow Celtic football strips. In the far corner, a huge television was showing a silent hurling game from the Irish Republic. In between hung a series of portraits. The heavy Victorian frames were grubby, but the subjects were recognisable enough—the pantheon of Irish independence; Collins, Connolly, Wolfe Tone, De Valera. The artists faced them from the other wall, above the line of booths; Synge, Joyce, Yeats, Beckett. The referee was the Pope, his spotlit picture slightly askew, high on the wall above the toilet door. I let my eyes drop back to the dozen or so drinkers. Was there an obvious candidate for my questions? I peered along the line of stools. The faces said nothing to me, but between one set of tunes stopping and another starting, I heard the flat vowels of America mix with accents that had been old before it existed; Cork, Dundalk, Donegal.

*Chair of Celtic History And Culture…*

Had Professor Jack been a regular here, along with his son, the fiddler? It would be surprising if he hadn't, I decided. Had he sat in this booth and listened with a father's pride? Or with an academic's insight? Or both...? I let my eyes find the brightly-lit stage which was the only exception to the comfortable brown gloom. The three unsmiling boys sitting on it, flat-capped and tweed-waistcoated, had launched themselves into yet another set of rapid-fire reels, *Master Crowley's, Cooley's, The Glass Of Beer…*

"They good?"

Mattie's question was earnest, interested. I hesitated before answering, found myself thinking of the old men in Derry Treanor's pub on Glasgow's South Side, where I'd been taught my first Irish tunes with such patient gravitas; *naw, young fella, it's a reel, no' a race…*

"I've heard worse," I said.

She permitted herself the half smile I was beginning to recognise; she'd become good at reading me. The music stopped on the thought. There was no applause. Unsurprised, the three players rose, left their instruments on their chairs, and made for the bar.

"So what now?"

The arrival of our drinks saved me from having to reply. The waitress was beautiful, a redhead with a heart-shaped face and a freckled complexion that couldn't have been anything other than Irish. She held her tray in one hand and wiped down the table with the other. The greeting was pure Dublin.

"Howya. You want to pay now, folks, or run a tab?"

I put a twenty dollar bill on the tray and tried to keep my voice casual.

"We heard Mike O'Malley plays in here sometimes. Thought we might get a chance to hear him."

She smiled. "Ah, Mikey, the roarin' boy himself. Ain't seen him in an age," she said, tossing her hair. "Last I'd heard he'd gone up to New York. Terrible man, don't know how he finds time to fit the music in at all. I'd say he'll be out all hours, lookin' for skirt. Chasin' it the length 'n' breadth o' Manhattan, I know him." She straightened up. "You folks want a refill, give's a nod over to the bar."

As her footsteps receded, Mattie's eyes met mine. I read the question in them.

"I've no more of a plan than you have," I said, quietly. "All we can do is start asking."

The boys who'd been playing sat down at the table nearest us, pint glasses in hand. They were laughing now, the banjo player and the guitarist teasing the boy with the whistle about getting one of the tunes wrong. Behind them, the pub's doors opened. A thin man with a brown face trusted himself as far as the edge of the long counter, then took a slip of paper from the pocket of his jacket. He consulted it, frowning, then called out.

"Taxi for Her—A—Git—Ty."

By the time he'd begun his third try, the ripple of laughter had reached the end of the counter. The fat woman assumed leadership.

"Why'n't they teach you God's own language?" she said, loud enough for the whole pub to hear. "Or ain't you towelheads got no schools in Eye—rack, or wherever the hell you come from?" She levered herself off the stool and leaned towards him. "H.E.R.A.G.H.T.Y! Spells Heraghty, don't it!"

He kept his dignity. "I come from Istanbul, madam, I never put a towel on my head in my life. Forty-one-twenty North Hudson Street, Arlington?"

She couldn't think of a riposte. Angry, she turned and shouted to the girl.

"Tell Andy not to forget the pizza. Pepperoni."

"Andy's gone, Bessie. Left two minutes ago."

The old woman gave a puzzled frown—and then, over the rhythmic rumble of the ceiling fans, I heard it.

A two-stroke engine. Overlaid with a tinny rattle.

*The exhaust… The scooter's loose exhaust!*

Mattie read my face. Her hand clamped down on mine.

"Whatever it is, *walk,*" she hissed. "Don't run. Don't attract attention."

As we approached the double doors, the taxi driver stood back, courteously. The minute we were through, we both ran for the SUV. As John started the engine, the last thing I heard from Pat Riordan's was the fat woman's complaining voice.

"What's the fuckin' hurry? Sump'n' we said?"

*

For the first time since I'd returned to Washington DC the temperature was bearable. The only heat I could feel was from the cardboard pizza box in my hand. *Would this work?* It was worth a try, we'd decided.

For we had nothing else. We'd caught up with the scooter two traffic lights away from the pub—and then promptly lost it again to an unexpected sudden right, up an alley none of us had expected. By the time John had managed to turn, it was gone. I ascended the steps to the apartment block, my footsteps loud on the concrete, then scanned the surrounding houses. Nothing, no one... I turned back again, surveyed the side. Twelve name slips were displayed beside twelve grimy bells. The name Heraghty was at the bottom, on discoloured card behind scratched plastic. There was a handwritten block letter codicil, faded almost to illegibility, taped to the wall by its side.

*WE DON'T WANT CUMPNY!!!*

I stared at it, blankly, then reached out. The bell was greasy to the touch. I heard its faint ring, somewhere to my left. I waited. No response. My thoughts raced in the darkness.

Had it been deliberate? The manoeuvre, the sudden right turn…?

I tried the bell again. Still nothing.

Had he known he was being followed?

More in frustration than anything else, I stabbed at the bell yet again, three times in rapid succession. Still nothing. I turned, let my eyes find the dark SUV across the street. What now? Back to surveillance of the Wenger van up in New Jersey? John had drawn a blank out in Bladensburg… I was almost at the bottom of the steps when the sound of a sash window being pulled open stopped me.

"What in hell's name d'ya want, disturbin' folks past midnight?"

The window was the nearest one to the left, only a few feet from the street door. She looked disembodied, her face still in shade, her body slumped forward over the sill like a rock fall. She was wearing a stained flannelette nightgown that had once been pink. I held up the pizza box.

"Connie said I should bring you this, Mrs. Heraghty."

The scowl was a cover for indecision. Finally, appetite won over suspicion. She nodded, slammed the window shut. I heard her progress through several rooms, then her footsteps, nearing the street door on the other side. Finally, it creaked open. The smell of alcohol hit me first, and then, through a six inch gap bisected by a security chain, I saw her face. It looked worse than it had in the pub, puffy and discoloured. Why? I squeezed the pizza box through the gap. She grunted her thanks, then paused. Her voice dropped to a mumble.

"Got no cash round right now."

"That's OK. Connie says sort it with her next time you're in."

She nodded, relieved, then started to close the door. Then she stopped and peered at me.

"I know you, mister?"

I ignored the question. "Is Andy around, Mrs. Heraghty?"

Suddenly she had energy. "Andy! Don't talk to me 'bout that li'l runt! Every last cent I had in the house! My disability cheque! The grocery money, the rent!"

The door slammed shut on her glower. As I reached forward to knock, it swung open again, without the chain. She flew out at me like a fury, a barefoot mountain of vengeance, then overbalanced. The mass of her was enormous, but I managed to catch her as she fell. It took all my strength to get her upright. I sat her down on the top step. When she could finally speak, the voice was a whispered croak between rasping breaths.

"After everythin' I done for him! My momma's pearls! My bracelets. My cards, all my damn cards!"

I got her up on her feet. She clung to me like a life raft as I walked her back to the apartment door. I left her leaning against it, then retrieved the pizza box. When I turned back to her, she grabbed it from me, glowering. And then she slammed the heavy door shut without another word.

As I strode back towards the SUV, I realised why her face had been puffy.

Bessie Heraghty been crying.

# 15

# BUSINESS

THE VERY AIR was perfumed. Its sanitised flow, subtly fragrant, pervasive, sighed around me, temperature-controlled and machine-washed, relentlessly on-message. I sat in the dimmed light at the back of the huge auditorium, the fiddle case on the next seat, the camouflage jacket from the pickup pulled tight around me. In one inside pocket I could feel my mother's letter, in the other, Seth's iPad. The stubborn bulk of Mike O'Malley's brown leather wallet was beside it, out of sight, but not out of mind.

The drive from Washington had been nine hours, non-stop. Sleep had once again become impossible, fatigue and speculation circling each other in my brain like punch-drunk boxers. I longed for rest. Was there an end in sight to all this? I reached for the wallet. Perhaps I'd missed something… I closed my eyes. When I opened them again, I found myself holding the iPad instead. I stared at it in confusion, then thrust the thing into the fiddle case's open flap. A long way below me, Ann Savoy and her nervous brace of assistants faced the darkened runway's end.

The spotlights came up in sudden brilliance. The audible thud of the switch caught the blonde girl by surprise, but training kicked in immediately. The smile was perfect, no one could have missed it. She cast it out before her at full wattage, careless of what it might catch, then began chasing it at a brisk lope. As I watched, it struck me that she was familiar. Why...? She approached the silent huddle of women purposefully, holding the lapels of the long black coat tight against her with one gloved hand, caressing its high collar with the other. And then she faltered slightly. Some vital imperative from the instruction manual had been belatedly remembered. Her walk changed. The hips swung wider, more sensuously, became a bare millimetre away from dance. When she reached the catwalk's end, she made an exaggerated stop and let her weight fall on to one leg. As her hand came down on her hip, she redoubled the dazzling smile. Then, in one deft movement, she twirled. The coat slipped from her shoulders and slithered down one arm until it was suspended by a single finger. How many hours of rehearsal had gone into that one move? A heartbeat later she began the walk back, dragging the coat behind her. The rear of the backless dress was a minuscule strip of sky blue, brightly bisecting the tanned length of her body.

Ann Savoy concentrated briefly on the retreating hips, then shook her head in a decisive negative. A sullen mutter climbed the raked banks of seats to me. The two young girls craned forward, pens in hand, to note her displeasure. The end of it rose to something near a shout.

"...goddamn amateurs! Tell Selina to send me someone who doesn't look like she's peddling her ass in a whorehouse!"

I heard a noise behind me. I turned. By the service door stood a slight figure in jeans and red hoodie.

Lou.

*

"Are you okay?"

The words echoed off the metal ducts which surrounded the stairwell. She nodded, looking down at her feet. She was wearing new trainers.

"I'm sorry about your father," I said.

A flash of the old defiance came. "He wasn't my father, I know that now. Aunt Rose ain't my aunt, neither, she's my mom. In a few weeks, I'm gonna go live with her."

"Where are you staying now?"

"Hotel. With Sandy 'n' Mattie 'n' John 'n' you." She stopped, gathered her scorn. "I hate hotels."

The awkward silence filled with Ann Savoy's shouting, the consonants stolen by distance and echo. The slurred wail of angry vowels was somehow more threatening than intelligible speech. Lou pointed down at the fiddle case.

"At least you didn't lose her," she said.

I smiled. "How do you know it's a *her?"*

She smiled. "You talk a lot in your sleep, remember."

Again, the silence enveloped us.

"I gotta say—"

"I should never have—"

She recovered first. Her eyes fixed on the square of khaki sticking out of the case flap.

"You finally got one, huh?"

The interest in her eyes decided me. I lifted the iPad and held it out to her.

"Yours if you want it. I've tried, but it's not for me. I hate computers as much as you hate hotels."

The shocked look on her face turned quickly into a grin. Its mockery was a reward. The last time I'd seen it had been when she'd come out of the second-hand shop in Wheeling. And then I saw the uncomplicated happiness slowly vanish. Head down, she took the iPad from me. When her face came back up, it was serious.

"I miss him, Alex." She paused. "He was an asshole, and he wasn't my father. But he was my dad."

*

The first person I saw when I went back into the auditorium was Sandy Hunter. She didn't hear me. She was sitting as far from the stage as she could get, holding an aluminium walking stick, watching the action below with an intensity that was three parts resentment to one part regret. I watched it give way to grimace as she shifted position. Pain? How much trauma would she carry from what she'd been through...? It was the first time I'd seen her since the shootings. Without warning, John's voice was at my ear.

"Detective's here." He read my reaction. "Relax, private, not a cop. Be good to have you in on this."

Watching us, the English girl's face was expressionless. John regarded her, just as dispassionately.

"You too, Sandy."

He strode away. I walked across to her and waited. She gave me a look that was just short of outright dislike, then levered herself out of the seat. The musky perfume I remembered from the farmhouse porch surrounded me as she leaned on the stick. Then, hesitantly, she accepted my arm. As we circled slowly towards the main doors, I felt her muscles tense with the effort of each step. Was she trying too soon? How long would she need the stick? Might she end up like Saul Morgan, forced to accept it forever, to make it part of her personality? As we progressed, her eyes never left the scene below. Another spotlit walk had begun. I catalogued it. Ann Savoy's annoyance was the same, the desperate scribbling to either side of her was the same, the coat and gloves were the same—but it took me a second glance to work out that I was watching a different girl. When the patrician voice came from my side, it was bitter.

"You realise what's happening down there?"

"What do you mean?"

"That no-hoper and all the ones before her—do they remind you of anyone?"

She watched it come to me; *of course...* She smiled, grimly.

"That's right. That heartless cow down there is about to lose her biggest asset, so she's looking for clones. Openly. Tomorrow is the last ever Rose Vannier show for Atlantic Style. The bitch is actually going to use at least three of these kids, just to rub Rose's face in it. To make the point that America's Sweetest Sweetheart is replaceable."

"Can you do anything?"

As she turned to me, awkward in her anger, yet another fresh-faced blonde hopeful arrived on the catwalk. Briefly we watched her begin. The English voice came again.

"I'd create hell if I thought I needed to—-if the truth wasn't so obvious."

"And what truth would that be?"

"That no one could ever replace Rose Vannier."

The voice's cynicism was laced with a definite undertone. Before I could probe, we'd reached the big double doors. She let my arm go and pushed them open with her stick—and the view pulled me up short.

The first pictures I'd ever seen of Rose Vannier, the triptych behind the Washington hotel bar...

Here, they'd been transformed into a twenty-foot high banner. I watched it billowing seductively on the air-conditioned breeze. A broad white strip made a loud diagonal across it.

*WELCOME AMERICA'S SWEETEST SWEETHEART!*
*GO GIRL!*
*ST. CHARLES MO. LOVES YA!*

Beneath it, impervious to the images, a white-haired man, elderly and tall, was huddled with John Walks-Over-Ice at a table. Its long marble top held a battered briefcase and a stack of papers. When he saw us, he broke off, took off his wire-framed spectacles and rose, awkwardly. He gave the fiddle case a suspicious stare, then offered a bony hand to each of us in turn. He was thin to the point of emaciation.

"Edward Staller."

The voice was dry. The solicitous way he ushered Sandy to a chair identified his manners as being from the same era as his suit. When I put down the fiddle, he gave me a quick glance of assessment. Then he donned the spectacles once more and went back to his papers. When they were finally in order, he arranged them neatly, took a small map of St. Louis from the briefcase and spread it carefully beside them. The dry voice was all business.

"Like I said, sir, it's all in here. Wasn't cheap, though, I have to warn you." He waited for a response from John, gave a nod when none came. "Our financial people traced Mrs. Heraghty's cards easily enough. Subject, subsequently identified as Andrew Aolfi, aka Alan Rhodes, Albert Delfino, used her VISA twice, once at a Mexican take-out joint in Reston, just off Route 267, then for a ticket at Dulles Airport—for a late American Airlines flight to Lambert St. Louis. We had an operative waiting when he touched down. No luggage. He must have called ahead, because he was picked up immediately by three young black kids, as soon as he reached the car park. Then..." He consulted the papers. "...Ford pickup, old junker, our operative followed it downtown to a house on the old streetcar line, location called Hodiamont Tracks, not the best neighbourhood." A bony finger stabbed at it on the map. "Three am they came out, all four of them, dressed in hoodies and overalls. My man got photographs, good enough for ID. They travelled about ten blocks, chose a derelict house and started doing their thing. No surprise. Once the pickup was full, back to Hodiamont. My man's still there. Nothing's moved, he says, not a thing, the whole day."

"He's good, your man?"

Staller's brow creased slightly at Sandy's question, but by the time he'd turned to her, professional politeness had erased annoyance.

"Ray Sorensen's one of our best, ma'am, been with us for over twenty years." He turned back to John. "We have contacts, we made a few calls. It wasn't hard to get a handle on this particular crew—all of them have records—and our informants have given us a pretty good idea where they'll be tonight, and when." Once again, the long forefinger circled a spot on the map. "This area, between Page Boulevard and Martin Luther King Drive, has many derelict properties. Word is, they're going to try two hits tonight. This'll be the first. We reckon they'll get there in about—" He consulted his watch. "—an hour, an hour and a half's time." He looked up at John. "On one aspect of this, Sorensen and I are of one mind. The Hodiamont Tracks house would be the wrong location to flush this kid out, place is a warren, too many exits. I think you'd be better catching him with the others. On the job."

John's face gave no reaction. Staller paused again, carefully let his voice become neutral.

"Could I ask, sir, if you or any of your people intend to be armed?"

John thought for a moment. "These boys, are they liable to be?"

Staller went back to his papers. He riffled through them till he found the relevant page.

"Leader's a kid called Terrell Fallon, seventeen. One conviction, armed robbery. A liquor store. Prowl car lifted him ten minutes after he'd done it. He had the usual Saturday night special, never fired it. The other two are his brother Bopper and his cousin JJ, both still minors." He looked back across at John. "There's no great history of gun violence associated with this type of crime, but it'd be a mistake to automatically assume there'll be no weapons around." His voice became diplomatic. "I'm sure you know that, here in St. Louis, we've had our share of racial problems recently—and it's upped the ante on the street, made things less predictable. On balance, I think it'd be better to let the police handle it. What these kids're doing is definitely illegal, not to mention extremely high profile—it's a crime that gets a lot of coverage, huge outcry in the liberal press, wanton destruction of the city's historic fabric, all that. After they've been arrested, you'd have no problem at all if you want to sit in on the interrogation, I can arrange it." He shrugged. "A few hundred bucks spread around, that'd take care of it. If we move fast, it could probably even be set up before anything begins. One call to my contact at—"

Sandy Hunter's English tones broke in again, emphatic. "Cops would be a mistake, I'm sure of it—especially in this city, especially with black kids, for exactly the reasons you've given. I think police action could be too heavy-handed." She turned from Staller to John. "We only have one shot here. You've already lost this boy once. Lose him again and we're finished."

Staller's annoyance was openly visible, now. Carefully not looking at the English girl, he handed the report to John and folded the map into his briefcase. The loud snap of the lock seemed like a rebuke. Finally, he faced her.

"I'm ex-force myself, ma'am. I'd have to say I think you're being somewhat less than fair."

The standoff lasted a few seconds. Neither of them backed down. Then, without acknowledging defeat in any way, Staller turned back to John.

"We've done what we were contracted to do. If you want anything more..." Again he shrugged. "You're paying the bills round here, it's entirely up to you. If the work's to go on, though, we will need a brief—a detailed brief."

The silence was taut. The ring of a mobile phone broke it. Staller took it quickly from his inside pocket, his face neutral as he listened.

"Three in the cab?" he said, finally. "Subject in the back?"

The voice at the other end talked at length. Staller finished the exchange with a terse grunt, then looked at each of us in turn.

"That was Sorensen. They're moving." His eyes settled on John. "Earlier than expected. I'm afraid that means you have to decide right now."

John turned to me. "Fraser?"

I didn't hesitate. "No guns. And Sandy's right, keep the police out of it."

"Why?"

I felt Staller's gaze upon me. "Instinct," I said.

Somehow, the single word had authority.

"I agree," John said, turning to Staller. "Just us, you and your man Sorensen. No police."

Whatever he thought, Staller's face stayed neutral. "And the lady here?" He gestured at the stick. "No offence, but I suspect she'd slow us down."

Sandy Hunter flushed red—then got herself under control. Completely. Poise recovered, she rose. Then she leaned down, lifted my fiddle case and looked at me.

"You can leave this with me."

She paused, deliberately didn't look at Staller. His face gave no indication of victory.

"Ma'am," he said politely, lifting the briefcase.

*

In the elevator, I turned, expecting to see her watching us. She wasn't. She was leaning on her stick once more, the fiddle case in her other hand, looking up at the three huge images. The fury in her face was open, now, but something else had joined it.

And suddenly I understood the undertone I'd heard earlier. Mattie's words came back to me.

*America just damn well upped an' fell in love with her…*

Was it possible to be close to Rose Vannier without being in love with her? It was true of John. It was perhaps even true of Saul—and now I was sure it was true of Sandy Hunter.

*Was it true of me…?*

Without warning, I was no longer in an elevator in a bleak convention centre, I was back on the North Carolina shore, watching perfect beauty emerging from the waves...

The vision died as soon as it had formed. As the scented air claimed me again, I found Sandy Hunter's eyes, locked on mine.

She was in control again, all emotion hidden. I saw a hard carapace, impenetrable. What lay beneath was something she had fought too long, instinctively I knew it.

The lift began to close. I saw her bow her head, then turn and begin to limp away from the billowing images.

*

The blows were muffled, the steel heads of the hammers padded with cloth, but the makeshift silencers did nothing to diminish force. It only took half a dozen strikes. The minute the two holes appeared in the roofless house's side wall, metal cables with businesslike hooks on their ends poked through from the interior.

The two hooded figures who'd been hammering busied themselves connecting the hooks to the pickup's towbar. The vehicle's engine revved. I heard the cables twang taut and watched the boys run, laughing, scrambling to either side. With a loud rumble, the wall bulged out, then collapsed. As the dust cloud rose, the driver reversed the truck across the remains of the house's lawn. Where was Andy? Finally I saw him, clambering over the rubble, coughing. He was still wearing his Redskins t-shirt.

"Understand the method now?" Staller asked, his voice a whisper from the seat beside me. "If brick isn't locked in vertically by a roof or a lintel, it doesn't take as much as you'd imagine to dislodge it. You set the building on fire first—they'll have done that a few nights ago. That separates the brick from the interior structure. On business night, you bump it with your vehicle to dislodge any last connections, you make your breaches and thread your towrope through. Soon as it's towed, as you saw, the wall just falls over. It usually comes apart in big blocks, then the impact of the fall breaks most of the bricks away from each other. The only tools you need are a couple of sledgehammers, a few pry bars and wheelbarrows. As long as you've got a truck with enough power and springs which can take the weight, you've got it made."

"They get cash from this?"

"Brick rustling is steady money—going price for a truckload's about three hundred bucks. Most of it goes to Alabama, Florida, South Carolina." I heard a tinge of sadness find the dry voice. "Our city's being stolen to build sunbelt subdivisions, Mister Fraser."

John's metallic voice came from the radio. He was in the other car.

"How do we do this, Staller?"

The detective lifted the transceiver. "You're sure you don't want the rest of the crew?"

"We have no interest in them whatsoever."

"Then we just separate your guy out. Best time'll be when the brick's stacked in the pickup. Hierarchy helps us. There's only three places in the cab, your guy looks like the Johnny-Come-Lately—he came in the back, means he'll leave in the back, on top of the brick and the tools. If we confront them once they're loaded and the first three are installed, I'd reckon Terrell and his boys will have no compunction about taking off before your man gets up behind. With yourself and Sorensen in the other car, we're four. Even if he runs, we can take him."

The squawk came again. "Okay, you say the word."

"Give me Sorensen," Staller said.

I heard a chorus of crackles from the other car, then the words *partial block,* then *go on my count, flasher and siren.* Staller caught me looking at him.

"Illegal, sure, impersonating the cops, but it'll help if these kids think that's who we are. Gives us a split second of edge." He peered back at the work going on round the pickup. "Another five minutes, ten at most." he said. "Open your door. Be ready to run."

We watched. The boys had organised themselves efficiently, two to throw the bricks, two to stack them on the truck's flat bed. They worked hard and fast. Finally, the pickup was crammed as full as it could be. Two of them gathered at the nearside front tire. I saw one of them kick it, and just made out the end of an animated discussion about the state of it. It ended in a hi-five, then the three black boys began piling into the cab. Where was Andy? I heard Staller's voice, barely more than a whisper, beside me.

"Four, three, two—"

The pickup's lights came on. It began to roll.

*"Go! Now!"*

As planned, the siren and the light from Sorensen's car confused everything. Before Staller and I had made ten yards, it had screeched to a halt. I saw the pickup try to swerve, the boy Andy launch himself, then fall heavily as his dive missed the tailgate.

The doubtful front tire disintegrated into flying strips of rubber.

*"Shit!"*

Staller's expletive drowned in a grinding of metal as the pickup's wheel rim smashed into the kerb—and then the sound of a gunshot stopped us both. I heard glass splinter, the pickup's engine roar. It careered forward and hit Sorensen's car side on. The impact was a jagged crash that turned into a tortured animal squeal as the pickup shunted the car across the street. Suddenly there were running figures and more shots. The car's windscreen starred. Slowly, its passenger door opened. John staggered out, clutching his arm. I watched him shake his head, then sway—and fall.

It galvanised me. As I ran, I saw the boy Andy, stumbling

away into the mouth of the unlit alleyway behind the houses. *How badly was John hurt?* Staller's hand grabbed my arm, spun me round. His face was furious.

"No! The kid! Get after him!" He saw me hesitate. "Dammit, man, it's my fuckup! I'll take care of our guys, don't argue!"

*

*Fifty yards? Seventy?* How long was the alley? Thanks to the red shirt I could just make out his figure. I sprinted, the sound of my running feet thunderous in the enclosed space. Was I gaining? I saw him stop, stagger to the left. Why? Again, I ran, full tilt, at least twenty yards—and found myself facing a wall.

A dead end. He'd boxed himself in.

Left? Right? Over a wrecked wooden fence to my left I saw a black hole, framed in white, up a short flight of stone steps. A back door? I stopped. Was this the way he'd gone? The rippled surface of a puddle gave him away. What to do? I could still hear the siren. Somehow, it deepened the silence confronting me. Slowly, I crossed what had once been a kitchen garden.

*

Inside the wrecked house, the smell was decay, rotting wood and disintegrating plaster. I went through another doorway, its contours blurred by huge brown growths which looked as though they could breathe. I came into ghostly light and a faint breeze, found myself overlooking the street through the remains of a wall already robbed of most of its brick. I stopped, listened. All I could hear was the ongoing noise from the crash at the other end of the street.

And then, over my head, faint but definite, a creak.

Him? It had to be... He was somewhere above, trying not to be heard as he moved. I picked my way across the caked dust of the floorboards until I found the staircase, a grand affair of marble steps, its wrought iron handrail torn away. I stopped, trying to think it through. Up and confront? Or wait till he thought he was safe and came down? Up, I decided, anything else was too chancy—there might be an external fire escape, or another way to scramble down outside. I cast around for something to serve as a weapon. One of the handrail's metal stanchions lay loose. I lifted it. Slowly, looking up, I began my ascent. At the top, I found myself on a wide landing facing a trio of heavy doors. To my left, another flight of stairs, narrower and wooden. Was he on this level, or higher still? Again, a creak from above.

Silence was more difficult on the wooden treads. I kept my back to the wall. As I climbed, I felt the staircase begin to move beneath me. How stable was it? When I reached the top, I saw I was in a space which was open to the elements—the house was roofless. I was in the remains of an attic, the stars winking down at me.

"What the fuck you d'you want, bro?"

He was kneeling at the remains of the gable end's fireplace, his face ghostly with brick dust. He was holding the right side of his ribs with his left hand. A faint trail of blood was coming from his mouth.

"O'Malley," I said, straightening up. "I want Jack O'Malley."

He looked at me in surprise, then tried to laugh. It turned into a wince.

"Oh, that's funny, bro, real funny—Jack O'Malley, the one guy nobody *ever* wants. Makes sense, I suppose—one mad mother lookin' for another. Houndin' me outta my nice little Mick job in DC, though, doggin' me halfway across the country, that's kinda over the top." He looked me up and down, sizing up the bar in my hand. "Couldn't even let me alone to get myself a stake, could you? Just a few bucks—desperation bucks. Where's the harm, poppin' a few bricks with my buddies? Nobody gets hurt." He shook his head. "My own damn fault—I should never've let myself get spooked in Riordan's when I recognised your fancy-ass fiddle case." He spat out blood, then grimaced. "Ribs, man, that's a real bitch." His eyes closed. "Shoulda known. Whole deal started goin' south the minute you did your Superman number an' knocked Mikey off the pillion." Eyes still shut, he managed a mirthless smile. "Hope she was worth it, bro. Hope she fucked as good as she looked."

He coughed again. A pink bubble of blood grew at the side of his mouth. When he looked up, I could see him trying to read me.

"Here's the deal. I'm guessin' you don't really give a damn about me, right? So how about you front me, say five large, let me disappear, an' I'll tell you where you can find the nutty professor."

I considered it. *Pay for information?* I hated the idea, but how else could I get him to co-operate...? Slowly, I approached the kneeling figure.

"You don't tell me, you *show* me."

He shook his head. I took another step nearer.

"No deal without it. And no deal means cops."

A noise came from the pocket of his jeans. A phone. Before I could react, he had the thing in his hand. He stared at the display, then tried to laugh again.

"What's so funny, Andy? Show me."

As my hand reached out for the device, I saw his eyes become dreamy above the smiling mouth.

I didn't expect the knife. The first I knew of it was the glint as it scythed across. Only a desperate swipe with the iron rod deflected it from my shins. He prised himself off the floor. The voice was a whisper.

"Ain't over till it's over, bro. Guess that's the American way."

As I stumbled back he came forward, phone in one hand, blade in the other.

"Serendipity, I'd call it. Now you're more 'n' just a persistent bastard with a fiddle."

I kept my eyes on the knife. *What was he talking about?*

"Now you're at least twenty large."

*What the hell was he talking about?* I backed away, parrying with the bar—until my left foot slipped behind me. *The stairwell!* I nearly overbalanced. He lunged forward, missed by a fraction. It was enough. I caught his arm, heaved him round and slammed him against the brick of the other gable end. He roared with pain—and then his rage conquered it. The knife came up, high, ready to stab down.

I rammed the iron bar into his chest.

The crunch of bone was an evil sound, the gurgling cry that escaped him, worse. He hung there, his shocked gaze shifting slowly from the knife in his hand to the rusty length of iron pinning him to the wall.

And then a tearing noise began, somewhere below. It was terrible, agonised. The floor began to shake. The sound became louder, a rending, tortuous. A thunderous rumble enveloped it. Beneath me the boards shuddered, then sagged. As I fell forward they began to buckle, then wrench themselves free of the joists beneath, nails exploding like bullets.

And then the world disappeared into a vortex of noise and dust.

*

I found him, half buried in the remains of the top storey. The collapse had crushed his chest and legs, but it had played a strange trick on his face, cleaning off the dust and grime. He looked at peace, almost angelic, once again the handsome boy, half black, half Italian. *Was he dead?*

My fear of touching him drowned in panic. My hands began tearing at the bricks. *O'Malley! I had to find Jack O'Malley! How—*

His eyes opened. *Had I thought the words or shouted them?* I watched his mouth try for a grin.

"Same problem, bro…" he whispered, "…every damn time." His hand snaked up, grabbed my wrist. "Good on the playbook, never could get to the goal line."

Whisper turned to cough, cough turned to a spray of blood. I wiped its obscene warmth from my face. The phone was still clasped in his other hand. I prised it loose and read the text.

*The Scotsman. He's near you now. Usual rates plus twenty. Ten minutes to accept or it goes to someone else.*

*J.*

The muscles of his hand jerked in a final spasm. A last gout of blood, dark and viscous, welled up from his chest.

The life left his eyes.

# 16

# BLUFF

THE DARK CORNER of the empty roadside restaurant was safety. I sat, staring down at my empty coffee cup, trying not to think.

*The blood, the final gout of black blood…*

Muttering voices brought my head up—a trio of elderly women, white, overweight and arthritic. They scowled at me in unison, as though the dining room was their private space. I watched their expressions ripen to open contempt at the state of me. A distant part of my brain reacted. *They're right, a beggar in rags, a man who spent the night hiding in a derelict house….* As soon as they were seated, their heads craned towards each other in cabal—until John came through the door, carrying my fiddle case. I watched a three-second parade of emotions—shock, fear, distaste—march across their faces, then scurry into hiding. The nearest of them dropped her napkin. It fluttered to the floor like a flag of surrender. He sat down opposite me.

"Good news," he said, softly. "No official search, you were never there, Staller's contacts kicked in. A couple of thousand spread around, St Louis's finest never heard of you. They caught Terrell and his crew, all three of them. Official line on the boy Andy is he died in the incident, end of story."

*Good news… Andy…*

I became aware of John Walks-Over-Ice looking at me, closely. It was a look I'd never seen before. What did it mean? He put the case down by my side and let his eyes follow mine down to the sling supporting his other arm.

"Clean break," he said. "Cast'll come off pretty quickly. Car's outside, we can talk there."

We got up. The case in my hand was relief, but his words... *Why weren't they in sync with his lips?* When he reached the three women, he stopped. With one fluid motion, he bent down and picked up the fallen napkin. When he placed it on their table, they all but physically shrank from it.

"Ladies," he said, gravely.

We went through the glass door, out into the morning sunlight. Just before it closed behind us, I realised I'd heard one of the women speak. I had to concentrate to understand the words.

*Uppity* and *injun*.

*

The town of Alton's crumbling waterfront was a desolate half mile of dirt and defeat, all but void of people. We sat in the shadow of a giant grain elevator, watching the traffic roar across the big bridge between Illinois and Missouri. There was a faint odour of sewage. When John Walks-Over-Ice's voice finally came, it was blunt.

"You believe it was from O'Malley?"

I let my hand find the fiddle case. Its worn leather seemed the only real thing in reach. I heard myself answer.

"It was signed *J*. Seems obvious to me."

"Too obvious, maybe? We've established that the text came from a pre-pay handset, virtually untraceable, the kind you can buy in any gas station for twenty bucks. Why go to the bother if you're going to put a signature on it?"

The blast of a truck horn from the bridge punctuated the question. As we lapsed once more into strained silence, I saw that my companion's eyes were on me again. The expression on the hewn-from-rock face was a reprise of the one in the restaurant. Slowly, comprehension found me.

An assessment. A damage assessment.

I felt sweat trickle from my palm on to the leather.

A *doctor's* assessment...

The thought came as I closed my eyes; *don't let it become pity...* I felt his huge hand on my shoulder. The grip was firm, the shake, gentle.

"Fraser, he was trying to kill you. It was self-defence."

He let go of me. I watched his eyes find a place beyond the muddy water.

"My grandmother..." he began. "She wasn't Cherokee, she was Oglala Sioux, that's where I get the height. It's where the name came from as well, she insisted my grandfather take it. They married for love, but she ended up poor after he died, not really wanted by either side, her new tribe or the one she'd left behind. Lived out her days in a shack near a town called Iron Duff, North Carolina. Alone. It was the fifties, Eisenhower was beginning to push the freeways through. Her place was right in the way of I-40—machines, noise, lights, day and night, went on for months. She was never particularly stable in the first place. It pushed her right to the edge, but she had her antidote. Whenever she felt the madness coming, she'd get down on her knees with a brush and a bucket and scrub floor till she fainted. It was as good a principle as any."

He stopped. I watched him search for the right words.

"I'd say that's pretty much where you are now. You've had enough shock over the last few weeks to break ten men. For my part in it, the snake back at the farm, I'm sorry. But now..." He shrugged. "I could prescribe you sedatives by the dozen, or therapy, or drown you in psychobabble, surround you with the usual neurotic bullshit Americans think they need from their doctors—none of it would help."

He started the engine. The tyres squealed as he spun us round, across the railroad tracks and away from the river.

"I've only ever seen one kind of scrub brush that seems to help you," he said, gunning the car through the lights and up the steep hill. "Let's see if we can use it to buy you some breathing space."

*

Was it madness? If it was, then it was at least a madness I understood. Seated on a huge log, high up on the bluff above the river, I let it rule.

Jigs and reels, hornpipes and measures... From Ireland, from Scotland, from Shetland, from Cape Breton, from anywhere. *The Sailor's Wife, Sleep Soond I' The Mornin', The East Neuk O' Fife, The Spey In Spate, The Bird's Nest, The Flowing Tide, Jenny Dang The*

*Weaver,* dozens of others whose names I'd forgotten or had never known. As the wind tore at my hair I apologised to them—old friends, trusted henchmen, they deserved more respect… When I got to *Whisky Before Breakfast,* the red hand appeared in front of me. The shot glass was full of Saul Morgan's bathtub bourbon. I took it as an omen, let the fire of it push me on.

English tunes. *The First New Dutch Skippar, Daniel Wright's Hornpipe, Rusty Gully, Speed The Plough, The Presbyterian Hornpipe...* They had fine tunes, the English. Why didn't they use them more? Why were the Celts so afraid of them? So dismissive?

*Why…?*

I ran from the word, delved into the complex rhythms, the strange intricacies. *Come all ye,* I thought, *I need you, every one…*

Danish *Hoppsas,* German *Rhinelanders,* French *Gavottes,* Polish *Mazurkas,* a cavalry march from nineteenth century Ulster, another written in Finland during the Thirty Years War... The strings beneath my fingers were salvation, the bow in my hand, the frenetic rod which ruled them.

The first tune that reached back to touch me was a strathspey. It was called *Look Across The Water.*

It wanted to slow me. I let it. I could tell it was a new tune by its phrasing, but I had no idea who had written it, or why. It didn't matter. What did matter was the way it opened my eyes. Suddenly, the landscape before me was everything. From the Alton dockside, the Mississippi had been a sluggish sewer. Up here it was the artery that pumped life through a nation's heart, stretching North and South as far as the eye could see. I exulted in it. I played the strathspey's springing phrases over and over, changing, improvising, tugging at the rhythm, waiting for a sign—any kind of sign—that would tell me what should come next.

And finally, only one tune would do. I stopped, drank deep from the proffered bottle, and began. After my first time round it, I stopped again. How long had I been playing? The sun had tumbled a long way down towards Missouri's cornfields. John's voice came.

"That's what you played that first day, at the farm."

I stood up and walked, shakily, to the bluff's edge.

No hawk, plenty of high… A chain of barges passed on the river below. They looked like toys.

"Some kind of healing melody? Is that why you keep going

back to it?"

I came back to the log, sat and let the fiddle fall to my lap. I had nothing left. I was spent, I couldn't have spoken a word or played another note. He reached across. With great delicacy, his hands prised instrument and bow from my grasp. Once he had them safe, the doctor's look came again, but now he seemed satisfied. He rose.

"I'm leaving you the car. Before you move from this place, you sleep. Then you get back on the horse."

He looked away, over the river.

*Look Across The Water...*

The falling sun caught his eyes, made fire of them. The huge head seemed part of the landscape, ancient and wise...

"You get back on *immediately.* Because she needs you, now," he said, softly. I heard courage find his voice. "Maybe even more than she needs me."

*

The air in the hospital was as perfumed as the auditorium's had been. Only when a nurse or a doctor passed through the doors behind the reception desk did the whiff of anything more human escape.

Sandy Hunter sat on a worn leather couch, her leg at an awkward angle, her stick by her side. One mobile phone was wedged between shoulder and ear, the other was in her right hand, its shrill insistence demanding its turn. As I sat down opposite, I heard her intone the word *no.* The single syllable sounded more absolute in the plummy accent. Why? And why were we here, I wondered, instead of at the hotel? She ended the call, switched both phones off and looked at me.

"I know about the boy," she said, abruptly. "I need your side of it."

*I need...* Annoyance tugged at me at the peremptory tone. Who had she talked to? John? Staller?

"The boy is dead," I said. "O'Malley wants me the same way, he's prepared to pay twenty thousand dollars for it. Once you know that, you know everything."

Again, the stare, long, evaluating. "What I need to know is, do you intend to stay or go?"

The calm which had come with fourteen hours' sleep vanished. She read my face, then continued, impassively.

"Things have changed."

She reached down and hefted a thick wad of newspapers out of her bag. It landed on the table with a dull thud. I lifted the top one. It was called the *National Standard.* The banner headlines covered the whole front page.

*AMERICA'S SWEETEST SWEETHEART*
*—NOT SO SWEET AFTER ALL*
*MOMMA'S A HOOKER, BRO WAS A PUSHER!!!*

All of the other papers were the same; the savagery smug, the tone pious, the detail forensic.

"Ann?"

She nodded. "First one within an hour of the St. Charles show finishing. Hell hath no fury like a manager scorned," she said. "If Atlantic Style can't have Rose Vannier…" She shook her head. "That's why we're here. It's the nearest anonymous place I could think of—the hotel's a battlefield, camera crews, reporters crawling round the corridors, telephoto lenses and mics, notes under the door, cash for exclusives. Gallant Fox is the same—America at its lowlife best, greedy for disaster. And it's just beginning. My laptop and these—" She gestured at the phones. "—are all the office I've got left. I'm maybe an hour ahead of the pack. So help me here, Fraser. If I say I need to know your intentions, it's for a reason."

"And what reason might that be?"

She bristled. The comings and goings of the hospital surrounded our confrontation. She settled back on the couch.

"You selfish bastard," she said. "Don't you understand what it means if O'Malley's put out a contract on you?" She leaned into me. "Killers aren't neat. Killers don't give a shit about collateral. Just being near you puts her at risk. You should vanish, now. More danger is one thing she does not need." I watched her face fill with contempt. "And she doesn't need freeloaders, either."

The word was a physical slap. My anger flared. Through it, I watched her reach down again into the bag. Her hand emerged with a thick envelope and slapped it down on the table.

"The gravy train's derailed, Fraser. Walk away while you still can. There's eighty grand there, it's as near a golden handshake as you're going to get. Now disappear."

I stood up before rage could rule me. Fiddle in hand, I gave the envelope one last look, then turned for the double doors—just in time to see a van with a satellite dish cruise past. Sandy Hunter's voice, its tone brisk and businesslike, pleasant even, stopped me.

"Edwardsville, Illinois, car park opposite the library. She'll meet you there in an hour, she'll be in Saul's old Eldorado. Cab's waiting outside."

When I turned, there was no envelope on the table—and no sign on her face that anything remotely untoward had happened. Had I imagined it? The bribe? Dreamed it? What had just happened here?

A *test…?*

I watched her pull herself up, then begin hobbling away.

"Tell her she has to do press," she said, over her shoulder. "They'll never let go if she doesn't. And the point about proximity's a serious one. Think about it."

*

The air was clear—painfully clear, scoured by emotion. Everything that needed to be said had been said, rammed home with brutal force. We sat on the front seat of Saul Morgan's nineteen fifty-three Cadillac like boxers between rounds, exhausted, the crumpled newspapers lying on the seat like discarded bandages, hurt hovering above us in an invisible cloud. I'd broached the danger argument, repeatedly. Each time, Rose had rejected it—at first with logic, finally with anger; *Sandy had no right, unless of course, you want to go…* I'd said nothing about the bribe, or test, or whatever the fat envelope had been. The woman beside me had trouble enough.

"Do you have any recourse against Ann?"

"Legally?" She shook her head. "I doubt it, she's too clever to have left tracks. No, the best thing's just to take the lesson and learn it. A simple enough lesson—never put yourself in the hands of someone who loves your money more than they love you."

She took off the sunglasses, but kept the brim of her straw hat low. Despite everything, she still looked perfect, her hair tied back in a severe pony tail, her skin flawless. I thought of the first time I'd seen her at the farm, in tomboy mode—but that had been choice, this was disguise. It was hard, though, to think of America's Sweetest Sweetheart as the next best thing to a fugitive.

We looked out at the sunny town square. The small Illinois town of Edwardsville's annual Art Fair had pitched its neat rows of polite little tents around the fountain. Among the fashionable browsers, I could see at least three women dressed almost exactly as Rose had been on the casino table's *Vogue* cover. She saw them as well.

"What do you think? Would I make a passable Rose Vannier clone?"

Her voice couldn't hide its pain.

"How bad is it?" I asked.

"In money terms, I have no idea, Saul took care of all that. I'm just hoping there'll be enough to survive on. The rest...?" She shrugged. "People are taking a wrecking ball to my life, Alex. It doesn't feel good. I'd decided to leave it behind, anyway, you know that—but I didn't want to do it like this."

"What are you doing about Lou and Mattie?"

"That, at least, is sorted. They leave tonight, with John, he's good at disappearing. That's a skill we need, now. I can't have either of them at risk, they've suffered enough, they don't deserve to have their lives turned into the kind of three-ring circus this is going to become."

"And Sandy?"

"Just before you came, I texted her, told her to shut up shop. She's been trying to stem the tide, but it's useless. There's another apartment, back in DC. Nobody knows about it yet, Lee was supposed to move in there. She can rest up, try to heal. I think she needs it."

No longer indispensable... How would the English girl react to that...? *Exactly what had happened back at the hospital?* Beside me, Rose took a deep breath.

"When I heard about last night, when Sandy phoned me..." She stopped. "I was scared for you—for both you and John." She turned. "I'm scared for you now."

"And I'm scared for you. If me still being around resulted in getting you killed, or maimed... Or disfigured..."

There was silence—and then a high laugh forced itself out of her mouth. It was strange, manic.

"Rose—"

*"Christ!"*

The eruption of anger only lasted seconds, but the desperation of it shocked me. Fists clenched, she sat back on the seat. When I tried to speak again, she held up a shaking hand to stop me. I watched the tears run down her cheeks and remembered the barn back at the farm. Had her veneer of control always been so paper-thin?

And then I thought about myself, about the state I'd been in after the wrecked house... When she spoke again, her voice was toneless.

"John doesn't think it adds up. He's not convinced the text really came from O'Malley. Do you believe that?"

"I don't know," I said, quietly. "But whether it was from him or not, the text on Andy Aolfi's phone raises one huge question." I faced her. "How did whoever sent it know I was near the boy?"

The silence which descended was heavy; with doubt, with suspicion. Who knew we'd been hunting the boy...? Before either of us could find the courage to go further, there was a knock at the window beside me.

John.

He was holding up the khaki iPad Seth had given me.

*

The little screen seemed to be transmitting from the past, or at least from a more elegant version of the present. I saw an airy room, shafts of evening light warming the grain of dark wood. Bookcases? A library? Yes, I thought, an old-fashioned gentleman's library... In the foreground was a leather armchair. The screen darkened in confusion, and then a figure appeared and began settling himself. The camera finally focused on the face of a black-clad man with silver hair.

The face from the Ambassador Hotel...

The face from a black pickup on a Virginia back road...

Even through the device's tinny speakers, Jack O'Malley's voice sounded cultured, authoritative.

"You interest me, Fraser. Mostly, I try to steer clear of my fellow man. I don't like dullards or posers, and—apart from sex, of course—I'm by and large content with my own company. The exception comes when I meet someone I feel compelled to understand."

He sat back in the chair. Once again, the camera had to catch up.

"You are just such an exception. Since our paths crossed, I've made it my business to get to know your history, and there is, frankly, much in you to admire. Your persistence, for instance, your impulse to do what you think is the right thing without a thought for the consequences. Watching you tackle Mikey off the scooter..."

He paused. His eyes seemed to meet mine through the little screen. The conversational voice didn't change.

"The outcome was tragic," he said. "for you and me as well as for the kid. But the anger in you, that feral rage, that I can't help but like. Is it allied in some way to the music? Or is that just coincidence? That's a discussion I would have loved to have with you. In fact, if we'd met in some other way…" He laughed, easily. "…I might even have offered you a job. After all, we might be from different subspecies, but we're both outlaws, don't you agree?"

I felt the panic rise. *The obscenity of him…* How to escape it? The cultured voice went on.

"An avenger, that's what the animal in you keeps striving to be—that particular strain of bandit who's moulded by social injustice, but who then becomes more, much more. A *haiduk*—if I remember rightly, the term's Ukrainian. I recommend you E.H. Carr's book on the subject, perhaps you'll have enough time left to read it..." Again, he paused. "But we have to remember you're only a *haiduk* at your best, of course—the do-gooder in you, he's a tiresome distraction, holds you back, keeps you on the leash. Perhaps that's to do with the music as well," he mused, "it really would be interesting to explore it. But when you leave the knight errant behind, when you just let rip and the hell with the consequences, you're impressive. A killer by nature. Me, now," His voice became markedly more Irish. "I'm something much less complicated. It took fifty years and a lot of false starts for me to come to it, but I finally got there. To my own particular truth. To the fact that I'm a killer by *vocation.*" He gave a cold smile. "But of course, none of it really matters now, does it?"

Finally, he let his anger surface. He leaned forward.

"When it happens, it won't just be for my son, Fraser. If you'd died in the van in Wheeling, that would've been some kind of justice, an eye for an eye. But you didn't, and now you've crossed me once too often." His mouth broadened into a chilling smile. "You won't know where or when, you won't see it coming. For you, it'll be long and painful. For me..." The cold smile turned into a smug laugh. "...it'll be a pleasure."

The screen went black.

*

The three of us sat, very still. The Art Fair's tents had long since been folded away. John's voice came from the back seat.

"It hit your inbox about five hours ago," he said. "If Lou hadn't checked your iPad, no one would have seen it. It was an attachment to an email, to *steady@gmail.com.* You choose that address yourself, Fraser?"

I shook my head. "It came from the man who gave me the iPad. He can't be anything to do with this."

"Who else could have had access?"

I frowned, trying to think back. "When I went to Zion Junction," I began, slowly, "I didn't take the iPad with me."

Rose's voice came out of the darkness. "The trailer, at Demon's Lair. It wasn't locked. Sandy and I just walked in."

I shook my head. "If O'Malley was there, why would he have waited? He'd have killed me immediately."

"Which only leaves..." I heard worry find the deep voice behind me. "...the casino."

"It was with my bag while we were with Ann," I said, quietly. "I never touched the thing the entire time we were there."

The question hung in the car's darkness. *Could Jack O'Malley have penetrated all the security?*

It was Rose's turn to break the silence. "She's scared? Lou?"

The deep voice tried to soothe. "She'll beat it. She's a tough kid. Sure, seeing his face gave her a shock, but Mattie and I will work on her." Behind me, I heard its tone change. "Fraser. I owe you an apology. I really didn't believe the text on the boy's phone could be real. Now we know."

Rose's voice came again. "What should we do?"

John didn't hesitate. "Only one option. Nobody knows this car. You can get away clean, leave the rest of the circus behind. You have a head start—maximise it, grab it as quickly as you can. No cards, cash for everything—and we steal one leaf out of O'Malley's book. We don't use our normal phones or computers, too easy for either him or the press vultures to use as trackers. I'll go now, get you as many small denomination bills as I can lay my hands on—and a bunch of prepay phones, one for everybody, that way we can stay in touch. Once I've got Lou and Mattie safely stashed, I'll get to work. There has to be a way to get some kind of handle on this."

Rose and I let our eyes meet. The tightness that came into the big man's voice told me he'd noted it.

"As soon as I'm back, you go. You lose yourselves in the backwoods somewhere and keep your heads down." He paused. "And you take care of each other," he finished, softly.

# 17

# HARMONY

WE WERE ON THE road by midnight, the convertible's roof down, the slipstream bringing a blessed freshness as the car's ancient springs rocked us east along the arrow-straight blacktop. The Illinois map's blue highways sped us between waving walls of maize, ghostly in the moonlight, then led us at a snail's pace through deserted hamlets and one street towns. There wasn't a soul to be seen.

The only rule, we'd agreed, was to avoid the freeways—pursuit would be easier to spot on the lonely reaches of the back roads. We saw no headlights, but it was too soon for that to be any kind of comfort. All of it—O'Malley's film, the boy Andy's death, Ann Savoy's cynical betrayal—was still too raw. All we knew, without a word being said, was that we were running—but even though our eyes rarely met, we also both knew it wasn't from each other. It was a strange sensation, surreal, a prism filtering every perception. As my hands gripped the wheel, I wondered how much my life had changed.

*Alone…*

Was it still the only place I could stand to be?

The big Cadillac handled like a stately old boat, slow to turn, slow to accelerate, slower still to brake—and being virtually the only vehicle on the road made me slow to react. My concentration wandered. As I accelerated out of the township of Lebanon, I tried to work it all out. What would we need? Clothes? Food? It would take planning. If Rose's face was everywhere, I'd have to be the one who bought everything, we'd—

A brace of deer nearly paid for my distraction. I squealed to a halt and stared stupidly at their disappearing white rumps. I turned to find Rose looking at me, white-faced.

"Alex, you're out."

After the obligatory glance behind, she came round to the driver's side. I slid across the wide front seat.

"Here. For your head."

I took the sweater. As the car moved off again, I found myself enveloped in her perfume.

*No longer alone...*

*

I awoke to the sound of a stream and the sight of a green canopy of leaves shading the windscreen. Across from me, Rose was asleep, eyelids fluttering, a stray lock of blonde hair over one eye. I had a sudden urge to straighten it, to touch. Before I could do it, she woke.

"Where are we?" I asked.

"Farm track," she said, sleepily. "Somewhere just over the Indiana State Line, near the Wabash. We're just outside a place called New Harmony."

*New Harmony...*

The American sequel to New Lanark, the second of an enlightened mill owner's failed experiments in utopian socialism...

Without warning, I was eight years old again.

*My father's hand, heavy on my shoulder, the sound of my mother's heels as we walked along by the churning roar of the Falls of Clyde. His voice, patient, committed.*

*"...wisnae perfect, son, nothin' that depended on one man's sense o' justice ever could be, especially a man like Owen, who'd come frae privilege. But it was a start. Folks workin' here werenae treated like animals, they were given education and decent conditions, and they didnae have religion rammed doon their throats."*

*"You'll not poison the boy's mind, Andrew, not while I'm above ground."*

*"How could truth ever be poison, Mary? If the teachings of your Jesus mean anythin' at all, he'd've looked kindly on Robert Owen's Institute—mair kindly than on maist o' the pulpits raised in his name*

*across Scotland. Look around you and learn. Some day you'll see it. Some day the world'll see it."*

*His hand, rough and callused, ruffling my hair…*

*Hers, gloved and gentle, helping me over the stile…*

As I sat, humbled by the memory, Rose's voice came, tentative, wondering. "How come you've heard of New Harmony?"

"It has connections with Scotland. And with my memories. Of my parents."

Once more, she hesitated. "You want to tell me about them? Tell me about this place?"

It was my turn to hold back, but not for long. "There was a Welshman…" I began. "His name was Owen, Robert Owen."

*

We drove. And watched our back. And drove.

*Mt. Vernon, Madisonville…*

Of all the journeys I'd made since coming to this continent, the long day we now travelled into was the strangest.

*Paducah, Union City…*

A long day of twisting back roads through the Ozarks, of fast food bought hurriedly with averted eyes, of tattered maps and convoluted detours.

*Dyersburg, Humboldt…*

A long day of learning how to slip between the cracks of what America had let itself become.

*Beech Bluff, Scotts Hill…*

A long day of avoiding, at all costs, the screens and speakers, the relentless pumping out of prurient speculation.

*Hohenwald, Waynesboro…*

A long day of becoming accustomed to the inescapable nearness of each other.

Of learning boundaries.

Of learning when to skirt round them.

And, slowly, by halting trial and stumbling error, of learning when not to.

*

By the time darkness had fallen, we had see-sawed between silence and painful confidence, between catharsis and hands-on-the-wheel catatonia, for nearly twenty hours. My explanations of New Harmony and New Lanark had somehow let the floodgates open.

She told me more of the sunlit innocence of her childhood and adolescence, of the hardships of life with a baby before the break came, then of the ultimate heartbreak of being forced to deny her child. I found myself explaining my own life, expanding on the brutal potted history I'd given her the first night we'd met. It was something I'd never let out to another living soul apart from my father—the tale of my wife's betrayal, of how she died, the story of prison and my strange, windblown existence since. I even told her of my mother, of our estrangement, of my dread of her passing before I could at least attempt to make peace. We listened carefully, each remoulding our opinion of the other with every fresh revelation. Once in a while, the weight of confidence would become too much, and one of us would draw back. But gradually, the slow swing of the pendulum, resting longer and longer on its median of silence, ceased to threaten.

Once more, we didn't even consider stopping to find a bed. Fear of recognition was part of it, but there was also the unspoken pact between us.

The agreement that we were both scared.

*One room or two…*

An attraction to which both of us had given tacit admission…

A very real fear of the consequences if either of us, impelled by whatever lonely logic, gave in to it…

So, once again, we grabbed what rest we could on the Cadillac's bench seats, me in front, her behind. I lay, listening to exhaustion overtake her, hearing the whispered, childlike gabbles which escaped her as she subsided into troubled dream.

For me, though, sleep was impossible. The questions wouldn't quit. What did this woman mean to me? Could I make her fit into my life, could I ever be part of hers? I had always been in awe of physical beauty, and hers, limpid and pure, all but blinded me. Would chaos follow if I succumbed to it? It had always done so in the past. The music had been my first line of defence against the insanities I'd once surrendered to—but the restless nature I'd allowed to flourish along with it… Had it warped me, permanently? Was O'Malley's obscene little film, with its pinned butterfly assessment, right? Would some goad come that I couldn't control, that my innate rage would seize upon to wreak havoc?

Havoc that would kill any hope of love.

*Love...*

As I lay there, fingering the fiddle case's leather on the floor beside me, watching the first red fingers of dawn touch the long bonnet, the word seemed to write itself in letters of fire across the sky. Despite everything, I knew I still believed in it. Was I really close to the brink? And if I was…

*Take care of each other…*

The big Cherokee's voice seemed to haunt the old car. Were we rivals, now? Was I ready to face that? I stretched, got out of the car as quietly as I could, then reached back in for the fiddle. Cleaning her, that always helped me think…

The dawn chorus had begun. Fiddle in hand, I walked out into the middle of the narrow road and stood, listening. Why did it always seem to bring an echo? I watched the landscape solidify; trees, telegraph poles, the water breaking round the rocks of the Tennessee River…

And the surface of the road itself, winding its uneven way down towards the next settlement.

*Road. Open road…*

My hand tightened on the case's handle. Just me and the fiddle, nothing more to wonder about than what was round the next bend or over the horizon, how soon I'd find the right place to take her out and ply my trade… *Were those days gone forever?* A noise came from behind me.

Barefoot, dishevelled, hair tousled, one sleeve of her shirt rolled up, the other hanging loose…

I had never seen her more beautiful. The look she gave me began as a sleepy smile, but it became grave as she took in the case in my hand. Neither of us spoke.

*Love...*

Her phone rang.

*

Rose stood, the phone in her hand, a look of disbelief on her face. I heard John's faint voice at the other end, but then it drowned in her laughter.

It had its roots in the same hysteria I'd heard two days before, yet somehow it was a totally different thing. It rang out like a peal of bells, echoing effortlessly across the river—a thrilling sound, strong and clear enough to reach all the way to the rising sun. It was relief, I realised—and I also realised it was the first time I had ever known her truly happy. I wanted to prolong it, bask in it.

"John," she said, holding out the phone. "He needs to talk to you."

Still watching her, I took it. I had to force myself to concentrate on the deep rumble at my ear.

"Fraser? O'Malley's dead. His body came up in a trawl net three hours ago, out on Chesapeake Bay. Only a few miles away from where they found Lee."

I stared stupidly out at the river. "There's no doubt it's him?"

"None. His prints were on a lot of databases, FBI, police, at least a dozen states."

"How…?"

"As far as the local cops can tell, two shots in the back."

"How did you find out?"

"I have Saul's phone. Since Lee's death, he's had someone in the Virginia Beach P.D. on a retainer for anything which might be linked. We don't have details yet, we'll know more when the lab work's in."

The thoughts flew round my head. "Does this mean it's safe to surface?"

The pause at the other end was a bare heartbeat long. "Does Rose want to?"

Her laughter reached me again. Could he hear it?

"I don't know."

I heard him retreat. "I'll know more when I get to Virginia. Till then…"

Again, a pause. Once more, just like two nights before, I heard what it cost him to say the words.

"…stay lost."

*

The food—fruit, cheese, ham and fresh bread—was delicious. We'd taken a chance, driven into the town of Stantonville and found a market. We'd had a gentle, good-natured tussle over whether her baseball cap and sunglasses disguise was riskier than my hopeless attempts at an American accent. She had won. Now we sat, eating in the quiet sunshine on a cypress-shaded wooden bench. The pristine white marble of the Confederate Army's Shiloh battlefield monument was less than a hundred yards away, its bronze figures glinting in the sunlight. We were alone. I gestured down at the pile of tabloids she'd bought.

"Page four, now. How much longer before they stop caring?"

She wiped at her mouth with a napkin, but she didn't reply. I watched her hands tear another lump from the sourdough loaf, then fall to her lap.

"Alex," she said, softly. "I don't want to think about that yet. Any of it. It's enough to know the people I care about are safe. John said we should stay lost..."

Head down, she hesitated. When the request came, it was made with great dignity.

"Could we do that? Steal some time, enjoy not being scared? Just for a few days more, before it all starts getting complicated again?"

She paused. It took her a long time to work up the courage to finish.

"I'd like us just to be together," she said, quietly, "whichever way we want to be. While we still can." Once more, she paused. "Before choices have to be made."

*Choices...* The ache in her voice made sad poetry of the word. How much had the last few days cost her?

"Please, Alex."

I had an answer. Would it be the right one?

"There's one thing I still have to do—*need* to do," I said. "It's for my mother. It would mean more driving. Back to where you found me. Back to Arkansas."

Eyes closed, she exhaled, slowly. In relief? In gratitude? She nodded her agreement.

And then, without warning, something about the decision we'd just come to changed things. By mutual consent we turned away from one another. As we finished our food, I wondered what had just happened. Why were we both suddenly acting as though we'd consented to something shameful...?

I found my eyes drawn to the monument, to the figure of a gunner, still peering through the smoke which had covered this field a century and a half before. His hands were shading his eyes. He was searching for his enemies. I was doing the same, I knew, but the battlefield was different; my own thoughts...

*Where had the sudden strangeness between us come from?*

Was it to do with me, standing with the fiddle in my hand in the dawn light, looking down the road? Or was it about America's rabid confessional soul and its savage pursuit of her…?

Her hand found mine. The closeness it promised was everything. But the questions wouldn't leave me.

Did dodging Jack O'Malley's bullet mean we had avoided something?

*Or had we just postponed it?*

# 18

# AFTERLIFE

THE SLOPE BEHIND Zion Baptist Church stretched a long way up from the town's edge. Did the graves stop at the hill's top, or did they continue down the other side? I stood, breathing in the smell, that pungent blend of cut grass and spent fuel which would always bring back the Scottish lowland summers of my youth. I could hear the mower, but the echoes of the hills robbed it of direction.

Rose was already walking along the first row of stones. There seemed to be no particular chronological order, new white marble stepping into the gapped ranks of old grey granite to replace the fallen. Was that to do with the location? Open ground which held enough soil to bury—among mountains, it would be at a premium… The late afternoon sun was still strong. She called to me.

"Do you have any idea where?"

I shook my head. "I'm not even sure he's actually here, this is just the one church she mentioned. But for all I know it could be anywhere, maybe even a private plot."

She paused. "My fault," she said. "I'm sorry. I dragged you back into my mess before you could look."

We shared a quiet smile. The awkwardness between us had dissipated. Blame was something we had both left behind.

"All I know," I said, "is that I need some evidence of what happened to him. For my mother."

It was odd, saying the last three words out loud... Rose nodded, briskly.

"You take the left side, I'll take the right."

I watched her stride away. She was changed since John's call. When would he phone again? Once more, the question which had dogged me since Shiloh surfaced. *How long could we hide from the future?* Once more, I could find no answer. I turned my attention back to the headstones.

Five hundred graves? Six hundred…? More…? How long before dark...?

*

After the long days in the car, stretching limbs up through the hill's mown grass was pleasant enough. Occasionally, an inscription stopped me. They ranged from the arcane…

*John Jacob McFarlane 1822-1868*
*Angry with You to the last, Lord*
*Please forgive him*

…to the wry…

*Faith Keller 1895-1972*
*Always said she'd go first, never believed her*

…to the downright heartbreaking.

*Mercy Selby, Carl Selby 1934-35*
*Our Angels Have Folded Their Wings To Lie With Jesus*

Was Rose finding her own harvest of poetry? I looked across. She was lower down on the hill, slower than I was. Why did that surprise me? I saw her examine a stone closely, then move on and peer at another, her eyes barely inches from the surface.

Odd…

And then memory clicked in—the first night, in DC, she'd peered at me, closely… And again in the barn at Gallant Fox, and a few times since... The realisation brought a faint smile. America's Sweetest Sweetheart needed spectacles. I began to move on, the thought idling in my mind; with all the entourage around her, why hadn't someone taken care of that? Or had it been part of Ann Savoy's veto…?

Speculation died as I resumed my climb. Swatting away the insects, I trudged up past the memorials of Jamiesons and Caltons and Dalziels and Mowbrays, past stark anonymous crosses, past Masonic skull-and-crossbones epitaphs long since crumbled to grim illegibility, past simple flat stones set in the ground by families too poor to afford more than a rough chiselling of name and date. And then I came to Ezra Salter McClintock.

I stared at the chipped stone, canted over at a precarious forty-five degree angle.

McClintock…

*Jane.*

Would I see ever her again? Or Seth? A flashback came, *The Hawk That Swoops On High*, following me on the wind as I left Chimney Holler... Up on the high bluff above the Mississippi, I'd played it well, I knew, but her rendition of it, so fine and strong, so personal—that was, and always would be, unsurpassed.

"Alex!"

The urgency in Rose's voice brought me back. She was pointing to a large white plinth with a wrought iron railing round it. I ran across to her side.

*The Very Reverend George MacBeth*
*1934-2006*
*Pastor, Friend, Beloved Husband*
*Taken Before His Time*
*Founder KZTX Christian Radio*
*No Man Did More For The Lord*

The raw rush of emotion ambushed me. I stood, defenceless against it, numbed. It was Rose who broke my trance, first with the click of the camera on her phone, then with one simple sentence which pulled together all my confusions.

"Do you wish you'd known him?"

Before I could answer, the mower crested the hill. It slalomed down through the stones with the ease of long familiarity, then skidded to a halt beside us. The driver killed the engine, took off headphones and cap, then shook loose his white locks.

*Reuben.*

The old man from the radio station… By the time he'd geared

himself up to speak, I knew he was drunk as a lord.

"George! Couldn't keep away, huh?" Laughing, he swivelled round to pull his beer can from its holder in the mower's side. It was too much for his balance. He toppled from the seat and landed heavily on the grass, still laughing. As I tried to help him up, the laughter gave way to a suspicious scowl. It lasted until Rose lifted his other arm—and then, as he took her in, it morphed into a sly grin. He shook us both loose. A finger came up, wagged at me.

"An' with a purty lady, too! Lillian sure ain't gonna like that, George! Ain't gonna like that one li'l bit!"

"I'm not George, Reuben."

He scowled again, then turned away and spat. I watched the light die in his eyes. He shook his head, sorrowfully.

"Guess you're not at that, mister, guess you're not. So whatcha doin' here, the cemetery?"

"I'm George's nephew. From Scotland. I'm here to take a picture of his grave to show my mother. George's sister."

He made it to his feet, brushed off the grass, then got back on the mower. "You was at the station, I remember, now," he said, pleased with himself. "You're the Scotch fella give Lillian the heebies."

And then, without warning, he threw back his head and started laughing again, a long, uproarious cackle. He turned the key. The mower's engine burst into life. His laughter culminated in a joyful shout.

*"An' you think ol' George is dead, doncha!"*

*

The Shack was a down-at-heel wooden box with a much-mended door and a brace of taped-together beer pumps. The smell was cigarettes and sweat and alcohol. It was deserted, silent except for a distant whine of country music and the ticking of the Smokey The Bear clock on the wall. Only the minute hand moved, endlessly retracing the hour after midnight. Reuben burped, then emptied his shot glass in one. As the elderly redhead who'd been serving us for the last hour came out of the back room, he pushed it across at me. I watched her replace the ancient phone on its cradle, then lift her cloth and resume her wiping of the counter. When I gestured, she nodded. I turned back to the old man, determined to keep trying.

"I was told George died in a flash flood."

Reuben eyed me, warily. Once he'd reassured himself that the bourbon bottle was on its way, he forced out an edgy laugh.

"Sure, sure," he said. "A flash flood, ev'rybody knows that."

The nervousness in his voice was obvious. I fought for calm. Which was true? What he'd said in the cemetery? Or what he was telling me now…?

*Could George MacBeth still be alive?*

Was it possible—or had I just caught the tail end of an old drunk's fantasy? Whichever it was, in the hour since I'd tracked Reuben here, this tantalising choice of truths was as far as I'd got. As the woman's cheap perfume enveloped us again, his laughter turned to leer. I watched his eyes fasten on her breasts, then saw his fingers ride up the inside of her skirt. Without pausing in her pouring, her free hand swatted him away. With no great urgency, I noted. She stoppered the bottle. As she turned, he watched her rear and gave the sight the tribute of another belch. Outside, a car pulled up on the gravel. His brows came together in concentration.

"Gotta use the outhouse. Siphon the python," he said.

The woman snorted. Her voice was cruel.

"Wishful drinkin' again? Last time that worm o' yours was a python, the Kennedy boys were still checkin' out Marilyn's ass."

He ignored her, downed the bourbon in one, then staggered to his feet. The sleeve of his woollen shirt caught the empty glass. It shattered on the floor.

"That's your last," the redhead called after him as he stumbled through the swing door which led to the toilet.

"Fuck you, Lorraine," he shouted back.

She faced me. "Third shot glass this week, useless ol' bastard. What's a young fella like you doin' buyin' him liquor?"

The circular motion of the cloth was hypnotic. As I watched it, a cold certainty came to me; the question was more than just casual.

*How careful did I have to be, here…?*

I looked out of the open window, to the Cadillac across the street. Rose, her face masked by the inevitable sunglasses, was behind the wheel. I heard the toilet flush, then heard Reuben's unsteady shuffle.

*Moving away from me.*

Three strides took me across the room. I pushed the swing door open, then the steel one that led out to the parking lot. The big mower blocked my way—but I was still in time to see tail lights disappear round the next bend. I ran back inside. The cloth was still circling the counter top.

"Who did you phone?" I asked, harshly.

She went on wiping. I brought my hand down on hers. She made no effort to remove it. When she finally spoke, it was in a measured southern drawl.

"We take care of our own round here, mister. My husband might be a mangy ol' drunk, but he's *my* mangy ol' drunk, nobody else's. Don't exactly know what you were hangin' round him for, but my guess is, it's time you were gone. Reuben's got friends, here, good friends. The kind wouldn't take kindly to anyone puttin' the arm on him jus' 'cause he runs off at the mouth a little."

She freed her hand from my grip. As the hypnotic wiping began again, I heard the siren in the distance. She didn't look at me as I strode through the door.

I ran for the Cadillac.

*

*ZION JUNCTION*
*POPULATION 2714*
*THE LORD LIVES HERE!*

We sat in the layby where I'd finally achieved sleep after my first encounter with God's home in Appalachia. The moonlight made a pale sculpture of Rose's hands on the steering wheel.

"You really think he could still be alive?"

Had the man ever been alive to me? Ever been real? *A phantasm, a creased snapshot…*

"I never even knew he existed until a few weeks ago," I said. "All I know is, I can't ignore the chance that he might be."

"Why?"

I reached into my jacket pocket, took out the envelope and handed it to her. I watched her face as the reality of the photograph hit her. As she looked across at me, her expression was caught between wonder and alarm.

"Read my father's letter. It explains things better than I ever could."

When she'd finished, she folded everything carefully away and put the bundle down on the seat between us.

"I know this isn't what either of us expected," I said, softly. "Or wanted. But it's not your problem. If—"

The sound of the siren, nearer now, stopped me. As it faded away into the mountain echo, she reached for the starter. As she pulled us out on to the road, tyres squealing, I saw the determination in her eyes.

*

The house on Gethsemane Trail was a developer's idea of what nineteenth century Colonial might aspire to on a twenty-first century budget. Cramped and colonnaded, it looked like what it was—a sad attempt to gentrify an unremarkable brick box. The crossed flags of the United States and the Confederacy hung limply above a doorway that would never be quite grand or gracious enough, and the bulky air conditioning units, running at full tilt on the upstairs windows, rendered any pretensions to antiquity ridiculous. In the darkness, the building's security lights pulsed a steady red rhythm behind the misted fans of spray which arced over the grass. A small spotlight lit up the mailbox at the bottom of the driveway. Beside it, the iron lawn jockey's smile gleamed a nervous white, as though he acknowledged the fact that sprinklers had replaced slaves, but he wasn't convinced it was permanent.

The open double garage was almost as big as the house. It would have accommodated half a dozen plantation owners' carriages, but now its sole occupant was the massive SUV I remembered from the radio station. I was sure it wasn't the vehicle which had spirited Reuben away from the Shack, but that was all I was sure of. My eyes kept coming back to the luminous scarlet script on the plastic stake by the mailbox.

*ARMED RESPONSE*

Just how literal might that be…? And if the police were now on our case, as the sirens had indicated, how long before the trail of our logic brought them here? Rose's whisper came from beside me.

"What now?"

What indeed…? How solid was my reasoning? Mentally, I went over it again.

She was Reuben's employer.

I'd been quizzing Reuben about her husband's death.

The phone call from The Shack meant my probing was a problem to someone—someone with enough clout for the cops not just to respond, but to respond *immediately*.

That meant a prominent citizen, I was sure, a pillar of society… Who was that pillar most likely to be…?

It had to be the grieving widow.

As though triggered by the thought, the front door opened. A figure sidled out, small, slim, wearing a grey headscarf and a raincoat with the collar up. One gloved hand held a small bag. As she headed for the garage, I realised I was looking at Lillian Macbeth. Rose's voice came again.

"Does she always dress like that?"

"Like what?"

"Like an extra in a bad TV cop show."

We watched the woman hoist herself into the SUV's driving seat, turn the rear view mirror to face her, then lift something black to her face.

Sunglasses.

Rose's voice was dry. "Pretty much clinches it, I'd say."

We watched the headlights come down the driveway, then turn. As soon as the vehicle had passed the clearing where we were parked, she started the Cadillac.

"Shades, past midnight. Something going on, definitely."

I watched the tail lights speed away towards the centre of Zion Junction. As the Eldorado's ancient springs bounced us out on to the road, I saw the ghost of a smile find Rose's mouth.

"Sunglasses *and* disguise," she said. "Not too much anyone can teach me about that combination."

*

Unlike the Demon's Lair caravan park, the Mountaineer Lodge, ten miles further down the freeway, had definitely seen better days. It was dark and desolate, its cheap sixties panelling cracked and peeling, its pastel green facade obscured by a row of dilapidated dumpsters with a sad penumbra of litter. The only constant light was from the office, where the window's stuck-on lettering had lost the first two letters of the word *ROOMS*. Beside it, a small neon sign alternated between the legends *Cabins, Suites* and *Weekly Rates*. We watched Lillian MacBeth's SUV come to a halt beside it. As we drove past, she got out, but she didn't give the Cadillac a second glance. Rose swerved gently to avoid an abandoned patent leather handbag, lying beside a crushed lipstick and a discarded vodka bottle.

"So," she said, "the No Tell Motel."

I reached for the door handle. Her hand came down on my arm.

"No point giving ourselves away. She has to be meeting someone. Easier to wait, see who."

"And if we lose her?"

"A rig like that in a dump like this? Even if we did miss her, a few bucks slipped to the clerk would get us the cabin number. Trust me, Alex, I know these places."

The expensive purr of the SUV's engine made it academic. Once it had passed us, Rose followed. As our lights yawed across the potholes, they showed us the sad state of the cabins. Even danker and dirtier than the main building, their disrepair was regimented in barrack-like lines, lifeless and dispiriting. Our slow patrol revealed only clumped weeds, darkness and decay.

We found the big SUV in the last row. It stood halfway down, its perfect coachwork a reproach to its unkempt surroundings. Rose turned the Cadillac, then backed away as far away as she could, to the tarmac's perimeter. Once she'd killed the headlamps, the only light was a thin glow from the window facing the four wheel drive's vast bonnet.

"Alex."

Another engine was approaching. She grabbed me, pulled me down. The lights swept over us. I felt the heat of her body as we held each other. Finally, I dared a look.

A police cruiser. Once it had negotiated the chicane of potholes, it pulled up beside the SUV. Two officers, bulky in kevlar vests, got out. The room door opened on the first knock. Lillian MacBeth appeared, backlit by the glow. Sunglasses and headscarf had been discarded, but she was still wearing her coat. We were too far away to hear, but instructions were obviously given—and pleasantries exchanged. A faint peal of laughter reached us. I watched her unlock the room next to her own. Then the bigger of the two cops opened the cruiser's back door. With his colleague, he began pulling at something. The figure of Reuben, barely able to stand, appeared. I heard a snatch of drunken song as he was manhandled into the newly opened cabin, followed by more laughter. A few moments later, the two policemen emerged again. Leaning against the door jamb, the director of KZTX Christian Radio handed each man an envelope. I watched them nod their thanks. She waved them off and closed her door.

The silence in the Cadillac was oppressive. I came to a decision.

"It has to be now," I said. "I think we just saw two policemen being paid off for delivering Reuben. I've no idea what this woman's got in mind for him, but I'd hate to gamble on what comes next."

Rose nodded her agreement. "I'll go, she doesn't know me. I can—"

"No," I said.

She turned to me, brows creased. "Alex, I'm not just along for the ride," she said.

Before she could speak again I took both her hands in mine. "Think about what's happened to you in the last few days. Think about the tabloids. You saw these cops. If that kind of transaction's the norm here, do you think anyone's going to pass up ready money for a two-minute phone call? *Think*, Rose. One whiff of your involvement…"

The stubborn resolve didn't leave her face.

"If not for your own sake, then for Lou and Mattie's," I said. "Stay, be ready to move. We have no idea what we're dealing with yet, we might need to disappear. Fast."

After a long pause, she gave a reluctant nod.

And then, without warning, she reached over and pulled me to her.

*

The kiss, fierce and urgent, sexless, made an unreal blur of my walk towards the cabin. Only when I reached it did something approaching detachment find me.

They hadn't even bothered to close Reuben's door. The television was on. I stood, watching, listening. It was an old movie, but the figure on the bed wasn't interested in Humphrey Bogart or the African Queen. He was sprawled, fully clothed, snoring sonorously into his baseball cap. A line of drool hung from his mouth, and the reek of alcohol from him was laced with the sour smell of vomit. I went on to the next door. Hers.

No noise here, none at all. The light escaping beneath the curtains was soft. As I got down on my knees, a small lizard scurried away. I tried to look inside, but the angle made it impossible. I had no choice. Carefully, I tried the door. Unlocked.

I pushed it open.

*

Lillian MacBeth, hairbrush in hand, saw me immediately in her dressing table mirror. Her eyes widened, but only for a second—and then they seemed to glaze over. Her mouth shaped itself into a half smile. She made no attempt to hide it. Her hand brought the brush down, slowly, then exchanged it for the lit cigarette which lay among the mess of make up and perfume. Once she'd taken a long drag, she exhaled. The sound was something between release and sigh. She put the cigarette down on the table's edge, carefully, then bestowed a satisfied smile on her reflection before turning to me. Slowly, she crossed her legs. The silk sheen of her slip rippled with the movement. It took me a millisecond to understand that it was all deliberate.

*Sex…*

The wave of revulsion that washed over me was visceral. I couldn't keep it from my face. She laughed, then swivelled sinuously back round to the mirror, lifted a powder puff, angled her head to one side and began dabbing at her cheek. When her voice came it was playful.

"Not bad for an old broad, Fraser, don't you think? Caught the Adam in you, admit it—fired you up there, had you goin'. Had you goin' *real good."*

The last two words were a leisurely parody of seduction. She waited for me to respond. When I didn't, it tipped banter over into scorn. She shook her head.

"Just like him. Same reaction, same tightass bullshit."

As she reached for her lipstick, she laughed again. The sound was brittle, bitter.

"All here waitin' for him, wet an' willin', perfumed an' gift wrapped, an' he didn't even have the guts to pull the goddam ribbon."

The casualness of her contempt was chilling. The chaste kiss in the Cadillac, a bare hundred yards behind me, might have been a hundred years ago. When I spoke, I didn't recognise my own voice.

"So it was a lie. Everything you told me."

She shook her head. "Not a word of it. I was crazy 'bout the man, he could've had me a dozen times a day—on the desk, up against the wall, in the flower beds, Jesus be damned." She leaned into the mirror, began applying the lipstick. "'Cept Jesus was the problem, wasn't he? Far as George was concerned, gettin' it up for me—pardon my French—came a long way behind gettin' it up for the Lord."

She pursed her lips, admired the effect, then caught my eye again. Then she went back to sharing her self-congratulatory smile with her reflection.

"Oh, don't get me wrong, I got his Christian duty out of him, once in a blue moon. But it was always a chore, never a joy. At first I thought he might be queer, but then I realised he just didn't care. You the same?" Her finger rubbed at an invisible flaw on her cheek. "Another highland hunk, scared of sex? Runs in families, that kinda thing, doesn't it? Guess all the stuff we found out about you points that way." Again she smiled at herself. "Killin' your wife to get out of fuckin' her, though, I'd say that was a little drastic—though I do confess it made me wonder if George ever thought 'bout killin' me."

She leaned down, arched one foot delicately into a high-heeled black shoe, then repeated the operation with the other. Then she stood up, smoothed her slip, lifted the cigarette, leaned back against the dressing table and held up her right arm with her left. I watched the smoke curl up into her hair.

*Déjà vu… The sick room in the radio station, the same pose…*

Just a different costume. Her smile took on an edge of mockery as she misread my gaze.

"Stare all you want, Fraser, take a damn good look. Wanna fool around some? Try out sex with a senior?" She laughed, tossed her hair. "Hell, you're so like him it'd be like old times."

Was she serious? *Was she mad?* Once again, my silence broke her pose. She stubbed out the cigarette, viciously.

"You prick," she said, conversationally. "Standin' there, all smug an' buttoned up in your righteous little Scotch conscience.

You've no idea what it was like, have you?" She pushed herself off the table's edge. "Workin' night an' day, scrimpin', savin', fixin' the smile on your face to deal with every Baptist asshole came crawlin' outta the woodwork. Sweet talkin' every miserable store owner who thought Jesus owed him a grab at my ass along with a cut rate on his ads. Or sweepin' out the needles every week after the teenage junkie prayer breakfast, or gettin' the poison pen letters 'bout wearin' too much make-up." Two steps brought her across to me. "I did damn near thirty years of it—thirty years of scrapin' the dregs, bein' polite to redneck retards, smilin' at every kind of trailer park trash you can think of. Writin' idiot copy for rodent exterminators an' drain cleaners, promisin' the creditors another ten cents on the dollar next month." Her perfume enveloped me, heavy, cloying. "Why did I do it, Fraser?"

I said nothing. Once more it fuelled her anger.

"Because if I couldn't have George MacBeth the way I wanted him, *I was at least goin' to have what the bastard owed me!* I knew what I was worth! So I fought! Long 'n' hard 'n' dirty! I scrambled us up every damn toehold I could find to heave us outta the backwoods an' get KZTX accepted where it mattered. Do you have any idea what that took? What it cost?" She laid the flat of her hand against my chest. "An' then, when we're finally close, when we're just about respectable enough to get ourselves invited to the top table—the corporates, the big money boys up in Nashville, what does George MacBeth do? Good ol' Reverend George, conscience of the county, scourge of the backsliders, the preacher with the direct line to the Almighty! He decides to throw it all away! And why?"

She was shaking, now. Her mouth twisted itself into a thin line of scarlet fury.

"Because a goddamn snake bit him, up in the mountains! Because he survived—*an' because he finally had the excuse he needed to go crazy.*"

Her hands were gripping my shirt, now. The voice became a hectoring sneer.

"That's what he wrote me! What the *Lord* told him! *Leave it all behind, George, it's all the work of the devil! Go back into the mountains, George, test your faith! None of it matters, George! Renounce it all!*"

I broke her grip, pushed her away. She took a step back, swaying. Then, as though nothing had happened, she resumed her place at the dressing table and began examining her face again. Her voice returned to its matter-of-fact speculation.

"Would've been better if the rattler had just killed him. Or the coyotes."

Behind me, the door opened. "Didn't have no Moët, darlin', it'll have to be Californian. I—"

Josh. Security Josh. Tie askew, mouth open, he stared at me—and then his jaw tightened. I saw the champagne bottle become a club in his fist, swing up.

The camera flash whirled him round. In the doorway, Rose didn't flinch, just went on taking pictures with her phone.

"Gimme that!" he shouted, lunging at her. "Gimme that *right now!*"

She held up a hand. "Back off," she said, calmly. "Even if you get me with the bottle, it won't stop me pressing *send.* Straight to social media." She nodded at the older woman. "Your girlfriend can be a pinup on Instagram by morning if you want. Sixty million people, maybe more. Your choice."

The standoff's tension dissipated, slowly. The bottle began to come down. Confusion ruled his face as he turned to Lillian MacBeth. Shock had drained her of colour.

"Over there," Rose said. "On the bed. Both of you."

They obeyed. She came into the light at my side. I watched recognition claim them both—and then, as though the sight of her had exposed them to some strange magic, they seemed to diminish, to crumple into something smaller. What had achieved that?

Resolve? Courage? Beauty…?

No, I thought, none of these things, not here, not in America. There was only one thing which held such power in this strange country.

*Celebrity…*

I stared at them; Josh, still holding the bottle, avoiding Rose's gaze in obvious shame, Lillian MacBeth, arms folded protectively over her sagging bosom, staring catatonically down at the carpet. The memory of my mother's face claimed me, its sad auburn-framed beauty, her hands clasped before it in prayer. When the vision cleared, I saw only the sad thing that was Lillian MacBeth.

"The letters," I said. "Why did you send them back?"

Her head whipped up, the face twisted once more in scorn. Her body began to tremble. It was as though she'd been switched on again.

"Because he was *mine!"* The words were a hiss of venom. "No matter what he'd turned into! He didn't belong to the Lord, he didn't belong to Zion Junction, or his dumb sister—he belonged to *me!* He was *mine!"*

She was quivering with rage. Her gaze went back to Rose.

And read the pity in her eyes.

The spasm of shaking intensified. Was she going to break? Collapse? Slowly, the anger retreated from her features, until her face was completely without expression. She got to her feet. Two slow, robotic steps took her back to the dressing table. She sat. Jerkily, she angled her face away from the glass. Then she lifted the powder puff and began dabbing at her cheek.

"My uncle," I said. "Tell me where he is."

Silence. The only sound was the gentle snoring from the next room. The powder puff never stopped. Her face was vacant now, a death mask, a painted skull. It was Josh who spoke.

"The ol' bastard next door," he mumbled. "Ask him. He's the one took him there."

# 19

# DIAMONDBACK

THE HIGH, SLOPING edge of the spoil heap was like the wall of some separate domain, doomed and defiant, its colour an ominous darkness that was somehow deeper than black. The pines kept their distance. A furred expanse of yellow and green lichens reached out towards them from the forbidding rampart, a cankered no-man's-land of colour, strange and sickly. The bright orange pools which dotted it looked poisonous, more like a mixture of bile and blood than water. As I surveyed it all, the fiddle case felt odd in my hand, uncomfortable. It was as though the instrument knew there was something wrong with this place—badly wrong. My free hand reached for the pocket which held my other talisman, my mother's letter. I fingered the envelope's surface, but I didn't take it out. Was this the end of the road? Could he really be here? Could I deliver it at last?

The drive here had given me time for reflection, but it hadn't prepared me for what I was facing now. I watched a rusty car with a dangling headlamp bounce along the track that led to the largest of the pools, then line itself up with the two dilapidated vehicles already there. A man and a woman got out. From the back seat they brought out matching cowboy hats. Once they'd been donned, two large oblong instrument cases came out. Guitars? Electric guitars? As Reuben's hand pushed me down, further out of sight, they began to trudge up the narrow track towards the black mountain. Somehow the sight of them added to the unreality.

My uncle—my mother's brother...

In *this?*

For it felt beyond bizarre; to have quit the grim, gutted Scottish pit village of Fallin over half a century ago in search of a better life, only to end here, embedded in the diseased dross of a different continent's hunt for riches...

The Diamondback Mine.

A stirring of wind blew the rancid reek of the place in our direction. Reuben's voice, low and conspiratorial, answered my unasked question as we lay in the shadow of the trees.

"Sulphur. Pyrites. Residues, crap that weren't never pumped out when they stopped workin' 'er. Acid, most of it. Dangerous."

"If it's dangerous, why did you bring him here?"

He eyed me levelly. His chin came up, stubborn, unapologetic.

"No place else to take him—leastways, no place he was willin' to go." He waved a hand at the spoil heap. "Still belongs to him, all this. Diamondback come to him through his first wife. Couldn't sell it, weren't nobody dumb enough to buy—cain't be developed or built on, too polluted, too many workin's. Shafts weren't never prop'ly mapped, subsides all the time. No warnin'."

"Does *she* know he's here?"

He nodded. "Told her a week after the service, once I was sure I had him safe. She called me a liar, cussed me six ways to hell 'n' back. Then I give her the letter, the one told her he wasn't the Reverend MacBeth no more. When I put the watch down on her desk she went crazy, rantin', screamin' at me. Accused me of killin' him myself—till I showed her the photo." He laughed. "His head was still all bandaged up, but he was recognisable—an' he was holdin' the front page o' the Gazette, dated the day o' his so-called funeral. That shut her up," he said, with satisfaction. "An' after all the playactin' was done, all the lace kerchiefs an' lies an' fake tears, it suited her just fine to leave him dead—all that good ol' Nashville syndication comin' down the pike, all that top dollar piety—couldn't have no crazy Scotch preacher wreckin' that, no sir." He shook his head. "Money." Once again, his stubbled jaw found its stubborn set. "Money an' sex. She'd hated him for years, on account o' both. I knew it, but till that day, I never understood how hard it ran her. Never did find out what was in the casket they buried, neither." He stopped, embarrassed by the extent of his revelations. "Anyway," he mumbled finally. "there was no way they could afford to let folks know he was still alive."

"Who's *they?"*

"Her an' that slimy bastard Hart—Josh. Real prick, screw anythin' that moves, steal anythin' ain't nailed down. Shake his hand, count your fingers."

Josh.

An edge of worry added itself to my unease.

*Rose…*

Because we couldn't trust the police, she was still at the motel, guarding the two lovebirds in case they tried anything. Had I been wrong to ask her to do it? Could I have found another way? As I wondered, a subtle change came over the wind. It took a second to coalesce into sound, another for me to identify it as music.

The faint but unmistakable swell of an organ.

*The Mingulay Boat Song…*

The song known to every Scottish school child, a very close relative of *The Hawk That Swoops On High…*

"Ol' Brattleboro harmonium," Reuben said. "I mended the pedals an' patched up the bellows for him. He still likes to play. Means he's gettin' ready to begin,"

I barely heard his words. The eerie sound went on, stealing the present from me.

*The road to Gallant Fox Farm, the circling bird…*

*The high trail from Chimney Holler, the tune reaching up through the pines…*

*The bluff above the Mississippi, my fingers fighting despair…*

And then the melody changed. It became the fine air called *Monksgate,* the tune of John Bunyan's hymn, *Who Would True Valour See…*

Valour... It was a validation. I smiled. Once again, I found Reuben's eyes on me, wary—wondering, no doubt, if I'd lost my reason entirely. I couldn't blame him. I turned again to the black mountain.

*No one else would ever understand,* I knew. *No one could…*

Jane McClintock...

Rose Vannier…

I could think of no better examples of true valour than the

fiddler who'd saved my sanity, or America's Sweetest Sweetheart.

*

An hour later, my nerves were ragged from inaction, but the old man would brook no argument, we had to wait. As we watched the steady stream of cars and people. the wind-borne melodies eddied round us. So soft, so fragile…

*By Cool Siloam's Shady Rill. Over The Sea To Skye. Mine Eyes Have Seen The Glory Of The Coming Of The Lord. Jerusalem. Will Your Anchor Hold In The Storms Of Life. Lead, Kindly Light. The Lord's My Shepherd. Abide With Me. The Dark Island. Amazing Grace…*

Every one of them was a different ghost from my childhood. The hymns and psalms had been the battlegrounds of my mother's godly hopes and my father's atheist scorn, the secular tunes had been their treaties of reconciliation. Reuben's voice was like an elegiac counterpoint to it all.

"What he does here, it started out honest, you have to believe that, Mister Fraser. It's been taken over, now—*he's* been taken over. Seduced—by all the razzamataz, the music 'n' lights 'n' show. Never thought he'd have any truck with that, always thought he was anchored in the ol' ways, the ol' sermons. The ol' certainties, I suppose." He turned to me. "He ain't part of any reg'lar church—Pentecostal, Baptist, nothin' like that. Says he knows what's holy an' what ain't, the good book keeps him straighter 'n' any deacon or presbytery. But the crazies, they got their hooks into him all right, there's no denyin' it."

"Is it illegal?"

"Far's the law's concerned, borderline—though they been tryin' to stamp it out for more 'n' half a century now. Hunnerd buck fine over in Kentucky. Still legal up in West Virginia, no place else I know."

We watched the steady stream of humanity, men, women and children, heading slowly along the dirt track.

"Who are these people, Reuben?"

He didn't answer me directly. "Always been a faith for poor folks, this—poor *white* folks. The mix'll be the usual—most'll be genuine believers. Then there'll be the inbreds, a few thrill seekers, an' a few plain ol' mountain madmen—Appalachia's got its fill o' that partic'lar clan, all right. But there's some who're different. Paranoid."

The echo of a slammed car door reached us. He nodded down at the skinny young man who'd emerged from it. His baseball cap was on backwards, but a businesslike rifle hung over his shoulder.

"Paranoid an' *violent.*" He snorted in disgust. "They catch you, they suspect you're a fed or a reporter, you're dead in a heartbeat, your body down a shaft so deep nobody'd ever find it. That's why you don't go near him till after the service's done, till you're sure every one o' them rustbuckets down there's gone. Even then, you gotta be real careful." He faced me. "You still ain't told me what you want from him."

I examined him in my turn. The liver-spotted hands were shaking. How badly did he need a drink? He was an alcoholic, that was obvious—it had taken a day after his deliverance from Lillian MacBeth to sober him up. But alcoholic or not, Reuben sober was a very different proposition to Reuben drunk. I scrutinised every inch of the battered face beneath the white locks; the sunken cheeks, the rheumy eyes, the broken-veined nose... He met my gaze calmly. No matter what his demons were, I knew I was looking at a man who'd retained, in this one respect at least, his decency. I also knew he was as determined as he was dignified.

"First you have to tell me something," I said. "Is he sane?

It took a long time for the reply to come. "When I found George," he said, slowly, "he was as near dead's makes no difference. Snake'd almost done for him—no surprise there, timber rattlers where he was walkin' were huge, ev'rybody knew. How in hell he'd managed to fight off the coyotes after the bite, the Lord only knows. But if I hadn't found him when I did…" Again he fell silent. "Changes a man, that kind o' thing—changes a man *forever.*" He let out a long breath. "So, *sane…?* Who knows?" He shrugged. "We're talkin' 'bout a man who holds a big rattler up in front of his face every Sunday, dares it to bite him in front of a hunnerd people. Three straight years now, he's done it." He stopped, scowled at me. "Says it's his duty an' there ain't a damn thing in this world or the next'll keep him from doin' it. Talk to him any other day o' the week, it's spin the bottle an' see what you get. One minute he's a reg'lar good ol' boy, cussin' the government, talkin' corn 'n' sorghum 'n' feed prices. Five minutes later, he's cryin' an' roarin' 'cause he's seen an angel up in the sky. Or Jesus down the mine. Or Satan, any damn where."

He shook his head in exasperation at his inability to convey the complexity of it. Then his eyes found a far place. When he spoke again, his voice had filled with gruff affection.

"I just try to remember him like he was, Mister Fraser. When he first came here, when he was my friend. When he was a force for good, before that damn woman an' the religion business stole his life. When his preachin' was as much healin' as hellfire."

He looked down. I waited, but he had run out of words.

"I need to give him a letter," I said, finally. "I owe it to someone. Someone in his family, someone he loved, once." I paused, offered up a silent prayer that she was still alive. "Someone who's always loved him. A great deal."

His head came up. The old shoulders squared themselves in resolve.

"I'll make two conditions," he said, "You don't hurt him. An' you don't try to take him outta here. Diamondback might be hell to you 'n' me, but it's the nearest thing to a home he's ever had."

"Agreed."

I watched him choose his next words with great care. "An' I'll ask you to remember one other thing, Mister Fraser. Whatever George MacBeth's become, sane or not, he's still a Christian. By his own lights, a better one now than he ever was in his fancy pulpit down in Fayetteville, or in front of a microphone at the radio station. Lillian..."

Contempt stopped the pronouncement. I waited for him to continue—and then our attention was distracted.

The music. The wind was suddenly bare of it. We stared at each other.

"Means it's gonna start," Reuben said, slowly. "Can last ten minutes or all day, depends how much strength's in him."

He paused. I heard his voice change.

"You sure you're set on doin' this?"

"Yes."

He got up and brushed himself down. Then he unbuttoned the chest pocket of his dungarees.

"She give it me just before we left." He held out a folded sheet of paper. "Told me you weren't to have it till we were done here."

A note? A note from *Rose...?*

I took it, began to unfold it, then stopped as the implication of the old man's words hit me. The look which answered mine was calm, unblinking.

*Reuben was telling me he might never see me again.*

He turned, began walking away, back down the hill towards his pickup.

"Wait," I said. "I need to know. Why you're not coming with me."

He turned. I read the sorrow in his face.

"'Cause he took agin me."

"Why?"

"'Cause he knows."

"Knows what?"

"That I don't—*cain't*—believe in what he preaches now. Or the way he preaches it."

He turned away again. The sadness of his final words came to me over his shoulder.

"I'll give you five hours."

*

*Alex, you were so wrapped up in hope about finding your uncle that I didn't have the heart to tell you this. But I know I have to, in case anything happens. John phoned. He's on his way here from Virginia. He said I should tell you that the bullets which killed O'Malley came from the same gun that shot Saul and Nancy Bell. And that O'Malley's been dead for at least fourteen days, maybe more.*

I stood, holding the paper, staring at the last pencilled words, at the savage underlining of them. *Fourteen days*… How was that possible? My eyes went back to the pitiless landscape. What did this information mean? I tried to focus, but it was impossible.

The wind rose, drove the diseased stench of the black rampart at me without mercy. Acrid and corrosive, evil, it caught at my throat. It was the right wrapping for the cruel questions which finally crystallised.

*If Jack O'Malley had been dead for fourteen days, who had sent Andy Aolfi the text?*

*Was it the same person who'd sent the video to my iPad?*

I pushed the note into my pocket, lifted the fiddle case and began walking towards the Diamondback Mine. Until I'd finished what I'd come here to do, I couldn't let any of it matter.

*

The winding shed was a two-storey stone edifice, tall and solid, testament to the most stubborn of Victorian fantasies—that even the most brutal of work could uplift, and that the spirit of the worker, if the master provided the right setting, would soar obediently. I scanned the walls. No Dark Satanic Mill had been intended here, whatever fate had overtaken the place. The rows of high domed windows must have been grand, once, the sunlight streaming in through them. Now they were little more than bare outlines, black with the grime of a century's coal dust. Could any daylight at all still penetrate? Only through cracks and missing panes, I decided… The roof was a rough patchwork of corrugated asbestos sheets, loosely scarved around a tall chimney.

Nothing identified the building as anything to do with religion. I listened to the hubbub inside, the dread growing in me. How many people were in there? A hundred, Reuben had said… How dangerous was this? I was ignoring every one of the old man's warnings, I knew. Was the risk worth it? Was—

The sudden amplified chord was feral, a beast's roar of assault—a physical blow of guitar, piano, drums. A wave of feedback screamed at me in its wake. The shock of it made me stagger backwards. I stumbled and fell.

Eyes closed, on all fours, the breath knocked from me, I listened to the shouts and whoops which punctuated the frantic rhythm that had been unleashed.

I almost ran.

And then I opened my eyes. My mother's letter had fallen from my jacket pocket. It lay in the black dirt.

Accusing me.

Ashamed, I forced myself up, lifted the envelope and pushed it into the fiddle case's flap, then breathed deeply and took stock. At the building's far end, beside the rusted derrick which had once supported the winding gear's wheels, I could see the foot of a metal staircase. Through the thunderous noise, I picked my way across to it and stopped. My heart was thumping.

I had to *know…*

I had to *see…*

And as I climbed the rusty treads, the pounding music vibrating through the soles of my shoes, I admitted the truth to myself.

It wasn't just for my mother. It was for *me.*

*

The voice was male, balanced on a high knife edge between raucous and plaintive

*"Praise Him, He is the glory!*
*Ol' Diamondback, he knows the story!*
*Ain't nothin' to fear if you praise the Lord today!*
*Yes—"*

It was the song I'd heard on the road to Zion Junction—but there was nothing anodyne or saccharine about this version, nothing slick or cleaned up for product placement. A cracked window showed me the musicians. Their black behemoth amplifiers behind them, they made a semicircle round a plain pine table which held a foot-high wooden cross. In the strange, patchy light I watched the speed of their hands and the tension of their bodies.

*"—yes, Praise Him!*
*Ol' Diamondback says Praise Him!*
*Take him in your hands an' Praise Him!*
*Ain't gonna bite 'f you Praise Him—"*

On it surged, wave after fervent wave, verse and chorus, raw and skilled. It was hypnotic, urgent, a deafening fury. My eyes found each of the players in turn.

The singer, a crew-cut man with two forked braids of grey beard hanging over his bass…

The two guitar players I'd seen earlier, eyes tightly shut, facing each other as they traded lightning-fast licks…

A bespectacled woman who looked like a schoolmistress, pounding out stride rhythm on an electric keyboard…

And at the back, an ancient drummer, rake-thin, with craggy brows and a vicious face. He ruled it all, effortlessly, his sticks moving like hammered blurs of light. As I watched, a fat woman ran out from the front pew and wiped down his brow with the sleeve of her shirt, then stood beside him, beating the nearest of his drums with a massive fist, her huge breasts jiggling. His face showed no reaction at all.

*"No place to hide, old or young!*
*No place to hide from a serpent's tongue!*
*Ol' Diamondback gonna find you out today!*
*If Satan's soul gonna make you lie—"*

I twisted round and scanned the rows of people as much as my vantage point would allow. Applause began, heads craned round. As the music began to climb towards climax, a man appeared, thick-set, squat and powerful. He processed ceremonially through the congregation, holding an oblong box covered with a purple cloth. When he reached the table he put it down, then drew back the covering. His hands opened the clear plastic lid and reached inside.

*The head, the familiar trapezoid head...*

Fear touched me. The snake was gargantuan. I watched it rise, swaying gyroscopically, its black button eyes locked by some internal radar on the face of its shaman. As the rhythm intensified even more, the patterns of its body were granted passing perfection by the shafts of sunlight.

Like jewels...

Jewels that *coiled*, jewels that *slithered...*

*Ol' Diamondback...*

The song stopped, as abruptly as it had begun. I closed my eyes. A single sound reached up to me, familiar, chilling.

Jewels that *rattled...*

At the sound, the congregation roared. The music kicked in again, more frenetic than ever.

*

*Jesus... The Lord... Lucifer...*

The rhythm kept on, folding the names into trance, wrapping them in hysteria. Stillness of any kind seemed impossible. They moved incessantly, the first snake handler and another dozen, male and female, who'd joined him as more of the plastic boxes arrived. Shouting exhortation, they held the snakes high above their heads, they twirled round, they passed them from person to person, moving all the time in a curious static stomp that was a jerky parody of dance. Men yelled, egging each other on, weeping women held each other, children ran through the throng as though it was a moving adventure playground. The expressions I saw ranged from unabashed anger to intense joy. The fat woman I'd seen earlier now held a snake in each hand, stretching out her arms as though she was being blissfully crucified, her head swivelling from side to side, her face triumphant.

*Mine Eyes Have Seen The Glory…*

And then madness piled upon madness. A bald man pulled a small canister from the pocket of his jeans and attached a metal tube to its top. He turned a nozzle, the woman beside him struck a match. I watched her take the torch from him, let its white-hot spout of flame play over her hands.

*Lead, kindly light…*

Within seconds, half a dozen more were doing the same. I watched the sweat break out on the first woman's brow, but she didn't stop. I felt my mind begin to flee, to reject it all. *Mortification of the flesh, with a blowtorch? The middle ages, updated with acetylene…?* What could marry such blind faith to such organised insanity? A noise came from below. I spun round.

The figure at the foot of the stairs drove out all other thought.

A tall man, grey-haired, wraithlike, clad in the purple collar and black robes of a Scottish presbyterian minister. *The face…* I didn't know it.

And then I did.

Sudden joy, intense and delirious, ruled me—until I took in the hollowed eyes, the sunken cheeks, the deep red scar, from hairline to throat. It had clawed the face's whole right side out of kilter.

He found words before I did. The voice was a strange rasp.

"I have been expecting you."

*The accent, still Scottish...*

From the folds of the robe, a shotgun appeared. It wavered in his bony hands as it rose, but not enough to stop it coming to rest aimed squarely at my chest.

*

The twin barrels jabbed into my back and sent me sprawling down a flight of steps. I landed hard on an earth floor. I turned, squinted up against the light. The face above the gun didn't change.

"What have you done with my fiddle?"

The only answer to my shout was the trapdoor's clang. It left me in total darkness. As the bolt shot home, a musty smell surrounded me. I got to my knees, reached up and pushed, but it was solid. Where was I? A cellar? I tried to stand up, but there wasn't enough headroom. Gingerly, bent double, I felt above me. Mortar… Could I get through it? Not without some kind of tool… My disorientation was magnified by the dull thud of feet somewhere above. I could taste dust, the dislodged legacy of the dancers. I let my hands wander till they found a solid wall. Damp and slimy or not, it was still a relief to touch it. I crawled across and sat against it. The cold seeped into my back.

*I have been expecting you…*

How could that be? His wife, her lover? Had they got free of Rose? But why would they warn him of my coming? Reuben? I discounted it immediately. I trusted the old man completely.

*Five hours...*

Could I last that long? Would he return in time? And if he didn't…?

*Dead in a heartbeat, your body down a shaft so deep nobody'd ever find it…*

Above me, the rhythm came to another abrupt stop. The silence only lasted a minute. I recognised the Scottish voice.

*"…Faith, brothers and sisters, faith!"*

Through the chorus of approbation I strained to hear the next words.

*"…you have shown it, now I will show it!"*

Once more, roars of encouragement. And then the rhythmic pulse of feet began again.

But its purpose was different now. I couldn't see the dust, but I could feel it cloud round me. The sound got louder, the tramp of a march which had already reached its goal. It got louder still, deafening. The dust was raining down on me, now, stinging my eyes, catching my throat, choking me. A chunk of mortar hit my shoulder. I cradled my head in my hands—*was this hole to be my prison or my tomb?*

And then it all stopped. More silence. After a few seconds it was broken by a strange sound, a faint, collective sigh.

I understood. He had done it—challenged the snake, just as

Reuben had said he would… I opened my eyes. Darkness. Dust. Nothing else. The faint rasp of his voice came again.

*"Matthew 7 Verse 26 …a foolish man, which built his house upon the sand! Brothers and sisters, have I not shown you that this house is not built on sand!"*

A wild cheering and stamping broke out. It cowered me into a ball, then, gradually, it died away.

The silence which followed was different, somehow I knew it.

Eyes closed, I waited.

Nothing, only my own breathing...

Still, I waited.

And waited…

I had already lost place. Now I began to lose time as well. I felt the world spin. I forced myself to concentrate—on anything. Anything to keep the void around me from filling with panic. I fastened on to the words I'd just heard.

*Built on sand…*

Was that what I'd done? Built my house on sand? By assuming the brother my mother had cherished would be decent, benign? By imagining I'd be welcomed with open arms?

*Sand…*

The dust choked me, the word echoed round my head.

*Mattie, kicking it away as we talked…*

*Rose, walking the tide's edge…*

*Saul, the bloodied mess of him on the beach, his wounds caked with it…*

Saul. *Sand.*

My fears shattered. I was alert, rational.

Saul Morgan hated sand, he'd told me....

So why had he rammed his cane into it, as hard as he could after he'd been shot? Why was his last conscious act to grab a handful of it and grip it as tightly as possible?

*Sand…*

And suddenly I understood what had happened at Cormorant Cove, the only way the facts could possibly be made to fit, the awful, clever obscenity of it. Strength surged in me. I roared out my triumph.

Sounds answered—a door, opening, footsteps. Thin wafers of light draped themselves down from the trapdoor's edges. I craned round to left and right, peering.

My heart nearly stopped.

Plastic boxes, flat ones, different sizes... The shape inside the nearest one was *moving...*

As the footsteps disappeared, a fork of tongue flickered out through an air hole.

I was only a few feet away, on both sides, from dozens of coiled snakes.

*

By the time he came for me again, I was a wreck—shivering, drained of tears. I didn't try to speak to him, the part of my brain which still worked told me it would be futile. Could I function? I could barely make my legs carry me in a straight line—all I knew was that I could feel snakes. On my skin, in my hair.... Even the rain, the cold rain, so good and fresh, seemed filled with them. As the shotgun prodded my stumbling progress along the side of the building, I could hear his tortured breathing behind me. It had the rattle, the snake's rattle... *Were there snakes inside him...?* A tiny, rational voice in my head told me I was hallucinating. Would it stop? Ever? I tried to make out my surroundings, but all my eyes found were changing colours that blossomed out of the darkness. As they faded, I knew it was night. The vicious jab into my spine told me I'd stopped moving.

The big metal door was open. The gun pushed me forward.

The shed was empty.

I heard the door slam behind me, a key turn. What would happen now? I began to feel, to hear—the clamminess of my soaked clothes, the rain on the roof. The word *escape* came from somewhere, but I knew I had neither the strength nor the will. I stood, waiting. At least I was alone, I was sure of it. The only light was a dim flickering, somewhere ahead of me. I squeezed between the banks of drums and amplifiers, then stopped.

The back wall... I saw what had been hidden from outside. The inscription ran its length, illuminated by a phalanx of candles to either side.

*MARK 16.17*
*THEY WILL PICK UP SERPENTS WITH THEIR HANDS.*

Through the gloom beneath the words, my eyes found the harmonium. It was in an alcove, a small writing desk beside it. My fiddle case lay on it, open. A different fear came, one which was at least familiar. Quickly, I crossed the big room and lifted her.

Unharmed.

And then my relief died.

My mother's letter. It was lying on the harmonium's keyboard. It had been torn open.

Had he read it...?

Two pages, written on the heavy laid paper she so loved, were lying on the yellowed ivory keys beside the envelope. I picked them up.

Her script, so fluid, so controlled, so precise... Her signature, so small... Her words came to me; *a large signature is for the vain, Alexander...* A faint smell reached up to me.

Gardenia, her scent...

The world swam. *She was alive, she had to be!* When my senses returned, I found myself staring at the pages, still quivering in my hand.

I began to read.

*...and I repeat, I forgive you. I forgave you, in fact, as soon as you had left us and my mind had begun to recover from the shock. For years now, in letter after letter, I have tried to tell you.*

*So let us have it said, plain and simple. You were not in your right mind.*

*And the consequences of that are partly my fault.*

*Because I had seen your jealousy, your feelings of rejection. Why did I not act upon what I saw? Since the moment it happened, not a day has gone by without me asking myself that question.*

*The nearest I can come to an answer is not meant, in any sense, to be an excuse. I had thought your feelings natural, rooted in the fact that after our parents' death, I had been as much mother to you as sister. I thought those feelings would pass. I had no idea they had brought you to such a terrible place.*

*The guilt of that realisation has never left me and it never will, but added to it is a second burden, for I know your sense of rejection must have been doubled by my rage, then redoubled again by my peremptory order to leave. That was panic, George, pure and simple. I was not strong enough to fight it. You needed help, not harshness, not punish-*

*ment or condemnation. I can only hope that, out there in your New World, you found that help. As I said, I have long since forgiven you.*

*And I have prayed, daily, that you would find it in your heart to forgive me. I ask it of you again now.*

*We are both old, George. I suspect I might not be able to think of myself as old for much longer, for I am wracked with pain, and with every passing day, I can see the shadows of coming sorrow lengthening in my beloved Andrew's honest, Godless eyes.*

*There are others I have to ask forgiveness of, one in particular. Somehow I know I cannot find the courage to do that without having yours first. So please, I beg you, in the name of the closeness we once had, grant me it.*

*We both know there can be no greater sin than what you tried to do, but Our Lord's great love—*

I read the rest in utter disbelief. *How could she have kept this from me? How could my father have sent me to confront this?*

Behind me, the metal door opened. I turned.

George MacBeth stood framed in the doorway, his robes stuck to him like a second skin by the rain. The shotgun was in his left hand, the box which held the big rattlesnake in his right. I watched the snake move inside its plastic prison and fought my fear. My uncle propped the gun carefully against the pine table, then turned to face me. Despite his haggard appearance, in the candlelit gloom he made a figure of authority. When his voice came, its hoarseness was laboured.

"I have prayed. Up on the mountain, for clarity."

He came forward, put the box on the table beside the cross, then paused. I took in the pallor of his skin. How ill was he?

"I apologise for the incarceration," he said. "I had to be sure who you were, that you were not some trick, some device. The Devil may be loathsome, but no man should underestimate his guile. But now that the Lord has granted me His truth, we can begin."

Beads of sweat had broken at his hairline. His expression changed, became a lopsided sneer. The scar, I realised… It had pulled down what was meant to be a smile…

"I always knew you were with me, from the day I set foot in this Godless land. Since I saw the light and renewed my vows, here in the mountains, I have hoped this moment would come."

I stared at him. And then understanding dawned.

*I have been waiting for you...*

*I always knew you were with me...*

First Lillian, then Reuben... Now George MacBeth.

For the third time, I was being recognised not as myself, but as my *Doppelgänger.*

The rain on the roof, the rasp of his breath, the dripping robe, the livid scar, the snake's bulging coils... My mind had to fight its way past all sight and sound to get the words out.

"Who am I, George?"

He took a firm step forward. "You are the best part of me, the part which never aged, which never compromised. You are my conscience, disguised as my youth. You have come to examine the soundness of my doctrines, to hear me expound them."

As I watched the bright madness of his eyes, water began to leak from the roof. It dripped on the lid of the plastic box. I saw the snake stir, the forked tongue shoot out, probing. I forced myself to ignore it. My voice was a whisper.

"You've read what your sister wrote? You understand what you did?"

His eyes never left mine. He *had* read the letter, I could see it... I watched the warring feelings fight for control of his face—pain, sorrow, fatigue, fear—as sanity tried to reclaim him.

And failed.

His features contorted into a desperate scowl. "I am of God's Elect!" he shouted. "He has told me I cannot sin! Whatever I do is His will!"

My hand held out my mother's crumpled pages. It only fuelled his rage.

*"I was wrong!"* he shouted. *"It was not the Lord's voice I heard, it was the Devil's! You are his creature!"*

He spun round, reaching for the gun—and stumbled against the table. The impact dislodged the plastic box. It hit the floor. The lid sheared off. I saw the rattlesnake begin to uncoil, just as George MacBeth lost his balance.

And fell on it.

By the time I had grabbed his arm, it was too late—the snake had struck. And then, as my uncle cried out, it reared up before me. Suddenly I was within a foot of the trapezoid head, watching it draw back, staring at the black fork of tongue.

The strike was like a hammer blow to my arm—and then there was an explosion, thunderous. The diamond coils arced away like a cracked whip. As the strength went from my legs, I smelled the cordite. My eyes strained to search the gloom.

It lay by the far wall, sliced almost in two, a twitching mess in a long smear of brown liquid… As I watched its death throes, everything began to slow down.

*Its blood… Why was Old Diamondback's blood such a different colour…?*

I felt a sickening surge of heat. My gaze fastened on my forearm. Two neat holes… Why did I feel no pain? I tried to turn.

*Where was my fiddle? The last time, my fiddle had saved me…*

"Fraser!"

Somehow, I found focus; John Walks-Over-Ice, his face inches away from mine... I felt my knees buckle. His hands caught me, laid me down. I saw him turn.

Clarity came, bright-edged, razor-sharp. I saw my uncle, on his knees, holding his arm. I heard his whispered words as he stared up at the huge red man.

"Are you *Satan?*"

Voices came, Rose's, Reuben's. My eyes closed.

*The stone floor… Cool… My body… Searing hot, aching, my heart thumping, fast…*

"Fraser! Stay awake!"

John's voice, far away… I searched for strength. *I had to tell him! That I knew, now! All of it! The kidnapping, the killings…* I forced my eyes open, found myself staring into the eyes of a man, supine like myself, a few feet away.

*Who was he?*

And then I remembered.

*He was the man who had tried to smother me in my cradle.*

# 20

# VENOM

THE SMELLS, WARM disinfectant and gun oil, were overpowering. I stood beside John Walks-Over-Ice, leaning back against the breeze block wall of the sweltering cubicle. I was determined to stand, even though there was a chair. The heat was beginning to make me dizzy, but if John was affected, he gave no sign. The young black cop by the door, his District of Columbia Police badge gleaming at his belt, regarded him with barely concealed distaste as he chewed his gum, then turned his sour gaze on me. Did that make me the lesser of two evils? Through the two-way mirror, Sandy Hunter, hands chained to a ring in the middle of a steel table, was facing a pair of unsmiling detectives. She looked cool—stylish even, orange jumpsuit or not. The sight was surreal. It was as though she wasn't really here in jail, as though she was sitting backstage at a fashion show, making a leisurely decision about which gloves Rose should wear with which hat.

The bulkier of the two detectives, an elderly man with a silvered crew cut, killed the fantasy by leaning over his paunch to switch off the recorder. When he beckoned to an unseen figure, I saw the sweat patch under his armpit. A wardress propped the girl's crutch against the table and began unlocking her handcuffs.

I couldn't watch any more. I prised myself off the wall, my back slick with sweat. John's hand reached out to help me.

The young cop no longer bothered trying to hide his scowl. "Goin' somewhere, Chief? Not supposed to leave without the lieutenant's say so." He nodded at me. "We're gonna want to talk to your buddy, too."

John ignored him. "Fraser, you've had enough for one day. We're leaving,"

The boy hooked both hands into his belt, took a step to the side and blocked the door. John took one languid pace forward. The confrontation was silent, the huge Cherokee towering over the barely five foot black boy. Grudgingly, the chewing stopped. The boy moved aside.

"Thanks for your co-operation, officer," John said. "Please inform your superiors that Mr. Fraser will make himself available for questioning at a mutually convenient time, as will I." A white card appeared in his hand. "Tell them they should contact the firm of Morgan and Associates to arrange it. They will be representing us both."

In a last attempt at bravado, the boy snatched the card from the red hand. As I followed John out, I heard a barely suppressed sigh of relief.

*

"When did you know?"

The question took a while to register—because of the deep voice. It was out of place, it belonged to wilder vistas, larger, more primitive. It had nothing to do with a placid park bench surrounded by runners and dog walkers, by pairs of laughing young women in trainers, jogging along a man-made path between stately trees. In the distance, Abraham Lincoln's lugubrious face regarded us from his marble armchair. He looked ancient, exhausted. I had to fight to get the words out.

"In the crawl space. When my uncle…" I stopped, forced myself to close down memory. "A bible quotation. About sand," I finished.

John pretended he hadn't noticed what the words had cost me. His red tie had been freed by the breeze from the confines of his immaculate suit jacket. He tucked it back in and straightened it.

"Staring us in the face," he said. "Sometimes you just can't see the wood for the trees. Sand. *Sandy.*" He shook his head, smiling. "Saul Morgan, world champion determined old bastard. Even when he thought he was dying, he tried to tell us who'd shot him."

The pressure in my chest began to ease. I could talk.

"How is he?"

"Out of the coma and a lot better, no thanks to the woman we just left. We found nurse's scrubs and syringes in her apartment—my guess is she was going after him because he could identify her as the shooter. She must have got the mother and father of all shocks when she heard he was still alive."

"What would she have used?"

"She wouldn't have had to use anything, just inject an air bubble, induce a coronary. In all the confusion of an emergency response, she might just have got away with it. If the hospital staff had bought it, she'd have been free and clear."

The ensuing silence was broken by the laughter of a young woman in power suit and heels, talking animatedly into her mobile phone as she strode into view. She gave John a glance of frank admiration as she passed. It elicited a polite smile. As she tossed her hair and walked on, I found myself wondering at the disparity of reactions my companion provoked.

*A young policeman's contempt…*

*A laughing girl's admiration…*

Voices found me; Rose's, the whispers of the women in the roadside café in Illinois…

*Forbidden fruit.*

*Uppity injun.*

Would the day ever come when race didn't matter in America? Suddenly I was glad that, despite the very real things which divided us, John Walks-Over Ice and I had finally managed to jump the wall into friendship. Would it last? *Could it…?* I realised he was talking again.

"…but she's a bearcat for nerve, you've got to give her that. She goes to Lee with the idea of killing Rose so Lou can inherit. They bring in O'Malley. When it screws up because of you, she hitches her wagon to O'Malley's, despite the fact he's even crazier than Lee. The two of them try again, kidnapping the kid. Nancy Bell foils that by letting Lou go. They kill Lee—or maybe she does it on her own—then the Bell woman turns up to petition Saul. When that looks like it's going to screw everything up, Sandy shoots Bell to keep her from talking, then Saul, because she's convinced he's too smart not to work it out. Then she puts one through her own leg to frame the woman she's just shot."

The urge to to know all of it came. For the first time in days, energy flowed into me.

"Why did she kill O'Malley?"

He shrugged. "Money, perhaps? Who knows? But her next move was real genius. She gets Andy's number from O'Malley's phone, sets the boy up to kill you. It could have worked—and even when it didn't, it made it look as though Professor Jack was still alive. Then the film sent to the iPad confirmed it."

"But surely O'Malley meant to send that? It must have taken time to set up, planning."

He smiled. "Sure. But why waste a good threat just because the man who'd made it was dead? Like I said, genius. If his body hadn't turned up in the ocean, we'd still be looking over our shoulders for him. There's still a lot we don't know, though. Perhaps we never will." He hesitated. "Or perhaps she'll tell you."

"What do you mean?"

"She's asked to talk to you. Alone. Says she won't talk to anyone else, lawyers, friends, anyone at all, until it happens. Prosecuting counsel's agreed, as long as they get a transcript. Will you do it?"

*Why…?*

His phone rang. His face told me nothing as he listened, but when he ended the call, somehow I knew.

"That was the hospital in Little Rock. I'm sorry." He paused. "Your uncle. He didn't make it."

My chest... It was tight again. An ache began in the puncture marks on my left forearm.

"If it's any consolation, the bite only speeded things up. He couldn't have had much longer, Alex, maybe a few months. He'd spent three years living on top of what was, to all intents and purposes, a toxic dump. All sorts of tumours, he was riddled."

The ache in my arm became a full-blown burning, the stench of the Diamondback Mine seemed to come from nowhere. *Would it ever leave me…?*

My eyes found the presidential statue again, imprisoned in its massive, cold cupola. The hard, hollowed-out eyes stared back at me, impassive.

The energy drained from me.

I wondered if I looked as old as Abraham Lincoln.

*

The jail sounds, harsh and metallic, surrounded us. In the distance I heard a toilet flush, then an angry, echoing diatribe which ended with the word *bitch*. It was all underpinned by a single anguished female voice, steadily sobbing.

It made a strange aural frame for the glassy calmness of the woman across the steel table. Catatonia? Full-blown insanity…? I wondered, but only until both notions drowned in her mocking smile. It turned into a forensic examination of my face.

"So. In the wars. Want to tell me about it?"

My silence didn't faze her. She sat back as far as the handcuffs allowed, the chain rattling loudly across the scarred metal. The perfectly elocuted voice was calm, its Cheltenham Ladies' College English more beautifully modulated than ever.

"When you first showed up at the farm, I thought about you, Fraser. Wondered if you were worth—" She tossed the black mane. "—a little effort. After all," she said, "you had the body, you looked the part—and you had that chip on your shoulder, that truculence thing, always such a lovely challenge. The bad boy CV did no harm, either, it was impressive. Add all of it to the fact that there weren't too many other options around—John only had eyes for Rose, of course, and Lee, well…" She gave an eloquent shrug. "He might have been a ladies' man once, but when I was with him, his ego needed even more stroking than the rest of him. And anyway, he'd passed the point of no return—he was more interested in getting high than getting laid. All in all, not much fun for a girl. You'd agree?"

Once more, I said nothing.

Once more, Sandy Hunter bestowed her mocking smile.

Around us, the background sounds amplified once more into brutal narrative; running feet, a ferocious metal clang, a shouted order, a cry of pain.

"Not the quietest spa I've ever booked in to," she said. "I don't think it would suit Rose, do you? How is she, by the way? Everything back to apple pie normal for her and the kid, now all the fuss has died down?" She shifted in her seat, languidly. "And how's it going for you, Fraser? Your hopeless passion, I mean." When I didn't reply, the smile widened to a sneer. "You didn't really think you were hiding it, did you? If you'd wanted to do that, you should have taken the money."

So the bribe had been a test. Of my feelings… Anger came to

my rescue.

"Did it hurt, shooting yourself in the thigh?"

It hit home, but I was only given a split second to perceive it. The hard shell was immediately drawn over, the spark of reaction buried beneath it.

"I should have had you on the porch, that first night," she said, lightly. "But I'm glad I didn't, now. When you ran, it was obvious what a wimp you were. And yet it's obvious you're not without courage." Again, the smile. "A wimp with balls. What a strange mixture. Typically Scottish, is it?"

I sat very still, remembering the brief John and the lawyers had given me; *as much information as possible…*

It seemed laughable, now—it was obvious there wasn't the slightest chance of any information at all. This woman had no intention of letting a single fact slip out of her control—unless it suited her purpose, whatever that was. This was pointless. It was time to bring it to a close.

"Why am I here?"

The slow release of breath was the only sign of triumph she allowed herself. "You think you've got me pigenholed, Fraser, don't you? Like in some old western. I'm the bad guy in the black hat, Rose gets the white one, takes it off once in a while to let the plebs see the halo. But how much do you really know?"

Without warning, she stood up and leaned across the table, as far as the chain would allow. As the sudden movement triggered an alarm bell, I saw the long scar on her abdomen. The door crashed open.

"Ask her, Fraser."

Four hands, black and strong, grabbed her, thrust her back down in her seat. She didn't struggle.

"Ask her about the Ambassador Hotel. Ask her how it all—"

The bigger of the two wardresses slapped her, hard, then turned her scowl on me. "Visitation period's over. You need to exit the facility immediately. *Sir.*"

They unclipped her and began marching her away. She managed to turn her head at the door. I was granted one last mocking smile, then Sandy Hunter disappeared.

I couldn't move. I sat there, my chest gripped in a vice of struggling breath and pounding heart, surrounded by the clanging and yelling, the sobbing voice, the reverberating symphony of despair and defiance.

But at least I understood now, why I'd been summoned.

*Hate, the flip side of love…*

Ann Savoy's revenge had been about money, Sandy Hunter's was about love. If Rose Vannier wasn't to belong to her, then she was to be spoiled. Tarnished.

Irredeemably, so that no one else would ever want her.

*Had it worked…?*

I got up. With a heavy heart, I admitted to myself that I only knew one way to get to the truth of the Ambassador Hotel.

*

John let the stethoscope fall back to his chest. "Nothing to worry about," he said. "It's reaction. Snakebite can be pretty traumatic, things can take a while to stabilise. Lucky for you she didn't have much venom—snakes kept in captivity, especially ones which have been badly mistreated, often don't. So it's not surprising, but it's not dangerous, either. One last test."

His face became serious as he wound the cuff round my biceps. He pressed the blood pressure meter's button. As it tightened, he spoke again.

"I hated killing it, Fraser. I know there was no choice, but they're the most misunderstood creatures on earth. Rattlesnakes only strike if they're provoked or frightened."

The question forced itself out of me. "Really? Which option applied to the one that killed Lennie Dutroux?"

I didn't even know where the impulse had come from. As he pressed the meter's release button, he gave no indication of hearing the question. The pressure eased. When he faced me, the stone face was firmly in place. For a long time, neither of us spoke.

"It wasn't a rattler, it was a big cottonmouth," he said, finally. "After I saw Dutroux get on board, I put it at the door of the main cabin, then called to him. He tripped over it when he came out. The bite was immediate, the effect…." He shrugged, scribbled figures on his pad. "Cottonmouths are among the most venomous of the common pit vipers. If it hadn't killed him, it would certainly have incapacitated him long enough for me to tip him overboard." He released the cuff from my arm. "But it wasn't necessary. As soon as the business was done, I rescued the snake and cut the cruiser adrift."

"What did you do with it?"

"The snake? Put it in the water, cottonmouths are fine swimmers. No reason for the animal to suffer for doing a good job. Of controlling vermin," he finished.

Before I could speak again, he was back at his desk. I looked out through the surgery window.

Gallant Fox Farm, serene, beautiful in its early afternoon sunshine… It looked back at me as though nothing had changed, as though nothing ever would.

But it had.

I hadn't asked in accusation and John Walks-Over-Ice hadn't replied in anger. He had confessed to murder, in detail.

He had just trusted me with his life.

As I reached for my clothes, an unfamiliar sound came from behind me. I turned. As I was buttoning my shirt, John was taking his off. The blue jewels of the turquoise-studded tool belt flashed as he fastened it round his waist.

*Work…*

Once again, the question came of its own accord.

"Can I help?"

The big hands paused.

"You OK with heights?"

*

There was wind. It was tricky, it only gusted when I came up out of the shelter of the wall on to the top rung. It had caught my load of planks on every trip up the ladder, making a sail of them, forcing me round and threatening my balance. This time was no different. I thought I was ready for it, but still I almost fell. As I steadied myself against the guttering, I tried to work out how long it was since I'd been up on a roof with a load on my shoulder. Twenty years? Twenty-five? The hammering paused. John's voice came from further along.

"Can't get the help these days."

Our eyes met as I heaved my load up on to the slats and began pushing the planks along to him.

"Best you're going to get for the money," I said.

A small smile found his mouth. "Here."

I caught the plastic bottle of water, unscrewed the top, drank, poured the rest over my sweating neck, then stretched.

And felt it. For the first time in months, a simple contentment.

The wind on my aching muscles, the smell of sawn wood, the sound of John's hammering…

The future could wait, the present would do for now. As I threw the empty bottle down into the skip, I heard the sound of hooves. Rose, on the bay mare I remembered. My heart swelled—and then my euphoria evaporated.

The question, the Ambassador Hotel...

*When would I find the guts to ask it?*

She nudged the big horse nearer us. A few yards behind, Lou appeared, looking doubtful on the Appaloosa. America's Sweetest Sweetheart threw a blissful smile up at us.

"And what would the crew like for lunch? Mattie's cooking. Some new recipe, smells great. I've got the name of it."

Her hand reached into her shirt pocket and took out a note, then paused as her daughter caught up with her. Rose leaned over to take the Appaloosa's bridle.

"It's okay, honey, you're not going to fall." She patted the horse's neck. "She knows the way back up to her stable, just let her lead you up there. Piece of cake."

The girl said nothing. Her miserable look encompassed us all.

"Honest, you don't have to do a thing," Rose went on, "just dismount at the block. Remember I showed you how to do that?"

Lou nodded, unhappier than ever. There was nothing of the streetwise kid there, now, I thought. *Was that good?* I'd miss it, I realised. We watched her, perched stiff as a board on the patient horse's back as it picked its way up the path. Rose shook her head.

"She's never going to be Dale Evans, that's for sure."

"As long as you're happy being Roy Rogers, she doesn't have to be," John said.

They shared a smile. Rose unfolded the note, brought it up close to her face. Then she frowned and let it fall. As she closed her eyes I could feel the frustration coming from her.

"You need glasses," I said, gently. "It's time you admitted it."

Silence. A long, long silence.

When her eyes came up again, I saw she was crying. She looked away, to the figure of her daughter on horseback, nearly at the stable block.

“Tell him,” she said.

Eventually, John’s voice, quiet, gentle, came from the other end of the roof.

“Rose is going blind, Alex.”

# 21

# COURAGE

"FUNDUS FLAVIMACULATUS. Inherited. It's the most severe version of a condition called Stargardt's Disease. It's a kind of macular degeneration, gradual loss of light, particularly to the centre of the eyes. It usually happens to much older people." She paused. "Except with this variant, it's not so gradual and I'm not old. At the moment, there's no treatment—there's stem cell research going on, but the results are still inconclusive. And even if some kind of drug does get to market, it's unlikely to kick in fast enough to do anything for me."

She was sitting on one of the massive reclaimed oak beams in what would, one day, be the main living space of the half-finished house. The roof slats threw a strange geometric light over her features. It looked like the bars of a cage.

*Or the window of a cell…*

Angrily, I thrust the memory of Barlinnie from me. It was nothing compared to the perpetual prison she was facing. When she saw the expression on my face she looked away, up at the sunlight. The tears were gone, now.

"How long do you have?"

"Before I can't function without help? Before I get to 20/200, the legal definition of blindness? It's a lottery. Could be twelve months, could be more. Psychiatrist's advice is to live quietly, take it one day at a time." Her voice hardened. "Shouldn't be too much of a problem, living quietly—I can't see the phone ringing off the hook for a catwalk model with a white stick and a guide dog, can you?"

Silence. I watched the dust motes, floating round her with balletic slowness.

"When did you know?"

"Eight days before the night we first met."

The precision of the answer was more chilling than any despair.

"No indication before then?"

She shrugged. "Nothing the opticians couldn't put down to *Anno Domini,* middle age dogging me, peddling spectacles. The plan was contact lenses. Ann wouldn't have glasses."

It was no solace that my surmise in Zion Junction had been right. I turned to the space which would soon be a window. The wind's breath was gentle, the view across the valley to the waterfall, breathtaking. *How long would she be able to see it?*

"Mattie doesn't have it, which means it must have come from my wonderful late father." The scent of her found me as she arrived at my side. "Mister Lennie Dutroux. No end to the man's generosity," she finished, quietly.

"So the sunglasses aren't just for disguise?"

She smiled, sadly. "No, not just that. The lenses are treated to take out certain wavelengths of light, it's supposed to help. John's idea, keep speculation to a minimum."

"Why didn't you tell me?"

She folded her arms. "Part of the fantasy. That you and I would ride off into the sunset together, make love, make beautiful babies, turn Lou around, replant Mattie's old life in better soil." She turned, faced me. "The fairy tale. That I was normal. That you were. That a future together was inevitable."

"And my feelings? Do they come into this at all?"

She looked at me, calmly. "I know your feelings, Alex, maybe better than you do. You think I didn't see the way you looked at the road that morning? With your fiddle case in your hand? You really think I'd take that away from you? That freedom?" Her hands reached out, took both of mine. "Do you imagine I could live with being the death of that? With sitting, blind, staring into the dark and wondering if that look's on your face? While you're standing beside me, glad I can't see it? How long do you think we would last?"

"Rose—"

She shook her head. "No," she said, quietly. "It's a done deal, the decision's made. I've let myself be panicked into enough bad things as a result of this, enough selfishness. I won't add more. I won't destroy the essence of someone valuable. Someone I love."

*Love…*

Through the silence, a desperate shout forced its way up from deep inside me. *Fight! Show her you can change, show her she's wrong…*

But I knew she wasn't wrong. I heard myself speak.

"What bad things?"

Slowly, the hurt of those three words enveloped us. When we finally faced each other, we both knew we had arrived back at the Ambassador Hotel.

*

"It was a bad time—the worst." Nimbly, she picked her way up through the jumble of rocks, the water splashing over her boots. "We were waiting for the judgement on the lawsuit against the factory owners—the real bastards, the fatcats in Dubai and Qatar who own most of the Bangladesh sweatshops. It had cost millions—not least because a lot of the international retail chains had funded their defence, secretly."

She read my puzzled look as she reached a hand down. She pulled me up, her grip strong.

"There was a time when people talked about Big Oil and Big Steel," she said. "Now it should be Big Fashion. As an industry it's as paranoid as it is powerful. Anyone who makes a serious move on its profits is going to be a target, supermodel or not. Raise the price of a t-shirt by a dollar? Just to pay someone in the third world a decent wage, or give them a safe place to work?" She shook her head in disgust. "I wasn't sorry I'd decided to take them on, not for a minute—but the upshot was we were so far stretched, we really didn't know which way was up. There was a strong possibility the entire Rose Vannier operation would go under, Saul laid it out for me on the phone from Dhaka. It was the first time the word *bankrupt* had been used."

We'd reached the waterfall's top, now. She stopped, breathed deeply and closed her eyes.

"The results of the eye tests came the same night as that call."

I heard a lark, then a blackbird. Both their songs seemed beyond music, preternaturally clear over the tumbling water. *How could such beauty and such cruelty exist in the same world?* I fled from my thoughts. Facts were easier.

"Who knew? About your sight?"

She reached down, scooped up a handful from the stream and doused her face.

"Only John and me."

The tone of her voice told me there was more. I watched the dripping water darken her shirt as I waited. When it came, she could no longer disguise her misery.

"And then I let it out."

*

The path through the pines skirted the ridge's edge. It was fragrant, resinous. The strewn needles crunched beneath our feet.

"John had taken Mattie into DC, she had a hospital appointment, she'd just been diagnosed as type two diabetic. Neither of them was answering their phone. Saul was halfway round the planet. I was here, alone." She spun round to me, her face earnest. "You know how people talk about panic? Like it's instantaneous, just one single moment of madness? Mine lasted a day—one day of the words *bankrupt* and *blind* echoing round my head, one whole day of chaos, of absolutely no control over myself. I'd never been in such a state before, not even after Paul and Mimi died. I'd've burst if I hadn't told someone. I even thought of talking to Lee or Ann, that's how desperate I was. In the end, there was only one person left."

The path came to an outcrop of rock at the ridge's edge. She sat and let her legs dangle over the drop. The whole settlement of Gallant Fox was laid out before us like a child's toy farm. Smoke was rising gently from the chimney.

"Sandy," I said.

She didn't reply. Her eyes never left the view.

*

"I trusted her. She'd been with me for years, ran my life like clockwork, between her and Saul I never had to think twice about organisation. She even took a knife for me once, a crazy out in San Francisco. It was beyond brave. She saw the guy pull out the blade and just launched herself in front of me, she could have died." Her voice filled with frustration. "But despite that, there was always something… Something holding me back, some kind of chemistry that stopped me crossing the last line, making a friend of her. Does that make sense to you?"

"Yes," I said.

It was the way I'd felt about John Walks-Over-Ice until a few days ago. She frowned.

"Ever since the truth came out about her, I've wondered if any of this would have happened if that had been different." Again, she hesitated. "If *I'd* been different."

The ache in the last phrase was palpable. I broke in on her reverie.

"The rest of it. Tell me now."

Head bowed, she went on. "When I phoned she came, immediately. I wanted to be measured about telling her, to be dignified, but as soon as I saw her, I just went into meltdown—shaking with tears, half crazy. Once the first rush of it was over we made a fire, outside, and as the sun went down we started drinking. After the first few it just all came out—like a dam bursting. Torrents of stuff, on both sides—feelings, regrets, confessions, all the crap women keep hidden, all the insecurities which only come in the small hours."

"Did you tell her about Lou?"

She shook her head. "No, not that, at least—but I told her damn near everything else. How scared I was, and not just of the blindness. How was I going to provide for people? For Mattie, Lou, Lee, Saul, her, everyone who worked for me…? She listened, she sympathised. She let me cry on her shoulder, literally."

"Did you know she was in love with you?"

The wind gusted, blew the pine needles round us.

"Not until she tried to kiss me," she said, softly.

"What did you do?"

She shrugged. "Fled. Just abandoned her, left her there in front of the fire. I remember stumbling up the stairs, falling into bed and crying myself to sleep. And then in the morning I felt awful about it—one more humiliation on top of everything else." She stopped. "Don't get me wrong, I'm no wide-eyed innocent, I knew there had been women in her life as well as men. But I'd never imagined, not for one second, that she was carrying any kind of torch for me." She gave me a wan smile. "But then, I was never exactly the world's smartest about love, was I?"

I said nothing. She turned away, stared into the middle distance.

"For the whole of the next day, I didn't see her. Then, that night, she appeared again. This time she was the one in tears. She'd made a mistake, she said, she'd read the signals wrong, all she'd wanted to do was comfort me. Could I ever forgive her? We both knew it was a lie, but it seemed like a big enough fig leaf for us both to hide behind. And the truth was, I felt guilty."

"Why?"

She took a long time to answer. "For treating her as though she was invisible," she said, finally. "And for not being able to respond, because I'm not into women." I heard her voice change, become flat, emotionless. "And that's when she told me she had a way out for me. A plan."

"What kind of plan?"

Without warning, she let out a savage laugh. It was loud and ugly, on the verge of hysterical, the same sound I remembered from Saul's Cadillac.

"*Plan…* It's a good word, don't you think? It makes it sound like something you could track, assess. Something you could tick off by stages on a clipboard."

She was crying now. I saw her mouth quiver as she forced the words out.

"It's what I thought you were, that night at the Ambassador—*the plan.*"

I didn't understand. Her voice came again, grim with self-loathing.

"I thought you were the man who'd come to slash my face, so I could claim the insurance on it. All thirty million dollars of it."

*

The words seemed to come faster now. It was as though confession was easier in the dark.

"She knew people, she said, people who knew people. It was simple, it would be made to look like a stalker—we'd had the guy in San Francisco, there'd been others, all the top girls get them sooner or later. So it was entirely credible. I'd be left with a knife scar on my face, maybe another couple of superficial wounds to make it look frenzied, but nothing worse. It would hurt, but only until I got to an ER. The attacker would have instructions not to make it worse than it had to be, he'd be a pro, he'd know exactly how far to go. All I had to do was be at a prearranged place at a prearranged time. Ten grand would take care of it."

Her face was ghostly, now. I was glad I couldn't see it.

"I said, what about the eye diagnosis, there would be files, records... She said it wouldn't be a problem, they could get rid of them. That should have told me, right then, that it was bogus." She turned to me. "If any claim at all was made, the warning bells would go off the minute those test results came to light." Her eyes dropped. "There was never the slightest intention of anything to do with insurance."

"But you fell for it."

"Hook, line and sinker." Again, she avoided my eyes. "Looking back on it, I realise I was just desperate to believe—that there was a solution, a way out. She was clever, she saw it. She knew she had one shot, and she grabbed it with both hands. I had no idea about her and Lee, I'd never heard of Jack O'Malley. I just nodded my head, Sun Bonnet Sue, the perfect patsy. I even told her how grateful I was. I set myself up to be murdered."

"And Lou? Why was she there?"

She hung her head. "I'm probably more ashamed of that than of anything else. Camouflage, to make the day look normal. I was to send her off in a cab at a certain time, then just wait in the rank outside the hotel. But before I could put any of it in train, it got all messed up. Because of her, taking your picture." She stopped. "And then because of you. Because you fought for me, saved me. Because you're the bravest man I've ever met."

The water, the crickets, the insects buzzing in the night air… They were the witnesses to her confusion. And to mine.

"And when you got back here?" I said, finally.

"She brazened it out. Said the only reason it had gone wrong was you. You, you, you… She was livid, she was adamant—the two boys would never have used a gun if you hadn't been there, the one on the pillion would just have done what was needed. With the knife."

"You didn't remember that the gun was the first weapon to come out when the scooter came down the rank? Or that the knife was still inside his jacket?"

Again, the bitter laugh came. She shook her head.

"I didn't remember a damn thing—I was too busy panicking. I was just so relieved it hadn't actually happened..." She shook her head. "...and so terrified and so confused." She paused. "She played it beautifully. It never occurred to me I'd been set up, not for one second."

There was nothing I could say, nothing which would make it any less brutal. When the moon came out from behind the clouds, I saw her face. Once more, it was wet with tears.

"So now you know," she said. "I'm a criminal."

"Join the club" I said, quietly.

I put my arm round her.

"Alex..." she began. "Can you understand? What I was trying to do? A few hours of pain for a lifetime of security? For everyone I loved?"

"And the damage to yourself? To your face?"

The minute the words were out, I knew they were wrong. She stiffened, pulled away from me and got up. She took an envelope from the back pocket of her jeans and laid it on the carpet of needles beside me. A bitter laugh escaped her.

*"Damage...* You think that's what matters to me, Alex? My face? How many blind women have you ever seen look in a mirror?"

I was stunned. I stumbled to my feet and tried to catch her arm.

"Rose—"

But she was gone. I slumped back down again, listening to the sound of her clambering down the rocks.

*

*My uncle's God-inspired madness... Lillian MacBeth's desperate efforts to prolong attraction... My father's quest for a last gift to set at the feet of the woman he loved... John Walks-Over-Ice's stoic refusal to abandon his feelings... My mother's search for forgiveness...*

*America's Sweetest Sweetheart's attempt to beat fate and take care of her own...*

Noble. Futile. Insane...

As I sat on the ridge's edge with the night breeze tugging at my sleeves, watching Rose Vannier walk along the stream's bank in the moonlight, it all crowded in on me. Which adjectives applied to which story?

*Which applied to my own?*

Were the New World and I done with each other? I watched her steady progress. She had almost reached the bright oasis of Gallant Fox Farm. She had given me much, I knew, so much... She was a remarkable woman, unflinching, brave.

How could I atone? How could I make her understand it was the damage to her spirit I cared about, not the damage to her looks? Once again I unfolded the single sheet of paper which was the last of her gifts.

*The Kenilworth Clinic, Banbury, Oxfordshire. 01295 987333. Admitted the thirteenth of March. Responding to treatment.*

My mother was still alive, America's Sweetest Sweetheart had traced her for me. I watched the porch door swing shut behind her and wondered if I had seen her for the last time.

And then I remembered her last question.

*How many blind women...*

I knew the answer.

*One.*

# 22

# FEARLESS

THE CANE WAVED, imperiously.

"Perhaps we might progress a little further, Alexander. As far as the flat rock, if you would be kind enough." The southern voice became ironic. "It would seem that, after a lifetime of happily occupyin' various dens of urban iniquity, I have finally let the Baptists claim me. I find myself strangely drawn to the redemption of rushin' water."

I pushed the wheelchair across to the outcrop where I'd first seen my fiddle in Jane McClintock's hands. John was kneeling on it, reaching down to the water with athletic ease, Once I'd applied the brake, Saul twisted round and smiled up at me.

"A fine stream," he said. "Clear an' cold, just the way I like it. I look forward to enjoyin' a modicum of it in my bourbon tonight."

John stood up. The plastic bottle dripped from the big red hands as he stoppered it.

"Should keep you going a few days."

"The ration your quack hospital colleagues are allowin' me, my friend, it'll keep me goin' for a few months. But a man—especially an unreconstructed ol' reprobate like me—must be grateful for small mercies."

He settled back in the chair and surveyed the scene before him. From the other side of the rain-swollen torrent, Steady gave him an unimpressed look, then bent his head and returned to the serious business of cropping the half moon of pasture. I looked down at my charge in the wheelchair. He was thinner, much.

"So," he said. "I expect you're wonderin' why we've come to disturb your rural tranquillity?" He opened the box file on his lap. "I apologise for the intrusion, but, as your lawyer, I deemed it necessary."

He prised out an oilskin packet, struggling with its weight until John took it from him. As it reached me, the faint smell identified its origin. I fought unease as I opened the flap; a book, a sheaf of papers… I drew the leather-bound book out first.

*THE PRIVATE MEMOIRS AND CONFESSIONS OF A JUSTIFIED SINNER :*
*WRITTEN BY HIMSELF*
*WITH A DETAIL OF CURIOUS TRADITIONARY FACTS AND OTHER EVIDENCE BY THE EDITOR.*

The Private Memoirs and Confessions of a Justified Sinner, James Hogg's seminal novel, Scotland's least understood masterpiece, published in 1824. Without warning I was back in the cold gloom of the Diamondback winding shed, hearing my uncle's madness...

*I am of God's Elect! He has told me I cannot sin! Whatever I do…*

The Antinomian heresy, the ultimate Presbyterian perversion—that God had created an elite cohort whose every sin was written off in advance… I felt the sweat on my brow as I opened the book. The margins of every page were annotated in minuscule writing, crabbed and spiky. Saul's southern drawl seemed to come from very far away.

"An interestin' work. I confess I thought the protagonist had the makin's of a fine attorney. The other literary masterpiece you're holdin', Alexander, would appear to be the sequel, The Private Memoirs an' Confessions of a Justified Snake Handler."

I drew the huge mass of paper from the bag. It must have been three times as long as the book…

"That such a cogent description of religious madness might inspire the real thing," Saul went on, "is a connection I leave to the psychiatrists, it does not concern us here. All you need to know is that both of these items were found among your uncle's effects, in this packet, with your name on it. I have taken the liberty of readin' through the manuscript, in case of legal implications, and I'm relieved to tell you there are none—or at least none an Alabama shyster like myself can find. The entire tome is, in fact, barely comprehensible—the sad detritus of a seriously disturbed mind. The term *Antinomian,*" he said, drily, "is the only consistently legible word. It features prominently once every five pages or so, usually underlined or circled."

John's deep voice came. "And the mine?"

Saul's mouth broadened. It was a faint reprise of the sly lawyer's smile I remembered from our first meeting.

"A mess." He turned to me, suddenly serious. "Be glad, my friend, that your uncle's generosity didn't involve you in it. He did, however, achieve the last and deepest laugh."

I waited for him to explain. The sly smile widened further.

"The Diamondback mine now becomes the property of Mrs Lillian MacBeth. The cost of the environmental cleanup's in the billions, the arguments have already begun between her an' the state of Arkansas on the issue of liability. That, she may well slide out from under—but I imagine the controversy is likely to rage for years. The legal costs alone will be enough to bankrupt her. She has also been charged in the matter of her late husband's false burial."

The packet in my hands seemed to become heavier. She had been a large part of my uncle's destruction, I knew. I could not find the slightest vestige of sympathy for her. Saul's hand went back into the box.

"The only other thing the Reverend George Macbeth left you was this."

I stared; his bible…

The gold-edged pages looked just as pristine as they did in the faded Scottish photograph I had carried for so long. I laid the Hogg book and the sheaf of papers down on the rock and took it. When I opened it, the fly-leaf's handwritten sentiment stared up at me.

*Luke 6, 37 : Forgive, And Ye Shall Be Forgiven*

Directed at himself…? Slowly, I looked around me.

The cabin, the stream, the pasture…

I tried to take strength from the honesty of it all. *It would be the whitest of lies,* I thought, it would bring comfort. What sin could there be in that? But could I make my mother believe it was meant for her? I had to, I realised.

Voices came from behind the cabin. Rose emerged, Seth's huge bulk close behind.

Her eyes were closed. Her walk was slow and stately.

She was fanning the ground before her with a white stick.

Seth smiled at us and put a finger to his lips as he followed her. Jane's voice came from the edge of the hog pen.

"Stick's less important than your ears, girl! Use 'em! Listen to the water, you've done this three times now. You know where it is!"

I felt my heart beat faster and smelled her perfume as she passed, inches away from me, sweeping before her with the white wand. She stopped. She was exactly at the stream's edge, my uncle's papers at her feet. When she opened her eyes and took in the three of us, she looked shocked, anxious.

And then her smile came.

It wasn't America's Sweetest Sweetheart's smile.

It was Rose Vannier's smile.

Her new smile, the one I'd come to know over the week we'd spent here with Jane and Seth. It was a smile of dogged persistence, a smile which acknowledged that each accumulated triumph was to be savoured.

Before anyone could speak, Saul turned the wheelchair and propelled it forward. Firmly, he took the white stick from her hand and handed her his Malacca cane in its stead.

"I do not recall," he said, "any clause in our contract which requires the most beautiful woman I've ever seen to be, in any circumstance, less than stylish."

*

I listened to the car driving off down the hill, then, once the sound had died, I turned back towards Chimney Holler.

I thought about John Walks-Over-Ice as I walked. The understatement of the quiet farewell nod we'd exchanged didn't bother me, it had been enough—after everything we'd been through together, neither of us needed more. I would miss him, though. He had become a constant in my life, a compass. He was a better man than I would ever be, I knew. I found myself remembering the first tune Jane had given me, *Lost Indian…* As I walked back up the track I wondered if the title applied to John. And if it did, would it always? Or was there a chance his patience might find its reward once I was gone…? If that happened, how would I feel about it? I came round the last bend.

And saw her. High above me, eyes closed and arms outstretched, on one leg, the other horizontally extended behind her. It was a ballerina's pose, its stage, the flat rock where I'd hidden from the sheriff.

A goddess's pose, a monument to resolve…

I stood there, my heart in my mouth. *The fall… It could kill her…* And then I realised that my fears were nothing compared with her bravery. I waited, drinking her in.

A week, now, since the confessions of the waterfall... A week of confusion, of gradual withdrawal, of acknowledging our closeness and shying away from it at the same time. A week of finding our footing in a world where balance had once again shifted, where we both had to learn how to be single units again.

Up on the rock, she opened her eyes and saw me. I saw her let the pose die, become a mere mortal again.

Neither of us smiled. I was leaving in the morning.

*

We played. In front of the big fire Seth had built by the stream's bank, Jane McClintock and I gave our all to each other, everything we had. Without stint, because we both knew this really would be the last time.

*Drunk At Night and Dry In The Morning, The Richmond Cotillion, The Inverness Gathering, Natchez Under The Hill, Short Life to Stepmothers, Last Gold Dollar, Aird Ranters…*

It poured out of us in a torrent which rivalled the stream's, raw and clear and unstoppable, a proud procession of tunes with minds of their own, works of rough art which seemed to decide, independently of us, whether they would consort or confront. And when we had slaked each other's need for music, for the ultimate closeness that only melody could bring, we stopped and rested and looked into the flames. And then, inexorably, we began again. Finally, hours later, we played it, the tune which had come to mean everything.

*The Hawk That Swoops On High…*

It was an ending, we both knew it. Once it was done, I brought out the rosin holder and used it on my bow. Jane smiled as she heard the familiar sound. She reached out and touched the cracked ceramic surface.

"Still workin' for you, Alex?"

"Of course. You want her back?"

Her fleeting half smile was quick, generous. "You know better 'n' that," she said. "Gift's a gift." Gently, she took it from my fingers. "I'll steal a lick back from her, though."

I watched the brisk competence of her hands as she ran her bow along the rosin's familiar groove. It seemed the right time to give my thanks.

"The help you're giving Rose—"

"Hush, Alex." She let bow and rosin come to rest in her lap. "Wasn't nothin' but a joy," she said. "It was a fine idea you had, bringin' that girl here. A generous idea, an' she's already got ahold of everythin' I got to give her. Only so much teachin' to be done, anyways, 'cause each blind person's darkness is their own. Individual. Unique. I swear to you, though, whenever she comes to visit, she won't want for help if she needs it—nor love, neither, 'cause my heart's already gone out to her." She paused. "What I'm sayin' is, she'll be tret like she was my own. But I doubt that kind o' help's why she'll come again."

"What do you mean?"

"You can be pretty blind yourself, Alex," she said, softly. She pointed the rosined bow up through the darkness, at the flat rock. "Can't you see? She's already moved on. She's sittin' up there now, watchin' the sky, listenin' to us. Takin' strength from the music an' the stars. Honin' her courage, sharpenin' it up for the tough things she's still got to face. Tellin' her daughter. Tellin' her mother. Workin' out the best way to do what she has to, to carry on." Once more, she shook her head. "No," she said, "no matter how sweet Rose is, an ol' blind woman's copin' ways ain't what she'll come back here for."

My silence told her I still didn't understand. When her smile came it was sad and sweet and gentle, all at once. She reached over, traced the contours of my face with her calloused fingers.

"You're a fine man, Alexander Fraser. The reason Rose Vannier'll come back to Chimney Holler is 'cause she knows when she's in my company, she'll always have a piece o' you."

*

As the sun found the sky over the flat rock, we walked to the edge of the clearing. Fiddle in my right hand, bag hooked over my left shoulder, I stopped and looked down the winding track. Seth had offered to drive me to the station, but I wanted to walk, to leave at my own pace. I turned. Before I could say anything, Rose's finger found my lips.

"Not a word."

The kiss trembled. Salt found the taste of it. I stood back and wiped away her tears. Her eyes met mine, then she let her hand fall.

"Go," she said, simply.

I turned. Eyes closed, I let the breeze find my face.

Walking away was beyond hard. Inside the fifty steps which took me to the first bend I wondered, a dozen times, if I was doing the right thing. Finally, I stopped. When I looked back, she was still there, hugging herself. I turned again and forced myself forward, round the road's curve, out of her sight.

And then it came.

I heard the rush of passing air before I saw it. It glided across my path and disappeared into the pines. I stood, waiting. And then I saw it again, wings spread wide, rising above the road, soaring up on the thermal.

*No,* I thought, fiercely. *Don't watch over me! Go back, watch over her! She needs you now!*

I put down my things. Two steps took me back to the bend.

Rose was gone.

I looked up into the sky. The hawk was gone as well.

I shouldered my bag, picked up my fiddle and started to walk.

# THE AUTHOR

BRIAN McNEILL, born in 1950 in Falkirk, Scotland, has long been acclaimed as one of the most creative forces in his homeland's traditional music. In 1989, not content with his roles as performer, composer, songwriter, music producer, teacher, musical director and band leader, he added novelist to his resumé with *The Busker.* His manic schedule in the late eighties meant that most of the book was written on aeroplanes. A second novel, *To Answer The Peacock,* based on the same character, the rootless drifter and street musician Alex Fraser, appeared in 1995. *...In The Grass,* featuring shape-shifting detective Sammy Knox, arrived in 2006. The next two instalments of the Busker series, *No Easy Eden* and *The Hawk That Swoops,* are now published for the first time in eBook and paperback format. His latest work, *The 90th Kill,* has also just been published in both formats.

His audio visual shows, *The Back O' The North Wind,* about Scottish emigration to America, and the sequel, *The Baltic Tae Byzantium,* which explores the influence of the Scots in Europe, have won wide critical acclaim, and his continuing connection with America's Lone Star State led to him being created an honorary Texan in 1998. In 2017 he was inducted into the Scottish Traditional Music Hall Of Fame.

From 2001 to 2007 Brian was Head of Scottish Music at the Royal Scottish Academy of Music and Drama. Recently his home town of Falkirk honoured him by carving two lines of his song *The Lads O' The Fair* in stone, at a viewpoint looking over the town.

# A Note from Brian

Thanks for reading THE HAWK THAT SWOOPS. I hope you enjoyed it and if you did, I'd love to know what you thought of it. If you wish, you can send a review to:

www.brianmcneill.co.uk

If you want to stay updated about any of my fiction—or about any of the music I make—please go to the website above and join my newsletter list. It appears four times a year.

The current list of my other books is as follows.

*

## THE BUSKER

## Book 1 of the Busker Series

Alex Fraser is a rootless drifter who lives by playing Scotland's traditional music on the street. He makes his home wherever his fiddle might earn him a few coins. He's a man hiding from life, haunted by the death of his wife, which he caused. After serving his sentence in Scotland, he decides to try his luck in Europe.

In Switzerland he befriends another busker—Max, an old accordionist. Max tells him a story, a puzzle rooted in the Spanish Civil War. It's a tale of kindness and brutality, involving a German intelligence unit, a rescued child, a painting and a huge inheritance. Max, dying, charges Alex with solving the puzzle.

The maelstrom of violence and greed he uncovers is byzantine, daunting and ruthless. It pursues him across a continent, makes him confront love again, and ultimately forces him to believe in his own worth as a human being.

*...The Busker is a fast-moving thriller in the Hitchcock mould, sending its title character, Alex Fraser, on a desperate chase around Europe pursued by both the police and a ruthless gang of killers determined to prevent its hero uncovering a secret that goes back to the brutal Spanish Civil War incident which opens the book. Fraser, a loner with secrets of his own, makes an interesting hero, while Brian provides enough European atmosphere, intrigue and adventure, including a tense escape scene over the pre-reform East German border, to make for an exciting read. ...a fine debut novel.*

*Dundee Peoples' Journal.*

You can buy *The Busker* either as an eBook or a paperback on Amazon.

*

## TO ANSWER THE PEACOCK

### Book 2 of the *Busker* Series

Alex Fraser is in Rennes, in Brittany. While busking, he's accosted by a mad beggar. The episode ends with his violin in pieces and him being worked over in a police station.

But it gets worse. Suddenly he's a target. Why? And why would anyone want to steal his clapped-out car? Or pursue him at night through the port of Concarneau?

Or plant a priceless antique violin in his battered fiddle case, in place of his own wrecked instrument?

The mysteries intensify against the web of conspiracy spun round Nathalie Gwernig, the beautiful daughter of a dead Breton nationalist hero. Torn between his growing love for her and his need to find his own fiddle, Alex finds himself unravelling the hypocrisies of an English stately home, fighting ancient rural cruelty, and being pursued by both authority and a deadly political extremist.

Finally, his quest takes him back to Scotland. It forces him to revisit his past, before ending in a bloody confrontation on a Hebridean island.

*It's a breathless thriller that gives us an insight into the mind of the musician, as well as showing how a skilled writer can pace a plot... ...The novel explores the themes of Breton and Scottish nationalism, and the present state of the Gaelic language. The story is more than the fight to retrieve a lost musical instrument: it is about injustice on a wider scale and the need for cultural harmony, without the violence that sometimes attends political causes. Some of the freedom fighters in this novel are sinister characters, who have allowed their personal prejudices to become entangled with their politics... ...There are Buchanesque overtones in the way that the plot unrolls, and in the way that the principal character defends his honour.*

*To Answer the Peacock is an exceptionally well crafted story that holds its interest to the end.*

*The Herald.*

You can buy *To Answer The Peacock* either as an eBook or a paperback on Amazon.

*

## NO EASY EDEN

### Book 3 of the *Busker* Series

In Germany, Alex is given a lift by Abigail Eve, a black US Air Force captain. They stop at a fast food restaurant in the town of Rothenburg. A few minutes later, three junkies come in. After creating a scene, the kids run off, followed by a concerned nun, and then as Alex and Abigail leave, a bomb explodes, killing her and hospitalising him. He wakes to find Gunther Klein, a reporter, at his bedside.

After Alex is discharged, Klein investigates. Who was the nun? Why were the junkies in the restaurant? To keep Alex safe, Klein sends him to his ex-wife Sigi's family, but when Alex discovers Sigi is part of what happened—and that the US military want to arrest him—he flees. In Rothenburg train station, trying to make the price of a ticket to anywhere with his fiddle, he meets an elderly black man. It's Abigail's father, jazz trumpeter Luther Eve, come to see where his daughter died.

With Luther's help, Alex escapes to the old East Germany, where he uncovers a plot between ex-STASI officers, a cynical American soldier and an ex-terrorist who has assumed a startling new identity.

Drugs, misplaced idealism and family betrayals come to a head in Hamburg's red light district, where Alex must make the hardest choice of his life.

You can buy *No Easy Eden* either as an eBook or a paperback on Amazon.

*

## ...IN THE GRASS

### Book 1 of *The Sammy Knox* Series

In the deceptively sleepy Cotswold town of Cadisham, there's mischief afoot.

When Lady Letitia Moresby, the society stripper, finds that her python, Justin, has been stolen, she calls in Sammy Knox, glamorous private eye and witch's familiar. Sammy, who can change with ease between cat and human, is, as usual, broke, so she takes the case with alacrity. With the help of her teenage charge Libby (a trainee witch, but she doesn't know it yet) and Scrapper, a grizzled escapee from an animal testing laboratory, she begins to investigate.

The trail, which leads her through zoos, gravel pits, scrapyards, accountants' cupboards and assorted bedrooms, involves a resolute bunch of rescued felines, a languid tiger with ambivalent motives, a venal tax inspector with an individual take on rubber stamping, and a sweet but dim bloodhound.

Who would have suspected the leafy Cotswolds of harbouring so many dark secrets...?

*Sometimes we like to mention the existence of people who shouted loudly and without getting tired „over here" when talents were distributed. Ex-Battlefield Band musician Brian McNeill is one of these people, but we don't want to use up precious space by enumerating all of his talents. Suffice it to say that writing is one of them... ...In The Grass is full of speed, funny and thrilling: highly recommendable.*

*Folker.*

*Sensuous, cunning super-sleuth Sammy Knox is unmatched in the detective genre. Brian McNeill's brilliantly crafted story and fantastic cast of characters will transport you to another dimension from the very first page. Pure magic!*

*Carol Hird.*

You can buy *...In The Grass* either as an eBook or a paperback on Amazon. Book 2 of the series, *...In A China Shop*, is in preparation.

*

## THE 90TH KILL

All the teenage Samuel Cadogan ever wanted to do was draw—but after the death of his father, a Pennsylvania coal miner, his family explodes in a maelstrom of child abuse and violence, and he finds himself on the wrong side of the law.

He runs. For the next six years he supports himself as a sidewalk artist in Boston—and then circumstances force him to flee even further. In the US military, under his new name of Lemuel Brecon, he discovers he has one outstanding talent. He's a world-class sniper, a natural killer.

Dishonourably discharged after serving in Iraq, burned out and barely existing on the street, he's approached by two high-ranking and high-minded ex-officers who want the re-election of a corrupt and controversial president stopped. They know Brecon's talents, and they lure him into their plot with the possibility of revenge against those responsible for his family's disintegration. Finally seduced by the promise that they will find his missing sister, he agrees to be part of their scheme. But for all their professed principles, the way these officers manipulate him is as merciless as it is cold.

This is a story about the cynicism and ruthlessness of America's elites, about the intertwined nature of its political process and its gun culture—and above all, it's about the stubborn courage of individuals and their determination to resist, to fight for their humanity as the juggernaut of American power does its pitiless best to grind them down.

*You can buy* THE 90TH KILL *either as an eBook or a paperback on Amazon.*

*

## THE HORSEMAN'S WORD AND OTHER STORIES

A collection of shorter fiction, based mainly on the speech and dialect of Brian's Scottish lowland home town of Falkirk.

1913. Love, loss, inheritance, religion and magic; the simmering tensions not far below the surface of a lowland farm…
1958. A courageous schoolgirl's simultaneous discovery of her heroine's surprising secret and her own morality…
1966. The rough community of a working class pub coming together to protect one of their own from exposure…
1967. A teenage boy's complicated coming of age between bedroom and building site…
1972. A student whose moment of rebellion teaches him the painful difference between slogan and reality…
2016. A wronged and implacable cat taking revenge on mankind, only to discover the real depth of human cruelty…

*The cover story, The Horseman's Word... ...is almost reminiscent of Thomas Hardy... ...You can tell from every sentence that the author of these stories is a musician. Every story has its own melody and it resonates.*

*Karin Braun, Writress Corner.*

*Includes a glossary of Scottish words and phrases.*

You can buy *The Horseman's Word and other stories* either as an eBook on Amazon, or as a paperback from Brian's website. The paperback is also available from Songdog Verlag in Switzerland.

In English:

*http://songdog.ch/buch-detail/the-horsemans-word-and-other-stories.html*

In German:

*http://songdog.ch/buch-detail/the-horsemans-word-schottische-storys.html*

An audiobook, read by Brian, is also in preparation.

Printed in Great Britain
by Amazon